ABOUT THE COVER

There is something uncanny about the cover picture which you may like to know.

The cat is called Acorn and had a twin brother Chestnut who sadly disappeared just before his third birthday. But if you look to the left of the picture he appears to be jumping out of the bush.

Also this shot was taken in the dark with no light source, no street lamp and nothing for the flash to reflect.

Apart from the added wisp of mist the photo is untouched.

To Tracey

Best Wishes

Jabberl

ACKNOWLEDGEMENTS

Our grateful thanks go to

Karl Strickland of the
Leicester Theatre Group

Proof Readers No 1 and No 2
(No 3 is being sacked!)

TABBIE BROWNE ABOUT THE AUTHOR

Tabbie Browne seems to have been writing all her life in one way or another. She didn't have the fear of compositions, later known as essays, at school and would err on the side of writing too much rather than too little.

Although she likes to communicate with people, she has learnt that it sometimes better to sit back and observe the way they act.

She also believes in listening to your vibrations, if you don't get a good feeling when you are with someone, there is probably a good reason for it.

So she follows her instincts much more now, being older and wiser and having found out the hard way that looking for the good in everyone doesn't always pay off.

Other books by Tabbie Browne and published by UKUnpublished
All available in paperback and for Kindle.

White Noise Is Heavenly Blue
The Spiral (sequel to above)
The Unforgivable Error

Visit www.tabbiebrowneauthor.com

ISBN: 978-1-84944-180-3

British Library Cataloguing in Publication Data.
A catalogue record for this book is available from the British Library.

Published by UKUnpublished.

UKUnpublished
.CO.UK

www.ukunpublished.co.uk
info@ukunpublished.co.uk

NO - DON'T!

By

TABBIE BROWNE

CHAPTER 1

"Oh, I'm so excited, I'm really looking forward to the next connecting, where is it?" Sadie's friend shrugged "Calm down, you put too much faith in these things. Anyway if your Ma had wanted to send you a message, don't you think you'd have had it by now?"

Jo's laid back attitude sometimes flattened the younger one's enthusiasm for a while, but it wasn't long before she bounced back, such was her drive to get closer to her dear mother, to know she still loved her, thought about her, even missed her, sad as that would be.

"Anyway," Jo continued "as I've said before, you are too excitable, they probably wouldn't home in on you. In any case, what would you say to her?"
For a few moments Sadie was deep in thought, then listed all the things she wanted to say but never had. As she gathered her wits, the words tumbled out in such a torrent, Jo had to stem the flow explaining there would never be enough time to cover all she wanted to impart. She left her with the promise that she would let her know as soon as she had located a suitable venue for the next attempt.

Little did Sadie guess how much of a good chance she had of connecting to the other world, but Jo dare not let her find out, for this schemer would suck out all the information she could from unsuspecting victims, then use it all for her own pleasure. Over time she had become very adept at conning willing recipients into thinking the long awaited messages had come from their loved ones, when in fact she was toying with their emotions because their minds were open to believe whatever they wanted.

She always homed in on the latest arrivals to the spirit world as they were most vulnerable, being unaccustomed to their new state. When they became wise to her antics she would move to pastures new, and there was never a shortage of new fodder. Such was her skill, she never took ones like

Sadie to a genuine medium as they could spot her immediately and would be aware of her tricks. For this she used the 'play actors' as she called them, the ones who just made money out of conning their public, and used them to prove to the newcomer that connecting wasn't that easy. So whenever she told Sadie she had found a séance or similar, the poor youngster had no chance whatever of getting through to her mother. She would have been better visiting her in the home they had shared, for that was where she felt closest to her.

But this was one little drop in the older spirit's evil ocean, and she immediately was contacting other little flies in her spider's web draining their memories for future use.

Bert nearly threw his newspaper on the floor in exasperation.

"No. I've told you before woman, I'm not going and nor should you. It's a waste of money, you're just lining their pockets. Charlatans, that's what they are, the whole lot of them, and it's idiots like you that encourage them." He gathered up the pages of the paper, slapping them flat and putting them back in order, wishing his wife would open her eyes to what she could be getting in to.

Avril Harker finished clearing the table in silence. In all their thirty one years of marriage, she had never seen him so agitated, you'd have thought she had asked for the moon or something stupid to see him carry on so. There was no harm in going for a bit of entertainment and it didn't cost as much as going to see a film these days. Muttering to herself in the kitchen as she put the washing up in the bowl she felt she had to explain that it was all alright.

"It isn't as if there's any harm in it, just a few folk sitting round looking for a bit of comfort." Although she had never received any messages personally, the lady who usually sat on her right had had a few, and the gentleman opposite heard from his wife only last week, and it must have been right because of the things she said. That medium, Mrs Simpson, Astral Anne, as she was known at these meetings, said things that she couldn't have known, so how could she not be gifted?

"Too earthly Bert Harker, that's what you are," she snorted as she dried the plates "do you good to lift your spirits to higher things, well, you're not keeping me down. There's things you'll never know about." When she had tidied up, she made two cups of tea, took them into the lounge and put Bert's on the table beside him. A grunt was all she got in return so she picked up her book and they sat in silence, each in their own little world. Every now and then he would cast a quick glance in her direction but she was too engrossed to notice. He tried to read the title but she had her hand covering most of the letters, so he relaxed and let his mind wander.

What had changed so much recently and why? They had gone along quite happily since they married, had two children who now had their own families who always seemed to be dashing about doing things, but he and his wife didn't seem to be that close now. Had they ever really done anything together? They had kept themselves respectable, paid their bills on time, never wanted things beyond their means, and taken most of what they had for granted. Was that it? Had they taken each other for granted, not really stopping to think if they even loved each other any more. Avril had worked part time as well as bring up the family and he had worked fairly long hours but he couldn't remember them being close.

The holidays had come and gone, with the annual stay at the east coast, because that was what they did. They never thought of having a change, going somewhere else, no, they always went to the same place, ate the same food, and played the same slot machines.

Again he looked up, and for a moment studied his wife's face and realizing he never really looked at her. Now he could see she was showing her fifty four years. The wrinkles were starting to appear and she was developing a tired weary look of someone ten years older. It reminded him that he would be sixty five next month, and the thought of retirement had mixed emotions. Although he could take things a little slower now, he didn't want to give up doing things altogether and toyed with the idea of doing some light gardening work which would earn a few bob to help out.

"What are you staring at?"

Her voice made him jump as he came back to reality.

"Oh, just thinking, about retirement and that." He shuffled the paper.

"You could find a hobby, or tidy the garden up a bit." She sniffed and went back to her book.

"Well I was just contemplating that, gardening you know, I'd like that."

She looked up slowly. "I think everyone should have something that makes them feel better about themselves."

He had a strange feeling this conversation was going to take an unexpected turn any minute.

"That's why I go out, to my meetings."

"Meetings! There're not meetings, they are séances, be honest with yourself. It's a pity you couldn't find something more worthwhile. There's plenty of decent groups out there for people like you if you look for them."

She thumped the arm of the chair. "What do you mean? People like me?"

"You know very well. Sad old housewives, spinsters, widows, all sitting around waiting to hear something that's not there. Look at yourself woman, you're getting as bad."

"So that's how you see me is it? Well let me tell you I deserve a bit of enjoyment in my life, I'm not ready to sit down and be idle just because you're ready to. A bit of gardening may be all you're looking for but I want more out of life." Her face was becoming more flushed as she grabbed her book and flouncing out of the room called over her shoulder "I intend to make up for all the years when I came last, well now I am going to be first." Bert was left with the echo of the slamming of the door which put an abrupt end to the discussion preventing him from venting any further anger.

Jo certainly put 'Astral Annie' as she called her into the play acting zone. The woman may have had an odd twinge of spiritual connection, but it was only a twinge. Everything else she either found out, or made up on the spot knowing full well that nobody could argue with her, for what did they know to the contrary? She would never be a television personality or known nation wide for her practices, she wasn't clever enough to cover up her shortcomings and would soon be detected as a fraud. But the little meetings she held locally gave her a bit of standing in the community, and more to the point brought in a few pounds for the little luxuries of life. Nothing much was known of her background. The older inhabitants of the small town remembered something about a husband many years ago, but he seemed to have gone off somewhere, it was all very vague. She still wore a wedding ring and continued to use the name Mrs Simpson, as she didn't want to appear to be an old maid who had never known marital status, and for all anyone knew she could still be married. But it wasn't anyone's business and she kept her knowledge to herself.

So this was exactly the kind of connection Jo used when she ferried her victims through the contact process. Souls such as Sadie couldn't hear messages being sent from the earth world, they had to rely on Jo relaying them, trusting her completely, so eager were they to make contact with those left behind, just as their grieving families still on earth were doing to get in touch with them.

Anne Simpson flicked the long handled duster over the furniture in her sitting room. She didn't like the modern word lounge as it suggested idleness, and she often used her grandmothers' word 'parlour' when no one was listening. When she conducted her meetings, she didn't go in for the round table nonsense with people all holding hands in the dim light as she felt that would invite criticism. She felt it was putting her own mark on proceedings to do things a little differently to what was generally expected, so she let visitors sit around the room wherever they felt comfortable, and without any physical contact with anyone else. If a couple came together they may want to hold hands or put a consoling arm around one another, but that was entirely up to them. One gentleman who had been coming for as long as Anne could recall, always sat on the chair nearest the door. He gave no reason, and as the offering, the term used for the fee, had to be paid before the meeting, there was no problem if he needed to leave before the end of the session. The fact that he had always stayed for the entire sitting made the host wonder if he had one of those conditions that meant he had to arrive at a certain time, sit in the same place, and leave at a precise moment, but whatever it was she was glad of the custom. The only problem was, that because he did not partake in any conversation, she had no way of finding out any of his background, so she had never ventured to suggest she had a contact for him.

Jo hovered around the room as the woman busied herself in preparation for the afternoon arrivals. She had been in presence on many occasions amusing herself with this lady's antics and had found the venue tailor made for her own use. This would be the ideal spot to bring young Sadie and pass on a message from the mother, or so the young one would believe. The sweet feeling of deception boosted her ego and she was about to leave when she was drawn to the chair usually occupied by the strange man. Her whole presence jumped, sending ripples through the air in the room. Someone was sitting there.

As she regained her composure, she realized they weren't actually sitting, but hovering just above the seat and their focus was aimed directly at her.

"Who the bloody hell are you?" Her thought travelled straight to the image.

"You don't know?" The return thought hit her almost before her own question had been transmitted.

After taking a few moments to regain her composure she ventured "Should I?"

"If you are good as you think you are…" the unfinished sentence hung in the air almost throwing the next move to her.

Anne cast a glance round the room and with a satisfied nod to herself went out into the hall, closing the door behind her, blissfully unaware that she had not been alone. A good indication of the extent of her true psychic ability.

Jo kept herself at safe distance from the other presence, trying to estimate who this could be, obviously someone who knew her, probably from earth life, but not necessarily. The nearest thing to a spiritual laugh fluttered around the walls of the room making it impossible to pin point the actual source. As Jo was not the most patient of beings and still didn't mince her words or thoughts even in her spiritual state, threw the next question with a fair amount of force.

"Well, you arsehole are you going to tell me or not? Please your bleeding self." She was trying to work out just what she was confronting. Gender was merely used only if identification was needed when trying to connect the various worlds through messages. She would have to try a new approach as a thought suddenly came to her. Changing her tone to an enquiring softer level she asked "Are you anything to do with that quiet chap?"
The air started to pulsate. "It depends what you mean by 'anything to do with' doesn't it?"
Exasperated by now Jo flung the thought "Oh I'm not here to play bloody party games, I'm going."

As she left the area, she felt the uneasiness following her, almost as if she was being targeted for something, but what? Was someone trying to get revenge for a false message she had delivered. Well, if that was the case, why not just come out with it, instead of all this cloak and dagger stuff. She did wonder whether or not to return later for the meeting as she didn't relish the idea of coming into contact with this – whatever it was – again today. Also she would have simpering Sadie in tow with the view to passing on a message to the mother for her, and she didn't want to look silly in front of her, if this thing should start playing thought games with her during the session. Curiosity got the better of her as she returned to where Sadie was carrying out small spiritual tasks given to her by higher authority.

"We may have to leave it for today," the thought brushed passed the young spirit.
"Oh No. Why? You promised we would try and make contact today." The disappointment came bubbling out. "I was so looking forward to it."
Jo calmed her a little imparting "Things aren't quite right, you know, where we were going. I have your safety to think of and I can't put you at any damn risk, or…." she added as an afterthought, "your Mother."
"I don't understand." Sadie, had she been in earthly form would have been in tears by now, but the feeling of being let down weighed just as heavily on her.
"Next time, I promise." Jo tried to be kind but she dare not take a passenger where there was a threat.

As she left the area, she knew she had to visit the meeting. She had encountered many passing forms, good and bad, but when something was being focused on her alone, she just had to get to the bottom of it. The entity must have known of her haunts, which was why she sensed its presence in one of her familiar meeting places. So it must have been there before, but why hadn't she been aware of it until now. Her whole being was concentrated on these questions as she formed her plan of action.

Bert's mother never shortened his name. "Bertram, what are you doing?" or "Bertram, have you finished your homework?" were familiar calls in the household. His name was always uttered on a high note, followed by whatever question needed an immediate answer. His father had never taken a hand in his upbringing, mainly because his mother ran the entire household and treated her husband much as she treated her son. She ruled and nobody ever dared to question her. In his early years, with his child's open view on life, he experienced many unusual things, feelings, senses, but nothing he dare ask either of his parents about. Once he had been chastised for talking to someone who wasn't there, only he knew they were there, it was just that his parents weren't aware of it. He tried talking to the local vicar at the church, but the man went and had a quiet word with the mother, and Bertram was told never to tell lies again or he would feel the wrath of God. In addition he no longer trusted the vicar and knew that nobody would ever understand the things which only seemed to happen to him.

One day when walking home from school with one of his few friends, he had a terrible feeling of dread and without speaking grabbed his friends' arm and pulled him off the pavement and into a nearby garden. The lad tried to pull away shouting at Bertram for his actions but at that moment a car mounted the small pavement and came to rest inches from where the boys had been walking. Both stood shaking for several moments.

"H-h-how did you know? The friend was almost crying, but before Bertram had to admit his premonition the driver had got out and ran to the boys.

"Are you both all right? Either of you hurt?" He looked them up and down and laid a hand on each.

Bertram found his voice first. "Thank you Sir, we are OK, aren't we?" The other boy just nodded.

The driver said "It was a miracle you dived out of the way, but tell me what made you do it?" If he expected an explanation, he wasn't going to get it, for Bertram just shrugged and the two lads almost ran past him as they headed for home not even wondering why the car had veered in their direction.

This and other events in his young life made him aware that there was much more going on around him than seemed to be affecting anyone else. He wasn't sure he liked the feelings he had, and it tended to isolate him from lads of his age as he didn't want to talk to any of them about it for fear of ridicule, but he grew up having a distrust of all things he couldn't explain. This was the reason he tried to put his simple minded wife off her new addiction. He was happy enough for her to join the flower arranging class, or the water colour instruction evenings at the night school in their little town, but when she was introduced to Madam – whatever her name was – the foreboding which he had so long buried, began to rise to the surface again. But he couldn't tell her why he objected, he just wished she would get fed up with the idea before it was too late.

CHAPTER 2

Milton Warner sat alone in his study flicking through some of the fan mail which had been carefully sifted by one of his faithful office team. Representing the other end of the scale to Astral Anne, Milton was not only very gifted in the spiritual world but could sense it if anyone was testing him as to his powers. He had always been spiritually aware, and coming from a religious family thought nothing of his unusual talent.

"Auntie Win is going to ring you." he would say to his mother as she did the ironing and sure enough, within five minutes the phone would ring. Mother never mentioned the fact to her sister as she wasn't quite so understanding about such things and would have put it down to coincidence.

As the years had passed, Milton's gift became widely known, quite accidentally he thought, for he didn't broadcast it but people soon got to know of his premonitions and were fascinated by things he told them about themselves that he couldn't possibly have known in the normal sense. Strangely, he never thought he was different, almost believing that everyone was the same. At first he was asked to speak at small local meetings, this was how it was put to him, but what they really wanted was a sitting in public, with everyone hoping they would get a message.

It wasn't long before the local radio and television channels hooked on to the idea that this could be good audience bait and he soon became a national celebrity. All the hype seemed to wash over him as he seemed to concentrate solely on the people to whom he was relaying messages, and equally on the ones sending them from other existences. But before long he was deluged with fan mail, requests for sittings and some requests which were better put straight into the waste bin. As he was now earning a living from this source he decided to employ a couple of old friends who had been made redundant from their jobs, and let them take care of sorting the fan mail, management, and any thing else which needed doing. Life was becoming very hectic and tours had to be arranged along with promotional material and Milton realized that now his life was not his own.

As he started to look at the letters in his hand, one stood out from the rest and he put the others back on the desk and was drawn to the beautiful handwriting before him. But what startled him was the date. This letter had been written five years earlier, so why had he only just seen it. It couldn't have been lost for all that time in the fan mail, for the lads always made sure nothing was left that long, so the only other explanation was that the sender had inadvertently put the wrong date on it. Slowly he started to read.

Dear Mr Warner,

I have followed you for many years and feel you are the only person who can help me for no one else will believe what I have to tell you.

This is not a joke. I am going to be murdered. I don't know who it is and I don't know why. It may even be by accident.

I know you have the gift, and when I have gone I will contact you and I want you to help me track down the person who is going to do this evil thing.

Don't ask me how I know this, even I don't know, I only know I don't have much time.

Please do not refuse me

Thank you for reading this.

Yours sincerely

The letter was signed by a lady or young girl he imagined, for there were only initials but no name. Of course she would think that when she contacted him after her passing, he would know. This particular communication was playing on his mind as he quickly read through the rest of the pile for there was one problem. Although his mind could be open to receive, it didn't mean that she would have the power to get through to him, for it was a two way thing, similar to the fact that it is no good phoning someone if they don't pick up their receiver.

And there was an even bigger problem. In general terms the next life is referred to such as 'this world and the next' or 'in heaven and earth' which suggests only two existences, whereas in fact there are many and earth is not necessarily the lowest of the platforms. But beyond earthly life a soul could be in many forms, or in many different worlds which is why it takes a true medium to be able to filter the messages through in the correct way. For example, if two trains are leaving Birmingham and one is going to Liverpool, the other to Leicester, there is no point in someone waiting at Leicester to meet a passenger if that passenger is on the train to Liverpool. It is the same with messages. They have to come through the right channel or this is where the play actors get things messed up and at the same time leave themselves as targets for contacts they would rather not have.

In Milton's office there was a notice board on the wall near his desk where he could pin various things which, although may seem to have no significance now, could have an important bearing later on when he was faced with an unusual problem. Some had been there for years, but he would not part with them for what was time? Only something we split into fragments for our convenience, but time is everlasting so who knows when that odd little piece of material, or a discarded bus ticket could fit into the last piece of a mental jig-saw.

He pressed a lever on his desk. This lit up a sign on the panel outside the room meaning that he was mediating and must not be disturbed until the light was off. After stroking the letter and getting the feeling of a young lady aged about twenty, he held it to his forehead for a moment concentrating deeply, willing her to give him some clue as to her identity. He lost himself in thought, completely oblivious to anything physical. There was quite a buzz of activity with messages and contacts being made around him but passing him by. Eventually, as though someone had been in presence watching the action he knew his spirit guide had been scanning the passing waves to no avail.

Many people are aware of their spirit guides and can give an accurate description of them regarding their race, background and in depth details of their time spent on earth. Some believe the guides are Chinese, others say they are North American Indians but in Milton's case he was French. Of course he had been with the medium since his earthly birth but it took a few years for them to become mutually acquainted. This spirit had taken both male and female forms during his earth lives and although had also lived in Belgium and Germany, retained his French connections and accent in his present state. Now he was hovering over the letter, letting his being pass through it trying to glean a scrap of information as to its origin. Milton leaned back in the chair his head relaxing into the padding.

"Jean-Paul, what do you make of this?" Milton didn't need to speak, the thought was enough to communicate and as words were not being used, the idea was transmitted in a fragment of time. Equally the reply of "Nothing" was also imparted in an instant. For several moments the two examined the paper but it was as though someone had cut the line to any possible identification. After about half an hour, Milton opened his eyes and sat up leaning on the desk.

"Looks as though it will have to go on the board for now." His musing was greeted with a silent agreement but as he took a pin to fix the letter to the board he stopped dead.

"Did you feel that?"

A strong feeling prevented him from piercing the paper with the sharp object. Jean-Paul sent a ripple through the air towards one of the drawers where plastic sleeves were kept. Taking out a small one, Milton very carefully laid the letter inside then pinned the bag to the board. The whole atmosphere seemed to settle once this was done.

Daryl, Milton's longest serving and trusted helper looked up and saw the light was off. This meant he could now take in the proposed plan for the forthcoming tour and have it approved before making the necessary bookings.

There was a waiting party ready for Jo when she returned to her duties. She knew she should not have gone off on her own when it was task time and was always being admonished for it. The higher powers always tried to say it was for her own good as she had a habit of attracting trouble, but there were those amongst them who were of the belief that there was so much time needed to keep the peace in their own area, that there was no need to go stirring up unrest when there was no call for it.

"We all know what you are trying to do Josephina, and you have to stop it. It won't help you know, revenge never does." One of the senior spirits took charge as soon as Jo appeared.

"I know that." She hated her full name and the use of it always put her on edge, but of course they knew that, so why do it unless they were trying to annoy her?

The next in line drew her forward. "We are afraid for you, you may be experienced compared to some, but you are still very young in the whole existence, you don't know what you are tampering with."

Jo was feeling very patronized now. "Then why don't you tell me? Is it something only you lot are privileged to know? If I don't know, how can I be on my guard against it? And what I am looking for can't be that bad. It's only the same as it was when I had a bloody body only now I don't do I?"

The last words came out in such a stream of frustration and anger, the surrounding area trembled and it took a while for the higher ones to calm the vibrations to their original level. There was a significant silence then the high power moved nearer.

"A decision has been made Josephina. Until further notice you will confine your movements to the areas to which you are allocated. To put it plainly, you will not frequent any earth happenings or try to seek out information from that source. Do you understand?" This was most definitely an order, but Jo would have to go through the process of conforming or she would never achieve what she needed.

"Well?" The high one was waiting for her answer.

"Suppose so." If Jo had still been in bodily form she would have crossed her fingers behind her back, as she had no intention of giving up now. The only good thing was that it gave her a perfect excuse not to take Sadie with her to the meeting and she still amusingly referred to herself as being 'grounded'. But she knew that somehow she must find a way of escaping the eager powers who would be watching her every move from now on.

Up to now, Avril had asked her husband to drive her the short distance across Mayfield, the little market town where they had lived since childhood, but as Bert became more and more opposed to her going to her meetings, she knew she had to find other means. There was no direct bus route to Astral Anne's house and it was too far to walk there and she didn't relish the idea of coming home alone if it was dark. Sometimes the meetings would be in the afternoon in the winter which helped but she felt vulnerable when out by herself so she had formed a little plan. If Bert had hoped that by not taking her she would stop going, he had better think again because this was her little bit of pleasure she wasn't about to let him interfere. Had she only known his reasons she wouldn't have set foot in Anne's house, but he couldn't voice them, she wouldn't have listened, for when she had her teeth into something she was like a dog with a bone. She wouldn't let go.

Over the weeks Avril had got to know the group of regulars who attended and at first nobody spoke to anyone much, they came deep in thought and left in much the same state. After a week or two a few "Hello's" or "Good Bye's" were exchanged but little else. They were a funny lot really, but if she could cadge a lift, she wasn't bothered about the pleasantries. As she stood now doing the ironing, her mind travelled to the various individuals who went on a regular basis not even thinking about the ones who had come once or twice but decided it wasn't for them. There was that strange quiet chap who was always there first, no matter how early she was, and he never spoke or looked around the room. When she really thought about it, she couldn't have described him to save her life because he never actually looked at anyone, and when the meeting was over he turned towards the door, presenting his back to the assembled company, gave a small grunt and had gone. She smiled to herself as she thought he almost seemed to wrap himself round the door rather than pass through the opening. He was very strange and made her feel uneasy. Fortunately she didn't have to sit next to him as his was the only chair next to a rather large sideboard, and as everyone seemed to commandeer the same seat each time she sat near another lady in the bay window. This woman was polite but didn't put herself out to speak unless spoken to but had mentioned her name was Gerte which, she imagined was more than enough information she had to divulge.

There were two high backed armchairs, either side of the fireplace, one in which Anne sat and the other was taken by a young man, not bad looking, but left you with the feeling he was trying to learn as much as he could about this business for his own means, rather than coming in the hopes of getting a message. He was extremely affected and really loved himself which didn't go down very well with the rest of the company, with the exception of the quiet fellow who probably didn't even know he was there. Avril imagined that Anne allowed him to attend as it was another few pounds in her pot, so as long as he behaved himself she would tolerate him for now. The seat at the other end of the sideboard, to Avril's left housed the most lonely and solitary lady anyone could ever meet. She had breeding and didn't look short of a bob or two but it was anyone's guess just how old her clothes were, her hair was done in the most old fashioned style and to look at her she gave the impression of either just coming off stage from a period drama, or someone who had let the recent years pass her by, which wasn't far from the truth. She had introduced her self as Miss Taylor-Barnes which, judging by a few nods rang a bell with the others but no one could quite place her. This left a two seater settee on the wall opposite the window. This was the target for Avril's lift, for she had noticed Mr and Mrs Isaacs always came in a car and she had learned that they had to pass her road on the way, so when she thought the time was right she would very unassumingly get round to the subject. They seemed pleasant enough, at least more pleasant than the rest of the visitors, so she may just be lucky, and Bert could sit and vegetate. With a little snort she switched off the iron and put the clothes to air and set about preparing the evening meal.

As the steam from a saucepan crept towards the window, the woman stopped in her tracks.

"I've told you Bert Harker, you can't stop me doing what I want, and your silly games won't make the slightest bit of difference." She shouted the words to the air for she was alone, but facing her in the steam was the word "DON'T" written across the window. Thinking he had rubbed something with grease or wax on which would only show up in this situation she reached for a cloth to wipe the window but to no avail. In the end she grew so cross she flung the cloth in the sink and yelled "All right Bert, you can clean it before you have your dinner." The sound of the saucepan boiling over didn't help her temper and she was still fuming when her husband came home from work.

"Well, you've got some dinner, I don't know how I'm sure." She met him with this outburst as he walked in the door.

"Let me get in woman, nice greeting I must say. Now what are you rabbiting on about?"

Avril wasn't in the mood for questions, or stalling.

"You know very well. I suppose you think it was funny. Well, let me tell you, I don't."

Bert was a little rougher than he intended as he took her arm and directed her to the kitchen chair.

"Now, slowly, quietly, do you mind telling me what is going on? I'm tired, I'm hungry, I've had a right old day at work, so without shouting, say what you've got to say. All right?"

Avril was shocked at this side of Bert, he may be awkward but she had never seen him like this before. His manner had calmed her down somewhat so she thought she had better explain and see that he had to say for himself.

"The window." She hoped that would be enough.

"What bloody window?"

"The one in the kitchen of course, the one you messed up."

It was Bert's turn to sit in a chair. He didn't like the way this was going and his intuition told him caution was needed.

"Avril, listen to me, I haven't done anything to the window, inside or out, so very slowly tell me about the window."

She related the word in the steam and as she finished Bert sat staring ahead, his face a mixture of realization tinged with fear. He knew why the word was there but if he tried to explain it to his wife she wouldn't believe him, and what's more wouldn't heed any warning it was giving her. Whoever had guarded him all his life was guarding them now, and whatever lay in store for them because of Avril's latest interest could mean danger to one or other or both of them. It must mean that his guardian knew much more than was being imparted and Bert was not going to go against this or any other warning.

They ate the dinner almost in silence and Bert knew that in some way he had got to intervene, but how?

Sadie was feeling quite low when she realized there was no hope of her getting through to her mother. She thought that up until the last minute, Jo might just change her mind and take her with her, but now with the other spirit being taken to task it seemed the end of the any chance of contact for a while. She got on with the jobs allotted her, simple ones for now but as she became more experienced she may take on the more sinister and dangerous work only given to those who had reached a high enough level in their current existence. Within one form of existence those on higher levels can travel down to the lower ones, but the lower ones cannot climb to levels above them. Different forms have different rules but Sadie was in the state of not long having moved from earthly form so she was on the lowest level of the next format.

She suddenly became aware of a presence close by and felt filled with the most soft and lovely feeling she had ever experienced.

"Don't be startled. How are you coping?" The message was received into her being and she knew she had only to think the answer and it would be understood.

"I am doing all right, I think." She didn't want to appear too assured as she didn't really know what was expected of her yet.

"I'm sure you are. Is there anything you need to be explained?" The presence seemed to be taking form around her in a very protective way and continued "it is very strange to adapt to a totally new way of living, for that's what it is, but in a different kind of living. You realize you don't sleep now, but you do have to rest, just the same as before."

Sadie was very relaxed and comfortable. "Yes, I know I have a lot to learn and it's easy to feel very alone, but I like comforting the new ones and I don't feel so sad for them now."

"You miss your mother." The thought was short and to the point and caught the young one unawares.

"Very much, I want to let her know I am well now, not ill any more and I feel so very free after the pain, but I can't."

There was a pause. "We have all wanted that, but - and this may be hard for you to understand at this moment, it isn't always the best thing."

"Oh? Why?"

"Let me make it as simple as I can, for it is not a simple subject. Everyone in earth form will have a parting from something or someone they love, but they have to learn to come to terms with it. Some sadly don't but we won't dwell on that for now. Now let's take you for example, you are doing very well, you have been taken from your familiar surroundings and lifted to a new environment completely and are adjusting bit by bit to what you have to do here. But you have no distractions. If you were visiting your mother regularly, and you saw her upset, it would hold you back and you couldn't progress at your normal speed."

Sadie felt she had to interrupt. "But I'm not the one left behind."

"No, but it is just the same. Your mother likes to think you are close, but if you were contacting her all the time, she could not move on with her earthly life. Now do you see?"

After pondering for a moment she asked "Is that why it is so difficult for the spirit world and the earth world to contact each other?"

The presence rippled amusement through the area. "That would be a very useful tool. But not really. You see it isn't always that difficult to make contact."

"What?" Sadie was amazed.

"I thought that would surprise you. Many, many people could tune in if they wanted, not just to this spirit form, although this is the easiest as it is the nearest, but some could reach out to other existences."

"And do they?" The young one's attention was riveted.

"Not much. They could but don't realize they can do it. Mainly because their lives are so cluttered, never giving their thoughts time to send or receive."

"Oh, that's a pity isn't it?"

The presence liked this fresh young person and would try and guard her from harm which meant keeping her as far away from Jo as possible.

"Yes it is. But children often pick things up or sense them because their minds are still open, listening, learning always enquiring. Trouble is, when they grow up they get out of the habit or put things down to coincidence."

Sadie felt the presence slowly slipping away and she sent out the question "Will you come again, I'd like to learn more."

A warm glow surrounded her as she felt she heard, almost like a gentle breeze "I never really leave you."

Jo's superiors knew full well this hard hitting, often foul mouthed spirit refused to obey orders, which is why they had 'grounded' her. Some, just a little senior to her had been paying particular attention to several of the so called séances on earth, not to watch the spirits being called upon for messages, but the not-so-wholesome entities they seemed to attract. To an errant spirit these were open doors to start spreading their evil ways, and the practice was growing worldwide because ignorant earth dwellers were feeding the habit. It would all start very innocently until one or several fiends would home in on one particular sitting which provided easy pickings. They dare not go near the genuine mediums as they would be sensed immediately and engulfed by protective spiritual guards who would oust them in seconds. So by banning Jo, it was certain she would find some way of going down to the next meeting to find out who had been in presence, thus doing a worthwhile job of work on their behalf. They would have to make sure, without making it too obvious, that she could get away undetected, but that was easy enough, a slight fracas in another area could pull some of them out of the way for long enough.

Little did Astral Anne or any of her guests realize what was in store for them the following evening.

CHAPTER 3

The television studio was buzzing with activity as the crews made ready for the filming of the next programme "Messages" and the assistants were briefing the audience in a green room as to the layout and procedures on set and also giving them a health and safety speech. Eventually they were escorted down corridors in to the studio and asked to take their seats as quickly as possible leaving the three seats at the front right hand side free. Any wheelchair users or visitors having difficulty climbing the elevated seating could sit in the front row on the left.

There had been the usual little hiccups with the set up and the director now wanted everything tightened up and moving as soon as possible. One of the staff explained there would be a short rehearsal for the benefit of cameras and lighting with a stand in for the medium. When all this had been completed to satisfaction the audience was asked to be ready to give a warm welcome to the star as soon as 'Action' was called. Within seconds everything was rolling, the announcement made and Milton walked out to face the throng. He never sat for these performances but always had a break half way through, although with the necessary cuts, television viewers never knew.

He suddenly stopped dead in the middle of the floor his hands to his head. The crew never questioned this sort of behaviour but had never seen anything quite like it before so took a quick glance towards the director who motioned them to keep rolling.

Milton slowly raised his head and his right hand started to lift towards certain part of the third row up. He never pointed. His mother had always said it was rude to point and this stayed with him all the while he was growing up, so he always held his hand, palm upwards as though he was about to receive something.

"Do you have something in your bag which never leaves your side?" He was directing towards a lady but his eyes were closed. He waited for the faint

"Yes." Slowly his lids lifted at he was looking straight into the face of a lady whose anguish and sorrow was written so clearly.

"Would you mind coming down to the front please?" This was going to be fraught with terrible memories and he had some misgivings about calling her but the feeling was so strong he couldn't ignore it. The producer would have described it as good viewing material but Milton knew that at the end of it he would be totally drained. Daryl, out of camera shot was keeping a close eye on him and was always ready for the slightest emergency.

The lady had arrived and had been motioned to the left hand seat, but for some reason Milton asked her to put her bag on the right hand seat leaving a space between. He was now standing facing her and the audience but turned his head towards the bag. It was obvious to all he was visibly shaken and the close up shots made cameramen shudder. This was new. After a moment Milton reached out his left hand and the lady laid her palm in his. They both felt the jolt and it must have been visible, as the first rows facing him jumped.

"I will not ask your name for this is very private to you." When she had nodded in agreement he said quite quietly "I do not wish to cause you any further pain, but you are here for a reason, and I have to tell you what you need to know." She nodded, but the tears had started to flow, and as her face was being shown on the monitors, many handkerchiefs came out. Milton was trying to keep control as he felt he was being shaken from head to toe so he gently let go of her hand and stood back. Bending over slightly he asked if she was alright to carry on and she uttered a barely audible "Please."

"My dear lady, you have in your bag a small white handkerchief, I believe there is something around the edges, lace or embroidery, but that is not important." He took a deep breath. "There is a lot of staining on the cloth, I believe it is brown now, but it was once red. Am I correct?"
The lady was trying to cover her face with one hand but nodded.

"There are initials in the corner." He paused concentrating, his eyes closed. "I don't think they are yours."
The sobs could be heard all over the studio as parents in the audience feared what was coming next.

"They are the initials of your daughter."

"Yes." The lady could be heard in the stillness. "I can't bear to part with it. May I show you?"

"If you wish, but only if you really want to, it isn't important to what I have to say to you."
She nodded and he handed her the bag. Slowly she took out the cloth and held it to her chest her eyes glazed and far away.

"My dear, don't be shocked, her name was Pamela I believe."
Her head nodded but she didn't look up.

"Oh dear, you may not like this, but Pamela wants you to get rid of it……"

"No" the cry was heartbreaking, "I can't, I can never part with it."

"She is telling me it upsets her. Look at the picture of her on her swing, or the one of you both on the beach. Remember the happiness, not the sadness it has been too long now." Then very quietly, "It is holding her back."

Even with his experience, Milton wasn't ready for what happened next. The lady slowly undid the hanky and spread it on her lap and there in one corner untouched by the old blood were two embroidered initials, and they were the same as the letter attached to the board in his office.

After a moments' composure, he leaned towards the lady and suggested she think about the message in the peace of her home, but he noticed that already her eyes had lifted and he knew that if only she could have the courage to do this one thing, both she and Pamela would move forward.

He gave the sign to the producer that there must be a break and 'Cut' ended the silence as the crew started moving about and Milton was ushered to his dressing room, Daryl close on his heels.

"What was it?" He whispered as the medium sat down
Milton looked at his friend knowing he had spotted something odd in the proceedings.

"The initials, they were the same as on the letter."

"Oh my God, and you think……"

"What are we doing?" Milton almost jumped up, his normal thoughts returning. "I need to ask the lady how her daughter died. Don't you see? I have to know if she was…" he lowered his voice"….murdered."
He sat for a moment then said "Could you fetch her in here for a minute?"
Daryl put his head to one side. "Well, they do want to get on with filming, and besides, wouldn't it be kinder to the lady to ask her afterwards?"

"Hmm, perhaps you are right. Tell them I'm ready to come back would you?"
Opening the door a little Daryl called to the waiting crew member, "He's coming back."

The rest of the session went quite smoothly, some recipients of the messages were sniffing into their tissues, whilst others seemed elated but this was the usual reaction. Milton was pleased to see the lady hadn't left during the break and she seemed pleased to speak to him privately, almost as if it was a relief to be able to speak out at last to someone who understood her pain. Unfortunately though, her information was not what Milton was hoping for, because it seemed the poor girl had died about fourteen years ago just before her sixteenth birthday and it was from illness. So he was back to square one as regards the item on his board, but gladdened to see the lady's slight change for the better.

"I thought you said you had got a lift." Bert was not amused. His wife was getting ready to go off again and was asking him to take her and bring her back.

"I said I would arrange it if I could and I expect to do just that tonight, when I see the couple who come by here."

"You know I don't agree with all this."

Avril was getting very tense with this. "Forget it, I'll walk there and get a lift back."

"Don't be such a silly fool, you wouldn't make it."

All he got in reply was a hefty sniff. She had him in knots, either he took her which was much against his will, or he would sit worrying all evening as to whether she had got there alright.

"Just this once then and that's my last word."

Although she didn't want to accept, she knew it was the only practical thing, and she would come home with the Isaacs.

"Like I said, I only want to get there."

He frowned "And you're sure these folks will bring you home?"

She nodded, not being absolutely sure, but in her mind she thought they couldn't very well refuse, if she said she was stuck for a lift tonight.

They travelled in silence most of the way and Bert dropped Avril off at the end of the road as she always requested so he never knew exactly which house she visited. With a brief "See you later." she had got out of the car but waited for him to drive off before continuing her journey.

After paying her money she was ushered into the room as usual, but being a few minutes later than her normal time realized she was almost the last one to arrive. She sat down acknowledging the few nods, and said "Hope I didn't keep you waiting." She wasn't really late but felt she had to break the silence somehow for the air was very tense and she felt almost as though she had missed something but didn't know what. As she cast a quick glance at the chair beside her and noting that Gerte still hadn't arrived, she added "Oh, I'm not the last anyway." followed by a nervous laugh which still got no response. Anne let the atmosphere in the room settle then said "I'm afraid Gerte will not be with us today. One of her family has phoned; it seems she has not been seen since yesterday and naturally they are all rather concerned, so we will have to proceed without her." The young man made a small gesture which indicated he found that to be an obvious statement which wasn't very well received by some of the assembled party.

The usual quiet moment followed where everyone was asked to open their minds and relax to see what transpired on this occasion. Avril found it hard to concentrate. The slight upset with Bert was in the back of her mind, and she couldn't help worrying about Gerte. Suddenly she felt a very strong pressure coming from the empty seat beside her. It grew stronger as though she was being pressed towards Miss Taylor-Barnes. She tried to adjust her sitting position but the movement seemed to help the force and she hung on with all her might to remain where she was. From somewhere above her, a sound started to reach her almost like an order "Go. Go now." She covered her ears but the voice got louder and the pressure on her right side was so strong she couldn't fight it any longer, but just when she was about to scream, everything stopped suddenly and she was left almost weeping in her seat. As she slowly lifted her head and looked round the room, no one appeared to have had any notion of what had happened. If anyone would have been aware, surely it should have been Astral Anne, but she was in her normal state with a half smile on her face waiting to hit the first victim.

Jo had done all she could to get the poor woman to leave there and then but it was obvious this meek soul was totally unaware of the power around her.

"She's very vulnerable isn't she?" Another entity had appeared at Jo's side during this little drama.

"Oh Christ who are you, and how long have you been here?"

"Just someone like yourself who tries to protect the innocent, didn't want to interfere though, you seemed able to cope." The senior spirit had been monitoring Jo's movements since she had been in the earth's vicinity which was pre-arranged but carefully planned so that she did not recognize her companion. Many spirits on high planes are capable of changing their appearance at will, for some do not even have any definite form so take on what is familiar to the recipient.

"What made you choose this place?" Jo was curious after her recent encounter and was on her guard.

"No reason, I like to float round them all, never know what's about do you?"
Prodding for more information Jo asked "You haven't noticed anything in particular here then?"

"Think most of them have undesirables hanging around, wish these silly people wouldn't open the door for them. You know how it is when they get a foothold somewhere."

Jo's attention was now on the man by the door, the place she had noticed the presence before but all seemed calm but then something seemed to be materializing near the fireplace. Hovering for a moment, the mist then drifted over towards the window and stayed over the empty chair before whirling round at great speed disturbing every space available as though it had to consume all the contents. The senior spirit was able to notice through the melee that all the human forms including the medium were completely unaware of this, while Jo's attention was focused on the being, trying to ascertain what it was and what it was trying to achieve for it seemed like something trapped in a cage from which it was trying desperately to escape.

"It doesn't want anything here." she imparted.

"Don't be so sure." The highly experienced one was not deceived and realized this younger form had much to learn for she was putting herself in the path of danger without realizing it. "Pull back a little."

Not knowing why she did it, Jo obeyed sensing there was more to this than she had first thought. The mist was now positioning it self directly in the middle of the room, hovering, waiting, almost like an animal waiting to pounce. In a split second it was gone.

"Where the hell did it go?"

"It hasn't."

Jo turned her attention to the senior. "But we saw it leave."

"Did we?"

"Well it isn't here now is it?"

"That's how clever they are. Even you can't locate it."

"You're not trying to tell me you can still see it?"

There was a moments' pause before Jo got her answer but not in words. Another facet of the higher forms is the ability to do mentally what we expect machines on earth to do, that is, rewind, replay, slow motion, frame by frame but they do it simply by their own powers. So as the junior 'watched' the departure of the mist at a much slower pace, she saw it enter the man sitting by the door, the exact place she had encountered the other form, which meant this was one and the same, or was it?

"What's it doing now?"

"What do you think?"

"Waiting?"

"What else?" The senior drifted nearer then returned but had moved so quickly Jo didn't even notice the movement.

"To use the man for its own ends?" Jo was stabbing in the dark but couldn't think of anything else.

"Possibly, or it could be the man's other self, in other words, him."

"But how could I have seen it here before when he had gone?"
The senior paused then said "It is confusing to start with but the knowledge only comes with experience."

"But I didn't like the feeling when I saw him then, he felt evil, I don't know more than that. But I don't like him."
There was a moment of stillness then Jo asked "Why does he come here?"

"Could be any reason, Maybe he has a score to settle, or perhaps he needs a platform to take off from, and this is the right environment, there are many things, many questions but you cannot possibly know them all in your undeveloped state."

"I thought when you died and went to heaven you got all the answers." The presence was having such an effect that Jo felt she should calm her normal rant of swearing usually used to enhance her statements.
The senior's amusement rippled "As you are now finding out, your passing was but the first rung of the ladder."

"And how high is this bloody.....um ladder as you call it?"

"My dear, if you are at the bottom and look up, you will not be able to see the other end even if there are no clouds to hide it."

"And you are telling me, all the rungs represent different levels?" Jo thought this was all a bit much. "It's like starting a computer game and knowing it is unlikely you will ever get to the end."

"Very good. It is very much indeed like a computer game. You have to achieve certain aspects on each level to be able to progress to the next, and if you don't master them, you never move up."
The senior let a few moments drift allowing this to sink in then observed "Look, they're moving."

Every occupant of the room seemed to wake from slumber, everyone looking round at the other in bewilderment, including the hostess herself. She was quick to notice that something was different but was going to turn it to her advantage. Pulling herself together she said, "Well that was enlightening wasn't it?" The looks of amazement on all faces told her no body, even her, had the slightest inclination of what had gone on. She hoped for one moment that she hadn't nodded off but it didn't feel like that.

"I never expected that," she started "you never know do you?"

Mr Isaacs felt bold enough to ask "What happened I seem to have um…." He didn't want to sound rude by saying he had fallen asleep.

"You had a message!" Anne was feeling the water.

"I did, who was it from?" He turned to his wife. "Do you know?"

Mrs Isaacs looked very embarrassed "I –I 'm not sure dear."

Anne was feeling braver by the minute "You all had a message, that's what I can't understand, to have so many in one sitting. Miss Taylor-Barnes now felt she must ask "Please, can you tell me if it was my Mother?"

"You know it was." Anne found she could tell them anything they wanted to know, they would swallow it but at the same time, she would have liked the answer. However it proved one thing, she must have tremendous power to be able to pull this off and not remember any of it. She must have gone into a trance; that would be the reason she couldn't remember afterwards. So full was she of this new found gift, she failed to notice one set of eyes fixed upon her in silence. The man near the door stood up, turned and left.

Gradually the assembled group followed in silence barely looking at one another and only giving Anne a nod or a whispered 'Bye' as they went. As she closed the front door behind the last one, she knew everything felt different. For all her false bravado, she knew something strange had taken place and she couldn't help wondering if they had witnessed more than she had, also, would any of them want to return? A strange stillness crept over the place and for the first time she began to feel very uneasy, almost as if she was being watched. Trying to shake herself back to reality she made her way to the kitchen to make a cup of tea but as she reached the door she had the overwhelming feeling that someone was waiting for her.

"Don't be so silly" she shouted and threw open the door to face whatever it was, but the room was empty. Almost sighing with relief she switched on the small radio to make some sort of comforting noise and hummed along to the music as she put the kettle on. As she took the tea bags from the cupboard she heard a distinct whisper. She stopped. There it was again. She spun round trying to focus on the source of the voice then realized it was coming from the radio, and it was getting louder each time she heard it. At first she thought it was just one of those things they did with songs these days, sticking talking bits in that didn't seem to have anything to do with the rest of it, but it wasn't like that. This voice was repeating just two words.

"Stop it!"

Anne was trembling now, but the tone had a kindness about it which somehow put her at ease at little, so she turned up the volume to hear more clearly but it had gone. All she heard was music so she switched it off. After making the tea she was about go back into to the meeting room and tidy up but felt she couldn't go in there at the moment, she had to compose herself so she went into the front room and sat down to take stock of today's events.

Milton and Daryl arrived back at the office and were greeted by Simon Freestone, the other man taken on after being made redundant and who had proved to be a gem in his own right. He lived and breathed computers and was often accused of having no life outside of his screen. He signed his name Si Fr which first became the nickname cipher, but as he had the unfortunate condition of producing far too much gas for any one human being, Daryl referred to him as Cyberfart. He took it all in good part and said he had his own names for them but wouldn't divulge what they were. As nobody ever wanted to stop to make tea or coffee, a drinks maker had been installed and now the two helped themselves to a cup and disappeared into Milton's office exchanging words with Simon.

"He's got his nose into something again" Daryl observed as he sat down "but he's good." When he got no reply, his attention turned to Milton who was staring at his notice board.

"Where is it?" he shouted, "Who's had it?" and turning on his heels he stormed back into the outer room and marching up to the computer almost yelled at Simon "Have you been in there?" pointing towards the open door with his finger.

Simon was not one to be rushed. "Boss, the door is locked all the time you are not here. I don't have a key." He certainly had a way of stating the obvious simply and effectively making Milton deflate like a pricked balloon. He patted the man on the shoulder and murmured "You're right, sorry, just got a bit wound up." Simon just nodded and turned his attention back to the screen.

Milton went back to his office, shut the door and sat facing Daryl who was just as bewildered, so asked "Boss, do you mind telling me where what is, and who has had what?"

"The letter."

"The letter?" He was still none the wiser and Milton's manner was not improving.

"For God's sake man, the one you brought me in the mail, the one I told you was dated way back, the one I thought was the same person as that lady in the audience, how much more do I have to say?"

There was a pause as Daryl hoped the man would calm a little before he hit him with his next observation but Milton was not going to calm down.

"Well?"

Daryl took a deep breath. "I was only going to point out that I didn't see it."

"What?" The question came out like an explosion.

"You said it was in with the mail, but I took your word for it, because I did not see it. I just went on what you had told me."

The steam was almost coming out of Milton's ears. "But I put it on the wall, in that bag" and he turned pointed to the empty plastic sleeve still pinned where he had put it, "and we said……" His voice trailed off as he added "Ah - I was examining it with Jean-Paul."

"Oh, Jean-Paul." The reply was tinged with sarcasm. Milton cast him a quick look and carried on.

"You know what this means, I didn't see it in the physical, the message was given to me in the spiritual, that's why you couldn't see it, and why Jean-Paul could."

There was a moments' silence as the truth sunk in then Daryl asked "One thing I was puzzled about is you took it to have come from a young lady, but how could you know that, just from the feel of it?"

"You know, my niece, well she's in her late teens now but a couple of years back, all the girls seemed to write the same, sort of square and bold but very neat, well it was like that, not boyish."

"And you said she just put her initials, P something."

"Yes, but that's also strange, here.." he pushed a paper and pen towards the other man "…write your initials on there."

Bewildered, Daryl wrote DF then looked up for some sort of explanation.

"Now write mine." As he took the paper with the two sets of letters he said, "You see, they are side by side."

"And?"

"The ones on the letter were under each other P T. Now why would a young lady write her initials downwards? Hang on."

"Now what?" Daryl thought this was becoming more like a mystery from a novel.

Milton was smiling as though he had hit on something. "The paper was torn at the bottom, so the T could have been a J or I, and there could have been more." He slapped his forehead "Of course."

"Well I'm glad you know what it is, on something that isn't there, so to speak." Daryl finished his coffee and looked up awaiting some enlightenment.

"Going back to my niece, the girls were always putting names, or letters on their envelopes, you know sort of fun codes."

"Oh you mean like S.W.A.L.K for Sealed With A Loving Kiss, and stuff like that?"

"Exactly although I understand some of them were a bit ruder than that, but you see this may be the start of one of those, there again, a young female."

"Oh. But does it give you enough to go on?"

"Not me on my own. I need to be left now. Shut the door on your way out." Before Daryl could even get out of his chair, the lever had been pushed and the sign on the wall outside lit up showing the boss must not be disturbed.

"Give my love to Jean-Paul" was the parting shot as the man left the room but it fell on deaf ears.

With the hasty departure of the guests, Avril hadn't had time to make any arrangements with the Isaacs as to her lift home and she was standing alone in the street wondering what to do next. She had a mobile phone which she only used for emergencies as she never felt at ease with it, and she didn't really feel like asking Bert to come when she had said she would get a lift.

"Going this way?"

The voice made her jump as she hadn't heard anyone approaching, and a man who reminded her of the quiet man at the meetings was standing very close to her. It wasn't him but the resemblance had shaken her.

"No- No thank you. I'm waiting for someone." She knew her voice trembled but she couldn't help it.

"Getting dark early, nights are pulling in, shouldn't be out on your own lady." He wasn't moving away and he was so near she could almost make out a mustiness coming from him.

"As I said, I'm waiting, so you can go now."

"Oo, couldn't leave a lady on her own, wouldn't be right now would it?" He took her arm in a tight grip and started to walk her away. "Just take you to the main road, just a few steps, be safer there you will."

She was confused, from what he said he seemed to be helping her, looking after her, but at the same time he was pulling her away against her will. Should she shout out? Looking around frantically she realized there was nobody about. Her mind was racing, if only she hadn't come, if only she had let Bert fetch her, if only... The thoughts were interrupted as he seemed to be pulling her sideways.

"This isn't the main road. Let me go!" The realization was sinking in, she was about to be attacked and there was nobody to help her. Her vain attempts to fight back had no impact, for this man had muscles of steel and her blows were useless, also his grip on her arm was such that the whole limb was becoming numb. She attempted a scream but it stuck in her throat as she became more and more frantic as she was almost dragged off the pavement into a small alley between the houses. A few more steps and she would have been on the main road where there would have been people who would have at least seen what was happening. His spare hand was now up her skirt snatching at her knickers, his roughness hurting her as he tried to cover her mouth with his to stop her crying out. The relief when his hand left her soon turned to terror as he thrust her to the ground holding her down with the weight of one leg while he pulled down his trousers and was thrusting himself between her thighs. Her instinct was to fight him off but one of her arms was now under her back and as she tried to raise the other he hit her such a blow across the face, a numbness seemed to be creeping over her whole body. Her last awareness before passing out completely was the throbbing movement of his groin ramming himself relentlessly into her body.

Bert had been restless since dropping off his wife earlier and he had half made up his mind to return to fetch her in case she hadn't got the lift she planned. He knew she could be hot headed and would make plans before the details had been arranged, so it was quite likely the couple could not, or would not wish to give her a lift. Musing on these thoughts as he sat in his comfy chair, a thought, an idea, whatever it was entered his brain.

"Get the car out."

And again "Get the car out." After a while this changed to "Go Now!" and was repeated at shortening intervals.

Out loud he said "I'm going, whoever you are," then added "I wanted to go anyway."

The ten minutes it took him to get across the small town were not lonely because he felt the presence of whoever it was pushing him to get to the pick up point. Whilst he was driving he realized he didn't know the exact place where Avril went as she always made him stop at the end of the road, but at least he knew which road so he would pull in there. When he stopped the car and switched off the engine, the force pulled him from the car and pointed him up the road making him face the opposite pavement. In the vicinity he imagined he could hear a scuffling and ran towards it although he couldn't tell exactly where it was coming from. At the same time a young man appeared coming from the opposite direction. As he reached the alley he beckoned Bert and together they saw the man taking off away from the still form which lay on the ground before them. With only having concern for his wife, Bert was immediately on the ground almost sobbing as he cradled his wife's head.

"She's alive thank God." He looked up to speak to the young man but there was no sign of him so he imagined the brave lad must have gone in pursuit of the attacker. He didn't want to leave Avril but he knew he must get help and having no mobile, he got up and ran to one of the houses adjoining the alley and hammered on the door. The wife said she would call an ambulance and the police so he could get back to his wife and the husband would come with him.

Avril was slowly coming round by the time the ambulance arrived but would have to be taken to the nearest Accident and Emergency hospital which was about ten miles away. The police offered to let Bert travel with his wife in the ambulance assuring him he would be brought back to collect his car later. He welcomed this, not realizing he was going to be asked questions in due course.

Liam, the young man from the meetings had received the message from Tommy, his spiritual friend who had been keeping a close watch on Bert for some time. He needed to warn him that the man needed help. Whilst Liam had been protecting Avril during the séances, Tommy had been trying to warn Bert of impending danger. He had asked the higher powers if he could be one of his protectors, for wasn't it this man who had extended his earthly life by pushing him out of the way of a car when they were lads and he felt he owed him a debt of gratitude.

But it was guilt that engulfed Liam now. He should have stayed nearer to Avril until he knew she was physically safe, whereas he had guarded her spirit side knowing her vulnerability, but not considering her earthly dangers. He guessed her attack was nothing to do with the meeting, just chance, unless the man had targeted her for his own reasons. When Liam had been given this task by the higher powers, he imagined it would be a walk over, if not boring. He had already ascertained that Astral Anne had no powers whatsoever, and wondered why he had been ordered to guard this woman who appeared to have no more go about her than a church mouse. Another thing that was bothering him was the identity of the being that had tried to push Avril away during the sitting. He was aware of the other entity in presence and had not yet worked out its purpose, but was guessing that it was just using the set up for its own ends, whatever they were. Now he wondered if this other thing was more dangerous than he had imagined and another good force was also protecting his charge. Little did he guess that it was only by chance that Jo had been there, who feeling the weakness of this lady had tried to get her to leave as she would have no understanding of such deep things of other levels.

So if Tommy hadn't alerted him to stay close, Liam could have deserted his charge and would not have had the chance to chase the attacker. Now, leaving his body resting up against the fence, his spiritual part went in search of the sexual predator to track him down.

Sadie welcomed Jo as the latter returned to her own level.

"Was I missed?" Jo was scanning the area to see if she had been detected.

"No, lucky you, there was a big disturbance and most of the attention has been on that. But don't do that to me again, I was sure I would be asked where you were."

The disturbance had been carefully planned to allow her to wander and had she only known, the senior force at her side was one of those who had 'grounded' her, using a different form.

Sadie asked "Did you find what you were looking for?"

"Not yet, but I will. I won't settle until I've found the bastard."

The younger one was worried for she liked Jo and didn't want to see her in any kind of trouble, and she was thinking about her lecture when she was advised to let go and move on.

"Maybe, it will sort itself, you may never find him."

Jo wasn't put off that easily. "I will not rest until I find the filthy scum that robbed me of my life in such a disgusting way. I wasn't ready for this, and I am not prepared to move on, as you put it. I have a score to settle, and nobody is going to stop me."

"You frighten me Jo. Do you know what you are up against?"

There was a pause, then the answer came slowly.

"I will find out."

"Do you intend to kill him?"

"Oh No. Nothing as easy as that. I am going to scare the shit out of him while he is in earthly."

"Jo!"

"What?"

"You shouldn't say that?"

Jo observed the younger spirit with mild affection. "My dear girl, I haven't changed my attitude since passing. You haven't changed from your lovely sweet nature. We are the same as we were, and to put it bluntly, I was a pain in the arse when I was in physical, and I will continue to be an even bigger pain in the arse from now on. And don't look so shocked, you must have heard it somewhere before."

To see a spirit so embarrassed amused Jo and gave a moments' levity to the situation, but underneath she was more determined than ever to seek out this fiend. Although she hadn't told Sadie, she knew the identity of the offender, but she didn't know of his current whereabouts, that was what she had to locate. Where was he now?

The higher entities knew exactly what was going on, but Jo's search was cutting across their own observations which is why they were letting her have enough rope, not only to keep her satisfied, but to help them track a much more sinister being who could infiltrate every sector of all known lower levels. No one was sure just how high it could climb and this was something they had to find out as quickly as possible. The entity observed at Anne's had not yet been identified which was causing concern as most beings were known to the higher ones, so this had to be treated with utmost caution. On one of the higher levels a conference was in full swing.

"Don't you think it is unwise to allow this inexperienced spirit to get involved?"

"She is carefully monitored although she doesn't realize it."

"But she doesn't know she is being used, she will not have her guard up."

"That is why we must be in presence in some form at all times."

"We are putting her everlasting existence in peril, it could affect her ultimate transition."

"We can't stop her in her own quest. She is in our way. What choice do we have?"

"What do you suppose she would say if she knew?"

"I think her reply would be unprintable!"

The debate went on for many hours in earth time, but in their realm it took a mere fraction of a second.

CHAPTER 4

Anne was restless. She had not been able to settle herself since the meeting and her nerves were still on edge from the feeling in the kitchen and the words coming out of the radio. She sat alone in the front room deciding whether or not to go to bed but her mind was in a whirl. Should she go into the back room and tidy up or leave it until the morning? But if she left it, would she feel like going in then? She felt something had been in there with them all, but she had no idea what. Just as she decided to make a cup of cocoa and get ready for the night she heard a knock at the front door which nearly made her jump out of her skin. At first she wondered if she should ignore it, but after a moment another louder knock came. Slowly she went into the hall and peered through the spy hole. Two men stood in the porch. Making sure the chain was in place, she opened the door as much as it would allow and asked "Yes, what do you want?"

"Mrs Barbara Simpson?"

Taken aback at the use of her first name she said "Who wants to know?"

The older of the two men moved forward showing his identification.

"I'm Detective Inspector Grimes, and this is DC Bruin, could we come in for a moment please?"

When she hesitated he explained "I'm sorry it's late and we can understand you being wary, that's good, but this is very important madam."

"Just a moment." Anne slid the chain out of its housing and slowly opened the door. The D.C. also showed his identity card as he entered and they both stood in the hall while she closed the door.

"Perhaps you would like to come into the front room." She led the way and after waiting for her to sit in her chair, they both sat down.

The DI smiled at her and said "Just one thing before I come to the point, you are Mrs Barbara Anne Simpson?"

"Yes, I never liked my first name so I always use the second one."

"That's fine. Now, I don't know if anyone's said anything but there's been a bit of an incident a few doors down. Have you heard anything this evening?" The Detective Constable was making notes as they spoke and her attention was momentarily on him.

"Um, well I did hear a siren earlier, but that's not unusual these days is it?" Both men noticed how on edge she seemed and felt there was more here than was obvious at first glance.

Det.Insp.Grimes took out a notebook, flicked over a couple of pages then looked her directly in the eye.

"You hold meetings here I understand?"

"Well, I have a few friends round sometimes, if that's what you mean."

"And you had them round earlier this evening?"

Well...yes... but how did you know that, and what has it got to do with anything?" She was flustered now and her words were very garbled causing the men to give each other a knowing glance.

"Séances to be precise." The statement was curt and the inspector was looking less friendly by the minute.

"Well no, not really, it isn't like that."

The DC spoke making her turn her head in his direction. "Just what is it like then Mrs Simpson?"

"We just sit and talk about things."

"Over a cup of tea?" Her head had to turn the other way to answer the inspector and this started to have an unnerving effect.

"Well, no we don't have tea."

There was a moments' silence before the inspector asked "Just where do you have these - er- meetings?"

"In the other room." Her voice was fading and she wished he would tell her what this was all about.

"You won't mind if we just have a look." This was a statement not a question. She would much rather they didn't but they were already making their way to the other room leaving her no option but to either stay where she was or follow. As she went to get to her feet DC. Bruin said "It's alright Mrs Simpson, we'll call you if we need anything."

The men looked round the room without touching anything but taking in every detail of how the seating was placed.

"No table or candle or such like, do you suppose she only thinks of it as a meeting?" the DC. asked.

"After what we've just heard? No way, she's hiding something. Get her in here."

The DC returned to the front room and called Anne to join them.

"I'm going to stand in the hall with the inspector, and we want you to stand in the doorway and tell us exactly who sat where at your meeting. Can you do that for us please?"

"Well not entirely."

"Oh why's that?"

"Um, I don't know all of their names."

They had joined the inspector who said "But we thought they were your friends Mrs Simpson, are you trying to tell me you don't know the names of your friends who come here for a meeting."

She stood there lost for words so he continued "Tell us those you do remember." He held his hand out motioning her to the doorway.

"Well, Mr and Mrs Isaacs sit there on the settee and…."

"First names?" The DC had his pen poised.

"I don't know, they never said."

"Carry on please."

"Well, then in that chair is - oh he's a young man, Lee I think he said. Then I sit there and then it's Gerte, only she didn't come today, then Mrs Harker." She leant further in looking round the door and nodded towards the dining chair "That's where Miss Taylor-Barnes always sits, and that just leaves this chair."

"And does anybody sit in 'this chair'?" The inspector made the last two words very precise.

"Well, yes, um.. a gentleman."

The DC was still writing. "And does the gentleman have a name?"

"No. I mean he must have a name but he never said."

"Ok. Let's go back into the other room please." The inspector was looking rather serious now and she was feeling a little dizzy.

It was obvious that this woman was holding séances, meetings, call them what you will as the officers knew that if you had friends in your house you knew them by their names, not, as she kept repeating what they had said, or hadn't said. And the fact they always sat in the same place added to the picture.

When they had all returned to the front room Det. Insp Grimes addressed Anne whilst still looking at his book.

"The lady you say is Mrs Harker was attacked this evening just down the road from here."

Anne went pale. "Is she hurt? What happened?"

Ignoring the question he went on "She is in hospital receiving treatment, and of course she is badly shocked. From what we can gather it seems she had just left this house." He gave a few moments for the truth to sink in before continuing.

"Do you remember if she left alone?"

"Well, everybody left about the same time."

"Ah yes, from the meeting, of course." There was sarcasm in his voice which made her feel as though he didn't believe a word she was saying. He made some notes in silence and she noticed the DC was also scribbling like mad. After a few minutes DI Grimes closed his book and said "We will need to speak to you again, not thinking of going away are you?"

"No, I'm not going away." Her voice was very feeble now as shock was creeping in.

As they got up to leave the inspector took a breath then said almost as an aside, "Don't suppose it will hurt to tell you, be in all the papers tomorrow but a Mrs Gerte Schultz was found this morning just outside of town."

"Is she......?"

"Dead? Very much so. And obviously you knew her."

"P – p –pardon?"

Grimes had got the reaction he had hoped for, confirming the dead person was another of the woman's 'friends'.

"What happened?" Anne was almost in tears from the shock of it all.

"Sorry, can't give any details." His reply was curt and almost without feeling as though he wanted it to get through to her, hitting the nerve head on.

Milton and Jean-Paul were trying to concentrate but they were both aware of a presence trying to communicate. As usual there would be many passing souls, either trying to connect with loved ones and looking for a real source such as them, or just going about their allotted tasks. They likened it to sitting on a bench in the park where you would hear people in conversation as they strolled by, but none of it had anything to do with you. But this was different. The image of the voice was desperate, begging them for help. Reluctantly they put the matter of the letter aside from their thoughts and both tried to home in on this new request. Suddenly they both felt themselves pulled away from the area as though they were being dragged across rough ground at such a force they were unable to resist. This immediately had put them on their guard, for up to now there was no indication as to whether this was a good or evil entity, and they weren't sure whether to fight back or go with the power. Not that it would have made much difference as they were propelled with such speed they had no option but to await the outcome.

As quickly as it had started, the momentum stopped and the two found themselves hovering over a ditch. A covering had been pegged over part of the ground and a few men were busying themselves examining the area. Milton did not concentrate on how many there were, for in spirit if the concentration is not on the earthly, the earth image can become a haze whilst the attention is given to the other realm. It was the being that was hovering just above the cover that beckoned them nearer.

"Come, please. You must help."

Jean-Paul indicated they both move together slowly and as they approached the image they saw it was a middle aged to elderly lady. Her hand was outstretched.

"You must stop this." Her words bore such urgency.

"Who are you and who must we stop?" Jean-Paul kept the question very calm.

"It is here, I knew it, I have known it was coming. I've seen it before and what it can do."

Milton moved forward until he was close to her. "Please, tell us who you are."

After a slight pause she said "I was known as Gerte Schultz in this earth life, but they recognized me and cut my life short." Her head inclined towards the tarpaulin then she continued "They would know that would do little good, but they probably thought that I may speak out to the earth dwellers. But I am in equal danger now I am back in the ether."

Jean-Paul had been deep in thought. "I am confused. You said 'it' then referred to it as 'they'. Can you tell us just what this is please Gerte?"

"The biggest, most evil force you could ever face. We have been trying to trace its whereabouts for some time and we had got it down to this particular séance."

Milton felt he had to ask. "Isn't this rather a small insignificant venue, I mean if it is as powerful as you say, wouldn't it be going for a much bigger target?"

"Ah, that is what fools everyone on all levels. No need to bother with such a little problem. But I tell you, some have already got it under close observation."

Jean-Paul wanted to learn just how much she knew about how this force would operate and Gerte was only too pleased to tell him.

"Yes, it starts with a small, seemingly harmless spirit stirring up a bit of trouble, but there are many, many such cells, and they grow, some join up making a larger cell. Do I need to go on?"

"But what is their ultimate aim?" Milton was realizing this wasn't to be taken lightly.

She paused. "To turn all good to evil."

Jean-Paul knew straight away the implications. "So they start on the earth level, knowing it will affect the next spiritual level, climbing up as far as they can, like a virus, affecting everything on the way."

"And," she emphasized "the disruption reaches far beyond that."

"In what way?" Milton was trying to figure out how much more could be affected beyond the spirit realms of existence but Jean-Paul knew.

"The whole universe and beyond." His reply brought a stunned silence to the trio.

"I'm afraid you are correct." Gerte turned her attention to Milton. "Can you even slightly imagine a force so strong that it can upset the vibrations of space? The consequences would be beyond imagination."

It took a few moments for the realization to sink in then Milton asked "You said you had seen it before Gerte. What happened then?"
She looked towards Jean-Paul then back to Milton. "We stopped its climb just as it was leaving the earthly zone. But as I am sure you know, nothing can be totally destroyed."

"Its still here, is that what you're saying?"

"No Milton, it is not here."
Jean-Paul took over. "It had to be dispatched to the place where nothing can escape."
For a moment his friend was in thought then he almost shouted "A black hole! You sent it to a black hole."

The conversation was cut short for Milton was being pulled back to his body. He felt very annoyed at the intrusion as he wanted to know all about the previous encounter, but Jean-Paul assured him he would fill in all the gaps on their return. Gerte bid them farewell. They knew she was still bound to the place of her death for now but was satisfied she had reached someone of her own level and passed on the warning.

Milton opened his eyes, glanced round the room and satisfied himself that it had not been a physical reason for his return but more likely a spiritual warning to get back if danger was threatening. He opened the door to the main office and was greeted by Daryl who grabbed some papers off his desk.

"Oh great boss, you're available; I've got the details of the next tour, just a short one covering some of the local midland counties. Not as bad as the last eh?"

"As long as you haven't booked me into one of those pokey little meeting rooms again." They both laughed, as some of the early venues had been a little on the meager side, but that was long gone.

"No, Cyberfart's booked some good places, he's just printing off the chart now, and he's finished the advertising bumf, looks good."

"Thanks Simon" Milton nodded in the man's direction and was answered with a single hand raised in the air in acknowledgment.

"Oh and Simon could you have a dig around the newspapers while you're on there, check up on a Gerte Schultz, see if there's any recent reports of her in an accident or something." Again the hand went up, and Milton knew that if anything had been reported anywhere, this man would dig it out.

Bert had been told he could probably take his wife home. It was the day after her attack, and although physically a bit bruised she wasn't in too bad a shape but psychologically she felt violated and dirty. She was offered counselling but refused as she had had enough of the policemen's questions and all she wanted was to get back to the safety of their own little home and never go out again. Maybe for the first time in years she appreciated the sanctuary of the place and also Bert who was a good man at heart. She had never seen him so upset as when he had been brought in by the police after she was admitted to the hospital, and the look on his face when he was asked to leave while she was asked a few questions would haunt her for a long time.

He sat with her now waiting for the doctor to release her, gently stroking her hand and telling her everything would be alright once they got home. Her main concern seemed to him to be the fact she had been forced to tell the police the address she had visited.

"But they've got to know those things," he assured her, "just in case anybody there saw anything when they were leaving."

"I suppose so. Do you think she would mind, Mrs Simpson I mean?"

"All the same if she does, can't be helped. They've got to try and find out who......." his voice trailed off as he tried to put the image from his mind of some other man having sex with his wife.

"Yes I suppose so, but I'm alright."

After a minute he said "You didn't sort out a lift then?"

"Um, No we all left rather quickly I suppose."

"Oh." He didn't feel he could ask why and there was probably nothing in it, but something was niggling at the back of his mind, and he was still a little baffled at the messages to 'Get the car out'. If he was honest with himself, he knew he was being warned about something, and he felt deep down that he should heed it, but the question was - what?

"There's something going on here and I don't like it, I don't like it one bit." Det. Insp. Grimes threw a file on the table and looked at the couple of detectives watching him. "Firstly, we know that the Gerte woman was found in a ditch two days ago, then that Mrs......, um, Harker got attacked yesterday, now today this." His finger stabbed at the message that had just come in from the traffic section.

"The car down the bank" DC Bruin stated, "so its not just a run of the mill accident?"

"No, by chance I had been talking to Reg Wills, from traffic, married one of my nieces, and he noticed the name of the dead couple was the same as what I'd been telling him about this séance business."

"Hardly coincidence with that name." the other DC observed.

"Quite, now it gets better, or worse, whichever way you want to look at it." He got up and turned to the board on the wall grabbing a pen as he spoke. "We know the Gerte woman was found, in the ditch, right by the roadside but out of view, so any passing motorist would have been within feet of her but wouldn't see her." He hastily made columns and headed them with name, place, visual etc. "Now, the Harker woman was grabbed and dragged into an alley, just off the road, near to a public path but out of sight, because it bends a bit, I've checked and where she was found, you wouldn't have seen her if you had been walking by." He carried on filling in the board.

DC Bruin asked, "And the car that left the road was hidden."

"Absolutely. It had come off on that slight bend and gone down into 'The Hollow' as the locals call it, and there again any traffic wouldn't have stood a cat in hell's chance of seeing it."

"Do we know if they were killed outright?"

"Don't know yet, coroner's onto it."

The DC who had been taking all this in stood up and looked at the board. "Be interesting to know if the car was faulty."

"Certainly will?" DC Bruin had joined them "also do we know how they were found if they were so out of sight, except Mrs Harker of course."

"Interesting point Bruin, now that's another thing. The car was found by a chap coming up the hill from Norbury where it joins the top road and he saw part of the car sticking up, so he went to have a look and called us on his mobile, knew he couldn't do anything for them."

"And Mrs Schultz?" the two younger men chorused.

"Local farmer, his dog was going mad at the hedge and when he went round to see what was up he saw her foot sticking out. He was looking from the other side of the ditch you see, not from the road."

DC Bruin was musing.

"What's up lad?" The DI wondered.

"Well, sounds silly, but these two are almost to a pattern, where they were, the chance way they got found, but why was Mrs Harker different?"

"And," the other man asked "what's it all got to do with that astral person, apart from the fact they were all regulars at her weird stuff?"

"Good questions and we will find the answers but first..."the inspector looked from one to the other "I think we had better track down the rest of the bunch, while we can if you know what I mean."

"Do you want us to take one each?" DC Bruin had his notebook open at the ready.

"Not at the moment, work together, till we know what's going on. Dig out that young fellow who came to help, Lee or something, then that spinster, Miss Taylor-Barnes the woman said. Now the last chap Mr No Name, that might be a bit tricky but......" he stopped.

"What is it?"

"We don't want her holding any more séances but what if he just turns up? "He looked at his notes. "The first Tuesday of the month, that's when they meet, so if she can't get in touch with him, will he come?"

"Unless," DC Bruin felt he had to add "the news of the events puts him off." Grimes pointed a knowing finger at him and grunted, then waving them off he said "Keep me informed of everything, and I mean the smallest detail."

As the two were leaving he called out to the other DC, "You've just joined us from Levvington, right?"

"That's right sir."

"Sorry what was your name again?"

"DC Murray sir, DC Liam Murray."

"Where on earth did that come from?" Milton had returned to the office after a visit to the bank and saw a pair of brown eyes peering at him from under Daryl's desk.

"Oh, hope you don't mind boss, its my sister's dog, she's gone away for a couple of days and didn't want to kennel him. He's very good, he'll be no trouble, I would have asked but she sprung it on me and you've been......."

"Yes, yes, I get the picture, alright if he's clean."   Flop, the cocker spaniel would have melted any dog lovers' heart and as Milton stopped to get acquainted with him, the tail started to wag and he nuzzled the man's hand.

"Probably got fleas." Simon made the comment without turning from the monitor and although his delivery was always very droll Daryl jumped to the dog's defense immediately.

"He hasn't got fleas any more then you have, come to think of it you have been scratching a lot lately."

"Yes, all right you two?" Milton had to laugh at the love-hate relationship between this pair and he was still chuckling as he made his way to his own office. The door was closed which was usual when he was out, but before he got to the threshold Flop had dashed forward and now stood facing the door growling.

"What is it?" Daryl was at his side in a minute but turning to Milton said "Stay back boss. This dog is warning you of something."
They all watched as Flop sniffed round the base of the door, his hackles raised. Then he slowly backed away a few inches, turned and took the few steps to Milton and sat at his feet, his right paw raised.

"What do you make of that?" Simon had joined them and stood with his mouth open.

"He wants you to shake it." Daryl nodded his head towards Flop.
Milton stooped down and shook the offered paw. "Were you trying to tell me something?" He knew animals could see things that humans couldn't and he never mocked this kind of occurrence although many people did. The dog seemed at ease now but Milton wondered just what he may have encountered had Flop not been there to warn him.

"Have you put something for him to lie on, and does he have a drink?" He had turned to Daryl.

"Yes boss, his blanket is behind my desk and there's water in his bowl in the kitchen."

"Well little fellow, it's good to have you on the team." Milton stroked the soft head and got a loving lick in return.

"Fleas and all." Came from Simon who had returned to his usual position at his computer, but although the levity lifted the general ambiance in the outer office, Milton was wary as he unlocked his own room and made his way to his desk. He stood for a moment taking in the vibrations then turned to Daryl, gave him the thumbs up and shut the door. Jean-Paul was the first to observe the ripples in the surrounding space.

"Seems more like something passing through than actually making a visitation" he was floating all over the office sensing the strength of the disturbance in each part, "it's left a straight line of its route from there to there, no stopping."

"So this was just on the way?" Milton was also tracing the path.

Jean-Paul didn't answer immediately and when he did his companion knew it was something more serious than first thought.

"This was powerful, unusually so and I have to tell you my friend that there have been several of these extraordinary passings worldwide so I don't believe this was aimed at you or this place, we are as you say just on the route."

"Well I suppose that's a bit of comfort. I do like to know what I'm facing."

As they settled in the returning calm Jean-Paul indicated to the door. "Like the dog, it's good he's here, he won't miss a thing. Very sensitive he is. He'll also add to the protective aura."

"Glad you approve." Milton laughed and they both turned their attention to the business of the mysterious letter.

CHAPTER 5

The senior spirits were in serious conference for they were now certain which evil power they were dealing with, and with their combined past experience knew this thing would grow at an alarming rate and had to be stopped in its infancy, for if it became deep rooted it could almost infiltrate their ranks before they were aware, so diligence was vital.

Many thought that Jo should be removed from the scene and given work elsewhere but there was the opposing view that with her innocence they may not see her as a threat. For now the same senior would guard her, sometimes in different guises but if too many of their level were seen hovering it could raise suspicion.

Jo was floating a short distance from the Simpson house when her sentinel appeared by her side.

"Who the hell are you," she eyed the spirit with caution."

"Nan."

"Why are you here?"

"Why should I not be?" I do the same job as you, I am in the calming section, to keep peace and tranquility everywhere."

"I haven't seen you before." Jo was still a bit hesitant to admit she was anything but calming in any capacity so decided to play along and see what transpired.

"My colleague was here, bit of something going on so we take it in turns to keep an eye on the place."

"Oh the one that was with me, she told me a lot."

"We are always glad to pass on knowledge to those who will listen." The tone of the voice this spirit would have used, gave the impression of a hypnotic flowing melody that calmed and relaxed everything in her space.

Jo was feeling a little safer and said "Yes I can see the resemblance you have the same manner as she did."

Nan let a moment of silence go by then asked "What brings you to return to this place?"

Jo explained her first encounter with the entity, then the séance where she had felt an overwhelming urge to remove the innocent lady from the group.

"What did you find different about her?"

Jo didn't have to think of an answer. "She was more vulnerable than the rest, poor sod didn't seem to fit in, so something made me want to get her out of there."

"And you think that was all your own doing?"

"Well, wasn't it, what are you getting at?"

"It didn't occur to you that you were in fact helping another good force already in the room, and......" she paused to let it sink in ".....perhaps more than one."

This really knocked Jo. She hadn't expected to hear this and she was struggling to find the next question. Nan gave her a moment then explained.

"Let's take Astral Anne as she calls herself, you have already worked out that she has no power whatsoever so why do these people come here?"

"To get messages. Oh, but they won't, only they don't know that because she makes them up, and takes their money for it."

"Not much different to you then. Except you don't take money, you can't, you just get the satisfaction of playing with spirits who want to make contact and you bring them somewhere like this where the 'medium' cannot detect you. Am I right?"

"Seems you know all about me anyway." Jo weighed the thought with as much sarcasm she could muster. Nan paused again before she shot the next arrow.

"But even that isn't the real reason is it?"

Jo was getting a little angry at having her soul bared and she wanted to know how much this one knew about her motive.

"I expect you are about to tell me."

"You are determined to find the person who shortened your life, in other words your murderer; you do know the identity but you don't know the location."

Jo was piecing together all she had just been told and asked "And you people do?"

Ignoring this Nan went on "And just what would you do if you found this earthling?"

This brought Jo to a halt, for so intent has she been on finding them for revenge, she hadn't thought what she would actually do. The person was still in earthly form and she was a mere young spirit on a different plane who may not be able to make contact. It would be most unlikely she could frighten them or affect their life, so what was she going to achieve?

Nan cut into her musing. "Your time could be much better spent doing good and helping to stamp out a much worse evil. Look down there."
As she directed Jo's attention to the house she said "Do you see that darkening mist hanging over the property."

"I didn't at first, but now I can. Bloody hell it's changing shape and stretching out slowly. What is it?"

"Probably what you met the first time and what has caused the horror since the meeting. Quickly she listed the three incidents finishing with "And that is only the beginning."

Jo recalled she had quickly returned to her zone when the meeting had ended afraid she would be missed, so had not witnessed Avril's attack and when she learned of the others she asked "But didn't you say there may be other good spirits there?"

"I did, they may have also been in physical form and there may have been some just in spirit, but all would have been in danger from this tremendous force."

"Would I have been in big trouble if I had got caught up in it?"
Nan didn't want to touch on Jo's role in too great a depth so replied "Well as long as your superiors didn't know, no harm done. But I could get you on the team if you like, get permission for you to help us."

"You could do that?" Jo was a little wary but always liked a challenge, although unbeknown to her, as she consented to the agreement, the seniors immediately put their plan into action.

"Why didn't I see the mist before?" It was now so clear before her that she needed an answer.

"I have made you aware of it so that you will always know of its whereabouts."
After a moments' pondering Jo asked "Are there other things about that I am not aware of?"

"My dear, there have always been 'things about' as you put it but few people notice them."

"Then how will I know, if there's any danger I mean?"

"You will be shown when the time is right."
The young spirit knew she had hit a brick wall and would not find out anything more at present, but one thing was very clear. This conversation had only taken the blink of an eye in earth time, something she was having to

adjust to quickly, for speed would be one of their weapons in fighting this enemy.

"Come" Nan beckoned "we have been here too long already." Together they moved to an area far enough away to observe but not be apparent to the entity.

"Look at the way it sends out tendrils from its centre" she explained "that's how it controlled the deaths and the attack, but it won't stop there, it will have the next target lined up. Look there is one going out now, almost waving about as if looking for something or someone."

Jo felt she had to whisper, not that there was any need for they only communicated in thought, "Why is it centred on Astral Annie's place, and why hasn't anything happened to her?"

"She's just the base. They use many such places to home in then take residence while they start their plans of destruction."

"You say they, are there more of them?"

"You have just hit on the problem. Think of them as cells, each one growing as it claims its victims. Just one or two at first so that nobody suspects, but then cells join and form larger multi cells and so on."

Jo was staggered. "So you have to destroy the small cells before they get bigger."

"Exactly, and I have to tell you that there is only a certain period of time in which to carry it out, because when it reaches a certain stage we are almost helpless against it."

"How do you know all this?"

Nan wondered just how much to tell the girl so just said "Past experience, that is all you need for now, but heed my warning, never let your guard down against this thing for an instant."

Their attention was drawn back to the mist which was darkening and becoming much denser. Another limb was reaching out but not on the ground, it was aiming upwards in the direction of the area they had just left, groping the air as if driven by hunger.

"Come, we must leave here for now." Nan's will shot Jo back to her home zone immediately. "You will have to concentrate on how to do that, it will be vital."

Jo was a little taken aback at the transportation until Nan explained it was ultra speed travel and you didn't go from one place to another as you would on earth, but the thought transferred you instantly. She instructed her to remain where she was and think over all that had happened whilst she rose to the greater levels for conference with other seniors.

Bert had just gone out into the back garden to empty some rubbish into the bin when his neighbour popped his head over the fence.

"Awful business, have you heard?"

Bert wasn't sure what the man was referring to so he asked "What would that be then?"

His neighbour moved nearer until he was almost leaning over the fence. "That couple in the car, I heard they went off the road at The Hollow, fairly took the dry stone wall with them."

Something in Bert shuddered. "When was this?"

"Yesterday I think, only it seems they can't have been there long. Both killed of course."

"Do you know who it was?" Bert was afraid to ask for he had a sense that he would hear something he didn't like.

"Ah, the Isaacs couple, live in that house on its own just out the town, you know the one with the stone lions by the gate."

"Oh that one, yes I know the pair but they keep to themselves a lot, never did get to know them."

"Well," the man beckoned Bert even nearer and his voice dropped to a whisper "I have heard tell that they was into some sort of black magic and the like."

It hit Bert like a bullet. They must have been at the meeting, he didn't know why but he just knew there was a connection. Bidding a quick goodbye, he almost rushed back into the house, but slowed his pace as he came nearer to his wife who was resting on the sofa, her eyes closed.

"Avril."

Her eyelids raised "Oh Bert, what is it?"

He sat with one cheek of his bottom resting on the cushion and said very gently "Don't worry I just want to ask you a question."

She sat up giving him enough room to sit beside her. "What is it Bert, you look worried?"

"I only wanted to know the name of the people you said may give you a lift home the other night, that was all."

"Oh Bert, I thought it was going to be something about the........" she couldn't put the attack into words so he continued.

"Was it a married couple?"

"Yes, why do you ask? If you must know it was Mr and Mrs Isaacs, they have to pass by the end of our road because they live a bit further out, only I didn't get the lift did I?" She started to fill up with emotion. "If only I'd asked them, I wouldn't have been, well you know."

Bert now wondered whether or not to tell her now or let her find out. After a moment he coughed nervously and said "I am so glad you didn't go with them my dear."

She looked more confused than anything and a very quiet "Why?" left her lips.

"Well you will hear sooner or later. Him next door says they were killed, car accident, seems the man must have lost control and they went down into The Hollow."

She sat there with her mouth open and they both knew what her next question would be.

"Was it Tuesday, after the meeting?"

Bert felt a bit stronger now. "Well we don't know that, seems they were found yesterday but we don't really know when it happened. I expect the police will be piecing it all together."

Avril was nearly in tears, "This is all because of the meeting."

"Why do you say that? We don't know." Bert didn't want her going off on a tangent until things were proved.

"I got attacked, you said Gerte had been found dead, and now this. It's all to do with that evening, something wasn't right."

Bert was alert in a moment. "What happened? You must tell me, don't you see it could be important."

Tommy, Bert's guardian was interested in this exchange for although he considered Avril as not being the brightest when it came to things beyond her understanding, she had obviously picked up something from the meeting which told him it must have been pretty powerful for her to notice. He was now tuned into Liam's spirit relaying every detail of this conversation.

Avril was becoming tense at the thought of having to recount that awful night. She told Bert that she felt she had nodded off for a moment but felt she was being pushed away somewhere, but she tried to stay where she was, and when she came to, nobody seemed to have noticed but the funny thing was that they all seemed to have dozed as well. The only person who appeared to know anything was Astral Anne who said they all had received messages but there again nobody could remember, so what was the point of that?

Bert sat in silence for a moment. He knew something had gone on and feared an evil source was behind it. His senses were now becoming finer tuned than before and he knew he must open his mind to any warnings which may be sent to him. His thoughts flicked back to the message on the window that Avril had seen, the order to get the car out again haunted him. He stroked his wife's hand and said gently "Well you are better off out of it, you must try and put it away from your mind now."

"I wish I could." she thought as she closed her eyes and rested her head back against the cushion.

Tommy now knew he could use Bert's hidden power as a springboard to bounce off in the oncoming battle. This was often done and could put the dormant spirit at risk, but every source was needed to try and stop this thing, and Tommy was only too well aware of that. He was in immediate contact with Liam, one of the 'plants' at the séance. It had only been by chance that he was placed in that particular venue as the higher powers had tried to put someone in each vulnerable possible place where the thing could get a foothold. Some of the placements were in spirit but some very experienced ones who could temporarily assume bodily form were used as decoys hoping the evil would not suspect they were observing it.

Liam was well up the ladder and had taken many forms in the past, sometimes just for the moment, then disappearing without trace, but occasionally it had been necessary to take over another earth form for the time being, then departing when he had no further use of it. In this case he was combining the two powers, so the young man Bert saw beckoning him to the alley was the temporary body of Liam, but would not have known that the spiritual one had tried to pursue the attacker, retuning to this body in the alley moments later.

He now chastised himself for his complacency at the start, thinking that Anne's place would not harbour a cell in the early stages. Although there had been no air disruption, no signs of festering sin, he should have concentrated beyond the room for signs of development. But he also had to make sure that no attention was drawn to him as he played down his power staying under cover for as long as he could, but it was little solace.

As Tommy contacted him, they both conversed on the spiritual level and in seconds had the whole picture. They agreed they must consult with higher ones as more help needed to be on standby. The evil was still in the early stages, but they weren't sure just how long it would take to start joining and spreading. Liam was letting the physical DC Murray do the ground work for him and he would just home in and pick up any odd bit of information that the police had learned which may have passed him by.

The mist was growing quicker than usual. The high spirits had seen this kind of entity a few times but each encounter was slightly different and each one was worse than the last as though the knowledge was being passed onto another generation. There were many now scattered all over the country and as they darkened in colour it was a sign they were about to join to a nearby companion. The arms that had been observed reaching out were not only to attack the next victims they were like antenna, probing the spiritual for any sign of observation. The one that had settled at Anne's started by picking off the vulnerable creatures. It had left Anne alone as it needed to keep her house as a base for now, but it was trying to track Liam's movements for it had picked up the vibes as he speed travelled, and had observed the fact that his physical was not as solid as the mortals thought. The little spinster too was not as innocent as she would have one believe but she seemed dormant for now. However, she might as well be taken out of the picture just in case, so it planned her immediate demise, and with her living alone it would be a simple task, no witnesses. It didn't matter that these people would move on to the spirit world, for they would be no threat to it there.

That just left the quiet man. It would be a month before he was due to re-appear at the meeting but by then he would not be needed and the local police would have more on their hands than to bother about him. And the image of him used by the mist would have disappeared into just that – a mist.

There was panic in Milton's office suite. One of the venue's had been double booked and the manager of the hall was asking if they could change the date. Daryl was indignant.

"You are not dealing with a little tin pot performer; you are privileged to be hosting the biggest psychic event in the country. Get the other people to change their date, all our advertising is done and may I say, paid for so if we cannot have your venue you will be charged with our losses, and may I also say, we do not appreciate the kind of bad publicity this will produce. Now, young man, do I make myself perfectly clear?"

Milton stood listening with mild amusement as Daryl slammed the phone down.

"And what did the young man say?" he tried to suppress the grin which was pulling at his facial muscles. Even Simon had turned round for the reply.

"It seems boss, that some idiot had also booked a golden wedding for the main hall, they are regulars and didn't want to let them down, after all their date is only on one particular day whereas our dates can be anytime." He almost spat the words out.

"And so what is happening?"

"They will see what they can do."

"No good. "Simon spoke and although he didn't waste words, what he did say always seemed to get a response.

"Explain." Daryl tried to emulate his speech.

He received a withering look then Simon said "Can't rely on them. And do you want to share with another happening?"

"Oh, if they shove them in another room you mean, "Daryl was deep in thought "Hmmm, can't have that sort of drunken noise with this kind of show."

Milton had been observing all this then said very quietly "Have you actually got all the printed tour details back yet?"

"Not really," Daryl said "I was so mad that...."

"OK. Cancel them. We don't beg."

They were interrupted by the phone ringing. Daryl snorted as he picked up the receiver.

"Oh really, well can you just hold on one minute please, I'm not sure if Mr Warner has decided to cancel in view of the last call we had." He pushed the mute button and said "It seems the party concerned would want to come to your show, so are prepared to have their do the night before. And the chap that phoned before is the one who cocked up and is getting a right rollocking for it." Milton just smiled. "Is that the one in charge?"

Daryl nodded. Milton said "Explain how much we are in demand, but as he has gone to great lengths to put this right, we will accept, this time."

There were smiles all round as they listened to Daryl laying it on as to Milton's popularity and how people were begging him to come to their area and it finished with the promise of posters being sent as soon as possible and a truly wonderful evening.

"You worked that well." Simon returned to his monitor.

"Oh thanks, yes I thought I did it beautifully." Daryl was beaming and stroked Flop as he spoke.

"Not you."

Milton smiled as he went into his own office. "Bright lad." he thought as he picked up the chart for the tour. Jean-Paul indicated to the first item.

"You had better strengthen your defenses there."

Milton looked at the name. "Levvington, why what's going on."

"About ten miles from a mist activity, if it spreads that far by the time you are on, you'd be right in the thick of it and you'll need more protection than I can give you. It'll know it can destroy you regardless of your gift. Better think this over."

There was a horrible silence over the office as the two tried to decide the best course of action, then Milton said "I've never been put off by the threat of bad activity."

"This is out of our league, you know that."

"Have you ever encountered one first hand?" Milton wasn't one to shudder but something made a cold trickle run down his back.

"No, but I've been made aware of the extent of the thing. Don't know what it is exactly apart from an evil mist that grows and destroys all in its path, bit like a tornado."

"So what exactly happened before? You said when we were with Gerte about sending it away."

"The high and I mean very high ones dispatched it, but don't ask how they did it. All I know it was directed toward a black hole. And of course in essence it's still there."

After a moment Milton said "We've still got to go, and it may not have taken in that place."

"Don't say I didn't try to protect you."

A tap on the door broke into the conversation.

"Boss," Daryl was beaming "the first place on the route, Levvington have been on the phone, word has got around and they've had so many enquiries they think it's a sell out already."

Milton tried to look pleased as he said "Oh that's good, let's hope they are all like that."

As he left Daryl called over his shoulder "They always are boss."

"Well that's that then, no going back now." Jean-Paul imparted a feeling of impending danger.

"Funny situation" Milton mused, "Imagine the headlines Medium cancels tour because of a mist that is hanging around only you can't see it."

"It's no joking matter."

"No that's the trouble. But don't you find it ironic? The audience will be listening to me trusting the messages are actually coming through me, which they are, and never questioning it. But if I said that there was an evil hovering over the place waiting to destroy them, they would say I was mad or something."

"That's when the gift is also a curse n'est pas?"

Being a small market town, Mayfield couldn't offer very big pickings to the evil without causing a stir immediately, so it had to be satisfied with just making its foothold for now and waiting for the cells in the larger towns and cities to start roping in the smaller ones. Then they could unleash their true threat. In the past many smaller ones had become impatient and tried to take matters into their own hands and the overall objective had to be crushed in its infancy. As it was only a couple of weeks to the start of Milton's Midland tour, the likes of the Mayfield cell would not prove too much of a threat, but Levvington had already joined with another cell and by the time Milton was due to face the audience, there was a good chance that it may have joined with, not only a single but a double cell making it four times the size of Mayfield. He and Jean-Paul were only too well aware of this but had no way of knowing on what scale it reached at this stage, as of course   neither of them had encountered it first hand before.

The Mayfield cell was ticking over deciding on how to take the spinster out of the earthly picture. It had sent a tendril after her when she left the séance so it had located where she lived, or so it thought. Miss Taylor-Barnes may have appeared spiritually dormant but in tactics she was far superior to the evil mist. Timing her actions to the last second, she had led the arm to an empty property at the precise moment that one of her higher sources had distracted another arm, teasing it like a cat with a mouse. Immediately Miss T.B. had returned to her upper level, leaving the imprint of her spindly body to dissolve into the earth.

The mist was searching the property for the woman but realized it had been tricked which made it angry, not only for being cheated, but it knew the incident would have been tracked by the ultimate one who was controlling the whole of this operation from above. In a rage it flung tendrils out in all directions with no apparent target, disturbing the vibrations far up into the other realms. On noticing this and realizing this would jeopardize the plan, the ultimate evil power crushed the Mayfield cell and sucked its remains back to its source. The Simpson house was now abandoned.

DC Murray had returned to Levvington station briefly to go over a case which was due up in court. As he walked through the entrance his eye caught a small hand written notice. It was requesting extra cover for a psychic night, giving the date, time and venue as on a recent similar event at one of the pubs, people had left as though their minds were in another world and many weren't fit to drive. A bit like turning out time, except they hadn't been drinking.

As he entered the CID office he commented to the DC about the request.

"What's the panic about this?" he asked "It's at the Stratford Hall, big place properly run I should think."

"Have you seen who the visiting celeb is?" Murray's old boss Det.Insp. Holland entered the room.

"Oh Hello sir, no it didn't give it on the notice."

"Well, none other than the famous Milton Warner."

DC Murray gave a low whistle. "Coming here, I thought he only did the very large ones."

"From what I can gather, he's doing a short Midlands tour by popular demand, and we are the first on the route."

"Be a uniform job won't it sir?" The young DC asked.

"Hmm. But wouldn't be a bad thing to have someone there, could be there's more to warrant our attention than just crowds and traffic." DI Holland mused for a moment. "Don't suppose they could release you for the night do you?" his attention was turned to Liam, who in view of the events in Mayfield thought it couldn't do any harm to keep his mind open.

"I may even be off." DC Murray was totally unaware that the spiritual force of the same name was pushing the DI to send him as it would give him a host to use instead of having to materialize into his previous form.

"I'll have a word with your man. You're willing?" Holland realized he hadn't actually had an affirmative reply.

"Oh yes sir, I'll do it."

"Good man." Holland then turned the attention to the matters in hand and the thought of the forthcoming event slipped from Liam Murray's mind.

There was now great consternation in the upper realms. Although knowledge of the evil mist was limited, senior spirits had some idea from past experience of the way this thing operated, but something was different, very different. Miss Taylor-Barnes now in her normal spiritual form of Tabar had been very successful in not being discovered as a scout by the presence in the house. She had been placed even without Liam's knowledge, such was her extreme advanced power and had put herself in the position on the same wall as the quiet man with the sideboard in between them. Although in their realm this would not have been an obstacle it served well in the physical form and created a small mental block for the time needed. She had realized at the first meeting that this was no ordinary human, but a temporary vehicle being used by the cell, so she cloaked her identity with a talent known only to the higher levels.

Nan was also in conference listening to various reports of similar small cells being destroyed.

"It's none of our doing, we were still observing them and suddenly they had gone, but the others are combining as they did before so what's their plan?"

"Self destruction of the weakest." All attention was turned to one of the highest entities present. "We were aware that when you tricked your cell Tabar, it showed a lack of cunning and planning in the ranks, so they would know we are closely observing their every move. Lesser evils would want us to assume they were withdrawing, but this force is far too clever, No it's just reorganizing and regrouping on such a scale we haven't seen before."

"So what is our next move?" one of the others wanted to know.

"At the moment, we can still only monitor every single fact however insignificant. We are pulling in various help from far off star systems because there is one thing we still are unsure of."

Nan offered "Is it that we don't know its origin?"

"Exactly, and until we know more we can't just dive in and destroy because that would possibly have no effect whatsoever, then we are at the thing's mercy."

"So we still go back in a different identity each time?" Tabar knew the answer but wanted confirmation.

The high one warned "Only the ones with your power must get near, the rest must keep a safe distance, and I don't think you should take that junior with you any more." He directed the last words to Nan."

"Oh, if you think it best but she could be very useful as she progresses to higher levels."

"Taking out insurance for the future?"

Nan felt told off but said "Her innocence could be a distraction, they wouldn't think of her as a threat and we do guard her from a distance. Also she is very strong willed."

Her superior gave a pause for effect then almost whispered "If it is to our advantage, but only in the early stages, when it gets ugly, get her out or it could jeopardize the whole operation."

"Very well, thank you," Nan was relieved. She hadn't relished the thought of explaining to Jo why she couldn't accompany her any more, and the girl did have good powers of observation.

The meeting as usual only took seconds and those present departed to their own zones to carry on with the fight they knew would require every single part of concentration for it to succeed.

Tommy and the Liam spirit had almost programmed Bert's spiritual side to respond when they pressed the button. There are many people, some with a faint awareness of things beyond their understanding, and some with no knowledge at all but both are used to strengthen power when needed. Unfortunately, it is used by good and evil alike. At times of turmoil, those such as Tommy and Liam would immediately home in on hundreds, thousands, or even millions in Bert's dormant state and arouse the hidden power to boost their own. With the evil mist threatening, they along with other realms were building up as much backing force as was possible for it was likely the mist could be doing the same with those inclined to the wicked side. There was also the possibility it was pulling strength from outside the solar system, even to the lengths of far universes if this particular operation was important enough. But this was something all levels were eager to learn for it is easier to face what you know as definite fact rather than working on assumptions.

Bert seemed quite oblivious to anything going on outside of his home and while Avril seemed to make a little progress she had become confined to the house, not daring to step outside. They both hoped this would ease eventually but the doctor had warned it may take some time.

It was early evening and they both sat in the lounge after their dinner. Bert put the television on and was flicking through a few channels when the regional news caught his attention. The newscaster was announcing the tour of 'the famous medium Milton Warner', and as soon as he realized it was beginning in their area he quickly turned to another channel and cast a quick look at his wife. Her eyes were riveted to the screen and she had gone deathly white, for any reminder of her last visit to Astral Anne's left her in shock. Bert couldn't help being relieved, for if anything good had come out of the incident, it was that she had put aside any wish to have anything to do with things out of this world. He imagined the scenes they may have had if she had wanted to go to the Levvington evening, but quickly put them from his mind. He selected a re-run of one of her favourite comedy shows and sat back hoping she would get a little pleasure from it.

He was rather tired and rested his head back in the armchair. After a few moments he was conscious of someone beside him but he was being calmed so that he didn't jump or speak in alarm. Tommy was whispering to him in soft tones telling him that he would be needed soon and to build up as much strength as he could. For some strange reason he couldn't have explained, Bert didn't question this encounter almost as though he recalled the many previous ones and just added this to them. In his waking moments he was barely aware of the visits, more as though he had dreamt them, and he put a lot down to the worry about his wife which had been rather draining on him as well. But his early experiences told him that something special was going on and he was to be part of it. With a little snort he came to in the chair, looked over at Avril, but she hadn't noticed anything odd, so satisfied he settled back to watch the programme.

Flop had been acting very strangely. He wasn't aggressive or timid in any way but every time Milton walked in he moved to his side and sat there. The dog didn't venture into his office but often was waiting at the door for him to come out after a session with Jean-Paul.

"I don't know what's got into him, he's never done it before and he's fine at home, it's just here he does it." Daryl went forward to stroke him when he turned suddenly and barked at the phone.

"He's crackers." Simon carried on working, not turning his head.

Milton held up his hand as if to silence the man "Watch." Flop sat down with his eyes fixed on the phone. Suddenly it rang, and the dog's head spun round towards Milton.

"Hello" Daryl was still in a state of shock as he answered and after a short conversation, put the phone down slowly and almost whispered "It was the Levvington venue about the posters that was all." His gaze was enquiringly on the dog who lay down for a moment, gave a low growl, then got up and went to sit beside Milton again. He slowly looked towards the phone, lifted one paw and put it firmly down on Milton's foot.

"Well what in heaven's name do you make of that?" Daryl was getting a little uneasy at Flop's antics.

"I think I know." Milton looked very serious.

"Told you, he's crackers." Simon still didn't look round and therefore hadn't witnessed the little episode.

"I'll be back in a minute." Milton headed for his office but Flop was there before him, barring the door and whimpering now. "It's OK feller, I'll be all right." And he bent down to speak to the dog on its own level. They looked into each others eyes for several moments and only they knew what was exchanged. Daryl looked open mouthed as his boss entered his room and the dog placed himself in the doorway as if to guard him.

"Oh I'm really getting spooked out now. That's all I need a neurotic dog on my hands."

Simon actually turned round. "Chill man." Then an after thought "Handbags at five paces."

"Oh go powder your nose! And that's being polite as boss likes us to keep swearing to the absolute minimum."

Simon had turned back to the monitor but called over his shoulder "Got the message. You just told me to piss off."

Just how much further this exchange would have gone was anybody's guess as 'boss' appeared from his office a serious look on his face. Flop was by his side as he moved towards the kitchen.

"Well, I supposed you've asked Jean-Paul's advice so are you going to tell us?" Daryl was quite put out with the whole thing and needed some solid down to earth answers to put his own mind at rest.

"Either of you want a coffee?" Milton reappeared with a cup in his hand.

"I'll do it boss if you'll just tell us what the f…….." Daryl paused as he was about to utter words frowned upon. It wasn't that Milton was a prude; it was just that he never used words which could slip out accidentally when he was giving a reading. It was different if a message came through bearing expletives, but he was conscious of his image and liked to keep it clean. Therefore he preferred the lads to do the same whilst at work.

"OK" Milton handed him the cup and said "I need a coffee so I'll tell you while we have a break."

He sat on the small couch to wait for the drink and Flop placed himself at his feet pressed hard against him. When the coffee arrived Milton said "Perhaps you'd like to be in on this Simon." which really meant he didn't like talking to peoples' backs. He gave a moment for the activity to settle and made sure he had their undivided attention.

"I know you came to work here because you needed jobs and I didn't expect you to believe in what I do, however, over the years I'm sure you have seen and heard things for which there have not been apparent answers." He looked from one to the other but only got a nod from Daryl. "There are many things most people will, how shall I put it, not be aware of or not believe if they have experienced something out of the ordinary."

Simon almost sighed but thought better of it.

"I have to tell you that there is something going on which could be a danger."

"Who to?" Daryl asked.

"To whom." Simon corrected him.

Milton looked from one to the other hoping they were taking this seriously. "Everyone, well perhaps some of us more than others."

Daryl looked from the dog to the man.

"And you think he knows?"

"Pwaaaa." Simon was almost turning back to his work.

"No Daryl, I don't think, I know that he is aware of impending danger, that's why he is acting the way he is. You say he is fine at home?"

"Yes boss, just when he is here, and come to think of it he is worse when you are here. He doesn't guard me or Cyberfart, just you, so he does know."

There was a silence before Daryl ventured the inevitable. "How do you know of this - danger, did he tell you." His head inclined to the other office.

"We both found out together. That lady I asked you to look up Simon, the Gerte lady we saw her and she told us."

"Before or after?" Simon was still not wasting words.

Daryl didn't quite grasp the implication so Milton explained "After she had been murdered."

"Bloody hell!" As soon as the words had erupted Daryl apologized but Milton smiled slightly and said "Exactly, in this case."

"But I still don't understand. Why don't other people know about it?" Daryl was serious now.

"Because it is only known on the spiritual level and of course to those of us in body who are aware of our spiritual forms."

"Bit like that film." Simon was still facing them "Only they were aliens."

"So what happens now boss?"

"Well, I have to tread very carefully. I won't go into details but can I just say the first venue is at Levvington." Flop shot up at looked him straight in the eye.

"There he goes again." Daryl almost shouted.

"That's why I said it. He knows that the danger is there and he is trying to stop me appearing." As if to confirm it, Flop jumped onto the couch licking Milton's hand. This brought a very tense atmosphere over the whole room, even Simon looked as though someone had slapped him.

"So what are you going to do?" Daryl was looking at the flyers for the tour. Even Flop looked as though he was waiting for the right answer, but it wasn't forthcoming.

"We're going ahead as planned of course."

"Oohh" for once the two assistants were in agreement.

Milton slowly placed his cup on the table and silently observed the men as their minds tried to cope with the revelation, and he knew that neither were dismissing this as trivia. But his attention was being drawn down to the pair of faithful brown eyes which now held him in such a fixed gaze that he knew the dog was pleading with him to exercise caution. The front paw was draped over his knee but seemed to be holding him down as if he should not leave that place.

The governing power of the evil mist was being very selective. Any small cell which didn't perform to standard like the Simpson house event was immediately vaporised and returned to source for destruction. Nothing would be allowed which could provide even the slightest threat, for the tiniest weakness could bring down the whole operation. The practice was being well observed by the good powers but they were noticing several differences now. As soon as the single cells were being recalled, another larger one was appearing somewhere else quite a distance away. Also the colour of the mists was changing. Apart from the darkening as they started to join, the ones which had achieved a greater mass were turning to a deep shade of purple, and the largest to date were mixed with purple, deep crimson and black, the colours swirling like a growing storm. Even more frightening was the fact that the largest of all were sending down funnels like a tornado, never actually touching ground but giving the impression it was a rehearsal for later.

Superior powers such as Tabar, had recently witnessed what happened to the sub standard cells on their return. As punishment they were transported to the outer reaches of this universe then exploded sending their entire being into thousands of pieces each stretching many light years from the next making it impossible for them to ever rejoin or reform into their original state. This was classed as the ultimate punishment for upsetting the evil hierarchy. But the main question was still being asked. "What was the final target this time?"

CHAPTER 6

With the start of the tour only being a couple of days away, there should have been the usual nervous tension filling Milton's office suite, but instead of the normal excitement of looking forward to another successful run, the air was hanging with apprehension. It all seemed to be passing over Simon, whose head was bent over his keyboard in the usual manner, Milton was always deep in thought, and Daryl seemed to be bearing the burden of carrying everyone's nerves around on his shoulders. Flop's owner had returned but it had been decided to let the dog come into the office until the tour started as Milton seemed to have formed a strong bond with him and felt better with him around.

"I don't suppose anybody cares what I think or how I feel." Daryl's voice cracked as though he was about to burst into tears.

"Knickers at five paces." Simon muttered but loud enough to be heard.

"Well don't you worry about things?" If he expected a reply he was disappointed but at that moment Milton appeared from his office and perched on the edge of Daryl's desk. He waited for Simon to turn then said quietly "I have been warned not to go, call it off even at this stage, but I can't, I have to go regardless of the outcome."

"Why for heaven's sake?" Daryl's lip quivered "Because *he* said so."

Milton eyed him curiously. "If you are referring to Jean-Paul, no not because he said so, but because we both decided we needed to find out."

"What?" Simon wasn't going to waste words although he did look more interested than previously.

"We know something is afoot and somebody has to ascertain just what it is, it may save many people in the future."

"At whose expense, yours?"

Milton tried to change the flow. "If you are bothered about coming........." But Daryl cut in "No boss, I wouldn't let you go alone and Cyberfart likes to be on his own don't you?" All he got was a cold stare in return and Daryl couldn't help adding "Not that you ever know who's here and who isn't, no wonder you......."

"All right, all right." It was Milton's turn to cut in. "Let's keep some harmony here at least can we - please?" He looked from one to the other, received a nod from Simon and after a moment a sniff and a mumbled "Yes" from the other.

"Right that's agreed. Now Simon while we're gone keep your eyes peeled for anything unusual going on. I know Jean-Paul has a wide spiritual scope but you have a knack of picking out little bits that would go unnoticed to anyone else, and could be important. We have to watch every inch of the globe, not just here. You OK with that?"

"Spot on."

"Good, then relay anything to Daryl immediately. I mean that."

"Willdo"

Just as the air was settling into a more acceptable calm, Flop flew out from behind the desk and ran to the kitchen. Milton followed on the alert but when he reached the door he stopped dead. Flop's biscuits had fallen out of the cupboard and were spread across the floor. The dog hadn't attempted to pick up any to eat and stood frozen to the spot.

"What is it feller?" Milton bent down to his level and was whispering to him when he went cold, for the biscuits had formed the two letters making the word 'NO'.

The other two men had followed and upon seeing the message a silence crept over the whole area. After what seemed like an eternity, Daryl gulped and could barely be heard stating "It's a sign boss." Flop was the first to move, backing away slowly until he was pressed against Milton's leg and as they both moved in unison the others backed away slowly until they had returned to the main office.

Once they were back Flop returned to his bed and seemed quite unmoved by the whole thing almost as though he had passed on the message and could now relax. Simon would not show any more emotion than necessary and like the dog, it was all over and everybody could get back to normal and what a fuss about nothing anyway. He felt no need to voice anything and in seconds was engrossed in his monitor.

Daryl on the other hand seemed to be a nervous wreck so Milton indicated for him to go into his office for a moment to settle himself. As they were about to close the door Flop pushed his way in and found himself a spot near the desk.

"Now Daryl, I know people aren't the same and we all react to things differently but I do need you to hold it together over the next couple of weeks. It's only a short tour after all, we'll be back before you know it, safe and sound, so come on, you'll be OK when your mind is full of checking everything and running round like blue bottomed fly. You won't have time to worry."
Daryl looked him straight in the eye. "Do you know boss, that's the first time you said you need me."

"What? Now what are you talking about. I always need you." He stopped as he saw the man looking at him in such a fixed way he knew he had to pick his words very carefully.

"You are the best PR anyone could wish for, I rely on you for my organizing and back up, but I don't go round telling people I need them all the time. So get your brain in order." The last sentence came out like an instruction to be obeyed, not a request. The tension could be felt in the room and all thought of spiritual matters was pushed out of the way as Milton realized, not the first time that he had to tread carefully with this man. He had been aware of comments over the months but hoped that by ignoring passing remarks Daryl would get fed up and look elsewhere for his entertainment. He didn't want to be too harsh just now as he needed everything to be positive for the tour and he certainly didn't need this lad to be throwing his teddies out of the cot and not concentrating. When they came back, well - he would have to see what he could do to calm the waters then.

Jo was in her element. She had been given a job alongside one of the hierarchy to observe, what was now referred to as 'mist movements'. Nan had taken another form so that any evil scouts would not realize they were being observed by the same higher power and Jo was so junior in such matters they would give her little credence. There had been a deep discussion as to the nature of this task and there were those who still had some misgivings about having Jo anywhere near the activity due to her headstrong ways, but Nan had faith in her and knew just how she would play it. Advice was plentiful about the safety of the young spirit, but this had been carefully thought through and there was always a strong back up to withdraw her at a moments notice, although Jo would never be aware of it.

"Where are we going?" The junior asked as they seemed to be hovering in several places without having a preset target.

"All part of the plan. Keep your thoughts neutral." Nan imparted in an instant.

"Oh yes, they can be picked up." The silence that followed was instruction enough to never let her guard down for even a millisecond as it could spell disaster, not only for them but for the whole spectrum and beyond.

They hovered for a moment over the town of Levvington then darted away to an innocent little village which held no interest in their search, then on to a fairly large city never staying in one location for long. Nan had donned the appearance of someone junior to Jo thus giving the impression that these two flighty young spirits were out looking for fun or just getting used to their level of existence. This was quite normal behaviour which is why Nan had opted to use this innocent approach. Although Jo had been told her senior was 'in disguise' and she knew she was with a much higher power, little did she guess her true identity or the seriousness of the mission. Also she had been unaware that, during this journey, Nan had left her several times, changing location in such a split second and returning before even the surrounding space fabric had received as much as a brush past, never settling to make an indentation which could be traced. Jo on the other hand was leaving a perfect traceable trail along the pre-arranged route carefully set by the organizing powers.

It is thought by some that only matter can disturb, or leave an impression upon its surroundings but the entities of the unlimited number of various levels of existence leave imprints upon time and space, and when observed by the current living species who home in on such 'recordings', they are given the impression they have met with or received messages from people from the past, almost like being in contact with a time capsule. When a person looks through a photograph album or watches a movie device, they are not living in that time or getting a message, they are simply experiencing a snapshot of what was saved at that time. So when the beings such as Nan have the power to flit without leaving a proper trace, they are from a much higher realm of experience than the likes of Jo who would leave her mark as clearly as footprints in the virgin snow.

It was with this in mind that the pairing was agreed. Jo would be attracting the enemy as if saying "Here I am" while Nan was darting about at different levels finding out the source and destination of the evil mist. Jo was in plain speaking a decoy.

Nan had formed a mental map in her consciousness and imparted it back to her source, but now it was time for the next stage.

"We have nothing to do for a while, all seems quiet." She sent the thought to Jo.

"What does that mean?"

After a pause Nan played her next card. "No need to hang around, go off on your own if you wish, surely there is someone or something you would like to spend a little time with."

Jo couldn't believe it. "You mean, you won't be with me, I would be free to go where I want?"

"If you like. I'll stay here. Take as long as you want. These jobs can get a bit boring."

"Well if you're sure." Jo couldn't quite believe it but couldn't resist the chance to track down her killer when the opportunity was put in front of her.

"I'll get you if I need you." Nan sent a vibration almost pushing the youngster on her way and in seconds she had gone.

The message was on its way. Immediately sentinels were on Jo's trail observing from a safe distance ready to inform Nan of any unusual activity or danger. One particular senior took on Nan's form so as not to arouse suspicion as to why she was alone, but the being was cloaked from Jo so she was not aware of it. Such was the cat and mouse game that was beginning to unfold. Nan was now free to change her form constantly which would be necessary as she had to block any connection when she moved around leaving a cold trail in her wake.

Her communications sent a wave of consternation rippling through the area as more and more senior powers gathered to converse. Nan was observing a massive cell with its arms spreading out like tentacles covering most of the Midlands. There were smaller ones still being terminated as they were considered useless and it was obvious that only the strongest were being used for this operation. Even some which had been fairly strong to date were being disposed of and the main system seemed to be growing in strength and size by the minute. But it was still not possible to determine the purpose or the ultimate target and it was this fact that now had to be addressed with all possible haste.

The next message evoked even more concern. The tentacles appeared to being homing in on various unconnected areas. Six main ones were creeping towards meeting places, but not the same kind. One was aimed at a sports centre, another at a theatre in one of the cities and one at a hall used for events at Levvington, the one where Milton was due to appear shortly. With some surprise a church was in line of fire but on closer examination it was found that a television programme was due to be broadcast from there in two weeks time, so it would be full to capacity. When they studied all the venues, each one was due to attract large audiences and all within about two weeks of each other. So any disaster would hardly have time to be dealt with before another one would be activated and with no connection would anybody think that theirs could be on the list? There probably wouldn't be time to cancel any forthcoming attraction, and due to the costs involved, would the organisers want to?

Another dilemma faced them with the next communication. The texture of the main cell was changing. It was as though a fire was being lit from inside fuelling the arms sending more power to the six large ones, but at the same time building up another ten which were reaching heavenwards. Did this mean they were standing by for when the main six had operated or were they aiming at targets beyond the earth and just using this rock as a platform for an almighty universal disruption? But another question had to be answered. The colours emitting from the main cell had never before been encountered, being outside of every spectrum on any level. If evil ever manifested itself in any way, it was here, now. The swirling horrible mess of the mass was so objectionable, that anyone in bodily form would have been so sick at the sight, they would never have recovered from the experience but the danger now was that the earth dwellers couldn't see it.

It didn't take long to realize that help was needed from the true clairvoyants and clairaudients to try to convince the earth occupants that there was a lethal danger imminent, but that was easier thought of than may be practical. The theory in the hierarchy was that if there could be a massing of good thought, strong positive power, prayer, or any feeling given whatever name which could build up such a strong protective force around the world, this evil being could be dispatched thus protecting the earth for now. However that would produce only the minutest result in the enormous plan, for even if the evil retracted it would still go elsewhere to wreak havoc, still resulting in disaster throughout the universes and beyond. It would in essence, affect all levels of spiritual being and everything material in space.

"I just knew it, didn't I say weeks ago?" Laurie Small was throwing his hands in the air as he rushed from one place to another. He had organized many functions at the Stratford Hall in Levvington and every time there was a 'major disaster waiting to happen' as he reminded the staff constantly. It had become such a joke that the catch phrase became part of any event.

"What is it this time Mr Small?" The use of the title always ruffled his feathers even more and he turned abruptly to face one of the younger members of his staff.

"If you had been paying even the slightest attention Abbie, you would know that the extra chairs for the new hall haven't arrived yet and the 'do' is tomorrow night. We can't pinch any more from the smaller rooms or they'll all be sitting on each other's laps!"

They were joined by Johnny who was more than used to these outbursts and usually managed to calm the situation. He indicated with a nod for the young woman to leave and taking Laurie's arm guided him to the office. He poured a coffee from the drinks machine and putting it on the desk said very slowly "Everything is under control. You are panicking for nothing, as usual."

"But the chairs, the chairs"

"The chairs," Johnny paused to make sure he had the other man's full attention "are on the way as we speak."

"Then why wasn't I informed may I ask?"

"I was just coming to tell you that very thing, but I was afraid you were about to blow a gasket so I thought a coffee might do the trick."

Laurie knew this man was a good organizer and had his finger on every button, but he felt an underlying jealousy stirring in his gut because if he wasn't careful he would be only too pleased to step into his shoes. Unfortunately, his guard dropped many times when he let the pressure of certain situations get the better of him. For now he would have to keep this person in tow which meant having to climb down before he made an even bigger fool of himself.

"Oh, yes, very good, well at least something has worked out." With a nervous cough he soon cut back to the question in hand. "When are they coming?"

"Later this afternoon. I think it swayed it a bit when I told them who was appearing."

Laurie shuffled some papers trying to give the impression that the conversation had finished but was curious to hear more.

"Oh?"

Johnny smiled. "Why yes. I mean if they didn't come up with the service for such a well known celeb, would we use them in future when it might be an even bigger name?"

Not wishing to admit the man was right he changed direction.

"Well as long as they don't expect free tickets, I know what some of these rogues are like"

With a knowing smirk Johnny opened the door and called over his shoulder "Better just go and check on the catering arrangements in case there is another disaster waiting to happen."

Laurence, as he preferred to be addressed, watched him go. There was something in the man's calmness that was very unsettling, almost as if he was studying him constantly to the point that even when Johnny was off duty it was as if he was still in presence. Laurie got up and went to the personnel file and after flicking through a few folders drew out the one marked John Sellars. Something was wrong. There should have been a wad of forms which would have been filled in before the man could have been employed at the centre. He checked the cabinet to see if the paperwork had slipped out but there was nothing. Quickly, with an eye on the door, he looked through the files on either side in case anything had been wrongly filed but again, nothing. Racking his brain as to when the employment had commenced, he hurried back to his desk and began searching through the computer for employee details. In his nervous haste he made quite a hash of getting into the right files but finally came up with the name John Cellars.

"No that can't be right, it isn't spelled that way." He was muttering under his breath but realised that there was no other information stored and he sat in disbelief as he struggled to remember when John came, but it was almost like waking up knowing you have had a dream but you can't recall it.

A sudden knock on the door followed by Abbie making an entrance jolted him back to reality and he quickly cleared the screen.

"Here's those invoices Mr Sm....." she stopped half way into the room her mouth hanging open. "Are you OK? Do you feel alright? Can I get you anything? Should I call......?"

"No, No, Abbie – um – thank you I'm just a bit tired you know." He was struggling to explain.

"Well you do overdo it a bit. I mean you take it all very seriously." As soon as the words had left her lips she knew it hadn't been the right thing to say but from Laurie's view it was a life line. He went into a short rant about how it was a pity more people didn't take their jobs seriously and how lucky they were to have a job at all, until she whispered an apology and backed out of the room almost tossing the paperwork onto a nearby table.

Instinct told him he had been left looking silly on all counts and the only way to cope now was to get himself back in the driving seat and get organising. So the history of Johnny was put on hold for the time being.

Jean Paul had pulled Milton into his office and was now imparting the latest developments regarding the mist situation. At this stage the spirit was unaware of the intents of the superior level powers and had he known that

Milton was about to be targeted by them, would have been even more concerned, but for now he knew that the meeting at Levvington was going to need every possible protection that could be summoned. They were in thought conference when they were both aware of another presence in the room. Instantly they switched their attention away from the discussion trying to identify the visitor but it vanished from the area as soon as it realised it had been detected.

"What was that?" Milton actually spoke out. It was a few seconds before Jean Paul replied for he had tried to follow the trail but it was at too high a speed to leave a lasting print and had covered its tracks before he was even out of the room.

"Don't know, but it was a high one. The normal levels don't have that skill." After a moment or two musing Milton asked "A warning?"

"Or a tracing." Jean Paul was very uneasy as he was aware of the usual visitations and movement of transient forms but this was different. He was forced to admit "Nothing I have ever encountered."

"I was afraid of that. We usually know what we are up against." Milton shifted in his chair. "You were saying about this mist, mass or whatever it is and it is hovering over our venue."

"Go on."

"And Flop is doing his little best to warn me of something. Did you catch the reaction when I mentioned the name of the place?"

"The very reason I checked it out then and why I've been watching it since." Jean Paul was moving about the room "Don't forget though, Levvington isn't the only place, so why others, and how big is it?"

Milton sighed in frustration "This thing seems to provoke more questions all the time and the answer is always the same. We don't know."

"Be assured Milton, I'm bringing in every bit of protection for you that is available, there will be a terrific combined force forming a surrounding shield."

"But my friend."

"Yes?"

"What about the audience. The support crew. The staff. Don't they deserve as much protection as I?"

"Of course, but are they the target?" As soon as the thought hit Milton, Jean Paul knew that this aspect hadn't occurred to him until now.

Milton swallowed hard. "Why would anything be aimed at me personally, and there are other places you say, different gatherings, so it can't be anything to do with the psychic side can it?"

"No. No, I think I was being over cautious. Forget that."

Milton let a smile creep over his face. "I thought you were going to sound like Daryl for a minute."

"Not in a million years!" Then after a moment "I'll go now but keep your guard up and by the way, sometimes these amusing little obsessive guys can act as quite a good barrier. Their emotions run quite high you know."

"I'll keep him close, but not that close." On the slightly lighter note the two parted.

As soon as Daryl saw Milton's light change on the panel he was into the office like a shot.

"If he so much as stares at me that way again, I shall do something permanent to him"

Milton suppressed his mirth and asked "What's poor Flop done now?" knowing full well this was not the object of the man's outburst.

"Not him boss. The other creature."

"Calm down Daryl, he probably doesn't realise he's doing anything and if you react like this, well – he may do it just to get a rise out of you, so don't play into his hands."

"Hmm. Well see if I care. Anyway, I have some brilliant news boss."

As he appeared to be waiting for some sort of response Milton said "And are you going to share it with me?"

"What? Oh yes. We are totally and utterly sold out. The whole tour. People are fighting for tickets; you should see the prices they are asking on the internet!"

Milton frowned. "I don't like that. People should be buying them for themselves, not to cash in on our business."

"Well yes, that's true. But you know what you were worried about, I mean you thought something was wrong and all that, well I don't think you should, I mean what can happen with all those fans there. You'll be OK boss, you see."

Wishing he had the others man's confidence he murmured "Let's hope so."

As Daryl turned to go the door was flung open and an unusually flustered Simon stood in the doorway his hand gripping the handle.

"I think you had better see this."

The two men followed him to his computer and all froze at the sight. Flop had his front legs on the chair and was barking at the monitor. The background was a mixture of the most beautiful shades of red and blue merging to violet but their attention was focused on the centre of the screen where two words were flashing in large letters. "STOP NOW."

It could have only been a few seconds that the three men and the dog stared transfixed at the message but it seemed like an eternity. Slowly the letters faded into the background and a silence fell over the office. Milton felt he had to take charge and said very quietly "We had better add that to the list lads, and that includes you little feller." Trying to lighten the situation he bent and patted the dog lovingly. Flop responded by taking his paws off the chair, pressing himself to Milton's leg and then returning to his bed as though nothing had happened. For once Simon seemed unduly unnerved by this latest warning.

"I didn't do anything." He was still staring at the screen which had returned to his last programme.

"Well don't look at me, I wouldn't dare even breathe on your keyboard." It was Daryl's way of realising the built up tension and Simon would always be his main line of attack.

"Alright lads." Milton's manner had an immediate calming effect. "We all know nobody did anything, it's just part of what is going on. Let's be comforted by the fact that whatever – whoever it is that is trying to warn us is on our side. A good force."

He turned to Flop who had rolled over onto his back and appeared to have been fast asleep for ages. "He's let it pass. Maybe we should do the same."

An unsure grunt was all that was heard from the younger two so Milton clapped his hands and said "Right, lunchtime I think, Come on it's on me today."

That message didn't take anytime to register and the energy flooded the room as if someone had lit a match. Milton would have liked to get them out of the place for a while but not wishing to leave the dog on his own at this time, he told Daryl to arrange to have food delivered. "We can't take him into an eatery." He nodded towards the dog's bed and added "Don't think they serve his favourite." This brought normality back to the place and before long they were enjoying well earned nourishment. Only Milton felt the proverbial black cloud which he knew had not left and his mind was more on what Jean-Paul was learning than the usual one sided conversation going on between his employees.

There was now great agitation in the higher levels due to the increasing speed of the area being covered by the mass. Tabar was in conference with those who had previous experience of the being, and all were trying to estimate its course and objective. Reports were flooding in of huge areas worldwide which were almost being sucked into its control but there was still an overwhelming feeling of impending disaster. It seemed the rest of the solar system was clear so the focus was solely upon the earth and surrounding space. Yet the earth dwellers were still unaware of what was hanging so closely over them, putting down local accidents or deaths to a run of bad luck, never dreaming the source was from a greater power than they would ever encounter.

One of the high angels now imparted with somewhat powerful force the decision that it was time to call in all contacts who had any true psychic ability, preferably those with greater experience as those with limited skill could jeopardise the operation and even more importantly put themselves and those round them in mortal danger.

Instantly the messages were sent to every spiritual being on all levels which could be reached, hoping those on even higher planes would pick up the thread and act on their behalf. The word immediately reached the likes of Tommy and Liam who homed in on targets such as Bert who were dotted around like pins on a map. So adept were the spirituals that they could impart mass messages in one go instead of having to visit with each living soul individually, which in this case would not have achieved the required result even in their time zones. The message was to think very strong thoughts, pushing away any bad vibrations, pushing them upwards, pushing them far away. The thoughts must be concentrated not allowing anything or anyone to interrupt or change their way of thought. They must do this without weakening and must spread the force outwards beyond the planet still pushing, pushing. They could not be given a target and it wasn't necessary for in the past the combined efforts were soaked up by the high ones and they then directed the power to the evil as if they were being fed the ammunition needed to fire their guns.

Simultaneously, the higher entities targeted the likes of Milton, people long proven to have the gift of communication at many levels and Jean Paul was instructed to now be on his guard even more as he and his charge had been in contact with Gerte who had obviously been despatched as a threat to the mass. There was little doubt that Milton was on their list for attack and it was just a matter of time so he would receive particular attention from other sentinels. The fact that certain areas were being protected was of little consequence now for the evil, whatever it was would be aware of their procedures and would not expect any vulnerable source to go unguarded.

"Are you ready for tonight then?" DI Holland was washing his hands in the gents as Liam Murray entered.

"Yes, quite looking forward to it." He called over his shoulder as he went over to the urinal. "Got a feeling it might be quite entertaining."

"Don't go in for all that 'physic' stuff myself, but I suppose it's alright for the daft buggers with more money then sense."

Liam laughed. "Don't call it physic in front of the celeb."

It was Holland's turn to smile. "Do you reckon he'll have them all in a trance?"

"It's not like that."

"Oh you know about these things do you?"

"Only what I've seen on TV." Liam's spirit passenger of the same name was already in situ and he was careful not to impart anything to his host at this stage but he was glad of the chance to be on board with someone who could wander at will and not be pinned in a seat all night. Then he would use him to advantage.

Unaware of his audience Holland said "Got a couple of lads in the wings and we're telling the medium to keep well back on the stage. We don't want any silly people trying to climb up like we had last time."

They left the gents and started off down the corridor towards the briefing room.

"Oh" Liam smiled, "hardly the same kind of event, I mean he was a budding pop star and the girls did go a bit crazy."

"All the same, I'm not taking any chances, and we are still trying to piece together those deaths connected with that prat of a so called medium woman. So we don't want anything else bogging us down especially folks thinking they've seen the light or something."

Liam shook his head in mirth thinking that the expected audience would be coming in a totally different frame of mind to his superior.

After a quick reminder to the assembled room about recent events, DI Holland set out the plans for the evening's performance. He almost hurried through the designation of traffic officers at strategic points then turned his attention to the building itself. He stressed that the police presence was vital as the hall would be a perfect picking ground for thieves as the people's attention was going to be on the stage and not always where their belongings were placed. And he was keen to have plain clothes lads on the look out for drug dealing etc. as they were in the middle of a crackdown on the habit in this area. Finally he listed the handpicked men for protecting the guest and his entourage, leaving Liam and himself as 'floaters' to home in on anything major which needed added clout. Although he was still only a DC, the inspector had great faith in Liam and would rather have him at his side than some of the other 'plonkers' as he called them.

When the rest of the assembly had been dismissed, Holland indicated for Liam to sit down. "You – um doing anything before tonight's fiasco?"

"Nothing in particular. Any reason?"

DI Holland looked uncomfortable. "Oh sounds a load of balls really."

"What does?" Murray and also the other Liam detected something not quite right in the older man's demeanour.

"Oh – I wondered if you wanted to just pop into the hall, have a general look round, get the smell of the place, you know the kind of shit."

"With pleasure. Um – anything specific?" He looked enquiringly at Holland. There was a pause. Then very slowly getting up the inspector said "You know lad, I've probably been in this job too long, but you get a nose for things. Can't always put your finger on it, but you just feel something."

"And you do with this?"

"Agh. It's probably nothing but….."

"I'll go." Liam's interruption came like a shot. It was just what spirit Liam wanted, a golden opportunity to have a good scout round before the show so he pushed the answer out before Murray had chance to even think about it.

"Oh well, if you don't mind. Shouldn't think there's anything to worry about." Holland sat back down but added "Course, you'll let me know if…."

"Certainly will." Liam Murray felt it was unnecessary but what harm would it do and he had no other definite plans. Little did he realise it wasn't his decision.

CHAPTER 7

"We don't think it can be of this universe." The problem was reaching higher levels of spiritual understanding by the minute. All knowledge was being transferred to all upper levels to try and estimate the source of this tremendous evil power. Tabar was in conference with those on her plane for when the Astral Anne cell was recalled, it was traced for a moment then lost. She of course had to leave the area in haste, so it was left with the other powers to attempt a tracking.

"It has to be a time lock." All attention was suddenly directed to Za, a power so high, few of the lower levels had ever encountered him first hand. His being now encompassing the whole of the gathering as he entered the space.

"So this is nothing physical, even from another space area?" The truth was beginning to dawn on all the high powers in presence but it was Tabar who submitted the theory.

"As there is no living species in this universe or any other that has mastered time travel, it can only be another level of existence that can be using it." Another high angel added "Yes they still have the wormhole theory on this earth, as though one would travel down a tunnel to reach another time." Others in the gathering soon added their own contributions to the thought.

"A time lock? That has to narrow it down."

"Never encountered one. I can't be high enough."

"It's not a question of experience, it's where they are in operation."

"That's why it reduces the options."

Za turned his attention to one of his close attendants. "Briefly." Was all he implied and the next in command quickly explained the process.

"Those of you who have spent lives on the earth planet may have come across locks on canals for boats to move from one level to another. Some appear to form steps for the craft to ascend or descend, where some may be single locks." He instantly transmitted an image of such a procedure at an earth location where the act was taking place at that moment. Understanding rippled through the company as he continued "It is like that with time transference." He knew he would have to go deeper.

"Areas like galaxies or even whole universes have an allotted space, whether it be expanding or shrinking. Every one is touching others regardless of its size or shape, but it is always surrounded by several, unless one is totally encompassed by a single one but don't pay concern to that at the moment."
A slight tremor of wonder ran through the assembly and although some had knowledge of this there were always those yet to experience it. The high power continued without delay.

"With every area being in contact, at the point they touch is the lock. Now, nothing is in any space format is stationary, so the parts that are touching are moving, therefore the same part is not always in contact with the same place on another area." There was a slight pause. "In physical terms, if you had a large area of inflated balloons all pressed closely so that there was no air between them and the whole lot was moving constantly - do you understand?"
A general agreement was felt so he imparted "I have to point out that the space shapes are not like balls, they have a multitude of different shapes brought on by the constant movement, so one odd shape will determine the one it is touching at that point."
Za now indicated for him to explain how the transfer took place.

"At the point one space area touches another a transfer can be made to another dimension, but this is where the time lock comes in. When they touch it may not be the appropriate transfer moment. So there is a waiting time for the touching place to be absolutely correct, like waiting for the water level to reach the exact height."
A question rose from the company. "Wouldn't that take an eternity on some occasions?"

"Quite right. In some cases it may never happen. Also your area could be in contact with another which would be suitable but you may have chosen not to take that route, or you may never have been aware of it because you didn't look."
There was another pause while the knowledge was assimilated but Za prompted his aide to add the important part.

"The reason why earth man or physical forms from other galaxies have not mastered this is because it is not for the material body, only the spiritual forms."

There was a small ripple of discussion for a moment then one of the assembled members asked what most of the others were wondering.

"We understand this to a degree but is this really time travel?" It was greeted with a hum of agreement.

Za rose above them. "Do not make the mistake of giving either time or space limits. When you stand upon a planet like the earth and look out into the space beyond you are looking into the past, for the light you see has taken many light years to reach you and its source may no longer be in existence. Again when you stand without moving in one place you believe you are stationary, but in a short time the earth has spun and taken you with it so you are no longer in the same place as when you started in that position. So have you taken time with you or left it behind?"

After a moment he felt he must clarify the current situation. "Now you are aware that something is probably using this form for visiting and departing, you realise you must set your sights in all dimensions and not just restrict it to the events on this particular planet. It could be so adept that it is space hopping through time locks making it very difficult to monitor. But we do have the advantage of knowing it will keep returning to its objective, even if it is only a temporary one." Again he handed over to his next in command.

"This knowledge is but a minute part in the way of things but it is still far above the understanding of the lower levels, therefore you have been informed for you to take the correct action but it would be wise not to impart these thoughts to those who would only be confused because of their junior status."

There was the sense of a parting gesture and Za and his sentinels were gone leaving a feeling of slight amazement trickling through the meeting. All this had taken about one millionth of a second confirming Za's ruling about time and in an equally short period all had returned to their own levels, some not even having been missed.

The spiritual Liam was on board Detective Murray's physical, careful not to influence him until required. As well as taking stock of the Stratford Hall and its surroundings he was also aware of any movement on his other levels, so when a kindred spirit was at his side he welcomed the positive vibes around him. Jean Paul was on a similar level to him and now was making thought contact regarding the venue.

"You vetting the place as well?" The contact was warm and Liam, although being careful not to let his guard slip again felt trust in this being.

"Covering all aspects. You never know." He sensed this wasn't a chance meeting so he ventured "You got a particular interest then?"

Jean Paul was being equally wary but decided to test the waters. "You do know what's going on around here?" He felt the other person was still being cautious so he added "No time to delay, do you know about a mist that is hovering around these areas?" This seemed to relax spirit Liam so he relayed the Astral Anne saga.

"Ah, that makes it easier. You remember Gerte then?"

"Oh yes, and you do obviously."

The two combined thoughts to exchange their various experiences and immediately a pact was sealed. Liam pondered for a moment then said "This is bigger than we first thought and personal now, as your friend is the main attraction. But surely all this isn't just aimed at him."

"Don't think so for one minute but he is going to be in the firing line. We feel it is the large gathering which is the focal point, along with the others. But there is the other factor."

"Which is?" Liam guessed but wanted to know from this other source.

"Milton's genuine gift. Are they, this, whatever it is using him as some sort of connecting portal to the main evil source."

"And why just him?"

Jean Paul was quick to explain. "Oh I don't think for one minute it is him alone. I think they will use anyone whether in earth form or spirit to make their bases."

DC Murray had just about covered every inch of the centre but finding nothing untoward decided to go and have a substantial meal before the job started. He was about to go out of the door leading from the main hall when his mobile rang.

"Hello Murray, Holland here. Where are you?"

"Hello sir, just leaving the centre for a bite to eat then I'll be back in good time as arranged."

"Noticed anything?"

"Such as?"

There seemed to be a muttering on the other end of the line before the Inspector said "Oh I don't know. Just can't get this gut feeling out my bloody system. Well, see you later then."

They exchanged brief farewells and Murray, casting a last look round the place left the building leaving spirit Liam with Jean Paul. Barely had the detective gone when Liam felt startled. "Did you feel that?"

"Um. Keep your thoughts still."

They hovered in the foyer. There were still centre staff milling about putting the last touches to the place but this was not on that level.

"It's overhead." Liam's thought was a mere whisper.

"No. It's all around."

Together they slid into the main hall their spiritual senses primed. They were at the very back of the hall facing the stage, and the very spot Milton would be occupying within a few hours.

"What is it?" Liam, had he been in body, would scarcely have managed a faint sound and he felt a cold terror encompassing him.

"Part of the feeler which is attached to this place."

"What do we do?"

Jean Paul indicated for him to remain still as he felt a protective force passing them from all sides. What the two experienced in the next moments had to be described as 'a first' for them both.

The evil tendril appeared to be having its own dress rehearsal for later. Its fingers were prodding the stage in various places but with no apparent pattern then feeling around the wings and down into the auditorium but when it reached the front row it appeared to have hit a force field. The colours swirling down the lone limb were throbbing, mixing purple with blood red and black until it was a hideous mixture of these plus colours never seen by the human eye. After several attempts at pushing its way forward it slowly retreated and hovered just above the stage pulsating as if planning its next move.

Jean Paul and Liam took this opportunity to retreat from the building and were hovering a safe distance away from the centre. They were now both aware of the enormity of the feeler which until now had been invisible to them. The arm stretched way out of sight but appeared to be thickening the higher it went.

"Is that what they called the mist?" The understatement left Liam with disbelief.

"Looks like it. I have to go back to Milton now and warn him again."

Liam wasn't keen on being on his own at the moment. He wasn't naïve in the affairs of various evil entities but this was something he knew was a tremendous threat to every thing, living or spiritual. As if by way of an answer he was instantly recalled by his mentors leaving Jean Paul to return to his task.

Completely oblivious of the terror hovering above them, Laurie was still flitting about flustering almost everyone beyond reason. He had dashed into his office to find a particular piece of paper and was rummaging around on his desk when the door slammed shut. Giving it little thought he carried on searching until he grabbed the elusive note and made his way to the door, grabbing the handle with some force. But it was as firm as if it had been locked and bolted. Feeling very irate now he cursed under his breath and gave a final hefty tug, but to no avail. Frantically he hammered on the panels and within seconds the door was opened by Johnny giving him a bemused look whilst trying in vain to hide his amusement. There had to be a butt at which Laurie could aim his wrath and this man was in the firing line.

"And I suppose you think that was very funny, well let me tell you, your juvenile pranks may amuse everyone else, but they certainly don't amuse me."
With his normal calm manner, Johnny said very quietly "I heard you banging, well we all did, and I came to see what was wrong."
Laurie spluttered, as usual, mumbled a 'thank you' and to regain his composure pushed the man out of the way, his valuable little piece of paper in his hand.

Little did either of them realise this pantomime had been witnessed by a passing spirit wandering around on her own little errand. Now she surveyed the scene.

"Found you. You filthy disgusting bastard!" Jo hovered with satisfaction for a moment before being recalled by Nan to her original task.

The high powers had taken Nan to task as soon as she released Jo into the temporary watch of other protective sources.

"Didn't you feel you were casting her into the path of the 'thing's area?'"
A thought came immediately from another power "It could have tracked her back you, jeopardised our tactics."
Nan spread her being to emphasise her explanation, her reasons touching everyone in presence whatever level.

"When we were scanning Levvington I picked up a sense that Jo had homed in on something, nothing to do with this task but of her own objective. So, if she was wandering in search of this point of interest, her mind would, temporarily be on that and not on the mist."
"And of course she thought she was alone?" One of the group asked.
Nan agreed. "She did, but don't forget there was one in my image accompanying her for a while, clear to any high power but not to Jo, so her guard would be down feeling she had free rope."
"So why didn't they pick on your image?"
"It had then been replaced with two high powers masquerading as lesser spirits, the 'Sadie' kind, giving an air of inexperience and general inquisitiveness but not able to see the mist."
One of Nan's level asked "But surely Jo could see the tendril, after all you had taught her the observation power to see the mist in its earlier stages."
"Exactly."

There was a general trembling of air as this one word baffled the assembled party. After letting the vibrations settle she explained.

"That was all we let her see. Just a mist. Our powers round her reduced her awareness level, so she was not aware of the progress of the evil."
This caused even greater consternation.

"So she was heading straight for it without knowing its potential!"
A calming wave was sent over the entire throng. "Due to our decoy placements, and her apparent lack of experience, the evil paid her little heed once it had satisfied itself she was of no threat."

"But……."
The contributor was silenced. "Please remember, there were dozens of such spirits flying in and out of the place, some hovering to see what was going on, some passing through on another errand, and when Jo found her long lost foe, she would have been of no interest to our nemesis."

"How long after that did you pull her back?"

"Immediately. I took on the previous innocent form and said I was ready for her to return. Do not forget, she hasn't been aware of my true identity throughout this venture." Then added "She will probably want to tell me all about it when we next meet."

When the ripple had died down the highest power present brought the meeting to its point of issue.

"So now we have all been informed of the movements, the important fact is what did we learn of the evil?" This seemed to unite all to the matter in hand. Nan again took the lead.

"You will have received the thought images we sent of the tendril which although appears to be waiting, is growing in power by the moment due to the colour changes which we have experienced worldwide. We cannot observe the main body of the thing as it seems to be moving in sections, sometimes joining then splitting but always being controlled from a main source."
The high power now contributed. "Well one thing we do know. It is concentrating on and around the planet earth and its moon. Its feelers have been sent out to Mars and Venus but have been retracted, so it seems this is the only one it wants, or is suitable for its means."

"But it can't want it for inhabitation, not if it isn't physical. It could exist anywhere in spirit." This statement came from a middle level being.

"Not necessarily." The high power was very patient and directed the reply to this particular one. "If its space area has been destroyed or encompassed in anyway or merged with another, bit like a galaxy collision, it could be searching for somewhere to make its base. But it would take over completely."

Another question came forward. "But why take over a planet that can sustain life, why not one of the others in the solar system, or even one of the other galaxies?"

There was a definite pause before the answer came, but it brought the thoughts full circle.

"Think of the high power Za. What would he say now?"

Most of the company were in unison with a barely felt whisper in the air.

"It is governed by a time lock."

Whilst the outer office was a hive of activity with Daryl checking and double checking every detail for which he had responsibility, Milton's remained a haven of calm. Flop had gone home and he was already being missed by all, even Simon if he took a second to admit it.

"So that's all we know up to now, but it isn't pretty." Jean Paul was hovering near the notice board. "But this Liam will keep us updated, seems a decent soul."

"We can do with plenty of those." There was a hint of humour in Milton's voice but he was only too aware of the unknown factor of the event. He closed a file saying "Well I'm not sorry to be coming back here tonight. Glad tomorrow's is near enough so we don't have to stay away."

"You think you'll be safe here?" Jean Paul couldn't help reminding his friend that there could be a good chance he wouldn't be safe anywhere but tried not to elaborate.

"As much as anywhere I suppose, but there's nothing like your own bed."

A knock on the door broke into their communication.

"Hope I was interrupting something." Daryl cast his eyes around the room as if looking for Jean Paul. He was met with an unblinking stare from across the desk which made any comment unnecessary. With an embarrassed clearing of his throat, he almost whispered "Everything's ready boss. The stage crew are setting the lighting and sound as we speak and all the promo stuff is in place. Of course I will check it to make sure before we start, oh and your dressing room is down the corridor behind the stage area but it is locked until we arrive."

Milton gave him a slight smile as he said "Well it looks as though you have performed to your usual high standards." The look he received told him immediately he could have worded that better but to try and correct it would only be digging his hole deeper.

So he got to his feet and said "Let's finalise everything with Simon before we go."

Any chance of a vulgar reply on Daryl's part had been squashed and he followed feeling as though someone had poured cold water all over him. Had he only been aware that Jean Paul had given him a playful pat on the bottom as he left with the thought "Never mind dear, you'll make somebody a lovely wife. But not him"

Due to Simon's eye for detail, everything for the tour was in place. After today's event the two men would be away for about a week leaving him to hold the fort and sort any hiccups which had a habit of occurring. Milton stated that there was just time to return home for a shower and a bite to eat and put on his travelling outfit. This was not his 'concert' wear as he called it, that was already packed along with other items and these were under the care of the faithful Daryl.

Tommy, along with myriads of other spirits of his level and above had been weaving their little nets of contacts. Bert had long been connected and there were many like him who had some sort of inkling that something was going on but couldn't quite place it. He knew it was like the feelings and events in his past but he wished someone would explain it. Not all earthly beings were as tuned in as he was, not having the slightest notion they possessed any psychic ability, but it was just as powerful when harnessed, all adding to the overall tremendous power that was being held 'on tap' for the right moment. It was the job of the likes of Tommy to secure the subjects which would then be tied to a larger system, almost as if they were tiny streams which ran into small rivers and in turn became part of a bigger river and eventually running into seas and oceans. Such was the power of the small beginning. Add that to the true clairvoyants and clairaudients existing on the planet and in turn add the almighty power of the multitude of existence levels, one would think that nothing could stand a chance in the fight.

But in balance with the good there is always the evil trying to gain footholds in whatever crevice it can find. It was such a foe that was now facing the combined good forces, but the question remained. How large and powerful? And its reason was still to be determined.

A fairly large crowd was gathering outside the Stratford Hall and the earlier threat of rain seemed to have given way to a fairly dull day with quite a chill in the air. Many of the onlookers just wanted to see the television celebrity in the flesh and with the evening being a sell out, there had been many disappointed people who didn't get tickets but they wanted to catch a glimpse of him just the same. As the people started to spill over the small square in front of the centre, the police moved in to organise the crowd and keep the traffic flowing. The plain clothes men were already inside but trying to keep as far away from Laurie as possible.

"Has he got a fly up his arse?" Holland asked.

"He's definitely got something, but I'm not checking it?" Murray smirked then asked

"Did you hear what that chap Johnny said to him?"

"Go on."

"He said that the vibes had to be calm for the celeb, so he had best calm down."

"Bet that went down like a fart in church."

"Didn't make the slightest different, if anything it made him worse."

The Inspector nudged and pointed to the doorway. "They're letting some of the ticket holders in, oh well here we go then."

They moved to the corridor at the rear of the stage. "What time's his lordship arriving then?" Holland may have given the air of self confidence but inside he was churning. His 'nose' never let him down and he felt it wouldn't this time.

"Any time now, he's coming with his aide then one of our bods is parking the car, and staying with it."

Holland looked surprised. "What all night?"

Murray smiled. "They'll take it in turns I expect. Just being safe, you know with trophy hunters, vandals and the like."

"Um. There'll be plenty of them as usual."

The main auditorium was filling up quite quickly with people from all walks of life, some hoping they would get a message, some out of curiosity, many of Milton's followers and as can be expected the usual handful of sceptics. One person had bought her tickets as soon as they were on sale and despite recent events felt she just had to be there. Barbara Anne Simpson's seat was about halfway down the hall keeping her eyes towards the stage. She had no wish to socialise as she didn't know if there may be any relatives there of her former clients, and she didn't particularly want to be pointed out and would have much preferred a seat at the back but they had all gone. She didn't know what she would do if she had a message but thought it highly unlikely. Something had made her feel the need to attend tonight but again that was in doubt. Apart from being rather interested to see how a real medium worked she couldn't have explained why she was there at all.

A feeling of foreboding crept over her now in case the two officers from Mayfield would spot her, but then felt assured that there would be no need for them to be there as it was some miles away and they didn't use detectives for a do like this. Little niggles kept hitting her like needles and she considered leaving, but told herself she was just being silly and to sit back and enjoy things.

Johnny appeared as if from nowhere at the side of the two detectives.

"Mr Warner has just arrived. We're bringing him down the side entrance straight to his dressing room." He produced a key and stood ready to unlock the door on his arrival.

"Oh you can leave that with us." Holland held out his hand and was surprised when the key was not given to him.

"Sorry sir, my responsibility, and the door will be locked when he in on stage."

Holland was not going to be over ruled by this upstart. "And the key will be in your possession all the time?"

"Absolutely."

"Why not give it to his right hand man? Maybe they won't like a stranger having the run of the room."

Johnny eyed them both then said in very slow tones. "They are fully aware of the arrangements sir."

What exchanges would have taken place was anyone's guess, as at that moment Daryl opened the corridor door and stood aside for Milton.

"Good Evening Mr Warner, Daryl." With a slight nod to both Johnny turned and unlocked the room, standing aside for them to enter.

Milton paused to look at the police officers. Holland seized the opportunity to introduce himself and Liam, assuring them they would be in good hands.

"Thank you gentlemen." Milton gave them a quick glance in acknowledgement then added "If you will excuse me please."

"Certainly sir." Holland waited from the door to close behind them then turned on Johnny. "You on first name terms?"

"Well I have been agreeing the arrangements with Daryl, but you will have noticed I treat Mr Warner with the respect he deserves.

"Hmm." Holland beckoned the detective away and when they were out of earshot almost hissed "Why do I always get the feeling that little prick is taking the piss out of us?"

Liam Murray was on the point of saying that it was because he was doing just that, but changed it to "Well you know what some of these little Hitlers are like, full of their own importance, but as long as he does what he's supposed to do, and does it well, kind of leaves us to our own avenues." He didn't ask for or wait for a reply but walked off towards the foyer leaving the inspector little option but to follow.

Sadie was picking up Jo's enthusiasm as they busied about a task they had been set but the younger spirit knew her friend's attention was elsewhere.

"So what made you go to that particular place?"

There was no way Jo was going to admit it had happened almost by chance and with the hint of a shrug in her being she replied "Well, you know I'm good at these things so it was only a matter of time before I tracked the filth down."

"But what will you do now? You've found him but you can't do anything, so I don't understand why you are so elated."

"My dear child you are so naïve." Jo hoped the fob off would be enough but the youngster was having none of it.

"I only ask because I know you and I'm afraid you'll do something silly."

"Oh yes, Miss Cleverdick, and what would that be?" Jo was fishing now, eager to find out what was in Sadie's thoughts.

"I don't know? It's just that you are here and he is there, if you understand. Different forms of living. You may be able to get through mentally but you can't harm him can you, so isn't it time you put it to rest?" She was really hoping Jo would drop it but she should have known her better for it was only the start of a new chapter of revenge.

"I'm going to make the filthy pig suffer as much I did, and again and again until he will wish he was the one that was dead." This sentence was delivered with such a finality that Sadie thought it better not to pursue the matter further but she still worried for her friend, mainly out of ignorance, but felt totally helpless nonetheless.

The higher powers were fully aware of the evil's spread as it now covered most of the earth's land surface and had entirely enveloped the moon, but the hierarchy had also taken account of the fact that, for the present it was confined to solid matter not liquid. Many of the earthlings were totally unaware of the presence, but the likes of Bert had been enlightened as to the mist concept to prove that danger was imminent, but not shown the full extent of the progress as one of the main problems would be universal panic. Such were the powers of the other levels that they only let man know what they wanted him to know whilst cloaking the horrible factors.

On Milton's level, although occupying an earth body, his spirit could learn from other sources and still retain all the information in his waking time. Jean Paul only left his side briefly to try and gather as much up to date information as possible but he could only operate on the levels similar to spirit Liam and Tommy. Some information was filtering down from above but they felt they weren't being told as much as they could be and this was one of the main reasons Milton had little idea of what would be awaiting him that evening.

The tendrils now contained multiple cells of intelligence all collected and supposedly working to the orders of the control area, but as had happened in the early stages any commodity not performing to the required standard was eliminated. The various entities emitted their own colour hence the variety of mixing hues experienced by the high angels. Where the cells of one kind stayed together in harmony the colour would hold firm but as soon as there was any animosity between neighbouring camps, the colours would start to merge as each tried for supremacy. It is inevitable in such situations that some will be stronger and more dominant than others and those of this nature were trying to oust the weaker ones, resulting in the horrible mess of colour hovering over the stage of the Stratford Hall. The control source, although it wanted the most vicious mercenaries in its control, were aware that, by amassing many packs of this kind could result in an attempt to overthrow other parties thus diverting the concentration from the matter in hand, which at the moment was to await, and more importantly, obey orders from above, and not to take matters into their own hands.

Johnny was feeling satisfied with that fact that he had manoeuvred himself into such a position at the centre that he was proving to be more competent than the imbecile Laurie Small. He didn't necessarily want the man's position, he could achieve all he needed from where he was and this place proved the perfect setting for his requirements. Being just another member of the staff didn't draw any attention to him, and although he was making himself indispensible thus securing the position for a while he didn't mind others taking the glory for any of his achievements. It suited him only too well to fade into the background especially during large events such as the one about to explode onto the community. His only worry was that permission had been granted for the evening to be recorded for possible sale or even broadcast on television at a later date. But he imagined the emphasis would be on the celeb and the recipients of messages, however to be on the safe side he had wangled the job of 'dressing room attendant' as he called it and would confine himself to backstage during the evening. If the cameras were allowed in the dressing area, there would be enough people milling around Milton Warner and he could beat a retreat to a safe area. He knew the centre like the back of his hand and broom cupboards and the like could prove invaluable at such times.

His thoughts were shattered by Laurie steaming through from the auditorium.

"I've done nothing but drink and piss all day I'm in such a state." He was obviously muttering to himself and jumped on seeing Johnny. With a nervous cough he spluttered "Oh I might have known you were here. Well there's plenty to do out front you know."

Johnny eyed him up and said very slowly "This was my allocation if you recall. I am on Mr Warner's dressing room duty." His head inclined slightly towards the door.

"Oh well, yes, I –I just wondered if there was anything he wanted." Laurie made for the door handle but Johnny was there in front of him.

"It's locked at his request. Doesn't want to be disturbed while he is getting ready."

It irked Laurie to be kept out of things that he felt it was his right to be part of. And this man always seemed to outsmart him and as if to prove the point he added "Well if there's so many things to do out front, wouldn't you be better checking that they are done. Out front." The repeated emphasis on the last two words combined with the fixed stare, gave Laurie no option but to retire gracefully, except that his exit was anything but graceful.

"I'll swing for that man one day so God help me." He sniffed, threw his nose as high as he could in the air and re-entered the main hall.

If Laurie had got his wish and been in the dressing room, he may have had second thoughts. There were three present. Milton had made no secret now to Daryl that Jean Paul was very much there due to the unknown harm which may manifest it self.

"Just tell me where he is, I wouldn't want to sit on his lap." Daryl eyed up the only vacant chair.

"Not much you wouldn't." Milton was glad of the moment of levity but soon composed himself. "He doesn't sit anywhere."

"What just floats around. Well where is he now? Where are you Jean Paul?"

"I think we had better think of why we are here. I have to go on in a few minutes and I want my surroundings calm."

Jean Paul always watched Daryl with amusement. "Spiky little thing isn't he?"

Milton smiled which didn't go unnoticed by his aide.

"Bet he's said something rude about me."

Turning round and giving his general appearance a final check in the long mirror, Milton said slowly "And you never believed in spirits before did you?"

"Who says I do now? You probably made him up."

"Oh, right!"

Jean Paul went to make a rude gesture towards Daryl but Milton smiling shook his head and said aloud for effect "Don't do that to him, not fair if he doesn't know about it."

"What's he doing?"

"Nothing, nothing, just teasing." Milton gave a final pat to his hair and asked "Are they coming to fetch me?"

This brought Daryl back to reality. "Yes boss, as soon as everyone is seated," looking at his watch he added "any moment now."

If he had only known Jean Paul was patting him on the head whispering "There's a good boy then."

"Have we made an error?" One of Nan's level was making the query.

"If you mean by harnessing Milton Warner's energy to fight off the tendril thus leaving him vulnerable, don't worry. We've taken that into account."

"Oh." The reply was rather flat.

"We have brought in the back up, that is to say the ones whose latent power is being harnessed and combined to create a greater force around him."

Another spirit asked "But will he still be able to perform? Won't it block his communicating?"

Nan was still aware of the tightrope they were walking but tried to spread as much confidence as possible.

"That was one of our concerns but we will act as a sieve, trying to let through the strong positive powers and sadly having to reject any weak messages."

"Seems unfair, but necessary." The spirit was satisfied with the explanation and added

"But positive is the key, right?"

"On all counts and in every dimension."

On that statement which closed the meeting, the area was immediately empty.

CHAPTER 8

With a gush Laurie bounced the short way down the hall to the dressing room and waving Johnny to one side was about to knock on Milton's door when to his amazement it opened and he stood facing Daryl who, looking pointedly at his watch asked "Are you ready?"

"Oh yes, yes we are. Now I of course will introduce the guest speaker….."
Daryl raised his hand to silence the flow and cut in "As previously explained Mr Small, many, many times, our own stage crew, lighting and sound do everything. A proper introduction is used and Mr Warner is not a guest speaker, he is a celebrity and will be treated as such."
Jean Paul was so amused by this little performance he was portraying the act of clapping his hands until he got a stern vibe from Milton who was enjoying Daryl's controlled rant.

"So if you will be good enough to inform the stage manager, we will take it from there. Thank you very much." He gave a little wave to suggest the gopher ran along and did what was asked of him.

When he was at a safe distance, Milton emerged looking every inch a showman immaculate to the last detail and as he left the room Daryl nodded to Johnny to secure the room. Jean Paul did a quick flit to the stage and back checking the route was clear from any spiritual threat and gave Milton the 'go ahead' to proceed. He was aware the tendril was still hovering although it seemed to have retreated somewhat and the whole place held an air of pleasant expectancy, but he knew there was no room for complacency and must be on his guard continually.

The main lights in the hall dimmed slowly to about half their strength and gradually pale blue lights started to bathe the stage in an eerie atmosphere. They changed colour slowly turning the area into a totally different setting. There were two follow spotlights positioned in the hall ready to pick out any member of the audience commanding Milton's attention, not on full brightness, but enough to isolate a particular place without turning up the house lights any more.

"Ladies and Gentlemen." the male voice was husky and very provocative and had just the perfect tone to put people in the right frame of mind.

"Welcome everyone to this evening in the presence of one of the finest in his field. Please sit back, open your minds and witness the amazing gift of ..." the lights on the stage went off and as they burst back on full power ".....Milton Warner." He was standing in the centre of the stage arms outstretched towards the audience. The applause was deafening from the hall now packed to capacity.

The stage was a little higher than he preferred, Milton liked to be nearer his audience but this kind of venue didn't lend itself to any alternative for it would not have been practical to work from floor level and a lower platform couldn't have been erected specially as it would have taken up too much of the floor space, thus reducing ticket sales. However Simon had done his homework and had ascertained that there were steps leading up to one side from the auditorium so if Milton did need to call anyone in particular to join him, they could be escorted by that means.

A hush now fell over the crowd as he moved forward scanning the whole room. Jean Paul was at his side already homing in on several contacts. If not many were in presence they would pick up on the same spirits trying to get through, but sometimes, as in this situation there would be so many jabbering away trying to force their point home, that the two would be sensing many sources not necessarily the same, but they had a knack of throwing the information between them, so when Milton would point to a fixed place it was often because they had both agreed that was the strongest at the time.

Daryl was watching from the wings, guessing his boss was not alone out there but tending to keep his opinions to himself now as he felt he was becoming just a laughing stock to them. He knew where he was with Milton, or so he thought, but the other being. Was it fair for something to be around and not be visible to him? His mind was brought back to reality.

"There is a lady over there near the back." His hand went into its usual palm upwards mode. Everyone waited, some trying to take peek over their shoulders but not wanting to appear obvious while doing it.

"Louise." His call was quite harsh and a few started but he was aware that the woman had reacted with the full knowledge that he was singling her out. The dimmed spotlight trained on her and she raised her hand slightly.

"Why did you do it? Why did you throw your Mother's things in the bin?" The attack was quite fierce even for this kind of message.

The woman was trembling now. "I had no choice. She should know that."

Milton stood perfectly still and when he spoke again his voice had regained the normal lilting tone full of kindness.

"I'm sorry. She has gone. It was your aunt wasn't it?" After a nod from Louise he said "She didn't seem a happy person and threw the words at me in a temper then went. I am so sorry if this has distressed you."

"It's alright. She was a horrible person. My mother understood, she told me to do it. She didn't want the things."

After a moment of quiet, Milton told her to think of her mother's love and put any other thoughts from her mind. He knew the mother had since passed over and noticed she had been pushed back by this dominant aunt who seemed a much more powerful being and would be heard. He finished by assuring her that her mother was also near and still loved her dearly." The usual sobs of satisfaction and happiness could be heard as the spotlight moved from her.

There were so many sources trying to pass messages that even with the filtering by the higher levels the space around the hall was soon teeming with positive eager beings intent on their own purpose. Most would not be aware of the tendril due to their spiritual inexperience, some would be aware of just a mist but pay it no attention, whilst there were those now gathering who were only too able to see the full force of the evil still hovering about the centre. Some abandoned the chance of a contact this time and left the area in fear.

So there was no shortage of fodder for this event and Milton ploughed through as many as possible giving a variety of emotions to recipients. He picked up a signal from Daryl to wind up the first half when he had finished the current message. Jean Paul was somewhat relieved that nothing had intervened up to now and had received a flash from Liam that the thing seemed to be pulling back even further. Hoping it was all due to the positive vibes that had been put in situ he felt a moment's complacency but was prodded back to reality by a higher level, warning him not to loosen his grip for a millisecond. The source seemed very familiar but he couldn't place it and so put it from his thoughts to concentrate on the matter in hand.

During the interval the hall was buzzing with general conversation about the evening so far.

"Oh he's very good isn't he, I mean there is no way he could have known about my dad's shovel. Only I knew that."

"Yes and what he told that lady at the front, she was shocked I can tell you." The comments were various but always had the same conclusion.

"Well I thought he was good on the telly, but you never know do you, if it's being made up like, but here, well I don't see how it can be faked do you?"

"I think he's better in real life."

Even the inevitable sceptics were beginning to wonder.

"There's got to be a plant in the audience. Bet somebody was listening to us as we came in then told him what we'd said. That's how he does it."

"Oh I don't think that's it, anyway how would he know who to pick on?"

"Radio, those earpieces, that kind of stuff. I'm telling you it has to be a trick, but I'm buggered if I know."

Barbara Simpson hadn't relished the idea of sitting on her own until the second half so went for a little wander round trying to fade into the background as much as possible. She had considered leaving during the break as her nerves were getting the better of her and there seemed to be far too many people milling around with their excited chatter and her head began to spin.

"Are you alright?" A kindly young voice broke into her confused state. Abbie, who had been allocated the task of checking the ladies toilets for any undesirables who may be hanging around, laid her hand on Barbara's arm.

With a start she came back to her senses "What? Oh - No I'm perfectly alright but thank you dear for asking."

The youngster wasn't going to be put off that easily. "Only you do seem a little pale, would you like to come and sit down where it's quieter for a while?"

"Do you know, I think I would, I got a bit too warm for a while," and fanning her face with her hand whispered "flushes you know." Even she was amazed at how the lie came out but it would suffice.

With a guiding hand on her arm Abbie directed her to her own office and showed her to a chair. "How about a nice cup of tea?"

"Oh that would be lovely, if you're sure it's no trouble."

"You just stay there and relax, I won't be long." Abbie was about to go out of the door when it opened and two men came bursting in."

"Where's Small?" Murray demanded as he cast a quick look round the room and was about to dash out when he caught sight of Barbara. For a moment he hesitated but had to put the information spirit Liam was giving him to one side.

"Think he is with the star." Abbie was a bit taken aback at the urgency in his voice. Holland indicated for the DC to carry on and, waiting for Abbie to leave the room sat down opposite Barbara.

"Bit much for you eh?"

"No, no I just felt a bit dizzy, um hot. But the kind young lady is fetching me a cup of tea so I'll be alright in a minute."

"You going to be OK on your own? You're not going to pass out or anything?"

He got up and was already making his way to the door as Abbie returned. As she put the tea on the desk she asked "Oh sorry did you want one Inspector?"

He raised a hand in acknowledgement and with a shake of the head followed Murray who was indicating he needed an urgent word.

If Barbara's colour had been returning, it now retreated as quickly. She could see the same manner in this man as the one who had been to her house and with the rank of inspector he could only be a policeman, and the younger man must be one as well. Her hand shook as she lifted the cup.

"You know, I don't think you should go back in the hall, it's rather stuffy." Abbie was concerned for this lady who she felt would get overcome with the performance and end up in a worse state than she was already.

"I think I would be better off at home. You've been very kind to me."

The two chatted for a moment deciding on the best means of transport, while not too far away the detectives were in conference. Murray having located Laurie and dealt with some matter regarding security had almost grabbed his superior to a spot away from the main activity.

"That's her!"

"Who is?" Holland was baffled but keen to know what was going on. But Liam Murray was finding it hard to explain how he knew this was the woman Grimes and Bruin had visited. The inspector may have had a 'nose' for things, but it would sound a bit far fetched to say he had an inkling and must have seen a photo or something. Then he burst out with "Same description. DC Bruin was telling me before I came over here." He felt it was a bit lame for in truth he had no idea how he could possibly know. Spirit Liam had seen Barbara arrive and had been trying to impart the thought in his mind but with all the buzz in the surrounding air he had found it difficult to communicate it to him. So he had resorted to entering his body as a passenger thus having closer contact in thought. Having achieved his goal he had now left to carry on with sustaining the positive protection programme.

Holland was deep in thought for a moment then punched the air.

"That must be it."

"Must be what?" Murray wasn't entirely sure which direction this was going.

"I said something was bugging me, I knew it. All that you told me about that séance woman and the deaths over at Mayfield, and if she's who you say, there's got to be something funny going off."

Murray was still a bit uncomfortable with the fact he was certain this was Astral Anne but couldn't prove it, after all there were no mug shots of her, but he knew just as spirit Liam wanted him to. The inspector drew Murray a little closer and almost whispered "You don't reckon she was really into this sort of stuff and popped 'em off do you?"

"Surely not."

With a nod towards the office he said "What's happening with her now, is she going back in?"

"Are you hoping she does?"

"Hey, perhaps she is working in cahoots with the Warner chap and all this is a ruse to pick up info from the crowd then feed it back."

Murray eyed him, pulling back a little. "Is this your nose working now or do you really think she is on a par with the experts?"

"Let's get back. Anything else going on?"

They started back towards the office. Murray shrugged "No, pretty quiet on our side. Some of the lads have sorted out a few lively characters but most of the folks are here for the show, some are keen followers it seems."

The office door was still shut so Murray gave a gentle tap and started to open it when Abbie appeared from behind. With a quick smile to both she said "Oh well, that's that sorted now I better get back to Loo Patrol".

"Where's the lady?" The two men chorused.

"Oh someone offered to take her home, she really didn't feel up to any more."

"She's gone!" Holland didn't mean it as a question, more of an exasperated statement as he felt this woman had something to do with his instincts for trouble.

"Obviously." Abbie smiled and left wondering if he was getting a bit past it and should retire.

Murray was thoughtful. "May be absolutely nothing, and as for your theory, she wouldn't have had chance to pass on anything to them backstage so I reckon that's a non starter." All he got in return was a grunt but the senior was already making up his mind to go over and see the Mayfield crew at his earliest chance.

The movements of the mist were now giving a great deal of concern to the high powers. They felt sure the six main targets of the tendrils were about to be attacked. Too much homework had been done by the thing up to now and the concentration of evil power was undoubtedly building for some sort of planned action. When evil forces usually invaded any particular space area, they did it quickly, always using the element of surprise hoping to succeed in destroying it or taking it over for their own purpose. For this reason the combined good elements had to operate a constant monitoring of all aspects in all areas which is how they got early warning of this mass. But for now they had no option but wait and observe.

Jo had made several return visits to the centre. It had taken her what seemed an eternity to trace her rapist and murderer and she wasn't going to let him get away now, but still being unsure as to how she could achieve this, she was now biding her time until the perfect plan would present itself. She too had recognised Astral Annie, as she still called her but gave her little thought.

"She doesn't know her elbow from her arse." she mused as she hovered around the hall. Being a bit restless waiting for Milton to begin the next session she floated backstage and hovered near the dressing room. Johnny was still at his post but her attention was drawn to the closed door as if something was pulling at her inwards. Slowly she floated through and saw Jean Paul for the first time. Whether or not he had such a stunning appearance in earthly form she didn't care, she felt she was melting in his presence.

"Hello." The greeting came from Milton which made her almost jump with surprise.

"You can see me?"

"My spirit can, and hear you."

At this point she didn't know whether to give her attention to him or this other beautiful creature hovering nearby so resorted to her usual bluntness.

"My God if I still had a body I would be in a right moist state now I can tell you. Bloody hell!"

Milton couldn't hide his amusement. "I guess you are directing that to my colleague here."

"Would somebody mind telling me who the f...... I mean who are you talking to now?" Daryl's interruption reminded them that to his knowledge he was alone with Milton.

"Sorry, we have a guest Daryl and she seems rather taken with Jean Paul."

"I knew it. You've never told me what he looked like, now I know why."

Jo, still casting sheep's eyes but indicating to Daryl said "Puny little thing isn't he. Fancy you does he? Cor, if he could see this one he'd have something to worry about."

Milton was more concerned as to why Jo had visited. "Did you want to contact someone? Only you appear to have taken the short cut."

"No, I already know where the bastard is I've been after. I just felt pulled in here for some reason."

"What's she saying? What's going on? We've got to get back." Daryl was becoming more uncomfortable by the minute.

Milton raised his hand and said "Well for all those present, I think we should follow Daryl's lead and concentrate on the evening in hand." Then turning to Jo asked "What do we call you?"

"Me? Oh Jo."

"Well Jo why not accompany Jean Paul for the rest of the show and we will talk later?"

Her spiritual gasp of delight must have disturbed the surrounding air. She liked these people and was more than happy to remain, a feeling which was not shared by Nan at that moment as she would have liked her well away from the venue until they knew the mist's intentions.

When the men had first encountered Johnny on their arrival, Milton and Jean Paul had noticed something strange about him in the spiritual sense. Experience had taught both of them to always appear indifferent when they weren't sure as to the nature of such a being. As he was appearing in bodily form it didn't necessarily mean he was in the permanent bodily state or he could have been riding passenger for some reason, but they just treated him as normal keeping their suspicions to themselves in case he was able to intervene on their thought patterns.

Jean Paul now wished he didn't have to keep such a close watch on Milton during the second part of the evening, but at the same time knew he had to find out just what this employee was up to. He guided Jo to the wings and indicated for her to keep her positive energy at its highest level. His intention was to flit back and forth in the gaps between readings when he thought Milton would be at his safest.

"Ladies and Gentlemen, will you please welcome back.....Milton Warner."

The announcement was greeted by thunderous applause and Milton this time walked slowly to the front of the stage, paused for a moment then moved to the left hand side, that is the audience's right.

Quickly Jean Paul did a switch to the dressing room door watching for Johnny's reaction, if any. The man started as he realised he wasn't alone and not wishing to appear as though he was there on purpose, Jean Paul slowed and communicated with him in thought mode.

"This bit gets a bit boring, seen it so many times." He hovered for a moment waiting for some kind of response. The man was looking straight at him which confirmed he knew where he was and possibly his power level.

"Neither of you acknowledged me before, except in the physical." Johnny's reply held a tone very different to his working image. Gone was the calming efficient manner. Now he was accusing, almost putting his opponent on trial.

"Don't usually. There's so many different entities milling around, you don't converse with everyone any more than you would in earthly form walking down a busy street. You get on with your own business." This remark was thrown back as a challenge and was followed by a long pause.

As this had happened in a split second, Jo hadn't realised she had been alone and her host was soon back at her side. Checking all was well he returned to the corridor.

Johnny surveyed him closely.

"You are watching me."

"Ha ha, you have got a suspicious mind. Guilty conscience perhaps."

"I'm just doing my job."

"Then I'll leave you to it." As Jean Paul returned to the wings his thought was "Physical or spiritual I wonder."

Nan's group wished the spirit guide hadn't made this move as they had been monitoring Johnny recently especially as Jo had taken such an interest in the place for her own reasons. Nobody seemed able to trace his past at any level which was now causing concern as to why he should be at one of the places in the tendrils path. Swiftly they did a search of the other five venues to see if any other employee fitted the same profile. Each one had someone who had only been there for a few months with flimsy background, did the work to perfection but didn't shout about it, and as wages were paid from the local government straight into the bank, no one queried why they weren't receiving pay packets.

Nan's group realised that this had to be a pre arranged plant, put in the right place to report or even engineer any attack at the precise moment. The terrifying thought that hit them next was that these plants were not underlings, but all from a very high power merging in with the day to day happenings getting all the details they needed for the ultimate plan, which was why they had been untraceable on the lower levels.

"How many of them are there?" One of the group put the question everyone was now asking. The answer never came for as yet there wasn't one.

Jo was enthralled. "He's the real McCoy isn't he? How did he know that?"

Jean Paul realised the youngster wasn't picking up half the messages that were being portrayed but she was likable and he felt it worth trying to explain.

"You've been hearing some haven't you?"

"All of them, er haven't I?"

"Very few actually."

"Oh...what are you trying to tell me?" She felt quite flattened thinking she had been a part of all that she had witnessed.

"Your level will only catch so much. My level and that of a few others round us at the moment can hear and see much more, then think of those who are way above us."

"Bloody lucky lot!" What she would have come out with next was interrupted by Jean Paul pointing her attention to Milton.

"Something's not right. Stay exactly where you are."

He was immediately at the man's side pulling in all the surround good forces he could but something was fighting him trying to drag him off. He called for Tommy and spirit Liam to help but if they were in the area they couldn't get near him. From Jo's point all she could see was Jean Paul fighting an unseen force while Milton was struggling to keep a visiting spirit in the room who was trying to pass a message to one of the audience. His voice was strained.

"He is always with you, he... sends... his love....to..." his voice was fading and he appeared to be trembling. There was a gasp from the whole auditorium as he swayed for a moment then regained his composure. He knew the relative had left but felt he had to close the message in some way.

"I am sorry, he has gone, there were other spirits trying to get through and I am sorry he didn't quite finish but he was sending all his love to you, please remember that."

The hushed crowd now broke into applause believing there had been a strong presence at play and it was a normal reaction for this kind of thing. A few still believed it was a bit of showmanship. If only that's all it had been.

Within seconds all had appeared to return to normal. Jean Paul was at Milton's side encouraging him to build on what had just gone on so that no one would suspect the danger which must still be lurking. According to the watching crowd Milton had just received a contact which was so powerful it had shaken him but that's what they had come to see and they wanted more.

"Thank you." He stood straight now, his hands raised. "May I just explain please? Sometimes we get a person on the other side who is so eager to get their message through, it disrupts the whole air around us and if there are a few all trying at the same moment – well you saw what happened."

"Are you alright Mr Warner?" A voice came from somewhere in the audience. He faced the approximate direction and said "I'm fine now, thank you." As soon as he homed in on the speaker he felt himself being drawn to a man sitting to his right side at the on the end of a row near the back. As he lifted his right arm towards him Jean Paul reappeared and pulled his arm back down.

"Don't communicate with him!"

"What?"

"Don't ask, just ignore him whatever you do."

The audience, watching Milton's every move hadn't missed this interchange and he knew he had to give some sort of explanation.

"As you know, we all have a guide or spirit companion and I am in constant touch with mine."

"What's his name Mr Warner?" The same man was asking and Milton sensed he was fishing for information, but not in a good way.

"Don't tell him." Jean Paul was almost shouting in his own way.

Milton stood stock still, his eyes riveting towards the heckler.

"That is not important and I prefer to keep that to myself." Panning round the rest of the room he explained "Some of us like to divulge our guide, some of us like to keep them private, much as you do I'm sure in your physical life." Then carefully selecting one area he said with a laugh "I think there are one or two of you here who do not wish all your associates to be known. Would you like me to pick you out?"

The air filled with amusement as many laughed, almost relieved at the lightness of the situation whilst others visibly shuffled in their seats. Daryl was feeling more uncomfortable by the minute. Even he was sensing there was more going on around him than usual and for once in his life he almost wished he could ask Jean Paul what it was. Jo on the other hand was thoroughly enjoying the moment watching Milton's guide flitting to and fro and with her limited experience she knew that all was not well in the body of the hall. Recalling her experience at Astral Annie's, she felt very strongly that the same kind of force was at work here and being of quite stern stuff she wasn't too unnerved by it. She did wonder as she surveyed the entertainment, why she had not been recalled to other duties but wasn't going to let that thought spoil this.

Unbeknown to her she had not been alone for one second as Nan's sentinels had been interchanging and reporting back to the higher levels where observation on the main mass had been heightened constantly. Several other Johnny forms in different guises had been noticed dotted around the building and all seemed to be taking direction from him. So although the main tendril had receded, it was felt that it had 'beamed down' agents who would act under their leader, Johnny who was in turn the main source of communication from above.

Spirit Liam had managed to get through to impart this to Jean Paul and assure him that higher levels were also in position so he was not alone and they would make themselves known to him if necessary. Milton was trying to concentrate on the messages which were flooding in to the assembled hopefuls but was picking up the essence of what was going on. The Liam spirit now entered Liam Murray who was standing at the back of the hall with Holland.

"What was all that about?" The older man whispered.

At this point Murray was picking up a sense of foreboding and getting flashing images of a dark cloud hanging over the centre and for once he felt there was much more going on here than he imagined.

"Don't know but I tell you something."

"Shhh." came from the back row.

The two men acknowledged the person and quietly went outside into the foyer. Holland turned straight to his junior. "What is it?"

Murray shuffled. "You know your 'nose'. It's been bugging you for days, that something isn't right."

"Don't tell me you've go one now?"

Again Murray didn't know how to voice his feeling and if either of them could have seen spirit Liam almost shouting in his ear they would have had real cause for concern.

He almost muttered "I think I've got the same."

"What?" He went a bit too red in the face for Murray's liking but ignoring it he replied "I have been getting these- oh I don't know how to put it, not messages exactly but...."

"A nose. You're getting a nose for stuff. And if we both have over this there's got to be something going off. No doubt about it. Almost a relief I can tell you." After a moment he asked "What kind of sense you got then?"

Before he could stop himself, the spirit took over and the detective blurted out "There's evil here, it's been building up and it's going to attack. Tonight."

As soon as the words had left his mouth he stared at Holland and said "What did I say? Where did that come from?"

The inspector wanted to get some reality back into things and pulling at his tie as though it was choking him said "It's all this spiritual shit, never did agree with it, gets people's minds all mixed up, brainwashing that's what it is lad, brainwashing I tell you." He was becoming more agitated by the minute so Murray tried to get him to sit on one of the foyer seats and calm down but spirit Liam was yelling at his mind to get the public out of the place. Without giving it a second thought he said aloud "But why get them out, what danger?"

"Eh?" Holland almost slumped onto a chair. "Who the hell are you talking to now for Christ's sake?"

Murray stood there looking at him thinking "How can I clear the room on a whim? And if I do and nothing happens, I'm going to look a right prick." He pulled himself together and suggested, more than told, Holland that if he would like to sit there for a while, he would go back in and see what was happening, if anything.

He had only been gone a moment when Abbie appeared and asked Holland if he would like another cup of tea, saying he didn't look too clever.

"A copper never refuses a cuppa, that'd be good."

"I won't be long" she said as she turned to go "funny thing though, we've had more people tonight not feeling well than I can ever remember."

A bell went off in his head. "Oh, how's that then?"

She turned "Oh you know, dizziness, feeling faint, must be the heat in there. Several have gone home you know. Seems a shame when so many wanted tickets." With that she hurried off.

His brain was churning. What heat? It wasn't hot in the hall well, no more than usual and there were plenty of people who didn't seem overcome, but was that because they were so enthralled by the celebrity they wouldn't have noticed anyway. He made up his mind to ask how many had been affected when she returned. Then his mind shot to Murray. Was the man flipping his lid or did he really have a feel for things? He'd have thought he would have had more sense than to meddle in stuff when you needed to keep a clear head for reasoning things out, but that brought him back to himself and his 'nose'. He knew full well that in the past it had served him well on many occasions but he could never have said why he had these hunches, he just did, like many others he'd known.

"Here you are sir, that'll hit the spot."

"Ah that looks good -er - how many people would you say had gone then?"

"Oo let me see now, must be a dozen or more at least. Funny though."

"Oh why?"

"Well nobody wanted a fuss, you know didn't want to give their names or anything or put anything in our book like we're supposed to."

"Mmm – well thank you um….."

"Abbie."

"Right."

She fussed about putting a small table near him for the teacup.

"Now you just sit there and relax, I'm sure your friend can manage quite well on his own."

"Thank you again," he called but muttered under his breath "patronising little twat!"

His 'nose' was telling him that there was more than coincidence that people should be dropping like flies and he cast his mind back to the woman he had spoken to in the office, wondering again if she was involved in some way, but still none of it would fit into any sort of pattern yet.

A thunderous round of applause filled the auditorium as Milton asked a couple to return to their seats after having invited them on to the stage. His reading had been exceptional and should have dispelled any doubts as to his true powers for he was revealing facts that even they had long forgotten, so he could not be accused of reading their minds. This encounter had taken quite a few minutes and the atmosphere appeared to the spirit world to have settled to a normal level but the warning again went out to stay on guard even more as this was probably a planned way of getting them to drop their guard and protection.

The sentinels had taken it in turn to check on Johnny but each time he seemed aware of their presence which meant he was of a level equal to theirs or even higher. So they had upped the levels of the latest ones to see if he knew they were there, and still he registered them.

"So just how high is he? Nan was asked but by reply she said "And why have such a high power in placement. Which also asks another two questions?"

One of her number offered "Is the highest controller of the mass working from earth level?"

Another added "Or is the main mass even higher, and is that the utmost point or is the mass being controlled beyond the earth?"

Nan was worried. "Any of these factors prove it is beyond our control. Oh we can help but it will have to be of Za's level or even way above that."

"That high!" There was a general consternation as the truth was beginning to manifest itself. "But that is higher than ever encountered."

"Exactly. It is now a job for the ultimate powers."

Milton stood alone in the spotlight waiting for the hall to settle. There had been a standing ovation and rapturous applause following his final delivery and the place was literally throbbing with the vibrations. Although he appeared motionless, everyone connected with him knew something was amiss for he appeared to be shaking from head to toe and Daryl gave the signal for the curtain to close leaving the baying crowd with the last look at their hero as he disappeared from their sight. Immediately Daryl rushed to Milton's side and grabbed him as he staggered backwards. One of the crew helped support him as his legs folded and they laid him on the floor of the stage. Weakly he beckoned Daryl close as he whispered "It got me, right at the end it got me." as he passed into unconsciousness.

CHAPTER 9

Murray had been talking to Holland who seemed to have a theory that all the people feeling ill had had the same sort of drink. Whilst sitting quietly on his own he started with the fact that the astral woman had been giving a cup of tea then went home, and he had been given tea which hadn't revived him as normal. In itself the two things didn't have much bearing until he found from various sources that everyone who left had been given a drink of some sort and had felt worse. The thought also hit him that it was after he had the first cup of tea that he felt peculiar.

Just before the end of the show Murray had been listening to what his elder had to say then he suddenly jumped up, yelled "Oh Christ Almighty!" and dashed through the door leading to the corridor backstage. Little did he know it was spirit Liam who was pushing him to examine the water which had been supplied to Milton during the performance. As he reached the door he was met with Johnny in his normal stance across the door. He could hear the applause now rippling throughout the building telling him the show was over but he couldn't wait for them to come down from the stage.

"Open this door please. Now."

Johnny remained immobile giving him a defiant stare.

"You heard me. This is police business."

There was no emotion on Johnny's face and he said very slowly "I and only I have the key. I open the door when the gentleman returns."

Both spirit and physical Liam were working together now and before the man had chance to move Murray had him by the neck of his sweater and was shouting in his face.

"I don't give a shit about your made up rules. Now open the frigging door!"

"Open the door now." Daryl's voice rose over the top of him.

As soon as the key was turned Murray and Daryl rushed into the room and slammed the door. Quickly the detective learned of Milton's collapse and immediately explained why he wanted to take any drinks that Milton had touched then asked as to the state of his boss.

"Seems it was just a faint, he doesn't want any fuss and...." his head inclined towards the door "...he wants him out of here before he comes back down."

"I'll get the keys off him then." Murray went into the corridor but there was no sign of Johnny and the keys were in the lock on the outside.

"Whew, could have locked us in if he'd wanted," he said returning to Daryl who now looked a bit uneasy. "What's up?"

"Oh nothing, just that the boss says you don't know who anyone is and he was wary of him 'cos he thought he knew everything we said."

Murray let a slow whistle escape then asked "Your boss is quite quick on picking this kind of stuff up isn't he. I've been watching him, there's more going on than just relaying messages."

Daryl was obviously concerned about 'boss' so Murray offered to stay in the dressing room until he returned with him, knowing it would give him ample chance to collect anything he needed for examination. Spirit Liam was still guiding him as he had been flitting about during the show and knew where to direct his attention. The man's gaze was drawn to the waste bin which contained all the usual stuff, but in the bottom was what appeared to be an empty mineral water bottle. Looking round he saw one of the   plastic sleeves used for carrying various paperwork, and using a pair of scissors from the props and make up bag, he carefully lifted the bottle by the neck and dropped it into the sleeve. It had appeared to be empty at first but now he could see the dregs of a substance unknown to him and certainly not what you would expect in a water bottle.

Milton had to be almost carried back to the dressing room and it was obvious to all around him that this hadn't been just a simple faint. Unaware of the fact that the star of the show was not well, Laurie was flitting about trying to tell them that there were loads of people outside waiting for autographs and when was he coming because he couldn't hold them off much longer.

Although this was an unusual situation, Daryl could handle most eventualities so he told Laurie to go and tell them it would be dealt with shortly. When the man had reluctantly toddled off Milton said in rather a sharp tone "For goodness sake, do what you have to then get back here."

"You'll be OK?"

"I've just said so. Now go."

Daryl grabbed a handful of signed photos from the box and feeling a little hurt with the abruptness left the room in silence. Laurie was soon at his side almost as if he had been waiting.

"I thought I'd just make a little speech and then….."

"No need for that, I'll sort it."

"Oh….." Although lost for words, Laurie wasn't going to be left out of anything so followed Daryl as though they were attached to each other. Daryl found a place slightly higher than the crowd and held up his hand for silence.

"Hello everybody. I have to tell you that after most shows of this kind, Mr Warner is somewhat exhausted, as you can understand." There was a low groan from the crowd.

"However, he hopes you've had an enjoyable evening and he really appreciates your enthusiasm, so he has asked me to make sure you all get a signed photograph." This caused a happier murmur and soon the photos were dished out to the waiting hands. Laurie still had to put his spoke in "Now there's plenty for all, so don't push or you'll rip them."

"Oh shut up you old fart" came from one man which caused some amusement, but Daryl hastened to add. "He will be resting for quite some time which is perfectly usual so please don't wait, and have a safe journey home." There was a finality about the statement and some started to trickle off straight away pleased with their memorabilia.

As soon as he could, Daryl patted Laurie on the shoulder and said in a very patronising tone "Well I think you can handle this now don't you?" and hurried back to the dressing room.

Simon had been quite happy manning the office in the absence of the 'tour party' and welcomed the peace and calm of the place. Living alone from choice meant he didn't always welcome company and much preferred to sit with his faithful friend, his computer, be it at home or work. He didn't go much for the puerile banter he got from Daryl, but at least his own offhanded manner kept his workmate from casting the kind of looks at him that Milton seemed oblivious too.

They had obviously been in touch during the time leading up to the event but during the second part Daryl had been too preoccupied to notice there had been no usual contact from him. It was only now as he sat watching Milton's slow recovery he realised what a long gap there had been. Murray had gone, assured no doctor or ambulance was needed and as he left the room spirit Liam vacated his body and stayed in presence.

"I'll just check with Cyberfart, he's been a bit quiet." Daryl took out his phone. There was no reply as Milton was concentrating on getting back to normal using not only his own, but Jean Paul's and Liam's positive powers to regain full control, for he knew he was very vulnerable at present.

"That's strange." Daryl stood looking at the mobile in his hand.

"What is?" Milton's reply was barely a whisper but held concern.

"Can't get him on any number. The office one is unobtainable, and his own is just dead. Funny for them both to be off, I mean a land line and a mobile. If he can't pick up a signal he could be out of range but not the office as well. Doesn't make sense."

"Keep trying." Milton indicated.

Tommy arrived and was greeted by the two other spirits.

"How is he?" He was hovering over Milton's physical form knowing the man was aware of him being there but all of them knew his psychic side had been attacked. In an instant the three had surrounded him to strengthen the protective shield he desperately needed and were soon joined by some of Nan's level to boost the recovery.

Daryl was unaware of all the activity going on around him but guessed that Jean Paul was nearer to his boss than he could ever be. The jealousy that was building was not the kind of vibe any of the spirits needed for although very strong it wasn't of the positive nature to restore Milton and was a perfect route for any unwanted source.

Simon sat in stunned silence, his face fixed on his monitors. He would never be able to explain what had happened, for who would believe him? After his last conversation with Daryl, he had settled down to update their website, but before he had chance to even log in, the screen was filled with an image that was so horrible, even this calm man shuddered. He was watching a detailed form of the mass Nan and her hierarchy had been studying all along but this was a zoomed in image showing the individual cells operating like separate armies all fighting their way for power. At first glance he thought he had downloaded some kind of horror movie but remembered his hands hadn't hit any keys. Even the worse kind of animation couldn't have matched this and his mouth dropped open as he sat transfixed almost unable to move.

The close up shots of the beings seemed to be stretching out at him like a 3D image and he was so filled with terror he felt himself loosing consciousness. As his awareness returned he wasn't sure exactly what had happened, or how much time had passed. All he knew was that he was facing a screen in front of him bearing the words "You had been warned but you paid no heed. Now you face the consequences."

In vain he tried to hit keys to get rid of the message but nothing worked. For once he had no control over his computer or anything attached to it, so pushing himself away on his chair he grabbed his mobile and tried to reach Daryl but there was no signal. Still seated he wheeled himself over to the office phone handset cursing the fact he had left it on one of the other desks. He almost dropped it in haste and dialled the number without stopping to check if there was a dialling tone. It was only when he couldn't get through he listened before trying again and knew he had no chance of contacting the hall. A panic had taken over his whole system and he was cross with himself for not holding it together when it was needed.

Taking a deep breath he told himself to get a grip and go over to the door, open it and walk out to find a phone. His legs were like jelly and he had to support himself on the furniture until he was within a foot of it and only then did it hit him that the general office door was rarely closed when they were there, only Milton's door was usually shut or locked even. As his hand touched the handle the fear returned for he was locked in, alone.

The questions buzzing about in the very high levels now were centred round how the evil force had perpetrated its attack and what would the lasting effects be. They knew it had acted but there was no visual evidence and no apparent moment of impact. Nan's party had been monitoring Milton and knew he had been targeted but in what way?

Za had been in presence and confirmed that this was the difference on this invasion compared with previous ones, for the good forces still did not know what they were fighting and couldn't take preventive measures to stop it, as this was a new kind of evil. Whatever it had planted at the centre was obviously going to be repeated at the other five venues shortly, and as the mass was seemingly spreading over the earth's surface, the whole planet was at risk, or rather the occupants. If it was trying to take over the earth for its own use, there would be little point in destroying it, so was it the people who were in the firing line?

But the other point of discussion was that it wasn't confined to the earthly beings. This was more a combat on spiritual levels, so why bother with a piece of rock. Although certain spiritual levels were concentrated around the planet, it didn't mean they couldn't exist elsewhere so what was it trying to achieve? Before Za left the area he left a worrying thought. The target could be the higher levels so it had to remove the lower ones first starting with any below earth status from other areas, then any planet containing any sort of life, moving up to the levels Jo's spirit was on, up to the ones that Liam, Tommy, Jean Paul and Milton had achieved, several higher until it got to Nan or Tabar's, many more to get to Za, and even they were only the lower ones in the table. So if the evil was aiming even higher, beyond anything all these which were considered very high to most spirits, the threat was beyond comprehension.

Nan mulled over these thoughts but still something niggled her as though pieces of a puzzle wouldn't fit.

"If that is the case, why did it attack Milton's spirit rather than his body?" As her thought wave hit her surrounding group she knew she would never rest until they had the answers, but by then would it be too late?

Milton was in thought conference with his spiritual companions which was why he didn't want conversation with Daryl at present.

"What happened? I wasn't aware of anything." Jean Paul was the first to ask what they all wondered.

"It was near the end. They were all around the place. Didn't you see them?"

"Of course, it was teeming." Tommy cut in. "Always are at these dos."

"No, No. Not the usual ones trying to contact."

"What then?" Liam was getting frustrated.

Milton paused wondering how to explain this new phenomena. "They were dotted all over the place, in people, in the lights, in the ceiling, even in the floor."

Jean Paul took over. "Wait a minute, how did you see them and we didn't?"

"I don't know, I don't know." Milton's spiritual manner was nothing like his usual calm physical state.

"Well what were they like?" Tommy wanted to know.

"Not people." Milton's answer was met with a wall of silence.

Tommy offered, "Well some would say spirits aren't like people" Then after a moment

"You're saying they weren't like spirits aren't you, he is isn't he?" His attention went to the others. Jean Paul felt this was going nowhere and said "I think we ought to just let him spill it out with no prompting."

"What I need is to get out of this damn place. When are we going for Christ sake?" The words came out in his physical form with such a force Daryl almost fell over putting the boss's outburst down to his recent experience.

"Whenever you say. I'll just check the crowds have gone. Be alright on your own? Oh silly me, you aren't on your own are you?" He left the room with such a flounce all except Milton found it amusing.

"I don't know what they've done to me, but something is very wrong. Can you find out?"

"Of course, but the higher ones have already reported back so we should know soon." Jean Paul didn't have to be told there was a change. It was almost as if his companion had gone and a stranger had taken his place which was making him very wary as to what thoughts he expressed in his presence.

The innocence of Jo's spirit meant she had no chance of seeing anything other than the lower level of relatives and friends trying to communicate with their earth companions and a few times she had tried to intervene and pass on messages while Milton was dealing with the higher levels. It hadn't worked because she had never had the experience of acting as a messenger, much as she had tried to convince the gullible ones like Sadie that she did. But it had kept her fairly amused and as the evening drew on she was so impressed with Milton her attention was held almost totally on him, with the occasional drift to Jean Paul. She had been instructed to keep in the wings, not for any visual reason of course, but Milton liked a 'clean area' in which to work, having the stage fairly uncluttered with plenty of air space around him and even Jean Paul kept his distance for this reason which had left Milton unprotected.

Just before the unseen attack, Jo had been aware of someone at her side and as her attention turned towards them, she had an image of Johhny leaving the wings. She didn't know whether to follow him or stay.

"Oh let the pigshit go," she thought "plenty of time for him later" and turned her thoughts back to the stage. She noticed something had changed in that split second and she cursed Johhny for the diversion. Milton's whole aura seemed to have gone and she felt more than saw that his spirit was being sucked from his body while he was clinging frantically to keep it. Her instinct was to rush to his side but she was held back and lifted from the area and instantaneously realised she was back on her own spiritual level with some of Nan's group checking her over.

"I'm OK. Let me get back." She was fighting to no avail and was soon persuaded to calm down and report any slightest detail from her position on stage.

"You did well little one," one of the aides tried to console her but Jo wasn't having it.

"Yeah. Too right. Did well? What did I do?" She was taking some calming until Nan appeared briefly.

"You may have saved him." The statement brought instant hush to the whole party.

"But I didn't. You know that, don't give me that bullshit, I don't need it," then turning to the other one almost screamed "and don't patronise me you stupid git. You always treat me like a dog."

"Jo!" Nan was not amused now and knew the youngster needed a good shake up.

"What?" The tone was somewhat lowered.

"When, and only when you have gathered your wits, something will be explained to you which is very important, but for now we need whatever you can tell us from the 'ground' which I can assure you is far more necessary to the furtherance of mankind than any of your little tantrums." Nan had such a way with her that Jo felt as though someone had poured cold water over her enthusiasm.

"If I tell you will you let me back?"

"So that you can pursue that man?" Nan was one step ahead. "There is no rush, believe me."

Very reluctantly, because she knew she was beaten Jo related every detail to the listeners and when she had finished Nan said "I have to leave to confer with my elders, but I have left information for you. Please be courteous enough to listen."

"My God, she can be officious when she wants." Jo looked round the spirits who were all leaving bar one.

"Who are you?"

"Jorg."

"And don't you have some place to go to - Jorg?"

"I thought you wanted to know that 'something important' Nan was mentioning."

"Is that the same as the information?"

"It is."

"Well, get on with it then, oh sorry I have to be courteous." The last word was thrust out with such sarcasm Jorg was silent for a second then said "Perhaps you are not ready. Another time I think."

"No, No, I'm sorry, I didn't mean it. I'm listening."

Jorg almost gave her the equivalent of a mental body search as though he was estimating whether to continue, but this was all for effect as he had a job to do.

"The reason you wish to return in such a haste is that you have traced who you think is your rapist and murderer."

"Slight correction there mate, I know, I don't think. OK .Go on."

"I think it would be better if you let me finish before interjecting." He was finding her quite amusing and even likable and he was almost tempted to play her along for a while but he knew there was no time for those games.

"Inter---- what? Oh you mean me butting in don't you?" and thought "why can't the bleeder speak plain English?"

"Exactly. Can we manage that?"

"Well I can if you can. Spit!"

"Pardon me?"

"Sorry, I mean tell me…. ahem.."

"As I was saying, you felt that Johnny is the man who raped then murdered you, but I have to tell you Jo that is not the case."

The impulse to answer froze as he continued before the fact could sink in.

"You may not have come across this yet so let me just explain. The earthly body is no more than a vehicle we use to house our spirit form when we are on earth, and yes, we don't always use a body but when we do, and it has served its purpose, we discard it, or shed it if you like."

Normally Jo would have told him to get on with it but there was something rather compelling about this spirit that attracted her. Nan had instructed the being to appear as a rather handsome male knowing full well Jo would be forced to listen and this was what was now taking full effect.

He continued "As we progress, we still shed our covering for the want of a better description, so when you go to a higher plane you will leave behind a faint image of what you are now. Each time you ascend you leave a vehicle."

He paused for a moment knowing this had to sink in. "Now, let's go back to the earth level, just for a minute. Your old car was the one people recognised you by. They would know when you arrived because your car pulled up. But when you needed a new one, the same people would know you by the latest one wouldn't they?"

Jo gave an acknowledgment but still didn't interrupt.

"But the old one you left could have been bought by someone else and those people who didn't know would see it and think it was you driving."

"Ah. Can I say now?"

He was amused. "Please do."

"You're trying to tell me that this chap calling himself Johnny who looked like my uncle, was only using a body that looked like him but wasn't him. But how's that work?"

"You are getting the point." He refrained from saying "Well done" as he had witnessed the last outburst from that remark. "But now I have to move you on to something you won't understand at first."

"Bloody hell."

Hiding his amusement he said quite solemnly "The same is true, as I told you with other levels, so say I was to shed my current covering, and it lay around discarded, there are spirits who would take on that form and my image."

Again he paused giving her the chance to ask questions which were buzzing round her.

"Is that what can happen at séances and the like? I mean the people who come through aren't always the ones the relatives think they are?"

In agreement Jorg added "That is why it is so dangerous to play with what you don't fully understand."

"Oh Christ!"

"I'm sure he'd agree." The tone lightened for a minute but when Jorg continued he was deadly serious. "The entity you saw which you thought was your uncle wasn't the physical form, it was an evil spirit, we think of a very high level, using a departed spirit form to appear as human." He knew this would have a tremendous impact on the youngster so he let it sink into her memory.

"Wait a minute, hang on there. Have I got this right? You're saying he is dead!"

"You do have it right. We have found that he too was murdered, not long after you, so it was classed as a revenge for your death. But the killer has not been traced by the living."

For once Jo was completely silent as the truth hit her. For all this time she had been searching for this horrible man whom she had trusted all her life and who then had forced her to have sex with him, to do the vilest of actions to him and when she threatened to tell her parents, he killed her. And most of the time he had been dead.

"Well that solves one problem." She sounded satisfied now.

"You are thinking you now have the chance to get even, whereas you couldn't before?" Jorg was ahead of her and she knew it. "Forget it."

"But he deserves to be punished, the filthy….."

"He is not on your level and won't be."

"Well where the hell is he then?"

Jorg gave her the impression of a quizzical look and when she seemed stumped for an answer simply offered "Exactly."

"You mean…..?"

"Well what you imagine hell to be. He has to make atonement, but you will have no part of it."

Jorg escorted Jo back to her familiar area and left her in the care of Sadie who had progressed considerably and was the best person to whom she could pour out her feelings, questions, and still in a way, her frustration.

Milton crawled into the back seat of the car with his three spirit friends surrounding him. Daryl got into the driving seat and before he started the engine called over his shoulder "I still think you should go home first boss."
The reply was curt "I've said the office, I mean the office. You can go in and pick up the papers I want, check why the phones were off, and then you can take me home."
Daryl was getting rather unnerved by Milton's tone as it was so unlike him, in fact he couldn't remember when he had ever heard him sound off like this.
  "Well, you're the boss."
  "Glad you appreciate that."
After a few minutes driving Daryl ventured to speak his mind.
  "Personally, I don't think you are fit to do the rest of this tour, short as it is."
  "I don't recall asking for your opinion."
It wasn't only his aide that was staggered by the outburst, especially as it seemed to be giving Milton strength every time he uttered a cutting remark. The three exchanged thoughts to voice their concern and agreed to keep a close watch on him, even if it meant shifts in case one was called away. Daryl pretended he hadn't heard the reply.
  "You will get home, go straight to bed I expect and then be up in the morning to get ready for the other five days, and you have to stay away, you won't be able to get back if you feel rough and what if you're taken ill on stage?"
Milton let the tirade finish then said very slowly and precisely "Have you quite finished?"
Daryl shrugged knowing he was on a loser so felt it was better to sit back and get this journey over with as little aggression as possible, a feeling shared by his unseen companions.

They pulled up to the block containing the offices and Daryl stopped the car, turned off the engine and waited.
  "I'll show him I'm not going to be treated like a piece of shit!" he thought and waited for some reaction from the back seat. He didn't have to wait long.
  "There is a file on my desk, it's important, I need it."
Daryl sat perfectly still almost feeling the hatred hitting the back of his neck.
  "Did you hear me? Now move your ass up those stairs and get back here."
Still Daryl remained motionless then taking a deep breath said very cuttingly "Aren't we forgetting something boss?"
  "The key is here if that's what you are getting at, now stop pissing about, and go."

If Daryl had ever been afraid of being forthright before, the change in Milton's manner seemed to give him the confidence to speak up for himself plus the fact that Milton didn't seem too concerned as to why there had been no contact with the office for such a long time.

"I was waiting for the 'please', you normally have impeccable manners SIR!" Tommy was punching the air with a 'Yes' enjoying the exchange but Jean Paul indicated there was something more here than a banter, some underlying force was at work and addressed both spirits.

"Could one of you go with the lad? Don't like this." Liam offered "I'll go and try and get him back here as soon as I can."

Daryl very slowly got out of the car and shut his door then equally slowly opened the rear door and held his hand in for the key.

"Don't go poking around in anything that doesn't concern you. Get the file, relock the door and get your sad little rear back here. NOW!"

"Yes sir. Thank you sir. Whatever you say sir." The door was slammed with such force the whole car rattled.

Jean Paul watched him go, then thought "I said he was a spiky little thing, just needed bringing out." But his real concern was the change in his companion and he feared it may be irreversible depending upon what had attacked him.

"That's funny," Daryl mused as he climbed the flight of stairs, "Cyberfart's working late. Bet he'll be surprised to see me."

He guessed the general office door may be unlocked if his workmate was still there so tried the handle before feeling for his own key and wasn't surprised when it opened, but what hit him was the sight of Simon sitting in the chair facing him as if frozen.

"What is it?" he shook the man by the shoulders but got no response. He peered into his eyes but was met with a glazed look and he knew Simon didn't know he was there. Quickly he felt his wrist and was reassured when he found a pulse, but panic started to seize him as to what he should do next. In normal circumstances he would have rushed back to fetch Milton, but there again in normal circumstance Milton would have come in himself. Spirit Liam had registered the scene and immediately transferred to the car where he told the other two.

"I daren't leave him," Jean Paul indicated to Milton "could you both go?"

"Was going anyway, come on Liam." Tommy had already departed and the two were in the room instantly.

Daryl was trying to tell himself to take charge, the way he always did, and cope with this in a practical way so he grabbed the phone and called for an ambulance. His mind was racing as he took stock of the room. The computers were off, everything appeared in order, so what was Cyber doing sitting on a chair in front of an unlocked door. He could only think that he must have finished his work, felt unwell and was going to the kitchen for a drink, but it was all guesswork, he had no idea of what had caused this. It answered the question of why no one would have answered the phone, but it certainly didn't explain why both lots of phones were unobtainable. It was obvious something had happened, but what?

The ambulance arrived within minutes and Simon had to be taken down the stairs on a chair as he had no movement whatsoever. Daryl gave the crew Simon's details and said he would inform his family and check with the hospital later.

"You not coming with him?" one asked.

"No, I have to get the boss home, just finished a booking and he is very tired."

"Entertainer is he then?"

"Yes." Daryl didn't want to get into any deep questioning and as it was obvious Simon needed medical help he was rather glad when the ambulance pulled away. Left alone he had a closer look around the place but everything seemed perfectly normal. Tommy and Liam were scanning everywhere at such a speed the human eye wouldn't have registered their movements.

"We need Jean Paul. He knows this place better than we do." Liam pointed out and went back to the car leaving Tommy to guard Daryl. Jean Paul looked at Milton and asked

"Can you manage him?"

"Sure, don't be long though."

As Jean Paul arrived at the office he motioned for Tommy to join Liam as the greater protection was needed there and he set about on his own search. Daryl was going into the inner office to get the file little realising he was getting support from the one he was jealous of. The office seemed fine, and as it was classed as something sacred to the workforce neither of the lads would hang around in there and certainly weren't allowed in when boss was away, so it was rather unusual for him to be here alone. Jean Paul didn't want to be far from him but still wanted to have an extra check around this room. As he could move at ultra speed he finished his survey in the time it took Daryl to enter, leave and lock the door.

But something had caught his attention. There was something about Milton's computer that was different so he entered the casing searching for what it might be. He soon found something which rang alarm bells, and sent a thought wave to Liam for him to join him. Indicating the spot on one of the boards, he waited for the other spirits' reaction.

"It's the same." For reasons he couldn't explain, spirit Liam knew there was a remarkable likeness between what was in the computer and what was in

Milton's discarded water bottle, the one which the detective had removed for examination. Concern now moved them even quicker as they went to the office computers, Jean Paul diving into Simon's, then immediately he checked all the other electrical devices and lastly the telephone where it was connected to the mains.

Daryl had locked the office suite and was on his way back to the car when they joined him. The message had already been sent to the upper levels as to the findings with the conclusion that somehow yet to be determined the evil mass was using forms of electricity and possibly radio waves etc to communicate for its attack. So it wouldn't have been seen at all as Milton was using a radio mike during the performance. But they still couldn't explain why the same feature had appeared in the water. While the higher levels mulled over this latest theory, the three guardians now wanted Milton in his own surroundings where he could be closely monitored.

Simon's experience had left him in an apparent state of shock which had parallelised his entire being. He sat now in the examination room staring straight ahead oblivious to all around him, not hearing the questions being gently fed to him, and not responding to any touch. Also he seemed to have lost control of his bodily functions. Daryl's usual description would have been "The light's on but there is no one at home" which was actually the truth, for although the vital physical signs were there, his spirit had been snatched from its host and all that the doctors were examining was a vacated shell.

Det.Insp Holland was still hanging around the Stratford Hall long after the audience had gone. He sat with Murray on a couple of seats near the exit door watching Laurie still scurrying about doing something, it didn't seem to matter what as long as he was on the move.

"You still look puzzled." Murray was watching him closely. "I mean more than Milton Warner being taken ill. I guess that happens though, in that line of work."

"Hmm? Oh suppose it does, but that's not why we're here, not for all that physic stuff."

"Ha, I think you mean psychic." The mood should have lightened but Holland seemed to be like a dog with a bone, something was still niggling at him and he couldn't place it. Laurie was hovering around as if their being there was cluttering up the place.

"If that fart doesn't piss off he'll find my boot up his arse." Holland muttered but it was loud enough for all to hear.

"Well some of us have homes to go to, and we are very grateful to you chaps for your attendance this evening, but if you've seen all you want, would you mind awfully if we lock up the place." Laurie's face was getting redder by the minute and he looked as if steam might come out of his ears if he was not calmed down.

Murray stood up and looked down on him with a sickly smile. "Mr Small, I'm sure we are all very grateful to you for your co-operation, " the smile turned into a sour sneer "but may I remind you, we were here not only for your protection but to do our job, most of which is nothing whatsoever to do with you."

Before the man had time to respond Holland was also on his feet "We have seen all we need for now, but I will be back here in the morning at 10 o'clock. Please make yourself and your staff available."

"But it's Sunday! You won't get them all here tomorrow, and certainly not at that hour, Most of them will be in bed."

"Fine." Holland clapped his hands together. "In that case, you all know where the police station is, you can all go there." As he went to walk away he turned and added "At 10am. Sharp!"

"But....but..." Laurie's efforts to argue went on deaf ears as the two detectives reluctantly left the building.

"You got the names?"

Murray nodded. "All except that Johnny bloke."

Holland got into the driving seat of his car, Murray in the passenger side to be given a lift back to Levvington police station where he had left his own car.

"But you know his name?"

Murray got out his notebook. "That's the strange thing. Small says his name is John Sellers then changed it to Cellars, but he doesn't have any more info in his personal records."

"Well how can that be? Everyone has a file of some sort or he wouldn't have been employed."

"Must have slipped through the net."

"Load of bollocks!" The inspector was getting very short tempered, mainly with frustration of the whole business.

"Have you thought, " Murray ventured "that 'nose' of yours could just have picked up the fact that the medium was going to be overcome, ill, call it what you want?"

"Now don't play those games, you know damned well there's more to this business than that." There was a pause so he continued "You wouldn't have sent that water for examination if you didn't think it was important. Always found stuff the others had missed, that's why I was sorry you got moved. What made you look in his waste bin anyway?"

Murray smiled to himself. "Isn't that the first place we always look?" He was loath to admit he didn't know what had drawn him to it so quickly and spirit Liam had hardly made his presence felt. "Well, "he added "we'll have to see what the results show."

As they pulled into the station yard, Holland said "Might be a good idea to find out tomorrow if those who felt ill have recovered."

"I did think of that, but wouldn't it seem a bit odd if the 'bill' go knocking on doors for something that seems to them, well, a bit trivial?"

"Hm, it's got us by the cobblers hasn't it?" As they got out of the car he looked across the roof and asked "Any chance of....?"

"My coming over tomorrow? OK by me but what about....?"

"Oh I'll clear it with Charles, don't you worry about that."

"Ok then. By the way, you fully recovered now, you know after your funny turn?"

"I don't have funny turns lad, just a bit of blood pressure. Had it before. Good Night then."

CHAPTER 10

Daryl was in two minds whether to get into the office early and do his usual double check on the arrangements for the short tour. Simon's absence wouldn't have much effect today as all the groundwork had been done, the promotion material was packed as always and it was more a case of personal requirements and clearing any outstanding queries. He stood musing for a moment then decided he would be better keeping himself busy than just hanging around. The telephone made him jump and he grabbed the receiver hoping for some news about Simon.

"Oh Hello bruv, sorry its short notice, but would you mind having Flop for a couple of hours, I've got to take Jack to the hospital and I don't know how long I'll be."

"Oh No! What's he done?"

"Probably nothing serious but he's had a fall and complaining about his shoulder so I want to be on the safe side."

"We're leaving just after lunch, the tour you know."

"I hope we won't be that long and I wouldn't bother normally, only the dog seems unsettled so I don't want to leave him and he's alright with you, and Milton likes him."

Daryl smiled to himself, he certainly wouldn't be on his own with the mutt at his feet.

"No problem, do you want me to get him?"

"That would help, sure you don't mind?"

"No, be there in five."

He got his coat and bag and thought what a chain of events this was turning out to be. First Milton, then Cyber now Jack and to top it all, the dog's got a problem. He couldn't help but remember all the strange warnings they seem to have had and even his sceptic mind had to admit there was much more going on here than he felt comfortable with.

He soon arrived back at the office and put Flop's bed near his desk but the dog went straight to Milton's office door and sat looking up at the handle as if it was about to open. At first Daryl wondered if by chance the boss had come in before him in which case he was either feeling a great deal better or he was just refusing to give in. No amount of coaxing could drag Flop away and in the end Daryl had to resign himself to letting the dog stay where he was.

He gave a gentle tap on the door and called "You in there?" Silence. Slowly he tried the handle but the door was firmly locked. If Milton was there he certainly didn't want to be disturbed, but what if he was ill? Still unsure he thought he'd give it a minute then try again. Flop had now lay across the door as if guarding the room showing he had no intention of moving.

In spite of the daily squabbling between the two men, Daryl was concerned about Simon and decided to ring the hospital to see if he could get any news although they had said they would only give information to family. A sharp knock on the door made him jump and Flop sprang to his feet then sat upright, still on guard at the inner office door. Being Sunday, Daryl's mind was racing as to who could be calling and he felt a chill of apprehension as he opened the door, coming face to face with a uniformed police officer.

"Are you Mr Daryl Finn?" The lady asked in quite a pleasant way.

"Yes, that's me."

The officer introduced herself and said she was following up the case of Mr Simon Freestone who had been admitted to hospital the night before and asked if she may come in.

"Oh, Yes, of course, please do." he stood aside and offered her his chair.

"No that's fine thanks." She waved the chair aside and seeing Flop said "Friend of yours?"

"My sister's dog, I'm just minding him for a while."

Daryl was beginning to feel as though she had brought some bad news and felt pushed to ask "Is it about Simon?"

Ignoring the question she went on to ask when Daryl had last seen him or spoken to him so he explained about the kind of show Milton was doing and that they hadn't communicated since the interval.

"Is that usual? To be in constant touch."

"Well yes and no, you see if anything new comes up he lets us know, or if there are any special messages I pass them on to Milton, that's Mr Warner when he comes off stage."

"I see."

Having perched herself on the edge of his desk, she went on to ask in detail about his return to the office. It may not have taken long but it seemed like an age and he eventually began to feel like a suspect, although he had done nothing wrong. He watched her writing everything in her book then was forced to ask "Are you sure you can't tell me how he is?"

"I'm sorry, I don't know, perhaps you could ask one of his relatives if the hospital won't tell you, they don't normally. Right, you will be available if we need to ask you any further."

"But we're going on tour, today, well this afternoon for five days, it's only a short one just the midlands, not like our normal ones." He knew he was rambling now from nerves. She couldn't tell him to cancel, not now.

"Who's we?"

"Just Mr Warner and me. And of course the back up crew, you know for the stage and all the promotion stuff."

"You have a list of the venues?" Her tone wasn't what he would call friendly and he was worried what all this was about. Did they think he had done something to Cyberfart? That was impossible.

"Yes, yes of course. Most of the flyers are packed, hang on I have some in this file," and going over to the cabinet, he opened a drawer and tried to take some out. As he went to lift them they appeared stuck and he had to give them a sharp pull. He went to hand one to the officer and was surprised to see marks on the lower edges of the papers so ran his finger over them but they were dry and he passed it off as being a printing ink stain, although he hadn't noticed it before.

"I will need numbers where you can be reached." She looked up waiting, pen poised.

"You had better have my mobile, that's the main communication. Milton's, I mean Mr Warner's is always switched off when he is performing."

It only just occurred to Daryl that this police officer had shown no recognition or interest in Milton who was a nationally known celebrity whereas most would be licking at his heels.

"Right, that will do for........." her sentence was cut short by the immaculate appearance of Milton framed in the doorway."

"Boss, I didn't hear you come up. Oh you look so much better."

"Better?" the officer took a sudden interest. "Have you been ill?"
Even Daryl didn't recognise the man who now almost floated towards her. "Ah the perils of the job dear lady. My gift has the disadvantage of draining all my natural resources."

"And you must be Milton Warner, the renowned, um... psychic?"

"Oo, you underestimate me my dear, never a wise move. Right! Now as you appear to have finished your business, my man here will see you out."

"I didn't say I had finished Mr Warner. I need to hear from you about last night."

"No point. I was in one of my recovery states." He began to remove his scarf in a somewhat flamboyant manner and Daryl was now feeling most uneasy. This was not the Milton he had loved and served all this time. What he was watching was an egotistical show off.

The police woman showed no signs of leaving until she had her information so Milton very quickly explained how, after a very intense show he always had what he called his dropping period, where he recharged his batteries.

"Ask anyone who does what I do. They'll all tell you the same."
Daryl was still querying in his mind the 'always' bit. Milton didn't always collapse, yes he often felt a bit drained but never to the level of last night.

Eventually, although she looked anything but satisfied, the officer left saying they would no doubt be hearing from her and gave Daryl a reminder to keep his mobile on at all times. For devilment he was tempted to say it had to be off during performances, but thought better of it.

As soon as she had gone Milton headed for his office but stopped dead. Flop was standing facing him his hackles raised, baring his teeth and with a low growl deep in his throat.

"What the hell is that mangy creature doing here?" He almost screamed.

"It's Flop boss, you know him; you always liked him."
Milton stood perfectly still, staring the dog straight in the eyes. Flop still growling edged his way round to Daryl's desk keeping his eyes fixed on the man who now moved at his pace until he had reached his office door. Slowly feeling for his key he held the stare until he had unlocked the door and felt his hand on the handle.

"Get it out of here now. That is an order."

Daryl waited for him to back into the room and close the door before turning to the dog who was now cowering on his bed.

"What's the matter little feller?" He wasn't afraid to touch him for this wasn't the one who had set Milton seconds before. The little face looked up with soft brown eyes filled with love but also fear. Daryl cuddled the dog to him and soon Flop was licking his face and appeared to have returned to normal.

"What was all that about, although I think I've got a good idea mate?" Daryl was certain the dog had picked up the change in Milton, a change that the canine senses had detected as evil. So what was in the inner office? A terrifying thought hit him. It was something that he would be alone with for the next five days, and nights. A cold chill ran down his back and he wished for all the world that he could have Milton back as he was, for there was no way he could be attracted to this man, and his pent up love now turned to hatred.

Jean Paul hadn't left Milton's side for an instant and had been in constant touch with Nan who was relaying every observation to her higher powers. Because those on higher upper levels can only come down to certain lower ones, they have to rely on those such as Nan and those with her degree of power to act as a go between with any beneath her. In a way it is like those in the basement and ground floor of a building could communicate with the first floor, who would then talk to the fifth floor but those on the fifth couldn't come down beyond the first and would have to go through the occupants of the first floor to send their orders.

In this instance Za felt it wasn't enough, because of the severity of the matter to get the facts second hand and he knew desperate measures were called for so that the situation could be estimated nearer its source, that is those who had been affected to date. Za in turn had to report to his higher sources and at present there was nothing with any substance to tell.

Unbeknown to many, in certain realms there exist the equivalent of special task forces, those with such power they can flit to any level, take on any form if required, but usually are totally unseen, unfelt and undetectable. It is only in very exceptional circumstances they are called upon but in this instance Za had been ordered by his higher authority to use them. This information could not be relayed and even if it appeared that those in high positions were doing nothing, that's how it had to seem for the sake of the mission. This power force was now employed.

So as Jean Paul watched his friend sitting in his office chair, every inch of Milton's mind, body, spirit and surrounding space was been minutely scanned. To cover the whole area took no more than the blink of an eye and the force had what they wanted, and instantly they were examining the entire centre containing the Stratford Hall. Before Milton could take a breath they were returning upwards to their unknown base.

"What are you looking so gloomy about?" Milton addressed the thought to Jean Paul but did not look at him although he was more than aware of his presence and was getting a bit fed up with having no privacy whatsoever, the man was stuck to him like a tail.

"You have to ask that?"

"Oh there you go, worrying about nothing again." He was acting as if his companion wasn't there. Gone was the close harmony, the camaraderie they had shared for so long, that they even knew what the other was going to say or do.

"How do you feel?" Jean Paul tried another approach but was scrutinising his every move for even the way Milton was moving seemed strange.

"I feel as if I was being interviewed. No not that, as if I was being examined." For the first time Jean Paul left him and passed to the office. Daryl was busying about as usual but the young man appeared shocked and somewhat upset. Feeling pity for him he floated over and put a comforting arm around his shoulders. He wasn't sure who was the most surprised for Daryl froze, put his hand up to his neck and moved as if responding to a massage as if he could feel the pressure. Jean Paul quickly pulled away and simultaneously the man stopped as if he knew the feeling had gone and was looking around as if trying to find the warm feeling and bring it back.

"Where are you? I know you're there, I felt you. Please come back." Then after a moment "Are you who I think?" There was no response for Jean Paul had returned to the inner office where Milton was gathering things together and putting them in his briefcase.

"Enjoy that did you?" His words were cutting and filled with sarcasm.
Ignoring the remark Jean Paul threw at him "Well one thing's for certain, you've not lost your powers, so you can still go out and entertain the masses."

"Load of morons."

"But you always loved your followers."

"Who says I don't? I love them very much, they bring in a meagre living for me?"

"Is that what's it's become to you? You are despicable."

"Woah, hark at the little Sunday school preacher."

Jean Paul, by arrangement was now going to leave Milton and Liam and Tommy would be taking over. Noticing the severe change in the man's whole behaviour Nan wanted to see how he would act without his right hand spirit in constant attendance and thought that two would be better than one to monitor him. She would keep Jean Paul close to her for his opinion, after all he knew him better than anyone.

The Stratford Hall bore no resemblance to the hive of activity from the night before. Not a single staff member was present in the centre although the side hall had been booked for that evening. There was a strange eeriness throughout the place and the main hall was beginning to take on a mustiness although it was hard to estimate just what the smell was. The floor was covered with a sticky substance and the walls looked as though the building hadn't been occupied for years. But worst of all was the stage. Where the tendril had prodded earlier, the floor, curtains, equipment, in fact everything was covered in seething cells, dropped from the main body of the mass, almost as if, on its earlier visit it wasn't rehearsing, it had actually set the positions for the cells to 'beam down' at a later date.

Two of Nan's group were sending images back to her area of the devastation but one part demanded special attention. For just in front of the stage was a pile of indescribable mess, as though it had been picked over by vultures. This was all that was left of Laurie Small.

With all the emerging facts, a picture was beginning to form on the higher levels and it was clear that all their previous surmising, although correct in some way was only part of what seemed to be beyond their previous experience or understanding. Za had descended to Nan's level and was in conference with entities there and for them to relay as much information as was deemed necessary, to the lower ones.

"All the theories we have had, although confusing were on the right track, but even we couldn't have guessed the enormity of this." His solemnity spread over the assembly as he gave a moment for that part to sink in before continuing.

"From the information passed we now know that the evil mass has used every means of communication possible to makes its contacts." There was a slight stirring in the area.

"They are using electricity, fluids, buildings even the air, any substance known on earth." Again a hum of disbelief so Za went into more detail.

"We were all waiting for a massive attack that we would be aware of. It didn't come, it didn't have to. Let's take the Stratford Hall, the first of the major ones in England for example which bears the mark of others around the globe. It hovered above the place for a while but it wasn't idle. The fester was growing within it as it waited for instructions."

Worried vibrations were being exchanged by all and there wasn't a spirit present that didn't wonder just how bad this was.

"What we now know is that one of their higher kind had been placed in each of the targets, nestling their way into the background acting as a control and setting the positions for each kind of attack. Oh yes there were several, it wasn't just one sort, that's what wasn't obvious until now."

"And the Stratford Hall's was Johnny." Nan offered.

"Exactly! This wasn't a sudden thing it must have taken ages to plot. He was placing invisible homing thoughts around the place, so when the water invaders were given the order they knew exactly where to strike, also the electricity demons would hook up to their signal, but that is only part."

Nan had been waiting for this as she needed answers regarding Milton and why he wasn't finished off physically when it would have been a minor job for this kind of evil. But her answers didn't come yet.

"The evil then penetrated strategic points of the building starting with the physical like the chairs, the curtains, cups, even toilet rolls. Then, it went on to contaminate the air."

Someone had a question. "I don't understand, only some people felt ill, wouldn't the effects become obvious on a wider scale? Why be selective?"

Za was eager to explain. "Oh it wasn't selective. Not a single soul in the place would have escaped. One of the effects or all of them would have got to them in some way."

"But it hasn't killed them, so what has it achieved?"

"I understand your doubt, I'm coming onto that. This is the danger. All who were at that venue are now time bombs waiting to be detonated at will."

"What?" The reaction was unanimous.

"They have set this very intense evil loose through every possible source and will trigger it throughout the community. Just imagine, if there were four hundred people gathered and they go out and come in contact with ten people each; that is one way. Every person who turns on a tap or goes to the toilet will be in contact. When one turns on a light, or ignites the gas or breaths the air, they are all infected."

"So nobody is safe." Nan wasn't asking a question, she knew what was coming next.

Za turned in her direction. "I reiterate, every single person, even the detectives, one of whom has already spread the poison back at Mayfield as did the Barbara lady to the kind soul who took her home. Not much of a thank you was it?"

After a moment he said "And now to get to the higher realms, for that is what you are waiting for isn't it?"

She nodded, hardly able to concentrate for the overwhelming sense of what she was about to hear was taking over.

"We thought they would be moving up the levels, but we were wrong. This evil is attacking any level up to the one where I exist, and thankfully it hasn't gone higher.....yet. But depending on its capability it may have no boundaries."

"So this evil could be as powerful as any of our highest realms?" This came from another of those present.

"Why not?" Za paused "There is balance in all things and in all commodities. We all know where there is good there is evil. Who are we to say we are stronger, but the truth is we have to be."

He turned again to Nan. "You are concerned about your workers. You saw Milton Warner physically affected, but they got to his spirit and are now in charge of it."

"Why didn't they take his body?"

"No need. In his case it matters not whether he has a physical form, they have what they want, so why bother with trivia. And I'm sorry to impart that they may want him in body to go out and spread the evil himself. He does have a great following and that is another immediate source of communication isn't it?"

"And the others?" She was afraid of the reply.

Za didn't communicate for a moment then very slowly said "They have been in close proximity, and if the evil has possession of Milton's soul......" he let her senses complete the rest of the comment.

As Za left the area, Nan was obviously very upset and although had a great strength in her work, felt this was hitting her personally as she had always had an affinity with the lads and she vowed to fight this thing even to the destruction of her own soul to protect her charges.

"He didn't explain about Mr Small." One of the assembled passed the thought around.

Nan simply replied "I don't think he had to do you?" and left the horror of the poor man's final moments to their imagination.

With the Stratford Hall operation complete, the tendril had retracted to the main mass awaiting its next target whilst the remaining five of that particular cell were raring to go on their allotted venues, and although it still hung like a dark cloud over the area, the majority of earth beings were still unaware of it. Only the true mediums would have knowledge of its existence, if it had allowed them to, for it was able to cloak itself at will from lower levels, so not all would have any idea of its presence. It sat pulsating waiting for its next strike receiving the bearings from its placement.

Having planted its seeds in Levvington it had no need to concentrate further on the immediate area for the evil in place would spread itself like wildfire almost like a plague of locusts clearing all in its path, and this meant the residents were not safe from it for it was already in their midst like an unstoppable virus. If one form didn't get them, another would, for by using all means of contamination nothing could escape. Before long it would have everything in its grasp, people, animals, plants and even the inanimate objects which meant even buildings would harbour the satanic destruction.

The power would be released rather like a medication capsule on time release, so although some would feel the effects immediately there would be those who would be carriers until such time they were triggered making the whole process very difficult to calculate. But the end product would be complete devastation from which there would be no escape.

Daryl was getting rather anxious as the morning wore on. He knew it could take an age waiting to be seen at the hospital and it wasn't as if it was on the doorstep as his sister would have had to go to the nearest town large enough to warrant an A & E department. If only she hadn't split with her husband, he could be here now to help out. The telephone made him jump as it rang and he grabbed the handset almost dropping it.

"Hello."

"Hello bruv, just thought I'd let you know they've checked junior over and he seems ok but they want to monitor him for a while just to be sure."

Daryl gave a sigh of relief." Oh that's good. I'm so glad."

Before he could ask about Flop she said "Look, I know you've got to get off, so I've rung Dave next door and he says he'll come straight away and pick the dog up and keep him till we get back. He's just got home from night shift but he says it's no bother and he gets on with him."

An even bigger sigh of relief left Daryl as he said "Oh you're a star. Give my love to junior."

"I will. Think he's enjoying the attention. Dave should be there in a minute. Have a good trip."

As he put the phone down he couldn't help thinking "A fine tour this is going to be, with old misery guts in there." He felt a nuzzling at his leg and looked down into the most loving set of brown eyes imaginable. Slowly he bent down taking the dog in his arms and cried with sadness and frustration. Flop kissed the tears from his cheeks and fixed him with his familiar stare, but this was not a look of aggression it was a comforting look of pure love.

The sound of the lock turning in Milton's door made them both jump and as the boss man came out of his office, Flop positioned himself at Daryl's side.

"I thought I made it quite clear." The words were shot with such force they were almost spat at the pair. "That!"

Daryl was not in the mood for any attack on his innocent friend and replied very cuttingly for him "For your information Flop is being collected shortly and will be out of your way."

"Oh." Milton's tone changed completely. "Well that's what I asked for wasn't it? The creature doesn't like me, look at his face."
Flop was pressing himself against Daryl so hard that he had to steady himself on the desk to stop himself falling over, and he could feel the warning growl vibrating through his body. The expression on the dog's face had changed completely from a few moments ago and he was now on the defensive, protecting his friend from what was facing him, for the thing moving towards Simon's desk was not the Milton he had tried to warn previously, but an image so horrible he sensed that it could only spell danger for the younger man.

The elite task force was now occupied all over the globe and the reports being fed back to the high levels meant that if the good forces didn't act immediately in some way, it was possible there would soon be no earth and possibly no solar system in this area. But apart from the physical evidence there was an even more frightening prospect emerging.

Those on the spiritual levels but still in body were being ripped apart from each other so in the case of Simon and thousands of others like him, his empty shell was left on the planet but his soul had been transported via a time lock to somewhere unknown, meaning there was no chance of them ever rejoining. The horrible outcome for these poor victims could only be an existence alien to their familiar space area where they would float aimlessly worlds away from what they had known. As their physical could not travel through the time locks there was no alternative but to leave them to rot or be destroyed later.

Reports were also coming in of spirits on the lower levels being fed through the locks. It was believed that even the evil force couldn't estimate their destination as the whole process was random, depending upon where each sphere touched another, so nothing could be programmed and was, at this moment, pure chance. So it was deemed by the high levels that the evil was employing war tactics but was not in total control. For what was the point in despatching souls if they didn't know where they had gone? The answer was frightening. It didn't matter. All the evil needed was for them to be dumped somewhere far away where they could be no threat. Basically it was clearing the entire area.

Murray's phone ringing roused him from a lie in, something he didn't usually do but he had felt more drained from the night before than he first thought. Raising himself onto one elbow, he yawned and fumbled for the handset.

"Hello."

"That you Liam? Who you got with you eh?" The cheeky laugh came from one of his colleagues who had become a social friend recently.

"I should be so lucky." Murray pulled himself up to a sitting position.

" Hey Li, I don't mind doing you favours, especially when you say it is of the utmost importance, that is what you said as I recall…"

"Yeah, OK what you got for me?" Murray suppressed another yawn wishing his friend would come to the point.

"You're pulling my plonk man!"

"You got the bottle I sent, right?"

"I did, and I examined it straight away like you asked, but come on, you loosing it or what?"

"I don't understand."

"Water man. You sent me the dregs of a bottle of mineral water. Now what was I supposed to do with that when I could have been getting laid with some sweet thing?"

Murray had now swung his legs out of the bed and sat scratching his head. "Ok there was water, but what was that coloured thing? The strange stuff in the bottom."

"Look Li, think its time you took a holiday. There was nothing, do you get me, nothing but plain simple water."

"Then it must have been tampered with. Perhaps someone dropped it and put more water in…then….."

His friend cut in "Hold it. Hold it right there. Listen to yourself. You're sounding like a crazy person. The plastic sleeve was sealed, as you sent it. The cap was still on, as you sent it. Now what do I have to do to convince you Li, there was nothing but water. Now, I had some prints lifted off it and if you want to compare them with that celeb of yours you can, but don't forget there will have been others who touched it before he even bought it no doubt about that."

"Ok, Ok, look thanks for putting yourself out, I know it seems crazy but last night, there was something strange in that bottle which had gone by the time it got to you. That's all I can say."

"No probs, hope you sort it out, whatever it is."

They said their farewells and Murray sat for a moment pondering all the events and knowing something was going on that for now was beyond his understanding. If he had only known he was soon to receive a call regarding the Stratford Hall, he would have been even more concerned.

But unbeknown to him, there was no way his friend could have detected anything other than water, for as soon as the sample was in his possession the tiny mass had entered his own being and was now controlling his soul.

Milton watched Daryl put the final bags into the car with a smirk on his face.

"Hmm nice arse," he murmured.

Daryl spun round. "What did you say?" A few days ago he would have welcomed such a comment but the Milton he knew would never have uttered such a thing which was probably what the attraction had been.

"Oh nothing, are you ready?" Milton stood for the passenger door to be opened for him.. They normally had a driver but the regular man was ill and it had been decided that Daryl would drive for this tour as none of the distances were too far and he could still run things as usual.

"I'm not your servant." The younger man swung open the door but then walked round to the driver's side without offering to close the other.

"No," Milton gave a sickly smile "but you were very glad of employment, and if you wish to continue I'd change your attitude."

Little did either of them realise how much their spirits had been affected, for although Milton's demeanour had changed drastically, the new Daryl was going to throw a spanner in the works, for part of Milton's success had been due to the efficiency of his back up team who were responsible for the smooth running essential to anyone in the public eye. Now the antagonism developing between them threatened not only the next few days but the future success of the business.

Ignoring Milton's last remark Daryl was silent for a while then said very pointedly "I will really miss Cyberfart, he's our right hand man." Then under his breath "Not that you'd admit it."

"Woah, you've changed your tune. Thought you couldn't stand the man."

"He does his job well."

"And now you're missing him, how sweet." The sarcasm could have been cut with a knife.

They travelled in silence for some time then Milton said very quietly "I hope you've got a strong stomach." As he got no reply he continued "These next few days will be very interesting. Very interesting indeed." If he expected any reaction he would have been disappointed but he didn't care about anyone's opinion, he was merely making a statement. When Daryl did eventually speak it wasn't by way of a reply.

"How's your friend today?"

"Who might that be?"

"Who else?" Daryl turned the car at the next junction and headed in the direction of Birmingham their first venue.

"Oh you mean Jean Paul I suppose. Who needs him?"

"I imagine you will have hurt his feelings saying that. He's here I suppose?"

"Then you suppose wrong."

Daryl was concentrating on his driving but this was quite unexpected.

"But he never leaves you, except, well just to flit about the office." He was remembering the pressure on his shoulder, a warm comforting safe feeling.

"Well he isn't here now and I don't need him," then added quite vehemently "and I don't need the other two guards they've put with me."

"Oh – so Jean Paul isn't here?" The disappointment in his voice was very obvious causing Milton to throw back his head and laugh.

"My word, what have you two little love birds been doing?"

If Daryl hadn't been behind the wheel he would probably have got his boss by the throat and he now had to use all his self control to let the moment pass without further digs from the man he was beginning to hate with all his being.

Milton rested his head back and closed his eyes. His normal psychic powers were being harnessed by the evil intruder and it was now allowing him to see the mass which had hovered above him and the effect of the planted cells. Instead of the utter horror he would normally have felt, he was being hooked on the visions floating before him, not only the one where he had been attacked but the growing world wide devastation. He could hear the screams of the living, but he was feeding off the distress of the souls in torment as they were despatched through whatever time lock was in place at that time.

But he should have known that everything comes at a price, and this extra awareness which was acting like a drug on his whole existence, forcing him to be part of this enormous new power would have to be accounted for. He and many gifted psychics of his class were now in place to act as mass dispatchers. They would gather their audiences with no problem for there were thousands of followers always ready to attend the performances eagerly hoping for messages from loved ones, but this would be different. They would all get a message, a mass brain washing but they would not be aware of it and leave still believing this man was wonderful, and they would go back to their normal ways of life spreading the harmful virus as they went.

The answer to a question being raised by the high levels as to why the mass didn't just flatten the earth and cause instant death to all, was now taking on another sinister meaning. The evil was being selective. It certainly seemed to be destroying the bulk of its prey, but it may be keeping certain ones for its own purpose, and that would be the worse scenario of all. It was now apparent that Milton could be one of these.

Nan had ordered a watchful eye to be kept on Jo who, for now seemed to have escaped the evil clutches, but the knowledge that she could have returned to her level bringing the spiritual virus with her had to be addressed. They tried to keep her on the lowest of levels but she appeared to be gaining in spiritual power and was already being lifted to a higher level. This in itself caused concern for they knew she hadn't had the time or experience to progress at such a rate, which left only one speculation. She was being groomed by the evil force, not theirs.

CHAPTER 11

The secrecy surrounding the elite task force had paid off. Such was the power of this sector that they were now jamming at least one of the time lock gates, making it impossible for the spirits to be despatched by that means. However, the high levels were concerned that this may have a serious knock on effect on the way the spheres moved. As the whole galactic process was in constant motion, one tiny blockage by a stationary sphere could clog up the movement of the others touching it thereby affecting the ones touching those and so on. Bearing in mind they were of differing sizes, the larger ones covering many light years so although the action seemed to be the remedy, it wasn't a permanent solution. The elite force was more than aware of this from the outset and had included it in their tactics, but could not divulge their plans to even the highest powers.

Up to now the evil mass had felt in total control being powered by the destruction caused and its apparent take over of its chosen souls, but this latest action had created a major upheaval at its source for it had not imagined there was anything in this operation that could match its conniving, so driven was it by its refusal to believe it could be overcome. All previous attacks in other areas had gone without a hitch. They had selected the area, gone in, devoured everything and spat out the poor souls either to the outer limits of the universe, or aimed them at the nearest black hole, usually the one in the centre of whichever galaxy they were inhabiting. So this was not going down very well, mainly because something had the cheek to damage their pride, and was succeeding.

They also realised that if a time lock was stuck in a 'holding' position, the spirits pushed through could possibly return by that route until such time as the mechanism was released. But for the moment this wasn't a two way passage, as the elite forces had   installed a temporary block to stop any further souls being despatched meaning nothing could pass either way.

Simon's spirit, along with many others had just passed through the time lock when the halting system was applied and part of him was attached to the other side of the entrance. He watched as the other souls either floated aimlessly round him or were sent away at such a speed it was as if they had never existed. When sucked from his body he had no idea what was happening for there was no contact with anything physical so he had no knowledge of his empty form being taken to the hospital, or examined. He was in a strange alien world surrounded by hatred and his normal calm efficient self was now becoming a terrified form which felt as though it was being destroyed like a piece of garbage with no use now it had fulfilled its purpose.

Slowly he tried to fathom his position. Unlike the other poor souls he seemed stuck to the edge of the sphere and somehow took a bit of comfort from this. Also he seemed to be able to reason and think for himself so his logical side started to take stock.   It soon became clear that he had no form but there seemed to be a duplicate image of himself which was misty and of no substance but was him all the same and this gave him something to use as a base on which to work. On looking around he noticed that some of the other floaters were the same, but some bore no resemblance to anything he had known in his life and their images didn't follow any pattern. These were the souls of beings from other space areas who were passing through this sphere at this particular time but he hadn't grasped that aspect yet.

The obvious answer was that he must be dreaming and with all his might tried to wake up but when that didn't work he settled back to try and work out his next move.

Tommy and Liam were not having an easy time with their assignment. The Milton they had known seemed to have vanished completely and although his earth form looked almost the same, his spirit was changing into something hateful. Gone was the camaraderie between them and he was continually ordering them to leave him alone.

He now lay on his bed in the hotel room, shutting out any good connections with any levels for he felt in total control on his own and would reject any sort of interference from his familiar companions, his only emotion being of utter contempt.

Daryl was at the Conference Centre overseeing the arrangements. Normally Milton would have been there as he insisted on doing 'the walk' before a show. This consisted of taking the route from the dressing room to the stage and back several times. Then he had to familiarise himself with the stage area to get the feel of the place. He would sit on any furniture, check exactly where a glass of water would be placed and anything in that particular venue that may be unusual. So particular was he that the vibes were right and he felt at home before he set foot on stage in front of his audience.

But this was different. The stage and lighting crew were asking Daryl where boss man was and he had to make excuses that Milton was still tired after the last show which a few believed, but those who had been around for some time had their doubts.

Nan took this opportunity to send Jean Paul to check out the place knowing he wouldn't encounter his friend but it didn't serve much purpose as the upper levels now knew that the mass's attacks would be elsewhere. However, she was curious to learn how the evil would use Milton, and she was determined to cover every detail to find out as much information as possible which could be fed back and used elsewhere.

It didn't take Jean Paul long to know that the Birmingham venue was not affected in the way Levvington had been but there was something going on here which had the feel of a controlling force waiting for it's puppet to perform. There was no sign of a mass observing the place but something unseen even to the spiritual levels was definitely there. He returned to Nan and suggested that he may be on too low a level to identify it and it may need a higher power. Instantly she suggested Jorg could take a quick scan and he was there immediately but something seemed to be pulling him down to a lower level similar to that of Jean Paul and Milton.

"We meet again." Jo appeared at his side but her being was trying to merge with his in the most seductive way.

"What are you doing here?"Jorg was trying to understand how she could be communicating on his level when she was of a much lower one and he hadn't gone down to hers.

"Why shouldn't I be?" She was enveloping to him, restricting his spiritual movement. His thoughts raced but mainly he couldn't understand how she recognised him for he wasn't in the appearance of their previous meeting. Nan, monitoring his vibrations was beginning to realise Jo was being given higher powers to suit the evil's needs which was very dangerous as spirits have to progress by learning and experience and cannot rise to higher things until they are ready. This young spirit was in no way groomed for what she was being used for, but now she was in the hands of the evil force so who was to say what could happen?

"I have to go." Jorge tried to free himself and when she clung on even more he knew it was time for action. A message, undetected by her was sent back to source and he was instantly returned to his home level leaving her bewildered at her failure and the evil power angry at this simple act of being out manoeuvred.

Nan, to grasp the exact tactics being used asked Sadie when Jo had left.
"But she hasn't." was the reply.
"Not at all?" Nan was fearing the worst.
"Been with me all the time, never left my space."
"Keep your guard up Sadie. Thank you."
Gathering her immediate ones around her Nan shared her feelings before informing Za.

"They're either using a duplicate image to monitor us but using their power which is why Jorg had trouble releasing himself or the duplicate has replaced the one with Sadie and Jo has already been raised to our level. If it's happened at that speed she will probably already be able to go above us."

"Is she aware of what is happening?" the question came from the group while another added "the fact that she is using physical sexual means to seduce him on that level seems a bit extreme."

"Sadly she may know but because of the evil driving her she will be enjoying it. Due to her lively nature she would be an easy target for them to occupy."

"What a waste." The thought was unanimous.

As Nan prepared to send the message to Za she imparted "Don't forget the basic methods of temptation are not confined to the earthly body however pointless it may appear."

The seething mass was hovering over the second of this particular cell's targets, a cinema complex on the outskirts of Peterborough. The following Thursday a new release was being shown attracting full houses at every sitting and as the patrons left they would be taking with them a newer deadly form of the current virus for the evil had invaded the actual reels, and unbeknown to the human eye their brains were receiving orders as they sat enjoying the movie. The upper levels would soon learn that this force did not repeat it self but grew in sadistic power so by the time the sixth venue had been attacked the results of the Stratford Hall would have almost paled into insignificance.

The arms were now activating at the forthcoming events. After the cinema it was aimed at a charity run on the Saturday, a theatre in one of the larger cities on the Sunday then it would sit back for the weekdays building up for its finale. The following Saturday had wide television coverage of an indoor sporting event, and the next day again television attention would be at Ely

Cathedral for a service of hymns and sacred songs. It was not by accident that a religious item had been selected to close this operation. But this was only one of hundreds of cells now making the earth a sick planet, and attempting to completely control the levels leading outwards and upwards. In its own view it couldn't possibly fail.

Milton could feel the new power taking over his being but far from being concerned he was thriving on it. He had a new image, a new control or so he thought, little realising that every move was being not only monitored by the evil source but stage managed. His forthcoming audiences were in for a big surprise for the well dressed yet tasteful man was about to appear as a metamorphosis of his former self and few would put it down to the fact that seeing him 'live' was different to his television character. They were about to experience something frightening but compelling almost like a vampire sucking their life blood from them but taking control of them at the same time, except of course it was a much greater force in the driving seat.

He was now awaiting the delivery of a completely new wardrobe, comprising of a different outfit for each day of the tour. Nobody was going to miss him. The power had seen to that for in every garment cells were planted to add to the mass brain washing at each venue. They had turned him into a walking, living breathing form of the next stage of the virus.

Daryl was not only peeved at being left with the final arrangements, he felt he was grieving for something or someone but didn't know what, and the feeling was bringing out severe frustration which was manifesting itself as aggression. The crew knew he had his hissy fits at most shows but this was different and they were all picking up on it although no one was going to be brave enough to confront him with it. He was hardly the sort you could sit down and ask what was wrong, and although he may have welcomed a comforting arm around his shoulder the men all knew it wasn't theirs, much to their relief.

"Well, is that mike working or not?" He fairly bellowed across the stage.

"Will be in two seconds."

"Two seconds isn't good enough. I asked if it is working, by that I mean is it working as I speak?"

"Absolutely ducky!" One of the newer crew members soon wished he hadn't been so flippant for Daryl was now inches away from his face almost spitting his reply.

"If you want to continue working for Mr Warner, I suggest you take a lesson from the more experienced members of this organisation and keep that SHUT!"

Two fingers thrust forward and stopped just short of the man's mouth but the attention was on Daryl's eyes which seemed to blaze with fire as he spoke. Nobody could have said how long he had him locked in his gaze, but the whole place took on an eerie silence until Daryl moved away still holding him as if rooted to the spot.

Slowly the setting up continued but there was a change in the air and most of the crew felt very uncomfortable, something they had never experienced before. The foreman warned them all to check and double check everything so there was no possibility of any hitch. Daryl was now in the dressing room on his mobile asking if Milton would care to grace the place with his presence.

"My dear man" was the sickly reply "if I don't know by now how to conduct my performances, it would be a sorry state of affairs wouldn't it?"

"I was going on your usual pride in what you do. That's what's made you who you are, and what you are."

"And paid your wages, let's not skip the trivia." The tone had lost its silky smoothness and bore a harshness which raised Daryl's simmering temper to almost exploding levels.

"For which you have received more than adequate loyalty, not that you'd have noticed."

"Ooh tut tut, did we get out of bed on the wrong side this morning?"
Daryl had had enough. "Well at least it wasn't yours!"

"Ah now we're getting to it. You'd have loved that wouldn't you? Do you really think I haven't been aware of your sordid remarks and the lecherous looks you've always shot my way?"

"I wouldn't waste myself on the likes of you."
Milton paused to let the other man calm for a moment then almost whispered "Then you must be getting very choosy." He switched off the phone and turned his attention to which outfit would wow tonight's crowd.

"Big venue, big style I think." He held a suit in front of him studying the effect in the mirror. This would have been the last thing he would have worn recently but he wasn't making the choice.

Simon had been located by some of the good forces on his side of the time lock and he welcomed the company although his guard was still up as distrust niggled at his subconscious.

"Stay calm." The thought brushed over him in a warm wave and seemed to come from all sides. He tried to home in on the source but the vibrations were closing like a blanket almost soothing him to an artificial sleep.

"Who are you?" His soul asked, not realising he was communicating without speech.

"We're here to help you. Please do not try to move from where you are. It is most important."

"I've got to be dreaming, this can't be real."

The reply was soft almost like a breeze. "You are in a strange world and we will try to get you back to your own, but we can't at the moment."

"I feel as though something is holding part of me." Simon was realising there was more keeping him in place than whoever was with him.

"That may be your answer to freedom."

"Explain." This was more like the physical Cyberfart who didn't waste words. The good forces knew he still had fight and would use it when necessary.

"This may be hard to understand but….."

"Try me."

"Alright. There are bad forces operating and to put it in simple terms they have stripped your soul from your body."

There was a moment's pause before he asked "Are you saying I've died?"

"Not yet."

"Yet? I could then?"

"Not if we can help it." They let the thought sink in knowing this was more than anyone could grasp at one time.

Simon was relaxing a little. "So, what has happened, or is happening to my body?"

"It's ticking over physically, but there is no sign of recognition."

"Oh shit! I'm a cabbage? Is that what you're saying?"

"Only until we can get you back, and we will do all in our power."

"Wait a minute. Hold everything."

The suspicion was creeping back and he tried to do a sweep of the area to get some sense out of all of this but couldn't pinpoint anyone in any particular position.

"Why would you do this for me? I don't know you."

A ripple of amusement ran around him. "Do we only help those we know? There is a lot to learn both on this side and in your earth form. Many people spend there lives helping others. We are no different. Yes there are those who delight in hurting others, tormenting and generally getting enjoyment from seeing others suffer. But we are not of that sort."

"I must be in heaven then."

The air settled to a comfortable calmness before any further communication then one who seemed to be stronger was at Simon's side.

"You're wrapped up in your computer world most of the time. You don't like to get close to your fellow man."

"Hey what is this?"

"Chill. I was the same."

"What? Who are you?"

"Oh just a guy like yourself. But how do you think I manage now with no keyboard in front of me. Tell you man, it was scary at first, felt like I'd lost my arms and legs, to say nothing of my brain."

"What's your name?"

"Woah. That shouldn't bother you. Told you. I know how you think. But guess I've had to adjust. Not easy though."

Simon didn't appreciate the fact someone could see though his façade but he trusted this man, or whatever he was now, and wanted to know more about his present state.

"Can you tell me what is holding me?"

"Yes."

"Well are you going to?" Simon was getting a little frustrated little realising he was getting some of his own treatment back. Daryl would have recognised the exchange immediately having been on the receiving end many times.

The spirit whispered "Are you ready for a mind shock?"

"OK."

"To put it bluntly, you've time travelled."

"Oh don't give me that!"

"Ah! Knew it would be too much for your minute brain cell to cope with." He was goading Simon into keeping his fight and not letting him feel any self pity.

"No, No I'm sorry, go on....please."

"Ok, Ok keep your wig on. Well you can't time travel in your bodily form, or at least you aren't supposed to, but you can in the spiritual sense. Now it gets a bit heavy but hang in there. They have these things called time locks, you've heard of them in your sci fi stuff, but here it's a bit different."

"I'm with you up to now." Simon didn't want to risk losing the explanation even if it was all a bit much at the moment.

"OK. Well its too much to go into it all, but getting down to the base line spirits pass through the locks and whiz on to some place else. But it's a bit random you see. Some clever sods can plan it but we lower forms have to go wherever we end up. Bit like jumping on a bus only you don't know where you'll finish."

"Some mystery tour eh?"

"You got it man."

"So I've gone through one of these time lock things?"

"Yep."

"Oh." For once Simon was at a loss for words but his brain was racing trying to piece it all together.

The man gave him a few moments for it to sink in then added "Seems there's a bit of a riot going on and this lock has been blocked so we can't go through yet. Guess they'll free it soon though."

"Why am I stuck to it?"

"Ha, yes, now that's a bit of a dick-prickament isn't it?"

Simon was beginning to feel a slight relief that he wasn't on his own but the knowledge wasn't giving him quite the comfort he would have liked.

"Tell you what. Let one of my buddies tell you about that." Then in an aside said "Knows a lot more than me, you know what I mean?"

Simon agreed still feeling very apprehensive as another apparently male form was by his side.

"What my friend is saying is that you passed though the opening just as it was closing and part of you is trapped in the lock."

"But I don't feel any pain, oh but then I wouldn't would I?"

"No you wouldn't and there is a good chance as soon as the lock is free you will be able to slide back to where you came from. That's the good bit about having part of your spirit anchored."

Simon waited for him to carry on but was forced to ask "And the bad side? I take it there must be one."

"The bad side, yes, are you sure you want to know?"

"Yes I want to know it all."

"The bad side is…..... that the part of you which is held could be damaged."

"Which means what?"

"If you do return to your body your spirit may not be completely in tact."

Simon was silent. "I'm not exactly sure what that means or if I want to just now. Is that OK with you?"

There was no reply but he felt reassurance that he was not alone. The message was relayed to Nan who added it to the list of other like souls who sadly stood no chance of returning.

The elite force knew they had limited time to keep the lock on but they had another skill at their disposal which although widely used by lesser levels was not honed in the way they had perfected it. They could alter time, having it running at various speeds concurrently. So although on one side of the lock it could be travelling at one pace and a different one on the other side they could reverse the velocities which although appearing to go against all known natural forces worked for a time until they returned everything to normal running. They could also control the time in the lock itself. Their main controlling power now had everything in place to the millisecond still without any knowledge being transmitted in any form to anything outside of their select realm.

Daryl had returned to the hotel to change for the evening's performance. He was just brushing the lapels of his jacket when Milton bounced into the room.

"Don't you ever knock?"

"Shouldn't leave your door open lovely man, open invitation you know." He stopped suddenly and sneered "Oh you're wearing that old thing are you?"

"It isn't that old, and who's going to be looking at me?"

Milton shrugged. "Well you do have a point I suppose but I do like my entourage to be nicely turned out."

Daryl was not in the mood for any more quips and turned on him "I'm driving you to the venue for Christ's sake, not Buckingham Palace! I wouldn't be doing that if I could have got some other poor bastard to do it but guess what, Mr High and Mighty, nobody wanted to."

Ignoring the outburst Milton strolled across to the window and said to himself although loud enough for Daryl to hear "I really must do something about the garbage I seem to be employing these days."

"That garbage as you call it has been faithful to you, even when you were an unknown quantity."

"Things change dear heart."

"That's obvious. Now if there's nothing you want, would you mind awfully if I finish here." The last sentence was said in such a mocking tone even Milton looked a little surprised and wandered out saying "In your own time, if it's not too much to ask."

It was Daryl's turn to be shocked when he saw the outfit Milton was wearing for his grand arrival and even more when he saw the one selected for the show.

"Tell me this is a joke. Oh my God. I'm not driving you anywhere like that, and who do you think wants to see you in that .. that... Mardi Gras stuff."

"Ha Ha. You can be an old woman at times. Get up to date, people don't want that dreary look any more, they want showmanship and that is exactly what they are going to see."

"If they haven't already left in shock."

"Oh the jealousy is back. I might have known. Can't take the pace now. Too much for you is it?"

"Sod off!" Daryl wasn't sure if it was anger or the pain of watching this man ruining his image but he felt the tears welling up and dashed from the room.

Milton watched with sadistic pleasure. If he could raise such emotion in one person, what could he do with thousands in the palm of his hand? The world was his, but he couldn't have been more wrong.

The Exhibition Centre was buzzing. Milton's show had long been a complete sell out due to his warm charm and personal approach as seen national wide on television. The crew were quite nervous as to how the evening would go but some thought that his experience would shine through and all would be well and put his demeanour down to the Stratford Hall trauma. These thoughts were crushed when the wardrobe lady carried his outfit through to the dressing room.

"Tell me someone's brought the wrong clothes." One of the hands couldn't believe his eyes.

"Why, what's up?" Another said in passing.

"Are you sure we're at the right place?"

"Why?

"He's just arrived; at least I think it's him"

Before long the whole crew was buzzing, not with excitement but consternation, all wondering just what was in store and hoping they could handle whatever was thrown at them for this didn't have the feel of anything they had done before.

Liam and Tommy had been trying to monitor Milton but Nan had recalled them as he was becoming too aware of their every move and was now far above them in power making them seem like juniors to him. Jorg had been making several visits but Jo seemed to be following him as if on higher orders and as Jean Paul couldn't be used at present another sentinel was being posted.

Just above Nan's level, Ariel was often used for such jobs as she had a unique ability only perfected by certain spirits. She could split herself into several beings simultaneously, all completely different but each acting as strongly as a single soul. By the time anyone had worked out her strategy she had gone and had never been confronted by her prey. She had no one identifying feature and had duped the cleverest of evil powers in the past, therefore she was never recognised when she made a later appearance. She was now preparing to attack her next target, Milton Warner.

A worry now circulating on all lower levels was the apparent lack of action by the powers above. It was almost making certain sectors want to take the law into their own hands but the more experienced knew that often plans had to be put into place to ensure the success of the whole operation. Tabar warned that any little unwanted action however well meant could jeopardise the end result. She had seen many instances where this had occurred and now knew better than to interfere, especially in a case of this magnitude, plus she pointed out they were still not aware of exactly what tactics were being used by the evil. Assumptions had been made but she felt sure the upper reaches knew much more than they were divulging. This calmed the air for the time but she pointed out to Nan and Jorg that she could still sense the unrest and hoped something would manifest from above soon.

The main arena of the Exhibition Centre was buzzing with anticipation. Although the event had long been sold out, there was the usual stack of tickets being sold over the internet for prices way above the original. The atmosphere in the house was electric with excitement but if the audience could have witnessed the scene in the dressing room they would have been in for a nasty shock. Daryl had finally had enough and threatened to walk out there and then thinking Milton would be totally at a loss without him.

"Please do." was Milton's curt reply.

"You would let me do that so easily?" The hurt in Daryl's eyes was turning to anger.

"Just watch."

"But you can't operate alone; you've always needed me there. No wait! Let me correct that. The Milton Warner that I have been faithful to needed me, but you…. you are somebody I don't know. And what's more, I don't want to know. Ever!"

Milton smirked as the door slammed behind Daryl. "Well that's one bit of useless rubbish out of the way at least." He turned to look at himself in the long mirror.

"My God you are a handsome fellow." He said aloud but the words fell on a totally empty room.

Ariel had flitted in and out of the dressing room but never staying long enough for the man to know he was being monitored. She had taken in every aspect of the area and was now positioning herself at strategic points but only on a temporary basis for speed was her weapon. She noticed Daryl in the wings gathering up his belongings and homed in on him.

"Where you going? We're about to start." One of the crew asked.

"He doesn't need me or you, so you may as well all go." Daryl grabbed his jacket and was about to make for the door when one of the men blocked his way.

"If there's something we should know, you'd better fill us in and quick."

Daryl hesitated for a moment. "You had better ask His Highness. We are all shit!" and with that he pushed the man aside and made his way away from the stage area and headed for the nearest exit.

"Now what are we supposed to do?" The question came from the group.

"Your job would be acceptable." Milton's voice rose above the murmurs and all stood mouths open as they tried to take in the sight before them. One tried to suppress a titter but Milton's steely look soon took care of it. This was not the clairvoyant they had worked with all these years. It was if someone had produced a complete stranger and told them to stage manage a performance they had never seen and had no idea as to cues, lighting or anything that went to make up such a show, but to make matters worse the audience were waiting and it was time for curtain up.

The choice of the crew was to walk out, but somehow they were compelled to follow orders and on Milton's hand gesture the house lights went down and the stage was in complete darkness. The hush that filled the place was creepy and slowly a dim blue light appeared in the centre of the stage. Gradually people could make out a figure in the centre and as the brightness increased they realised there was a man but not the one they had come to see. Whispers ran round the seats.

"That's not him."

"Probably a warm up to start the show."

"Oh a supporting act."

"Give people time to settle so he can make a big entrance."

"He's never had that before though."

"I suppose they make changes or it'd be boring."

"I like him the way he is."

The figure had his back to the audience and was dressed in a long royal blue cloak and brimmed hat. Slowly he turned to face them and as he spread his arms to open the cloak they could see he was wearing a silver suit which was catching the light in such a way he seemed to be glistening from head to foot.

If the audience was shocked it was nothing to what the stage crew were going through for the lights appeared to be working themselves and when Milton removed his hat and threw it across the stage it disappeared with a bang and cloud of mist. This brought a gasp and a little ripple of applause from some who still thought this was a magician doing a little repertoire in readiness for the main piece. But the ones nearest to the stage could see this was no warm up, but what was this man doing? He needed no dramatics, he was a celebrity in his own right and gifted in his field and an uneasiness started to manifest itself spreading back through the rows until the whole place was in total silence.

Milton slowly removed his cloak and laid it on a settee. He turned and gave a small nod in the direction of the stage manager. Suddenly the lighting was under their control again and orders were soon going round the communicating mikes for the show to proceed as normal. He was walking to the edge of the stage his hand palm upwards as normal but instead of directing it to one particular place he let it scan the whole audience until the tension built to such an intense level that everyone felt they were about to receive a personal message. The effect was electrifying for every single person was motionless as if frozen in one position. Still the silence continued. The backstage crew seemed to be the only ones capable of acting normally for the sound crew in the house waiting to home in with a mike on any individual Milton might chose, were also rooted to the spot as if in a trance.

He stood feeling the power flowing from his body down his arm and leaving him causing a wave across the arena but that was not all. He felt himself growing upwards and outwards free from his body until he floated above the people spreading himself like a blanket until each one had been affected. He retreated now until he had returned to the standing position at the front of the stage.

For a moment the silence continued then the place was filled with rapturous applause, people jumping to their feet to applaud. The crew looked on amazed.

"But nothing happened." One whispered down their mike.

"Carry on, they must have experienced something, Lord knows what."

"Harry, what happened out there?" They were calling to one of the house staff.

"What do you mean?"

"Leave it. Talk later."

Milton moved to the left side of the stage and gave some of his usual style messages out to the patrons but something was wrong. With his gift he knew when relatives were trying to pass information, but what he was getting wasn't like this. He was being fed unpleasant things, things people would not want to be divulged in public or private. Something was either relaying the sort of message mediums ignore or it was all total fabrication and he was passing on a load of utter lies. Whatever it was, the receivers were getting rather distressed but Milton appeared to be thriving on it.

His voice rose as he directed his arm to one lady on her own.

"You are nothing but a tramp. You are living a lie. You are dirt!" The whole place gasped and a few started to leave. Suddenly there was a pressure in his back pushing him to the edge of the stage. He swung round but there was nobody on the set with him. Turning back to the audience he directed his attention to the lady but she seemed different, in fact he thought she must have moved seats but someone was where she had been sitting. Strange. Then he thought he caught sight of her in the front row, but that was not her. He looked around and she appeared to be everywhere but nowhere. Knowing he had to compose himself he moved back to the centre of the stage and when he raised his right arm the crew knew they had to kill the lights. It was announced there would be a break of twenty minutes when the evening's performance would then be resumed.

Ariel returned to her level within seconds to relay that she had been able to interfere with the power flow coming from Milton causing a mild disruption. Although she could have communicated without leaving the arena she knew the other forces would already be attempting to identify her and she needed to distance herself for a time. As she was such an invaluable asset the high levels suggested she used the 'flitting' system where she could appear in one form and whilst removing that one replace it with one of her others and so on. As she was adept at covering her wake, it was hoped any monitor spirit wouldn't know whether to follow her or stay with the new placement. As Ariel could perform this trick up to about six times, she could keep them on their toes for quite a period. She had already confused Milton with her appearances in his line of vision and was certain she had thrown the controlling forces off balance. Her higher ranks questioned whether she could glean enough information with this method and suggested using another placement to observe as back up. It was decided to hold two of Ariel's level in readiness so that if she had to retreat quickly one or both could slip into audience members and use them as shields for that moment, but all of this had to be done with speed and accuracy to avoid detection. Nan was ordered not to be tempted to approach Milton or anyone in his vicinity for the present, and this in turn was relayed to Liam, Tommy and Jean Paul.

Liam Murray was going over some statements in the office at Mayfield when the phone rang. Glancing at his watch he realised time had crept on and it was later than he thought. He picked up the receiver and as soon as he answered the caller skipped the pleasantries and plunged straight into the conversation as though it was of the utmost urgency.

"Hey, who was that chap you were telling me about over your way?" The detective had worked with him before and they had remained on chatting terms since he had moved to another station.

"Oh Hi Dave, which one?"

"You know, the one you were telling me about, that one who collapsed or something."

"Oh you mean Milton Warner. Him, that was last night. Seems he's gone off on his tour OK. Why?"

"Well, you didn't say what a weirdo he is did you? Thought you'd have said. My God, what a strange one."

"Hey, slow down. Sure you've got the right man here? The one I was with was normal enough just had a bad turn on stage or something, although something was a bit off about it all."

"Liam, we are talking about the celebrity aren't we, the well known medium, call him what you will."

"Yes, and he was just what we expected, very clever or shall I say the genuine thing, not some mind bender."

Dave paused for a moment. "How was he dressed?"

"What?"

"How was he bloody dressed? Was he in some sort of outlandish stage tinselly thing?"

Liam ignored the question. "Dave I don't know what you're driving at but in his appearance he was normal. Smart but - wait a minute we're not talking about the same man are we?"

There was a silence then Dave said very precisely "If you were standing where I'm standing right now in the Birmingham Exhibition Centre, you would be asking exactly what I'm asking. Because if what everyone here is seeing is your man, he's undergone an amazing transformation overnight."

It was time for Liam Murray's virus capsule to release its venom. For a moment he paused then said very calmly "I think you've been at that bottle again David. Relax - this man is entitled to liven up his act, thought he was a bit boring so maybe he's seen the light. Now, I suggest you get back and enjoy the rest of the show while some of us have to work." He put the phone down, turned to his computer and began to spread his evil seed throughout the entire police network. After a short while he gathered up his belongings and left the station for good, now following his inner orders to spread the malice to a much greater field. Little did he know that he had served his main purpose and could be disposed of at any given time.

CHAPTER 12

It only took seconds for major disruption to spread throughout the entire emergency services and the news reporters thought they were having a field day all trying to be first with the latest reports. What they didn't realise was that every communication they made added to the chaos and soon all the broadcasting companies were experiencing massive overloads of the unseen power destroying their very existence. No amount of reasoning or investigation by maintenance experts could explain what was going on, but the spiritual onlookers felt the sensation of utter helplessness as they watched nationwide institutions crumbling.

In some areas there was complete silence almost as if a tornado had swept through leaving its trail of destruction behind whilst others seemed to have been hit by mass panic causing human stampedes as workers tried to leave shops, restaurants and any place where people would have gathered for the evening.

Many sentinel spirits had been sent to evaluate from ground level the best plan of action but all reported that the evil had penetrated too deep to be able to remove it. Plus in each case whatever had planted the horror had long since left, so there was nothing to fight, but help was desperately needed for many of the victims.

It soon became apparent that by it attacking the emergency services at this stage would cause massive deaths as help couldn't be summoned, and if casualties were transported to hospital by the general public, there would be no means of treating them. Already the equipment in the intensive care units had shut off and throughout the hospital essential life saving means were useless. The Accident and Emergency Department was suffering especially, the staff at their wits end wondering how to cope. More and more tried to get into the place which was crammed, paperwork was being trampled and injured folks either screaming in pain or crying in fright. One mother with her child in her arms in the children's unit tried to escape but was pushed backwards until she was pinned against the wall fighting to protect her little one from the heaving mass.

Nan appealed to those above her to do something, she didn't know what but her frustration refused to allow this carnage to continue while no orders appeared to be given to halt it. She was told that steps had been taken and when she asked what, was told it was necessary to the situation not to divulge the details.

"Then perhaps you could tell them to get a move on, or all the souls will be here before their physical time is properly over."

Za imparted that he knew no facts but that it would soon end. Nan was neither impressed nor convinced and had never felt so helpless in her entire existence.

Milton was ready to continue. Cal, his stage manager took him to one side and said that there may be a problem. There seemed to be a huge power cut in the area which was affecting mobile phones, radios etc. and the police thought it not safe to go ahead in such a situation.

"What a load of bollocks." Milton started to walk to the edge of the wings.

"We can't go on if the police have stopped it."

"Watch me." And he walked straight onto the stage without even waiting for the usual dimming of the lights.

"What's he think he's doing?" The police inspector had appeared at the manager's control desk.

"I told him and he just walked on." Cal shrugged and pointed.

"Doesn't he realised this is about the only place with any electricity in the area."

"What?"

"Don't ask me? I don't know why but we can't have the mass panic of this lot trying to get out if it does bloody well go off."

Cal covered his mike and said very slowly in a whisper. "Then you go on and tell him because there is no way I'm going to do it."

Before either of them could say anything, Milton's voice rose until it seemed to touch the high ceiling, his arm was sweeping across again and it was only then one of the crew came to the control desk holding something in his hand, his mouth wide open.

"He's taken this off." The words were barely audible as he showed Cal Milton's personal mike and battery pack. Everyone's mouth was hanging open now as they turned to look at the performer who was speaking to the whole audience with a volume impossible without mechanical means.

"How's he doing that?" The policeman asked.

"He can't be, unless….."

"What?"

"Oh he must have swapped it, he's put another on. Hang on though…" Cal was studying the lights on his panel. "He isn't using one." The words faded away as he looked in disbelief.

"How can you tell?"

"There's no light on, and there would be."

Now everyone watching from the wings couldn't believe what was happening for Milton was being lifted from the ground. Frantically the crew were looking up to see if he was suspended but they knew no harness had been fitted to him so how was he doing this? It had to be a trick. The audience all appeared to be under some sort of spell and as he rose, they all stood with their arms in the air as if grasping to receive something from him. Even the sound boys in the house had put their equipment on the floor, taken off their earphones and were following the mass reaction. Cal was calling them to respond but there was nothing.

Now the whole place seemed to be acting like a massive heart beat that started quite slowly and increased in speed until the pounding could be felt not only in the arena but through the walls until it had encompassed the whole centre.

Cal and his team were wondering how they seemed immune to the effect for although the pounding was beginning to get unbearable they were still in control of their thoughts and actions.

"It's because he's facing away." The inspector said with no need to whisper now, in fact he was almost shouting to make himself heard.

Cal immediately called down his mike, "Keep at the back of him at all times. Don't let him look at you."

It may have seemed a strange order but the lads were only too pleased to do anything which would end this unsettling event, and the sooner it would be over the better.

But nobody was prepared for what came next. Milton suddenly became shrouded in a light so eerie it seemed to change his form completely but his voice was the most terrifying of all.

"I have you all. I have your souls." Boomed through the auditorium and as the words faded there was complete silence.

From the wings the men watched as he slowly walked from the stage. No one had noticed when he had returned to the stage level and Cal was waiting for the usual applause but none came. Following instructions nobody looked him in the eye as he left but it wouldn't have made any difference for his job was done. The inspector pointed at one of the house cameras.

"My God, look at that." And he rushed to the stage staring in horror at the sight before him. The entire audience including the sound crew and centre staff were all collapsed where they were. No one was unconscious they were all dead, just empty shells, their souls ripped from their bodies. Their spirits stolen by Milton Warner.

"Look, observe." The order hit the levels surrounding Nan and down to Jean Paul.

Everyone was scanning the devastation in their area but one important fact was being overlooked. Nan's thought wave went out with such a force it hit all around her.

"The pockets. Look at the pockets."

All attention now was not on the horror but the little havens which seemed to be untouched by this holocaust.

Jean Paul was the first to notice another factor. "There's two sorts."

Jorg agreed "Look, where the tendrils are pointing at the next targets in our zone, they seem to be OK although everything is in chaos around them. It's protecting them for its next hit. But you're right, look around elsewhere, away from those places."

Tabar almost screamed "There's a repair going on. Something is restoring it to what it was before."

"No it's not just that" Nan was scrutinising it closely.

"What?" was the chorus.

"I've only seen this once before. Something is turning the time back. It's not repairing, it's rewinding, and look how quickly it's spreading."

Liam and Tommy watched in amazement as this was all new to them but they needed answers.

"How can this happen?" Tommy sent the message up and the answer came from Nan.

"I can only think that it is the action we were promised but not given any details."

Liam was very curious "Can you explain?"

Nan and Tabar shared a momentary thought and both replied "Beyond our knowledge."

But that wasn't enough for the two younger spirits who started to fire questions expecting answers. Nan indicated to Tabar who dropped to the lads' level.

"There are some things we have seen which are best not broadcast for who knows when they may be needed again?"

"But...." Liam wasn't satisfied and felt they were being fobbed off.

Tabar expected this and was ready with her reply. "Also, there are many things which will defy your understanding at present, so we suggest we all work together along with whatever help is obviously being used.....by whoever." and with a warm feeling of support she returned to her own level.

Jean Paul had been quiet throughout this but had homed in on one word – whoever. "I think we should do as suggested."

"What are you thinking?" Tommy was studying him.

"Maybe nothing. Just a hunch."

"Such as?"

"I just feel that we could get in the way and ruin things."

"He's talking in riddles." Tommy realised he wasn't going to get much from his companion and turned his attention to the earth not noticing Jean Paul slip away to another area.

"Well, how are you?" The greeting was warm but filled with concern as Jean Paul greeted his companion.

"I feel like I'm in hell." Milton's spirit was shrouded in sadness. "I don't know how you got me out and believe me I'm grateful, but that!" He indicated in the direction of his bodily form and it disgusted him to such an extent that had he still been in residence he would have been physically sick, for this creature was everything he wasn't.

"Don't thank me, I could never have done it. We've got some greater power beyond our understanding to be grateful to."

"Do the others know I'm here?"

"No and it has to stay that way."

"Haven't they worked out that we are from higher planes than they believed?"

"No, they're not experienced enough yet, and they don't need to. I'm hanging around on their level to keep up the pretence at least until such time as it is safe for you to return."

Milton was very low now. "I can't go back to ....that."

"Maybe when you go back you won't be going back to......that." Jean Paul repeated the words to show he understood fully then added "You know, time tricks and that stuff."

After a pause Milton said "It's so different when it's you, you know. We've seen others but I never realised just what a trauma it all is."

"Let's just see what happens, at least you're safe here, and I can keep in touch."

"Thank you my friend."

"Stay cloaked."

"I will." Milton felt the warmth of their friendship surge over him as Jean Paul left and knew he must use all his concentration to protect his being from the mass, for it would know he had escaped its powers and would no doubt be hunting him. The carcass being used for their evil means had obviously been taken over by one of their own kind, but Milton was worried that all this would permanently damage the good name and image he had built up over the years. His only hope lay with whoever operated the time factors, for if his followers could be left with no knowledge of his false persona he may be able to return to his previous life style, but he knew nothing would ever be exactly the same.

He had watched Daryl's reactions to the imposter and felt quite sorry for him and decided that if things could get back to anything resembling normal he would be more understanding towards him. It made him wonder if some good force had pushed Daryl out of the way to protect him from the events at Birmingham but Milton knew that someone must act on his behalf to ascertain the man's whereabouts. There was no way he could leave his secure area so he would have to use someone with experience he could trust. The news of Simon had also reached him and he wanted to will him back to his proper side of the time lock when it was released but again he could not come out of hiding. With the odd visit from certain spirits he was assured that Simon was receiving all the support he could possibly have, and all would be done to return him hopefully with the virus destroyed.

The mass had made a big mistake in using Jo and trying to promote her beyond her capability for they hadn't reckoned on the good powers intervening. These had let her have a short length of rope to give enough time to work out the evil's intent, but just when it thought it had a foothold, the levels above Za had stripped it from her and she was now back to her own area under the care of Sadie. The anger spread through the air like a thunderstorm but when the evil knew it was beaten it retracted and appeared to have departed for now.

Sadie had such a good soul, she felt sorry for everyone and had proved herself during the chaos going on below, although when it reached the spiritual regions it was way above her and she was kept aside to care for the souls arriving giving them comfort through their unexpected transition.

For now she hovered around Jo who seemed a fraction of her former self, and Sadie wished she would regain her true personality and let a few choice words slip. Then she would know her friend was back. Although often embarrassed by some of the expletives, the younger spirit had to admit she had missed the little tirades which were all part of Jo and what she was. But if she could make her feel wanted and loved, maybe she could end up being the butt of her remarks and she would welcome that.

Daryl hadn't gone far and was in another part of the vast Exhibition Centre when he felt the heart beat pulsing through the building. The spirits removing him from Milton tried to get him as far away from the main arena as possible but knew they had to keep him inside the boundary to keep as much control over him as they could for outside he would fall prey to more virus communication. The effect of the evil on him at present wasn't manifesting itself but they were sure it wouldn't be long before he was triggered into action. They were not aware at this stage that he had been used as a back up to boost Milton's objective and now the imposter had built in strength and power, Daryl was no longer any use. But the change that had taken place in him since Levvington now stood him in good stead to fight back. Gone was the simpering 'yes sir' image and in its place stood somebody who was his own man, someone who could act for himself, not be another man's servant. The new Daryl was now emerging like a butterfly from its cocoon and he was ready to take on the world.

He felt the pounding heartbeat now and something - but he didn't know what - was making him form a protective shield around himself until he felt he was standing in an invisible transparent dome immune to any outside force or power. It was a calm feeling and he wasn't afraid and he also felt he wasn't alone. For the first time he had an inkling as to how Milton had received his messages for although there was no direct speech, he was sure someone was guiding him to safety and protecting him from something that was evil and deadly. He kept up the force from within him strengthening his protection all the time and it was only when he felt the extreme calmness subsiding he started to take stock of his surroundings.

There was panic everywhere with people either rushing trying to find a way out, or security heading in the direction of the arena which was resulting in a human stampede from all directions. Daryl found himself in a small room with a window in the door where he could see this mayhem but remain protected until the crowd had cleared. In his mind he was going to face Milton Warner and tell him exactly what he thought of him and state that now he was entirely on his own for from this moment Daryl Finn was not going to answer to anyone. As he waited in his safe haven his mind came down to earth and he began to wonder just what was going on and the thought crossed his mind as to whether in some way this had anything to do with Milton's performance. He couldn't have explained why because it was just a gut feeling, but somehow he knew it had to.

The message crossed the galaxy in a spilt second. The time lock had been released. Simon felt himself pulled back through the hole and whisked away at speed and although he had no body he was aware that healing powers were tending to the part of him that had been trapped. If all went well he could be restored to his body but time was of the essence and one good sign was that any virus affecting him seemed to have stayed on the other side of the lock leaving him free of it at present.

It was expected by the elite force that the evil would immediately fly through the reopened time lock, but they knew from experience it was impossible to guess exact movements from any foe. This one seemed very cautious, hovering around the area but not using it. After a while it seemed to be ignoring it although this could be a ploy.

The elite now executed the next stage of this particular angle. They were blocking time locks then reopening them at random so the evil could not work out where to go next and so intent were they at fathoming this latest hiccup to their plans that much of their attention was taken from their earth targets leaving the elite force to attack the virus forms worldwide.

The good spirits were observing this upturn and some were realising that the upper powers hadn't been as idle as they thought and accepted that secrecy had been their main weapon, but none had any idea of the source which was how it had to remain.

The evil mass may have suffered a setback, but this was something it would not accept and a vicious anger spread throughout its entire network. The good forces may be undoing some of its previous work thinking they knew what they were fighting but that was going to change, for the next attacks would be in a different form and something they would not dismiss so lightly.

Something positive was being monitored by the arch angels. A fact emerged that they hadn't considered as a possibility until now when it began manifesting itself. It had been thought that the virus was unstoppable, so when it attacked the results would be fatal and it would continue to spread indefinitely, also it would take a permanent hold on whatever or whoever it touched.

But what seemed to be the case was that once it had completed its assault, that particular source was extinct. Therefore it relied on each onslaught being totally successful, and leaving devastation behind it could close down or perhaps run out of power and the main evil control would concentrate on the next area. This left a perfect loophole for the elite force as it could repair or rewind the deserted areas. Although this would be a mammoth task it wasn't beyond their capabilities and who knows what backup they could muster? But while all this had to be masterminded there was also the problem that the next targets would be attacked in a different way and just what that would be was still a mystery.

Nan and Tabar had been deep in concentration and sent a communication to Za who was in presence immediately.

"In earthly terms, wouldn't it be wonderful to have a spy in the camp?" Tabar opened the meeting.

Za paused before replying "It has been widely used in our sectors as you know. Remember when it was almost proved in one of the world wars. We were afraid the secret was out."

"Weren't they still in bodily form as well?" Tabar remembered it clearly. "Then they would go onto the astral plane to spy then return to their bodies with the information."

Za gave her his full concentration. "And you are suggesting we do that now, with this?" He appeared surprised even through his calm image.

"It's a thought," Nan paused.

"But.....?" Za knew these two had something more to add.

"What if we already have?"

"You haven't sent one of ours into the source, they wouldn't survive, and we don't have anyone who is adept enough not to be traced." Za was becoming very concerned fearing they had been headstrong without permission, but something about their calmness got through to him. "I think you had better explain."

The two exchanged a thought then Nan continued. "Perhaps they have provided us with the situation." She let that sink in before saying "When they had control of Jo, she was clever enough to pick up things and tuck them away for future reference. She's quite a crafty one when she wants to be."

"Oh No! You haven't been using her already have you?"

"If by using her you mean sending her into the throng, no we haven't." Tabar was a little more severe than she meant and instantly realised Za did not appreciate her tone. She continued in a calmer vein "Sadie has been relaying little things she has picked up from her manner. Now we think Jo is keeping it all to herself for fear of attracting the evil to our level, but with the proper approach we believe she has important information which we could use."

"And you have tried?" Za felt he wasn't being told everything.

Nan was quick to assure him that no attempt had been made to get information as they felt a higher level should be in presence but knew he was too high to descend to Jo's normal one.

"Can she not be raised to yours?" Za enquired.

"No, she is safe where she is as they won't suspect she has imparted anything from there, and they would know by her actions."

"Then I think we must send Ariel, she has the ability. But one of you must conduct the session and not make Jo aware she is being watched. Keep your thoughts as clear as possible."

"We understand."

"Also there must be a distraction in case they home in, give them something else to chase. Ariel may fulfil that act perfectly."

This was the end of the meeting and Za had gone without further word, leaving the friends with their new challenge.

The work done by the elite force on the Stratford Hall left most people wondering if they had imagined the doors being locked and the strange smell coming from the place, for now everywhere looked the same as it had before the evil attacked. The only evidence of anything untoward was a stain on the floor where Laurie Small had perished. Sadly he had gone too long for his spirit to be retrieved and it had been taken to an area of rest for him to settle until the realisation set in. Other keys had been obtained and the usual staff, without Johnny, all gathered late afternoon to get ready for the evening's booking.

DI Holland arrived to see why they hadn't reported to the police station as requested. He was not in the best frame of mind as he had been delayed with the other problems in the area. His first question was as to Laurie's whereabouts.

"Haven't seen him. Caused us a right pain he has. No keys. He has them so we've had to get the spare set." Abbie was quite put out about it, but nobody seemed to wonder why this efficient manager wasn't there as usual. Holland looked around and asked to see the office. His 'nose' was telling him that there was a big cover up going on.

"I haven't unlocked it yet."

"Then please do so without any more pis.......um delay miss please. And the rest of you stay where you are until I tell you to move, and don't touch anything."

There was a general buzz of annoyance among the staff but they felt apprehensive all the same.

"Hey where's Laurie?"

"Dunno. Must have overslept."

"Not him. Don't think he goes to bed."

"Probably a vampire."

"Shut up, there's something not right. What's that old cop doing here again?"

There was a sudden hush as Holland returned to the group and started questioning them as to the whereabouts of the manager. When it was obvious none of them had any idea he told them to remain in the foyer for now while he examined the hall, stage and dressing rooms. He had got Laurie's details from the file and would use them in a moment but for now he had that feeling again that something had gone on but he had missed it.

All seemed normal apart from the mark in front of the stage and he called for a test to be taken without delay. He ordered the staff to cordon it off with chairs and not to allow anyone to touch anything near it until they were told, they could then go about their business. He had the strange feeling that nothing odd was going to be found as if all traces of evidence were being obliterated before he arrived at any given point. Sitting behind the office desk he rang Liam Murray's mobile but the line was unavailable.

"Well that's bloody strange." He said aloud then rang the Mayfield station to see if the man had gone into his office.

"He's around somewhere sir, must have nipped out. Shall I get him to call you?" The voice was helpful so Holland agreed but asked that the message was marked 'Urgent'.

"Done as we speak sir."

"Umm could you do me one more small favour?"

"Of course sir."

"While I hold on, could you call him on his mobile please?"

"Doing it." Then after a moment "Oh, it seems dead, I'm not getting anything."

"Thank you very much."

He sat back for a moment assured it wasn't just him imagining it, but things were not right. Small was missing, Murray was out of contact. It all felt like too much of coincidence. Also the whole atmosphere of the place was dead, there was no life, no feeling of activity in the air and his mind wandered back to Milton. Something was piecing together in his mind like a puzzle coming together. When the man arrived and while he was performing the place was electric, you could feel it. But now it was as if he had taken all the energy with him and left the building void of any emotion. His 'nose was telling him he was picking up something that belonged to another world.

It would only be a few hours before he would learn of the Birmingham fiasco and then he would know that this was certainly real but it was way out of his league when it came to dealing with it. How his tired body would cope with it would remain to be seen.

CHAPTER 13

The evil had planned that, even in these early stages it would have an upper hand, so the spanners being thrown into its works were not only hampering the overall plan of attack, they were making the source angry beyond comprehension. A power such as this didn't just get a little annoyed, it became an unstoppable hurricane, fuelled by the growing counter actions of its enemy. Secrecy had been the main tool and it still was important in the future planned assaults, but it hadn't reckoned on such an intelligence it was now fighting. Such strikes in other areas and on other planets had been fairly simple compared to this, so it pondered on just what it was up against and whether it would have to re think the forthcoming attacks. For once it wasn't only the good levels that were waiting for the next move in the game.

Some of the organising evil decided to pull back and try to estimate the source of the higher spirits but they were soon monitored and immediately diversions were put in place to throw them away from particular areas so within seconds the idea had to be abandoned and concentration was returned to making the next attack successful but on a more intense scale. Orders were despatched to all parts to speed up the operation and achieve total control as soon as possible. The good forces would have welcomed the knowledge that a degree of panic was creeping in and was a sign of weakness that would eventually give them a stronger hold over the evil.

Liam Murray was driving away from Mayfield at a faster speed than he normally would. He had to get away but he wasn't sure why. His mind was in turmoil for something was telling him he had done something very wrong and he struggled to sift his thoughts to know what. Everything seemed to be going blank apart from the fact he had been sent somewhere to do something. Spirit Liam had been sent to guide him away and get him to an area where they could cleanse his mind and get him back to normal but the virus was trying to take over and fighting to use this man one more time before disposing of him. The evil planted in him was stronger than the good spirit who called for help to oust the thing but he felt himself being drawn into Murray's body until they became as one, but both on the same destructive task.

The detective's foot was pressing harder on the accelerator and as he was driving along minor roads was in danger of losing control on the narrow bends. Suddenly he felt his hands being lifted from the wheel and as his spirit friend desperately called out again the car veered off the road, rolled down a slope and landed on its roof in a field.

Nan and Tommy appeared as the car skidded its last few feet, and immediately joined the two occupants.

"Too late." The sadness in Nan's thought was shared by Tommy who was helping spirit Liam to separate himself. All three surrounded Murray knowing his lifeless body was no longer of use for any terrible purpose, but welcomed him to their keeping knowing that he would now understand many things but needed the necessary time for adjustment due to his sudden transition.

The creature occupying Milton's body was now set on his course of destruction but of a totally different nature to the Birmingham performance. He knew the tour route details which had been easy to absorb in the short time he had been in body but he had not yet realised he was alone. Even the higher evil powers had missed the fact that the true Milton had left the scene and they just assumed that he was lying dormant unable to interfere with his passenger. Had the infiltrator been less full of himself and the sudden success of his mission he may have taken a moment to realise the situation for this was providing the perfect weak link the elite forces could use to their advantage.

He had left the arena, dismissing the crew with a slight wave of his hand and when asked about Daryl, just shrugged and said "Daryl who?"

The police inspector was so busy calling in back up to deal with the horror in the auditorium that it was only when he turned to question the crew he noticed Milton wasn't in sight.

"Get him from his dressing room, or wherever he is." The order didn't go to anyone in particular and nobody moved.

Getting very frustrated he repeated it only to be met with an uneasy shuffle from one of the younger stage hands. He turned on him almost shouting "Well?"

"Sorry, I think he went."

"WENT! What do you mean he went?"

"He – he always does after a show, it's very tiring and….."

"I don't give a shit about him being tired or anything else, I told everyone not to leave, did I not?"

The lad shrugged not quite sure how to react and was grateful when Cal stepped in.

"Sorry sir, we were all busy doing equipment checks, we don't watch the boss if you know what I mean."

There was a pause before the inspector said very precisely "Then would you please locate him and request the pleasure of his company, here and now!" The order bellowed across the stage and wings and Cal decided it would be best if he went, knowing full well the dressing room would be empty.

It seemed a futile task but the police wanted to make a thorough examination of the stage for anything at all that might prove helpful in understanding the tragic events. Everywhere had been sealed off and only certain officers were allowed in including as many coroners as could be traced. Up to now only a couple had been contacted and were on their way, a fact welcomed by the elite force who were busy setting up a plan of action to undo as much of this horror as possible.

The task was to rewind certain aspects alongside a freeze of current time, then readjust the two to run alongside until they were level and in conjunction with world clock time. Although many lower levels find this difficult to understand, it can be likened to runners in a race, one may speed up while another is jogging along at an even pace and may even stop and then be overtaken; but the leader could then slow down and eventually it may result in them crossing the finishing line together.

If they could reverse the auditorium to the point where the souls were seized and try to leave them in their bodies but freeze the current time, or even rewind that a little so that the police would have nothing to investigate, the times could be levelled so that the horror would appear to have never happened. This tactic has been used many times throughout time by elite forces without mere mortals being aware – until one day someone says "Do you know, I could have sworn you had said that before."

And so the plan was set. But one person not included was Daryl for the powers ruled that if he could remember these events it would stand him in good stead with his acquired knowledge which could be put to good use if he could only harness it and with the right tuition that should be possible. Jean Paul and Milton agreed that he deserved some recognition for the way he had stood up to the imposter, regardless of the fact that the virus had touched him and given him the will to fight, but that had been successfully removed from him and the new Daryl was almost unrecognisable from the pathetic creature that had arrived earlier. Now all the protective spirits had to do was keep him safe until he could be moved and not let him get caught up in the time adjustment.

For a split second everything in the exhibition hall and surrounding area went into time freeze while Daryl, locked in a protective dome was steered out of his hiding place and transported to his car and guided well away to a safe area.

He shook himself, looked around and tried to take stock of his present whereabouts.

"I must have dozed off." he thought. For a moment the events at Birmingham seemed like a dream and he found it hard to believe it had all been real. His car had been carefully positioned so as not to draw attention to any passing vehicle, and was tucked in a small lay by under a group of trees, a place many a tired motorist had used for a quick nap, or local couples had used for other late night purposes. Jorg was positioned in the front passenger seat, two other back up protectors were in the rear and another on guard outside the windscreen. So important was this operation that higher forces had to be used to ensure the split second timing was successful. Had Daryl been aware of such a presence he may not have got out to have a pee so willingly but the spirits paid no heed apart from still keeping the protective force round him every second.

When he got back into the car he knew he had to get his bearings for he had no idea where he was so he switched on the engine started to move off in the direction he was facing. The sat nav showed no major roads which surprised him and he toyed with the idea of keying in his home code to see if the direction gave him any clue, not only as to where he was but why.

He hadn't had time to gain any speed when he was aware of something which reminded him of the experience in the office when Jean Paul had been drawn to comfort him. He felt protected and instinctively put his hand to his shoulder but this time the feeling didn't leave him, in fact it got stronger until he felt his attention wasn't on controlling the car so slowed back to a halt, the engine still ticking over.

"Who are you?" He whispered. "Are you Jean Paul?"

By way of reply he felt a soothing sensation travelling the entire area of his body and mind and although he heard no words the message was a clear as if Jorg had faced him in the flesh and spoken.

"Don't be alarmed. We are here to help you, to protect you."

"What has happened?"

There was a pause. "Many things. Don't try to understand too much."

"It's to do with Milton isn't it? Something happened, it was as if it wasn't him."

"You're on the right track, but it goes a lot further than that."

For a moment they let Daryl gather his thoughts then he almost burst out "There's been lots of strange things happening, things we couldn't explain." Then after a moment he almost shouted "Is that what caused Cyber--- I mean Simon's – well what happened to him?"

"Very much so."

"Oh."

The sentinels kept up their guard during this but knew Jorg had to get to the point as time was still a major factor.

"Daryl. We can look after you but we need you to help us."

"Who's us?"

"You have worked with Milton long enough to know there are many things most people are never aware of. You know he can communicate with other worlds but so can many more people if they only let their minds be less cluttered."

"Well I can't."

"So how do you explain this conversation? Look around you."

Slowly Daryl let his eyes cover a full circle his head turning one way then the other, the realisation hitting him like a bullet. "Oh shit!"

"Or in other words…."Jorg's sense of humour was never far away.

Daryl's voice was nothing more than a whisper. "I'm talking to you but I can't see you."

"Well to be precise, until the 'shit' bit, you hadn't actually spoken."

"You mean I've been talking in my mind, people will say I'm crazy."

It was time to move him now without any more delay.

"Drive on, we'll direct you."

"We? How many of you are there?"

"Never mind, it's imperative you move at the moment. All will be explained, just trust us."

There wasn't time, or even a logical explanation why Daryl obeyed without question and he could never have given a good reason why he went along with an order from someone he couldn't see, but something told him that this was right and he would be in danger if he didn't comply.

Nan was pleased this operation had gone well and now consulted with her higher levels as to the next move. Jean Paul conveyed the message to Milton who had doubts as to whether his aide could handle it but realised this wasn't the old Daryl but a new force to be reckoned with. He also enquired as to Simon's condition and was assured he too was under the care of the good forces who would extract all the knowledge they could of his trauma and put it to good use.

Milton's physical body had left for Derby, the Monday venue knowing the crew would take care of their side of things and if Daryl decided to join him he would probably be told to get lost as he was of no use. He found the hotel where he would spend the night and as bookings were always made well in advance he knew he would have the best room available. He ordered the staff to carry his cases, leaving no tip and generally causing general annoyance by his high and mighty attitude. Those that had seen him before couldn't believe this was the same man. He looked similar but the Milton Warner known to millions was well mannered, quite generous and treated all alike but this man must be a look-alike for there was no way the same person could change so drastically. One young chamber maid complained that he had 'touched her up' as he passed but the manager told her she must have imagined it. It was only when she broke down in tears and he received other such complaints he realised the poor girl must have been telling the truth.

Having dismissed the staff with an offhanded wave, Milton stripped and prepared to take a shower before relaxing on his bed. As he stood with the soothing water trickling down his body he felt as though his entire self was being washed away with soap as it trickled down the hole. For the first time since the beginning of this charade he felt empty. Gone was the bravado that had carried him along on his wave of power and he searched for the true Milton inside but there was nothing. Knowing that he had supposedly squashed the medium and taken control he hadn't given it a thought that the spirit would leave altogether.

This evil puppet – for that's all he was to the high powers, couldn't work out that if the true occupant left, the body could cease to exist at any given time, that is it would die. A temporary occupant could keep it alive for a while, but if the original owner did not return by the time the usurper left, the carcass would be an empty shell. But all this creature knew was that he was alone. He couldn't boss Milton about or crush him because he wasn't there and all that concerned him was this feeling of utter isolation, something he had always feared even to phobic proportions.

This was being observed by Tabar who wondered if the evil powers had known about this when they put him in placement, which didn't seem to be the best tactic as the creature could jeopardise any major plan. But maybe they did know and used him knowing they had such a hold over him because of this weakness, and he would be easily dispensed with and replaced by a more efficient worker when it came to the more intense attacks. Perhaps he was simply the pace maker keeping the slot ready for the main runner at a pre ordained time.

The man in the shower quickly dried himself off and put on a long gown to lie and have a think about the events. Not feeling like mixing with the rabble, he had ordered his meals to be brought to his room, but as the feeling of loneliness increased he began to wish he hadn't. Milton himself would have welcomed the peace and quiet as he was always recognised and much as he loved his followers, he was always ready to chill out away from people at the end of a performance.

Jean Paul did a quick sweep of the room following Tabar's visit but the man on the bed was none the wiser and his spirit mind was not open enough to home in on such things, which is more than could be said for his controllers who knew every move surrounding this dummy. They knew it would draw attention from the good forces and were hoping they would be in presence to a greater extent than they seemed to be doing. Although the evil didn't want any confrontation at this stage, they did hope that their high powers could work out any strategy which was being planned, but the good force seemed indifferent, just taking the occasional peek then leaving. This was not going according to plan and they knew they would have to make the catch more appealing to get them to take further interest

For this was how they were trying to build up a full picture of what they were fighting, know your enemy, and at the moment they were learning very little and the lack of knowledge was hampering the immediate offensive. From experience they now knew that their previous attempts had not achieved the success they imagined they should have. Much of the devastation was being undone whereas it should have left entire areas completely barren and added to that was the fact that the good powers they had monitored appeared to be taking little part in what was going on, which could only mean one thing. There was a much more powerful unseen force at work and until they found out what it was, their entire operation could crumble.

The current occupant looked down at Milton's body which was in pretty good shape and realised that with such equipment he didn't have to be lonely at all. He rang down to the front desk and asked for a companion to be sent up and was astonished to be told that "this isn't that kind off establishment sir." Frustration and terror started to fill his being and he began to shake, his mind now playing tricks. Gone was the flamboyant persona he had adopted and enjoyed, but now he needed the basic physical contact and temporary affection of another soul preferably in human form so that not only would he not be alone but he could enjoy the pleasure this race seemed to have at their finger tips.

Jean Paul had picked up this vibration and knew he had to do all he could to protect Milton's body for the present, not only for physical reasons, but for the good name of his friend when hopefully everything would return to its previous state.

Det Insp Holland was in bed but sleep wasn't on his mind. Every time he tried to piece his thoughts together another question always rose to the surface. His arm went out to the empty side of the bed and he lay there wondering what his late wife would have advised. There had been many occasions when a case was bothering him and they had sat in the small hours talking over different aspects until the answer seemed to reveal itself. He used to joke that it was her psychic ability that hit on the truth because her mind was fresh and open to all avenues whilst his was so full of many ongoing jobs he couldn't see clearly. She would laugh and say it was only because she had put his mind in order that he had fathomed it out in the end.

He toyed with the idea that it may have been she who had been trying to guide him now. Maybe she had foreseen some kind of danger and was trying to warn him and perhaps that was what he was putting down to his 'nose' picking up something. With her prominent in his mind he lay back and tried to clear his thoughts completely in the hope something would emerge.

After about five minutes he felt himself being lifted up but the sensation was not unpleasant and he let himself be taken wherever this feeling was going. He was aware he was not in his body for that was still lying on the bed and gradually he was turned until he was floating face downwards with something protective on each side of him. They all moved as one gathering speed until they were over the Stratford Hall when, in a matter of seconds they showed him the entire events of the evening filling his mind with knowledge of the impending evil.

This was not a new experience for him but he was one of those who, when awake had no knowledge of their spiritual travels which was why bodily he couldn't work out what was happening but knew something had. He just couldn't remember what.

His sentinels were gradually appearing to him and he recognised them from previous trips and immediately put his trust in all they were showing him. They moved to the Birmingham arena and informed him of Milton's performance and the subsequent seizure of the souls, but also said this was not the end for there were good forces at work trying to reverse the horror.

Holland asked as to Milton's whereabouts but was told to be patient for there was something else he should see first. Of course this level believed Milton was still in body. They took Holland to the scene of Murray's death and hovered over the car for a moment.

"So that's why he didn't answer." The thought was almost a whisper and a sadness came over him for this was a promising officer who had a great future which had been snatched from him.

"Did the evil get him?"

His answer came from the car as the two Liams rose to join them briefly. Murray moved forward. "Sorry boss. Yes it did. I tried with all my might to fight back but it was so strong it took over until I wasn't in control. Guess it won in the end."

The other Liam joined him "It hasn't won. It's only taken his body, we will repair his soul, but we have to go." Turning to Murray he said "You have a lot of adjusting to do my friend" and with a small wave they had both gone leaving the area still and quiet until such time as Murray's body would be found.

Holland was then whisked away to Derby and found himself in Milton's hotel bedroom but was instantly removed to a safe distance where the trio floated over a countryside away from the distraction of earthly happenings.

"Why did we go there if we weren't staying, what was the point of that?" He was somewhat confused now.

"Only allowed a quick look at present." Was all he got in reply followed by "Did you notice anything in particular?"

It had all been a bit quick for Holland and he remarked that if they had pre warned him he would have been ready, but it was so instantaneous he only noticed where the man was in the room, what he was wearing and the fact he didn't look too happy.

"Not bad for a tenth of a second." One of his companions observed.

"So why go? What was the purpose? You must have had one or we wouldn't have gone, and come to think of it, it must have been important."

There was silence for a moment then one of them said, "We have to go but there is someone else coming, they can probably answer your questions."

He was never sure of the exact change over but when Tabar arrived, Holland felt such a strength coming from her, it seemed to enter his own soul and the strength was rising instantly.

"You must be quite confused." Her approach was very reassuring.

"To say the least!"

"There is a reason you have been called."

"And that is?"

"You must be aware you have served many spiritual purposes in the past although you aren't aware of them when in physical form, there is a reason for that too."

Holland was wishing she would get to the point but knew she wouldn't be rushed so he didn't interrupt but just agreed with a thought acknowledgment.

"Probably due to a past experience, there is something in you that the virus can't control."

"Ah now we're getting to it." It wasn't that he understood exactly but at least there was hope of an imminent explanation.

"It tried when you were at the Stratford Hall if you remember but it couldn't get a foothold."

After a moment he exclaimed "The drink. I did feel odd."

"You were monitored soon after because it was like antibodies fighting an invader and your body stifled it so it had no chance with your soul."

"Bloody Hell!" Although there was no speech the thought was strong enough to cause a ripple on the surrounding air and Tabar moved them to another area.

"I've a feeling there's more to come now, am I right?" Holland was getting a bit suspicious.

Nan joined them briefly and the combined power strength increased dramatically.

"You have a great asset. They can't touch you." She breathed.

Tabar was quick to add "We can use this in our fight against this wicked thing. Crush it before it creates any more devastation. Yes, we can and are repairing a lot of it, but how much better if it doesn't succeed in the first place?"

"But what can I do?" Holland couldn't see how he could be of help.

Tabar said "Many things if you are willing."

"We'll guide you of course," Nan cut in "you won't be alone."

There was a moment of stillness as Holland mulled it all over then suddenly he was being pulled back to his body by his light line. As the two escorted him to safety he called "OK, I'll do it" and he entered his body on the bed with the telephone ringing in his ears.

CHAPTER 14

As one ascends to supreme spiritual levels, the most important factor learnt on the way is never to divulge more than is necessary at a time, even to those held most dear or close. Although Jean Paul knew he and Milton were of much higher levels than most imagined, it never crossed Jean Paul's thought that Milton may be of an even higher level still. Many times Milton had been tormented by the fact he could not confide in his companion but that was the way of things and he knew he could not act any differently. Even now he had let his friend believe that he had been solely instrumental in extracting him from his body, whereas it had been timed to the split second using Jean Paul as the tool. Also he had to make sure he was in the secret holding zone when Jean Paul visited, but as that had to be very limited, it seemed to be working for now. One of his skills was the ultra high speed movement which is so instantaneous that an enemy would have to be of the same standard to detect it. Also he could freeze the time he was occupying whilst taking a full reconnoitre, then restarting the time after he had left. But much of this would be beyond Jean Paul's capabilities and not to put it unkindly, beyond his understanding for the full knowledge is only known by those who have achieved such status.

Up to now Milton had covered most of the area in this working zone and was aware of all the events and who was being used. He had been very instrumental in Simon's release but could not admit it to any source, now or ever for this operator was one of the highest of the elite forces deployed around the earth planet and much of his success was because of the utmost secrecy which would be forever cherished.

Another skill of this special few is the ability to be able to move through any level regardless of whether it be of the higher realms or the lowest forms and not have to feed information down in steps as used by the likes of Za down through Ariel then Tabar, Nan and Jorg and so on down to Jo and Sadie on the spiritual planes. But they can also penetrate the earthly and sub earthly realms if they wish although they only go below earthly ones in extreme cases. The term earth is not used in the physical sense, which is where the understanding becomes difficult for those not of their power.

When knowledge of the impending threat had reached the good spiritual hierarchy, Milton's earthly visit was planned well in advance as a distraction. As time is very different on other planes, the life time he would have to spend leading up to the attack was insignificant for he could flit spiritually from his body at will. If anyone had looked deeply into his past they would have found a normal human leading a fairly normal life, apart from his medium skills which many earthlings scorned, but this was the bait for the unknown enemy. Using past experiences the upper powers knew this kind of evil attack usually homed in on individuals such as true mediums to get a foothold then prepared for the kill which was exactly what had been happening up to this point.

In fact Milton had put himself right in the firing line as a guinea pig, knowing full well the consequences could be disastrous, not just to him but mankind as a whole. The levels around Za knew he had been placed but assumed he was obeying orders from above, little realising he was one of the organisers.

Milton was aware that by leaving his body for a significant earth time he could be in danger of not being able to return, he would die. But that was part of the plan for he would no longer need it and would be free to carry out his elite tasks. The exact moment was yet to be confirmed depending on how things developed.

He hovered now in his secret holding space then instantly moved to confer with those of the elite members of his team. In less than the blink of an eye they had decided upon their next move and he was back in case Jean Paul paid him a brief visit. But his friend was being quizzed by Nan and Tabar who had dropped to the level they believed were where Milton and Jean Paul were situated.

"But why shouldn't we know, he could be in danger?" Nan was very concerned and a little put out feeling she wasn't being told everything.

"I told you, some higher level said he had to go to safety, and I could visit him to keep him up to date." Jean Paul felt this was a bit of a lame excuse and knew he wasn't being believed.

"And can we know who this higher level is?" Tabar joined in.

"I don't know."

"So how were you told?"

Before Jean Paul had chance to reply Milton appeared. "Only a quick visit, I'm supposed to be under wraps. Need your help. Can you come?" He indicated towards his friend.

"Of course." Jean Paul was grateful for the interruption and instantly they had gone leaving the assembled pair even more bemused than before.

Back in the safe zone, Jean Paul was somewhat stunned for there was Milton waiting for him. As he turned to ask his escort what was going on he was confronted by Ariel.

"Many thanks Ariel." Milton thanked her warmly.

"Any time there's a problem….." she offered as she left.

"Sorry about that, had to get you out of there." Milton felt slightly amused.

"But how…. I mean…"

"I asked her to help, she can fool anyone."

Jean Paul relaxed for a moment then asked "But isn't that going to make them wonder even more."

"Probably."

"You don't seem very bothered."

Milton paused for a moment. "On the contrary, Nan is very protective and will need answers so we will have to give her something to stop her wondering."

"And how are you going to do that."

"Oh I'll work on it."

"Is that it?" Jean Paul was a little deflated but Milton couldn't be more specific at this stage so he told him he had better leave now but to make sure he was noticed around the likes of Liam and Tommy which was the level they were believed to occupy. He also asked that he didn't visit him any more than was necessary so as not to lead a path to him.

Having convinced his friend to go about his business as usual, Milton now settled to work out his plan.

The car was approaching Derby and as Daryl recognised the major roads a slight chill ran through him. Realising he didn't have to speak to portray his thoughts he sent the apprehension to his unseen companions. Jorg was expecting this and said "Keep going, you will be under our care."

"But this is the next venue."

"We are aware of that."

Daryl's new feeling of power was taking some getting used to and he was wondering if he was going to be able to cope with it for he seemed to be starting a new way of life altogether and still felt it must be a dream of some sort.

"Take the next left turn." Jorg was giving instructions and Daryl knew he had no option but to obey, for what else could he do?

Soon they came to a small hotel which was large enough for him to merge into the guests without drawing the attention he would have felt in a smaller one, but not so big that he would encounter lots of other people.

"Your room is booked Mr Freestone, Mr Simon Freestone." Jorg emphasised the 'Simon'.

"But that's Cyber's name – oh I get it, and do I give his address as well?"

"You do." Jorg was relieved Daryl seemed to be accepting the situation. "And if you answer any question in the way he would, it will save you having to indulge in conversation with anyone.

"Well he never did waste words. Oh God!"

"What is it?"

Daryl looked horrified. "I'm speaking about the poor bastard in the past tense."

"Don't worry," Jorg was amused "you'll have plenty of chance to make up for lost time when you two meet again." Before Daryl had time to comment Jorg said he had better go and sign in and get a good nights sleep before the next day and reminded him that 'Milton' had a show in the evening.

"But..." as the word left his lips, Daryl knew there would be no further communication for now and hoped his unseen bodyguard was still there as he got out of the car. It suddenly occurred to him that he didn't know if he had any luggage, but on checking the boot was relieved to find his travel bag still where he must have put it, but the memory was very vague and being tired he grabbed the handle, locked the car and entered the foyer.

A rather plain lad took him up to his room and explained that the kitchen was closed for meals but he could bring him some supper on a tray if he was hungry. The old Daryl would have been quick to pick up the admiring look cast in his direction and maybe would have read an ulterior motive into the offer but apart from needing to be on his own, his mind was not concentrating on such earthly things. Remembering Jorg's words he simply said "Thank you. Leave the tray outside the door."

The somewhat deflated porter pocketed the simple tip and closed the door behind him leaving Daryl alone – physically.

"Do not speak aloud." The voice seemed unfamiliar at first and yet somehow he felt he had heard it somewhere before.

"Who are you?" Daryl kept his thought silent.

"You have a busy day ahead of you tomorrow. When you have eaten get some rest. We will speak later."

"But – do I know you?"

The answer never came.

The elite forces were succeeding now in repairing the evil quicker than it could take hold but were still on the alert for any unexpected twist. The whole area around the Birmingham arena had been cleansed spiritually and the people in the immediate area had been reunited with their souls, a feat that even shook the likes of Nan and Tabar, but the operation would have been far above their capabilities so they thankfully praised whoever had achieved it. In such cases a massive brainwashing process has to be implemented so that those on the earthly plane believe enough to carry them on through their lives. They may wonder or challenge their knowledge but it is enough to satisfy them for now.

So everyone involved believed that the true Milton Warner had given the performance of his career and so his reputation was in tact at this precise moment. But there was the rest of the tour to take into account. It could easily have been cancelled, but Milton knew that he was the main target and would use all the bait he could to draw the top evil powers into his web, for he had known all along that they had acquired a certain insight into his status, but no one could possibly guess the extent. He would be using his faithful aide in the task in ways the lad could never have imagined.

Holland was awake. The call had been a wrong number and he cursed under his breath wishing he could have conversed longer with his spiritual companions. His new awakening was answering many nagging questions over the years. Of course it hadn't been his 'nose' that had often led him to a solution, he had been guided. It all made sense now and he was willing to tackle this problem because of his special immunity. He stretched out in the bed and ran his hands over his manly frame.

"I'm not ready for the scrap heap yet" he mused. "I can be of use, more than I would chasing petty criminals in this bloody job." His head turned to the pillow beside him.

"What do you make of it lass?" He smiled to himself then sat bolt upright looking again at the empty space in the bed.

"Do you know about this? Are you going to help me?"

The thought hit him like a brick, and even if it wasn't right, the simple idea of being on the same spiritual level as she might be, gave him all the urge he needed to get cracking on the job he had been selected for. His body may look old and tired but he felt as if his spirit had been given a new lease of energy and as the hidden memories of past experiences infiltrated his mind, he gave himself up to those waiting for him and by the time the fatal heart attack hit, he had departed to a new beginning.

Monday morning arrived with a distinct drop in temperature almost threatening an early frost but the staff at the Mansion Rooms in Derby were too busy getting ready for the evening show which was a sell out. News had spread that the Birmingham venue had been a huge success with almost a mass experience as though every single person present had received their own individual message although other details seemed rather vague. The press had been hard pushed to get anyone to speak of their experience saying it was private and only for them. Now hopeful followers were trying to get any seats which may become available through cancellation although it was virtually an impossibility.

The employees at the venue were guessing at what had been so special about the Birmingham show and it excited them to think they may have a repeat of it tonight. They would have worked for nothing to have a chance of seeing this celebrity in the flesh and maybe even speak to him. Two of the younger females were giggling as they went about their tasks.

"I've heard he's very dishy."

"Too old for you, you tramp."

"I wasn't thinking of shagging him!"

"No?"

"Well perhaps just a little bit."

"Wonder why he's not married."

One of the lads joined them overhearing the last remark.

"Doesn't need to I guess, listening to you two, he can probably get all he wants without."

"Like you, you mean?"

There's no knowing where the conversation would have gone, had the supervisor not entered at that moment.

"All right you lot, more work and less chatter, there's a lot to do."

As she hurried off to check the bar staff the lad muttered "Frustrated old bitch, she needs a good seeing to" then in a mock haughty manner said "I'd do it myself but I'd need to be dead drunk first."

The girls stifled their giggles and exchanged a few whispered comments about him.

The stage crew soon arrived and took charge, most of them still in a bit of a fog about the previous evening. When Cal joined them he noticed a slightly more subdued bunch of lads than usual. He was relieved nobody started asking question as he knew he had no answers. He had been tossing and turning all night wondering just what had taken place, but didn't feel it could be anything bad or serious.

His mind now went back to a job he was on when the whole audience was hypnotised, and most of the crew went under as well but couldn't remember anything afterwards. This was very much like that and he wasn't going to be the first to admit he had been affected this time, so the least said the better and they must concentrate on today, then let tomorrow just take its course. That had to be it. Milton had turned to hypnotism without anyone realising. He hoped the majority of the crew might work it out but some were too young to have had any previous experience of it.

"Oh well," he thought "perhaps now's the time to break them in. If you work with this kind of stuff, you've got to take what comes, whatever it is."
With that idea in mind he was ready for any questions that may be thrown his way.

Daryl had been lulled to sleep by his protectors but the first thing that came into his mind when he woke was the nagging question as to whose voice he had heard, or thought he heard before turning in. He had a shower and was dressing to go down to breakfast when he stopped, his trousers half on.

"It couldn't have been." He looked at himself in the mirror almost talking to his reflection. "It was Milton, but how....?"
He was almost correct. Ariel had sent the voice tone through knowing it would have enough of a ring of familiarity to settle him but without direct contact. She was making him feel secure in his spiritual awareness gaining his trust in this world which like so many others was new to him.

He finished putting on his clothes, had his meal and returned to gather all his belongings. It had been relayed to him that he must be involved with every stage of this tour, and regardless of how 'Milton' may react he must be as near to him as usual. He was now aware that the true Milton was not in body and although this was a huge aspect to understand, Daryl was assured that his guides and protectors would be there all the time and would give him instructions on how to act.

As he zipped up his bag, he felt an arm around his shoulder and he was slowly moved into a sitting position on the bed, his eyes closed. Instead of actual words, the message was portrayed by deep thought as Jorg drew close until he was merging with him, the sentinels protecting them from all angles.

"For your safety, we are going to clear your memory of most of what you have been shown. You will go about your work in your usual way exactly as before when you were on tour. If you have any rejection, you will ignore it. We will feed you only what you need to know, but you will do as we ask." He let the process take over before adding "But you will never be alone, you will be protected at all times."

Again there was a moment for the information to take effect.

But what Daryl wasn't told was that they could not be too obvious or it would draw attention from unwanted sources for the evil scouts would be everywhere and pick up immediately on any threat. It had been necessary for his inner self to believe he was safe in order for him to carry out this mission and he was now directed to go to the Mansion Rooms and wait in the dressing room assigned to Milton.

Slowly he realised where he was, gave his head a little shake as if to clear his mind and giving a final glance around the room he left for the unknown danger which lay ahead.

Sadie had sent a message by Tommy to ask Nan to contact her as quickly as possible for she still could not rise to those levels.

"What's up?" Tommy wondered if it was something he could help with.

"Can't say, and it may be nothing."

His curiosity aroused he sent the request immediately but hung around hoping to find out more because Sadie had become very efficient in her own field and only called for help if there was a good reason.

Nan arrived instantly and with a dismissive "Thank you" to Tommy turned her attention to the young spirit.

"What is concerning you?"

"Oh it may be nothing at all but when did you lift Jo up to a higher level, only I didn't think she was ready yet?"

Nan was concerned, knowing this hadn't happened and wasn't likely to for a very long time.

"Tell me why you ask." She wanted to get as much information as possible without alarming her, but she knew this was serious.

"Well, she still wasn't...well... completely stable as you know and recently it was very difficult to keep her concentration on the simple tasks you'd told me to give her."

"And....?"

"Well, I'm afraid I was concentrating on the intake from that flood in Europe and when I looked for her to help she wasn't there."

Nan knew this would take some extracting but knew she couldn't pressure her or it may take even longer.

"So what did you do?"

"I asked around but nobody had seen her, or seen her go anywhere and I didn't think she could have been lifted up and… I didn't quite know what to do…and I should have paid more attention."

So this was it, the girl felt responsible and was afraid to admit it.

"My dear, you can't watch everyone all the time and we do move around in a very different way to what you were used to on earth so let's sort this together. You did the right thing by calling me."

Sadie looked a little relieved as Nan continued.

"Right. Where was the last location – where you saw her last?"

Together they went to the position.

"She was here."

"And when would you say that was?"

Sadie thought then carefully explained the time in their terms. Nan recapped the exact details including Jo's manner and the colour of her surrounding space, and telling Sadie she had done very well and was right to call her, Nan left for consultation with Tabar.

After a brief exchange they sent a call to Za for help, for Jo could not have disappeared without trace. There were too many sentinels who would have sensed she was out of her limits.

"Do you think they've got control of her again?" Tabar was musing whilst they waited for Za's appearance.

Nan replied very precisely. "You know in worldly terms it's almost as though they left a chip in her which they could control at will, and now they've activated it."

"Oh don't." Tabar was horrified but before she could answer further Za was in presence.

"You need not concern yourselves about the spirit," There was a shocked silence before he continued. "I have been informed that she is being used elsewhere and will be returned when she has completed her task."

"But…" Nan's thoughts were racing and many questions buzzed through her being.

Tabar was quick to jump in "She will be in danger won't she?"

With a brief "No more questions." Za had gone.

Nan was angry. "They can't be using her against the evil, not after what she went through."

"I don't think we have any say in the matter, regardless of how we feel. We can only think on a positive wave for her and trust whatever is controlling this."

"What do I tell Sadie?" Nan felt almost guilty now.

"Do you have to tell her anything?"

"I'll just say she was moved to another area, but on the same level. Part of her readjustment process."

"Well that may satisfy her for now, but she's a caring soul and may not be convinced."

After a moment they agreed there was no alternative and Nan left to get it over as quickly as possible.

The truth was that Za had no more idea as to Jo's whereabouts than anyone else. He merely received his orders from the higher levels and in this case would have kept them to himself, had Nan not enquired, which was why she received such a non informative reply as he left. She and Tabar knew there was no good trying to trace the spirit but could only offer their love and protection to her, wherever she was. So after trying to give Sadie as reassuring an explanation as possible, she returned to her own level to await news from any area.

"Have we heard anything from Milton?" Tabar asked as she joined her.

"Nothing, and that's something else that I think we aren't being told."

"Wonder where he is?"

Ignoring the remark Nan had a sudden burst of inspiration. "Jorg is covering Daryl!"

"And?"

"There has to be a connection. When is Jorg due back?"

Tabar gave a mental shrug. "What are you thinking?"

"Just this. Where Daryl is, I bet Milton isn't far away."

"And you want to grill Jorg in case he knows something. But getting back to Jo, are you trying to tie her in with this?"

"Oh I don't know." Nan's frustration was nearly at boiling point. "Well we will both have to be extra alert, glean what we can from all sources. How else are we suppose to protect people, and….."she paused "we still don't know what the evil can do, or what it wants."

Tabar was silent for a moment then decided "We also don't know which side Jo has been allocated."

"But…"

"Oh I know what Za said, but he has a way of fobbing us off without proper explanations, so let's just hope and keep all our avenues of possibility open." Nan knew this made sense, her friend always did so she gave her a mental hug of agreement and they turned their concentration back to their tasks.

The 'Milton' occupant was awake but something was very wrong. If he had been afraid of being alone, he had more cause to worry now for he knew something was with him, inside the physical body and it was trying to remove him. Trying not to cry out he held on but he was being pushed from the inside until he felt his entire self being pressed against the shell as if threatening to burst through the skin. Suddenly the pressure eased and he relaxed wondering what was happening. Before he had time to gather his thoughts, another feeling was gushing over him and his attention was drawn above the bed. He rubbed his face as he knew he had to be dreaming. Floating above him was the most beautiful image of a young woman dressed in seductive black leather strips which barely covered the essential parts, and she was beckoning to him, her tongue moistening her lips while her eyes held him in an unrelenting gaze. Her arm reached out towards his groin and he felt himself instantly aroused as her fingers were calling him to go to her. His whole being was vibrating to an intense throbbing he couldn't control and gradually he let himself slide up towards her leaving another tenant to enter Milton's body at precisely the same time.

As the female shot away with her prey, Holland settled himself into the physical form, lifted the sheets, looked down and whispered "Not now, wrong time, wrong place" and with a smile let the body return to its relaxed state.

Nan would have further reason to be annoyed when she would find that her male protégée had been whisked away for other purposes but that was how this plan had to work for the evil to be overcome.

Souls like Liam Murray who had been taken before their allotted time, had to go through the adjustment process before being given tasks in their next stage of existence but Holland's body had reached it's run, and with him having been given the insight into his past experiences, he needed little or no time before he could be put to use. As this was a delicate operation using split second timing, Milton knew he could rely on this man to carry out this dangerous manoeuvre. Whatever Nan's plans had been for him, they could not compare to the important job he would be doing now.

Jo had the creature under her spell which wasn't difficult for he was of the baser element and prone to succumb to the slightest temptation, but she had in her hands a sample of the evil however small. Immediately they had cleared the hotel they were surrounded by members of one of the elite sections and whilst some took the evil pawn one way, others cloaked Jo and whisked her off to a safe holding zone.

The task for the elite was now to extract as much information as it could although they were aware it would be limited for the upper evil would not have been stupid enough to divulge its plans to one as naïve or dispensable as this specimen.

Jo was so pleased to be of use again as she felt she owed a debt to her own kind after being tainted with the evil. Those around her were still apprehensive in case any of it was still lurking in her, but whilst Milton was aware of this, there was no room for feelings and this situation called for tough measures, regardless of the cost. He knew that if anything had been deeply routed in her soul, they would reactivate it when required and he was almost dangling the carrot then whisking it away to draw them out.

Had Nan or any of her companions dreamt he was doing this, they would have been horrified. But they didn't and their innocence was just as important to the whole structure of the plan.

Holland got out of bed and took his first full look at his temporary body.

"Well, not bad, could have been worse." He couldn't resist a smile as he remembered Milton at the Stratford Hall. If he had known then that he would soon be the caretaker of such an eminent celebrity he would have thought that the pressure of work had finally got to him, but now – he was re-born and ready for battle.

"Better give this body a shower," he said to himself as he climbed out of bed and although the idea had a light hearted side, he was aware that this was going to be a very serious task and he didn't want to fluke it.

He was towelling himself dry when there was a delicate tap at the door.

"One moment please" he called softly, then donning a robe slowly unlocked the door and peered round the edge.

"Sorry to disturb you Mr Milton, only it's time for your breakfast." The young lad looked very apprehensive as he offered the tray.

Holland thought quickly, "Oh yes, must have ordered it; sorry I was very tired last night."

The lad had never been so relieved in his life, quite expecting a repeat of the rudeness experienced before. As he was beckoned into the room he took the tray to the table and turned to face Holland who was being prompted by his peers on how to act in order to regain his good name.

"Do hope my associate didn't alarm you last night."

"Your...your.. assoc...."

Holland put a fatherly arm round him "Can you keep a secret?"

The lad was excited now. "Ooh yes sir, you can trust me."

Holland was rather hoping he couldn't and that the lad would immediately relay everything he was about to say.

"Well," he moved away and then turned looking him directly in the eye "you see some of us have to escape from the media attention from time to time, and in order to do that, we have what we call 'stands'."

"Stands sir?"

"Stand ins. Impersonators. People who look something like us, so that while you are thinking we are in one place, we have a chance to chill out, you know be somewhere else."

The lads' mouth was opening wider by the minute, and now he wore the broadest smile possible.

"You mean that wasn't you last night. I said you looked different, you ask the others." He slapped his fist into his hand. "I knew it, I knew it."

If the situation hadn't been so serious Holland would have enjoyed this interchange but he knew the lad wouldn't be able to resist gloating to his workmates.

"But how did you swap, I mean he isn't here now, and I didn't see you at all."

Holland put his finger to his lips "I've locked him in the cupboard."

"Oh" then after a quick thought "no you haven't." He was laughing now and Holland was being hurried to get rid of him.

"Just a minute," he made his way to the wardrobe to get a tip but on opening the door he stood back in horror. "Is this what he was wearing?"

"Yes sir."

Holland fumbled in the jacket for a wallet but found some loose notes and gave one to the lad whose eyes opened even wider.

"Oh my   - thank you sir, you're the tops, I can't wait to......oh I mustn't say must I?"

Putting on a mock frown Holland whispered "Not a word" and put his finger to his lips.

As he ushered him out of the door he whispered in his ear "After you went off duty, my stand went out, and I came in. Satisfied?"

He sat down to enjoy his breakfast and his thoughts turned to the disgusting apparel in the wardrobe. He couldn't resist the urge to go and have another look and was relieved to find a solitary plain suit at the back, but his first instinct was that it would be too small for him, then prodded himself back to the current situation. He was in the body of Milton Warner, of course it would fit. It was his suit.

Finishing his breakfast he tidied the room then dressed and packed the belongings he wanted to keep. He left the garish clothes on the bed cast a final look round and went down to reception. It was obvious the word had already been spread for he was welcomed warmly by all the staff as they passed him.

The manager was at the desk ready to check him out and Milton leaned towards him and whispered, "Would you be so kind as to dispose of those appalling clothes my understudy was wearing. Give them to charity or something."

"It will be a pleasure Mr Warner, you just leave everything to me, and can I say what a delight it has been having you stay at our hotel." If he had grovelled any lower he would have been licking Milton's shoes and Holland found this rather amusing and unusual as people didn't always welcome visits from the police in such a manner.

"Arsehole "he thought but smiled back equally sweetly as he left a tip in accordance with Milton's usual manner.

"Thank God that's over" he thought as went down the few steps then stopped. How had 'Milton' got here? That was something he hadn't considered but his attention was drawn to a hand waving from the window of a rather smart looking vehicle which pulled round immediately and stopped in front of him.

"Morning boss."

"He's a runner for the crew, come to fetch you" was fed into his mind.

Milton threw his bags into the back and climbed into the front seat. "Thanks."

"S'alright. We wondered if you'd got here OK, so my gaffer checked and found you'd come in a taxi so he set me on to make sure you get there, if you know what I'm saying."

"Yes, yes, that's fine, thank you."

"That was some performance last night, knocked 'em dead you did."

The guides surrounding Holland wished the runner could have used another term, but it reassured them that his profile seemed to be in tact.

Holland thought for a moments then said "Well lets hope we can give them another one tonight," refraining from saying a 'repeat performance' as that was just tempting fate.

As they travelled, more and more information was being fed to give him a clear picture of the events and he was being coached as to how to act before and during the show. As Holland wasn't a clairvoyant or clairaudient, he was assured that one on a higher plane would be there with him and passing on real messages to loved ones so everything would appear normal. All he would have to do was be the front man and relay what he was told mentally, but at the same time be alert for anything that, by instinct seemed unusual or threatening. They soon arrived at the Mansion Rooms and the temporary Milton was ushered in to his dressing room to settle before checking the stage area.

"Oh Good Morning!" If the surprise was noticeable in Holland's voice it was nothing to the astonishment in Daryl's as he turned to look at his boss.

"Well, I can honestly say I am happy to see you," he was eying him from head to toe, grateful that the man had shed his peacock feathers."

"Daryl, I have a big favour to ask of you before it gets too busy." Holland was trying his best to act as much like the public figure he had seen before but of course he had no idea as to how to be with this man when nobody else was around.

"And what might that be?"
Milton himself would have picked up the new self assured attitude of his aide, no longer the servant jumping at every whim but Holland was feeling his way and it went unnoticed.

"Um, I seem to have packed very little for this tour. I need my show outfit. Any chance you could get hold of something, you know what I like," thinking "I hope to God he does".

"No problem, I'll have something sent over on the double."

"Good man."
There was almost an awkward moment when neither spoke but Daryl grabbed a plan of the stage area and moved two chairs together beckoning Holland to sit whilst he went over some the plan of the day.

"Pretty usual stuff really. The crew are all here getting on with things, then when you're satisfied with the set and your outfit has arrived" he grabbed a flyer "we go here and have a meal and there is a room where you can rest up until you come back for final checks."

"Your usual competent self." Although Holland was impressed and rather liked being looked after for a change, he knew he could not appear too overwhelmed as he was sure Milton would have taken it in his stride.

"You're doing just fine." The voice is his head was calming and very reassuring and it seemed familiar but he couldn't place it.

For now he took stock of the room with its own washroom, amply lit mirror and clothes rail. Simple and adequate for one evening but rather plain for someone of Milton's calibre.

CHAPTER 15

The evil's arms were still being monitored. It was hoped that the efforts to defeat it so far may put it off any further attacks, but this was not happening. The five arms from the existing mass seemed to be gathering strength as though harmful armies were being amassed to add strength to each one for a planned assault in the near future.

The one causing most concern for Milton was the one directed at the DeLux cinema complex in Peterborough, which was the adjacent building to where Milton was performing at his last venue of the mini tour on the following Thursday having played Nottingham on Tuesday and Leicester on Wednesday.

This particular arm was much thicker than the other four put together and that in itself had to have some significance, but again the question arose. When? Word had been received that it was already affecting the point directly underneath it but not spreading around the nearby area. This was something new. And what was so special about this target? The likes of Nan and Tabar thought it was just coincidence but Milton and the force knew better. His objective was working, and he knew it. Now was the time to put his plan into action and if successful would eradicate the whole thing in one fell swoop. There may be casualties, but he knew the risk and sometimes it was inevitable.

Although the spiritual forces on all levels were watching the evil sitting there pulsating and growing, it was only the elite forces that realised it wasn't confining its attentions to the surface of the earth but penetrating deep beyond the crust and was now injecting itself into the mantle. It was a possibility that it could even be aiming for the core itself, so this could be the new ploy to control the planet regardless of the spiritual activity surrounding it?

Milton was glad of Holland's assistance in keeping the attention on his physical body but it was only a matter of time before his enemy realised he wasn't there himself and they had probably even worked it out by now. But with using a decoy, Milton would soon know if he was the target, for if the evil was certain he was not in body, surely they would divert their attention elsewhere, so the next performance would be a definite indication.

As he mulled over all the facts, he wondered if they had tried to get him out to attack him on purely a spiritual plane, but the earthly devastation proved they wanted more. So maybe he was blocking the way to their success and by eradicating him, they would be left with a clear run to take charge of this space area, including the earth and everything surrounding it, even the whole solar system and possibly beyond.

He was pulled from his thoughts by one of the other elite forces warning him of their next attack. This was going to be a most dangerous manoeuvre and could have disastrous consequences if not successful. The message was passed down the ranks for all entities to protect themselves, a format used in cases of severe threat where each and every spirit in whatever form, strengthens their aura to maximum, the weaker ones taking cover with the stronger souls. Often a whole group would band together making an almost impenetrable shield. The danger in this case would be that no one could guess the outcome, and they didn't realise it wasn't only the evil they were in danger from but the effects of the elite attack.

Sensing Jean Paul was about to make one of his checks Milton instantly returned to his safe holding zone and awaited his friend. They quickly exchanged thoughts and it was agreed Jean Paul would monitor Holland and Jorg would stay with Daryl backed up by the minimum of guards. Ariel had been assigned to Jo, who may be called upon at any moment should the time be right. But for now all the higher levels had to prepare for the protection of every soul during the imminent onslaught, not that any knew what was going on, but that was the way of the elite.

Jo had been moved to an area well away from the action but could be returned in an instant when required. She was feeling more like her old self with the success of the recent little job fresh in her thought.

"So what do you think will be next?" She directed her question to her solitary guard, a rather dishy male by anyone's standards.

"Who knows?" the reply was warm and almost seductive.

Jo was getting an image of this spirit but couldn't quite make out any details as he seemed to be in a mist and was floating around, never staying in the same place for a second.

"Have we met before?" she asked.

"Would that make any difference?"

"God yes. I like to know who I'm sharing space with." The humour was exchanged but if she expected to get any sort of information she was disappointed.

"Me too." There was almost a tinkling laugh and the feeling that flowed between them was warm and loving.

"Well how about coming out of that fog and showing yourself. Come on let's have a bit of exposure, decent or otherwise." She was really feeling her old form returning.

"Would that make any difference?"

"Christ Almighty! You sound like one of those automatic machines that gives out the same message time after time."

"You wouldn't know me."

"I don't know a lot of you bods in this world, well not many at all to be honest, but I can still get to know folks."

"Especially handsome young ones." The laugh was in the reply.

"Now you're taking the piss." She was feeling like a toy being patted around at someone else's pleasure – someone she didn't even know.

Ariel was an expert at holding a target's attention and she now had this young thing in her grasp, and by not revealing an image of this dishy young man Jo thought was in presence, she could keep her interest indefinitely. Now and again she would give a quick flash of an impression to feed the girl's curiosity knowing she would be hoping for more. For now Ariel was without backup so as not to attract any attention to their location but she could summon help should she need it. So adept was she in her skills of transformation and communication, the enemy would have a hard job to keep up with her and on previous occasions were always following a cold trail. But she knew that an order could arrive at any time and she must be able to harness Jo's being in that split second, so that they would be gone before anything could trace the direction they had taken.

As Jo's capabilities were in no way able to match such a high spirit as her guardian, it meant that Ariel had to absorb Jo into herself and transport her in less than a blink of a human eye. That is they didn't travel along any given route, or fly on a flight path as earthbound people would understand, but transport from one position to another, almost disappearing and reforming elsewhere which was what made the likes of Ariel so difficult to monitor.

Nan and Tabar were consulting on the tactics which seemed to be operating without their knowledge. Jorg was being used which would seem to be in order but why Jean Paul whom they still believed to be beneath them in level should be working with Holland was a mystery, unless Holland wasn't important in which case they could have put him to better use. Had they known Ariel was in charge of Jo, they would have had further cause to wonder, for why would such a high spirit be allocated such a lowly one unless Jo was a danger from her previous evil contact? But the hierarchy never felt they had to explain to workers if they were not involved in any current plan, any more than Nan or Tabar would have confided in the likes of Sadie, but Nan always liked to know everything that was going on and would probably use all her wiles to find out what she could.

The spirit Liam, and Tommy were helping Liam Murray to adjust. He would normally have started on Sadie's level for a while but it was felt he needed the support straight away of the ones who had been protecting him so far, and if he could be helped to progress, he too could serve a useful purpose in the current situation. The likes of Sadie's charges were all very young in the spirit context and were often on their first transition so it was a new experience for them and needed compassion and care, a skill in which she was very adept. But Murray had already had a few earth lives and would not necessarily have needed the low level adjustment, so could quickly assume his level alongside his namesake but now simply using his earth surname.

Daryl had experienced no trouble in fitting 'Milton' out in suitable attire, not only for tonight's performance but others for the rest of the tour, knowing they would be well used on future events. Although Holland hadn't thought too highly of him before, considering him 'a bit of a prat' he had to admit that this man was responsible for much of Warner's success, for everything ran like clockwork and without him the show wouldn't have the professionalism it boasted. As he looked admiringly at the clothes, Holland's mind flew to the arranged lunch.

"God what does the man normally eat?"
Immediately the message was placed in his mind as to Milton's likes and dislikes.

"That could have been embarrassing." he thought but was reassured to know they had similar tastes. "Could have been awkward if he loved something I couldn't stand."
The answer was comforting. "It would have been sorted."

"I'm sure it would. Does he like a drink?"

"Not when doing shows. Just stick to coffee, no sugar."

"Ugh. Well I've had it before when I was trying to loose my belly, so I'll manage that."

"Also he doesn't smoke."

"Thank God I gave it up."

"Don't worry we'll guide you as to his habits at the time. He doesn't speak much while he is eating, nearly choked once so is very careful. That should make it easier for you to concentrate on what we tell you."

The next thing nearly knocked Holland off course. Taking advantage of his being alone and evil spirit presence not too active in the area at that precise moment, Milton returned to his body for a second, then left.

"Bloody Hell! What in Christ's name was that?" He leapt up from the seat trying not to cry out.

"Calm. We'll explain."

He sat down again. "Please do." His heart was pounding in his chest, but then he realised he didn't have either and decided it must have had an effect on Milton's body and it was that heart that had gone into overdrive.

"It was necessary for the owner to return to confirm he had not left the body for good."

The way the message was portrayed, Holland assumed the name had been omitted for a reason and by sending it in a nondescript form would not attract attention. There was a lot to learn in this world and if he had hoped for a little rest first, he would have been disappointed but he had taken on whatever was ordained and he was secretly enjoying it all.

He was brought back to earth by a tap on the door.

"Sorry to bother you Mr Warner but Daryl has requested that you take a look at the stage area, there's something he's not happy with." The runner didn't come in but peeked round the door.

"Right, tell him I will be there directly please."

"OK." and the lad disappeared without waiting to see if Holland was going to follow. Trying to walk with Milton's gait, which was something else he was trying to perfect, he made his way to the stage.

"Ah, boss" Daryl extended his arm to guide him to the front. "Don't like this, can you give me your opinion?" Although the term 'boss' was used, Holland couldn't help but notice that the words came out more like an order than a request.

"What's the problem?" he started then assumed an attitude he thought Milton would have used, "tell me, just what is it you don't like?"

This was normal to Daryl and Holland almost breathed with relief when he knew he had hit the right tone.

"Well just look at it." He was waving his arms almost panning the space from the spot where he was standing to the back of the stage. "This isn't deep enough. By the time your table and chair are in place, you're going to be wiping the noses of the front row. You need more air space – you're too cramped."

Holland stood still but moving his head from side to side following the track that Daryl had indicated. He stroked his chin to give more time for his instruction. Jean-Paul was in instant contact with Milton who sent back that he could cope with it.

"Hmm, see what you mean, but I'm sure it will work. We'll make it work."

"But boss, remember when you were in Edinburgh, the problem we had there?"

"But that was then and this is now. And as we seem to have no alternative, so be it."

Daryl opened his mouth to reply but before he had chance to utter a syllable Holland said

"Well it is I who will be out there, not you, so don't worry."

If Daryl felt put out he certainly didn't show it, on the contrary he seemed relieved that the old 'Milton' was back, for although Jorg had wiped certain knowledge from his brain, the memory of the false Milton was still there. As he told the crew to carry on, his mind turned over, as if he was trying to place bits of a mental jigsaw together. He could remember the spectacle Milton had made of himself, but now in his mind it was just the same person putting on some sort of act for reasons best known to himself. The idea of an imposter was being erased and for all he now knew, the object of his past affections was not only there in front of him but had always been. Jorg knew this part of the plan was now complete.

All levels were geared to protect themselves. Milton secretly hoped that the elite attack wouldn't interfere with his own plans, for it was likely that whatever the other team were doing, it wouldn't destroy the evil for good, whereas, if all went well, his would at whatever cost. He couldn't warn them of his own strategy as it would ruin everything and undo the years of planning to get this thing in just the right place to annihilate it. So he had to stay dormant for now and continue to plan his moves to the tiniest detail.

There was a hush. All levels from the earth up as far as Za's area waited. The earthlings felt as though a storm was brewing for there was an uncanny stillness everywhere especially around the giant heaving mass in the Midlands of England. Dark clouds masked the sun and darkness turned day into night, and although there was no solar eclipse, there might just as well have been.

Unbeknown to the earth inhabitants, the attack on the mass was like a giant vacuum sucking it away from its holding position in an attempt to drag it out beyond the earth's atmosphere and at the same time other forces were trying to detach it from its moorings, severing any hold it could have on the planet to whatever depth it had gone. It would then be despatched to the centre of the galaxy for its inevitable fate.

But this kind of operation, however successful in itself has an ongoing effect on everything connected with it, in other words it disrupts the very fabric of space and every thing however minute connected with it. Some felt the earth shake whilst in other areas tornados were wreaking havoc, volcanoes erupted and it seemed that more harm was been done than good. But which was the lesser evil? The elite's job was to rid the area of the mass but it wasn't a case of just sending it on its way, it had to be ripped out, before the next step of disposing it could be tackled. The shock waves extended into the spiritual levels and souls were in danger of being transported away from their holding or working zones, hence the warning.

From his highest point Milton surveyed the scene and knew this would be a set back for him.

"Unless……. I turn it to my advantage." was his first instinct. He could see that the operation was a failure, the evil almost growing with the energy being used to move it. In fact it was sucking the life force out of the elite squad until they had no option but to retreat while they could.

The elders of all levels were told to resume but stay alert as the mass may be expecting another onslaught and would be ready. It could also attack sooner than expected because of this and may take the opinion that it had been used as a feeler to see just what it could do. It would now know that the good didn't appear to be able to have any positive effect on it and that would in turn give it more hold.

It took a long time for the air to settle at all levels but the ripple carried on out into space and throughout the universe almost like a message that would keep going forever and this would, for whatever reason notify any element tuned in as to the attack. But with the vast amount of such messages filling space, it may never have much attention paid to it. So Milton weighed up the situation and knew exactly what he must do now.

The nurse looked at the patient asleep in the chair by the window. Not a bad looking young man, but the scars of whatever he had endured seemed etched on his features. As he opened his eyes, the suggestion of a smile flickered across his face and he raised himself from his relaxed position.

"Hello Simon." The nurse smiled back and turned her attention to the medication on the tray in her hand.

"Oh not more. I feel like a pin cushion."

"Don't worry, it's only a tablet, here have some water."

"It won't knock me out will it, only I ….his hand went to his head trying to remember what had happened "…I…I need to get my head together."

As if not wanting to be asked any questions she appeared to have ignored his remark and simply said "Come on now, doctor's orders" and handed him the small cup containing the drug. He toyed with the idea of pretending to swallow it, but guessed she might check his mouth so downed it with plenty of water and sat back giving the impression their contact was at an end.

When she left he sat musing, trying to grab any little memory he could to tell him why he was here. He had regained consciousness in what he thought must be a hospital, but he heard voices from somewhere saying he should be moved to a psychiatric ward. This jolted him to work to retrieve anything that would help. Had he had an accident of some sort, or a stroke? He was always being told that spending so much time in front of a monitor would 'do things' to his brain.

"How the hell did I get here?" Although he was thinking to himself, he almost expected an answer.

"Where am I? I don't recognise this place."

There was a soft soothing feeling creeping over him and he closed his eyes wishing he hadn't taken the medicine for he was finding it more difficult to remember anything now.

"Simon."

Suddenly he was alert, every inch of his body vibrated and his name came like a command for attention.

"Simon."

He tried to move but was held by an unseen yet comforting grip.

"Damned drug, why did I take it?"

"It is not the drug." The reply was almost like an automated reply to a question and there was silence as if it was waiting for the next one.

"Who's that?"

"Someone who's been looking after you."

"I know your voice but I can't…….."

"Simon. All will be told to you in time but for now you have to rest for a short while and do as we say."

"Who's 'we'?"

"You will be back to normal soon, you have progressed well. Trust."

"But I need to know more."

The warm feeling had gone and Simon felt alone but the experience had given him the capability of using his brain to put all the facts together that they were going to feed to him over the next few hours. It wouldn't be easy as he wouldn't understand the extent of the trauma he had endured, but they had to get his physical body dismissed from the hospital before he could be sectioned or committed to a mental unit. Work was already going on to feed false information into his records to prove that he was not insane but inject proof of overwork and eyestrain. Certain forces would work on the medical staff to ensure they were convinced enough to discharge him.

Then he too would be ready to fit into the plan.

The elite force returned to lick its wounds. Although it had not been absolutely certain it would succeed it had to be positive enough to believe it could, but never before had it encountered such a strength of force as this and the knowledge was all useful to build up a picture for future reference. Milton had already included the result in his formula for action but he was not going to execute his attack until the precise moment, for timing was the essential tool and he was doing his homework on all aspects.

He returned to his holding area where he would have an instantaneous meeting with Jean Paul who acted as coordinator for Ariel and Jorg giving Milton the complete picture with the minimum of contact.

Curiosity was the main enemy. Jean Paul knew Milton was staying at a safe distance from the evil but would never know just how important the information was he was feeding his friend. Had he ever guessed what a central figure he was supporting, he may have found it too overwhelming. He would fire the odd question to Milton to find out the general plan of operation from those supposedly above them, but was never given straight answers, even to the extent of pleading ignorance and being told he was just following orders. Although Jean Paul was often tormented with the lack of knowledge he knew he would only find out anything when the time was right, which wasn't always satisfying enough.

Having spent a relaxing afternoon almost alone, Holland felt a little happier about the forthcoming evening. Jean Paul had given him enough information to take the stage in a manner befitting the body he occupied and was happy enough to receive instructions to guide him through the procedure.

Fortunately, in that kind of entertainment, it was quite normal for a medium or the like, to pause whilst receiving messages and even speak back to the sender, so he could listen to what he was told by the intermediary and pass on details second hand, or even third hand if they were relayed via Jean Paul himself.

As he glanced at his watch he was conscious of someone next to him and he jumped up looking around but could see no-one.

"Don't be alarmed." The voice was in his head but he could hear it as plain as if the person was breathing in his ear.

"Who's there?" Holland stood still.

"We must be quick so listen carefully."

Holland's mouth opened as if to answer but closed as quickly. He nodded and waited, not questioning his actions.

"You are temporarily using Milton Warner's body, but don't forget that the real you is in the spirit world only and therefore you can be aware of much more around you now your inner eyes have been opened to the reality of your situation."

"Now I'm dead you mean?"

"Passed to another level is more accurate."

"Ok Ok. Now what?"

"We are making you aware of your guide, the one who will protect and inform you."

"Oh. You mean I will see him, or is it a 'her'."

"You may not see him at first but the more you become accustomed to your state, the clearer he will become."

"Oh, that sounds reasonable." Holland felt it was a rather tame reply but was at a loss to come up with anything better at this stage. It was all a lot to cope with, but he would, he had to.

"One other thing."

A feeling of slight dread flowed over him. Rather like the inevitable 'but'.

"Go on." He waited.

"You must always be on the alert. The more you see spiritually, the more you are open to attack by undesirable entities.

"There had to be a down side I suppose. Can you elaborate?"

"Don't worry too much for now, you will be well monitored but always be alert for that split second when something tries to get through to you, but it isn't who you think."

"Mmm. I think I follow. Funny business isn't it."

As the sentinel left, Jean Paul took up his post and Holland felt an immediate strength supporting him and now he could even place the source.

"I hope you're not watching while I go for a slash." he laughed to himself but realised the physical functions would have no interest for the 'other side' or so he hoped.

The ever faithful Daryl was waiting to escort his boss to the venue, assuring him that his show outfit was ready and waiting for him in his dressing room along with a supply of his favourite brand of water. Holland refrained from remarking about how efficient the man was as he felt Milton would have taken it as normal.

"Thank you, shall we go then?"

As they got into the car, Daryl's tone changed. He spoke as he drove off but keeping his gaze ahead all the time.

"Just one thing I think you should be aware of boss."

"Go ahead."

"Well, after you left, it seems there was a strange character hanging around. The crew told him to go, but then I found him hanging around outside your dressing room so I got the security people to oust him."

"What was he like?" Holland felt he had to ask but thought the watchers from the other world would already know.

"Funny really. I didn't know him yet......"

"Go on, there's something worrying you."

Daryl looked very thoughtful. "He was familiar, but I couldn't place him."

"In what way, his voice, his build?" Holland stopped there knowing he was going back into his policeman roll.

"Can't place it. But it's getting to me. I won't be satisfied until I've sussed it."

They drove on for a while then Holland said "Bet he won't have the gall to turn up tonight."

"He'll get his marching orders if he does." As if he'd had enough of the subject he rattled off some facts about the following three venues finished with a jubilant "And of course every one is a sell out."

"Be a bit worried if they weren't." Holland laughed and his aide felt a surge of the old Milton's true self which was only to be expected as Ariel swept through the car spreading the vibes Milton had instructed.

They soon arrived at the Mansion Rooms and were ushered in away from any crowds which were gathering in the hopes of still getting a ticket which had been returned for re-sale. As Daryl indicated for the dressing room door to be unlocked, there was a gasp from the staff member as the view from inside met them, for adorning the mirror were loads of cards from fans and on a side table the largest display of red roses in a basket. Dismissing the girl, Daryl held out his hand for the key.

"As arranged I hold the key for the duration of Mr Warner's time here."
She meekly did as requested and turned to go but cast a lingering admiring glance at Milton. Holland felt quite honoured, then realised it wasn't him she was ogling but someone else's body. But why not enjoy the moment.

Milton had done several lightning visits to the place, never staying for more than a millisecond and fortunately hadn't drawn any attention to himself, but having gleaned all the information he needed, he instructed Ariel to take over the important task he had set.

"Only get her at the very last moment." He imparted and Ariel knew exactly what he meant.

"You can't bring that dog in here sir." The front of house staff had confronted a man, very similar to the one seen earlier, yet different in many aspects.

"But he goes to all Mr Warner's readings. Sits in the front row. Is on the same wavelength. He picks things up. He warns him of bad spirits."

"Call the manager," the usher ordered and within a minute the man arrived.

"What is all this fuss?" he demanded.

"The gentleman says he takes his dog to all Milton Warner's events."
The manager turned to the man with an apologetic "I'm terrible sorry sir, but there are no dogs allowed, except guide dogs, and as this isn't of that category, it won't be allowed into the hall."

What happened next had everyone in the area spellbound for the dog stood up, faced the manager and held his gaze as if frozen by it. The dog then slowly rotated on the spot taking everyone into his gaze whilst his companion followed his line of vision but staying behind him so that the animal had a clear view in front of him at every moment. When he had completed a full circle, he sat in front of the manager and looked up into his eyes. The man on the end of the lead stood with the suggestion of a satisfied smile on his face and asked very slowly and quietly "So may we now be allowed entrance please?"
It didn't seem to come as a surprise to any of the crowd as the manager said "Of course, on this occasion, it will be permitted, due to the special circumstances explained."

As if released from a trance, the gathering carried on as nothing had happened and continued to make their way to the hall allowing the man and his dog to follow the usher to a seat on the front row, when having watched his master settle, the dog then lay, head on paws with his eyes fixed on the stage area.

Jo couldn't contain herself. Ariel, in the form of the same young handsome male was telling her she would be needed soon for another important role.

"Well let's hope it's as good as the last one only more satisfying, if you get my drift."

Ariel was amused by this young spirit, feeling she was like a breath of fresh air lifting the gloom which was only too apparent but she knew Jo was still in the recovery stage from the evil influence and must be carefully watched. The superior spirit knew it was not for her to question the moves of her elders and if Milton wanted to use the girl, that's how it must be, but she feared for her safety in the spiritual sense knowing it could have a never ending effect. She liked her and was determined to do all in her power to protect her.

Although Ariel was carrying out orders from an unknown high entity, she was still, and always would be, ignorant of Milton's status. The elite forces main weapon remained their anonymity and on this operation she imagined he was relaying orders from his superiors.

"Come on. You're wanted." Ariel got the message and relayed it to Jo.

"What're we doing? Where're we going?"

"Calm it for a minute." Ariel held her a safe distance away from the venue and explained.

"They want you to be an observer. Do you understand? You just watch and report."

"Yes, yes. Bring it on." Jo was eyeing this image with some desire that could impede the plan. Ariel knew she had to present herself in such a way that she could keep the spirit's attention solely on the job in hand without distraction.

"I'm not coming, I have other work." She noticed the disappointed look and knew this was the right move. Another companion is joining us. You will take orders from her."

"I suppose so." was the reluctant response.

Ariel used her talent of multi images and placed a slightly older female at Jo's side.

"This is Min, she knows what to do. Stay alert." And with that the male image had gone.

"Oh. So now what happens?" Jo tried not to appear deflated.

The image of Min looked at her for a moment then asked "Are you quite sure you're ready for this?"

"They picked me didn't they, so I must be wouldn't you say?"

'Min' sent a controlling vibe around her. "Let's get one thing straight young lady. This is not a pastime, it's not a holiday. This is serious business. Now if you feel it is beyond your capabilities, you had better say now, or you will jeopardise not only the whole operation but the lives and souls of many."

She knew she had Jo's full attention and if it needed a bit of animosity to keep it, that's what would be used.

"I know what you are saying." In bodily form Jo couldn't have looked her in the eye and she knew she had to toe the line or be sent back to the boredom of Sadie's level.

"Hm. Right. We are a team and we work together. I receive the orders and pass them on to you as you are not high enough to receive them directly. And don't take that personally, it is a fact."

"Oh, I wasn't going to," she had calmed a bit now.

"We are going to the next venue of Milton Warner in Derby."

"Oo good."

"To repeat, you will watch and follow instructions. No going off on your own course, you must, must, must stick to the rules."

Although Jo hadn't welcomed the swap in guardians, she felt the power and command of this new one and was beginning to feel a slight relief for the fact was dawning that this had the hallmark of something big and she knew she had to respect Min's seniority.

"I do understand and I will do everything as you say."

"Good," there was warmth in the word and Jo picked up on it instantly. "Well, if you're ready, we must be off. I won't be at your side all the time but you can call me in an instant. Just think my name, but I'm sure you know that." Ariel had to give the impression they had just met and that she was covering all angles, almost as if she was ticking things off on a list.

"Yes, yes, I'll do it. I'm ready for the action… I mean watching like you said."

All the higher spirits were perfectly aware that, even with the best intentions at the time, Jo was so headstrong, that given the opportunity she would take matters into her own hands because she felt that was the right thing to do. It was precisely this factor that Milton was going to use to his advantage. Apart from the task she had been given, which may have had some use but was not actually needed, she was the perfect distraction to any on-looking foe, so if a situation arose, or was manufactured and she took the bait, she could lead the enemy away from the important area for long enough for the major plan to be put into operation.

The likes of Nan would consider it fool hardy, but the likes of Nan were not in the elite forces and never had to make such important or instantaneous decisions as those of the choice few. The lower levels may wonder and criticise, but they would never have a glimpse of the select world for there had been many occasions when the intervention of such as Milton had saved the entire solar system and beyond including every spiritual plane in the surrounding area.

Jean Paul took the opportunity of having Holland alone while Daryl did his usual flitting making last minute checks before the show.
"There's something very important I have to make you aware of."
Holland focused on the mirror in front of him, Milton's solitary form returning the stare, but there was someone else appearing over his shoulder. He gave a short gasp.
"Who are you?" The feeling was soothing and calm and he didn't feel it could be harmful.
"The one who's been guiding you. You have been listening to my instructions."
"Oh God! Now I see you. What's your name?"
After a moment he heard "There is no harm in you knowing. It's Jean Paul."
There was no time for proper introductions or pleasantries and he continued.
"What do you see in the mirror?"
"Well, the Milton chap of course."
"Be prepared for what I am about to say. If you could see yourself as other spirits are seeing you, you would be looking at the same image."
"What? Not me?"
"It is necessary, partly for the protection of your own soul, but equally essential for any evil onlookers to think Milton is back in his body."
Holland leaned forward to get a closer look. "How do you do that?"
"Just one of our tricks. Just remember for now, you ARE Milton Warner and nobody else. Think as he would. Wipe your own identity. Everything depends on it."
The image faded leaving Holland still staring ahead. Something in his inner self told him that this was what had to happen, and the severity of the task flooded his mind. With unseen help from Jean Paul, Holland's spirit seemed to evaporate, and Milton stood up, turned to take his usual look in the long mirror and waited for Daryl's return.

With only minutes to go, the hall was buzzing with anticipation. The usual hope that people would receive messages from their loved ones was very evident and there would be a few disappointed ones leaving at the end. The man and his dog had not moved and both had their attention fixed on the centre spot of the stage area. Although raised, it wasn't so high that anyone had to strain their necks to look up.

Other people paid little attention to them as the earlier brainwashing had convinced them this was a perfectly normal occurrence, and they were more interested in their own affairs than bother with him. The person in one of the next seats had offered a smile but as he didn't turn his head it went unnoticed.

The doors closed, the house lights dimmed slowly and a hush fell over the whole room. At this point the dog sat upright, his gaze still fixed on the same spot. Jo had been brought in at this point and told to move anywhere except on the stage near Milton. This should have been familiar to her from her previous visit, but her spiritual mind was playing a few tricks as though something else was closing doors on her memories, yet opening new ones on things she didn't understand. Shaking herself, she floated over towards the wings noticing many souls hovering over the audience. As she neared the stage the entire hall was becoming crammed with eager spiritual relatives trying to be first to relay a message and at one point she felt impeded. As she managed to cross the front row, the dog's gaze followed her movements and watched her take up her position stage left, which was on the right as he watched. The man also was studying her and after a while she found this a little unnerving, but Jo's rebellious side shot to the fore and she returned the 'look' until they both returned their attention to the centre of the stage.

"Bloody cheek." she muttered to herself, "have they never seen a ghost before?" As soon as she had the thought it dawned on her that they were the only ones who had even recognised her presence and she began to feel a bit uneasy again.

"I'll have to keep my eye on those couple of weirdoes." she thought but as Milton's arrival was announced she turned her attention to his entrance.

"Oh I remember him. How could I have forgotten?" Her mind was playing all sorts of tricks now and she felt she was opening memory boxes trying to place him more clearly.

"Couldn't have shagged him, I'd have remembered that." Then after a minute "Wish I had though."

Ariel was flitting in and out of Jo's being, and could never cease to be amused by this girl but it was time for more serious matters and she pressed the spiritual button to start the process using all her positive power for the protection of this innocent pawn.

CHAPTER 16

Milton stood in the centre of the stage with a dim light beaming down on him from directly over his head. As Holland had made his way from the dressing room the truth had hit him. Not only did he have the appearance, both physically and spiritually of Milton, but he was feeling every aspect of the earthly body. He had barely had time to get used to his new state before he had been planted back into a living breathing earthling and it was rapidly becoming very familiar with it, for as Jean Paul had instructed, he was now Milton Warner. The phrase kept repeating itself until he was actually believing it.

He stood motionless waiting for the crowd to settle. Any previous worries he may have had about how he would perform vanished and his arms lifted slightly as he moved forward a couple of steps. Jean Paul had promised there would be a medium helper who would relay messages for him, but that was of no consequence. He felt alone and confident.

Jo watched excitedly, her vibrant energy attracting any passing entity who may wish to home in on her. She was falling under this man's spell and was resisting the urge to rush forward and …..and what?

"Wish I'd got a body, I've give him something to remember me by." The frustration being stirred up in her by Ariel was sending ripples around her space and reaching out as it was fuelled more and more.

Milton had homed in on a lady to his right and was relaying a message from her Mother which immediately brought tears to her eyes and hankies were being grabbed by several now. Ariel was on her usual form. Not only was she focusing Jo to draw attraction to Milton but she was the instigator behind the readings. It wasn't easy with such a mass of eager spirits but she had learned to be selective and chose the most entertaining and realistic ones. She didn't need to be near him but projected her thought as she travelled around.

That would have been enough for most spirits even of high levels but Ariel was insatiable. She was like a sponge. The more she was given to do, the more she seemed capable of, a talent which was often used when too many presences would have ruined an operation. Also she didn't question but carried out any task to her limits knowing she was a small cog in a much bigger pattern. Her ability to divide herself into completely different beings yet still function perfectly in every form simultaneously was a skill acquired by only a few.

Jo, although she was transfixed with Milton decided to take a peek around the rest of the hall. She floated from the wings and was drawn to the man and his dog again. The dog sat up and they both stared in her direction which was ignored by the audience near them as they were now under Milton's spell hoping they would be next for a message.

For a moment Jo remained where she was, just to the right of the stage but near the first row of seats. She would never know why she didn't just ignore them or carry on with her little wander, but something made her return to her original position at the in the wings.

"Stupid morons." she muttered. Why do they have to flock here in such a bloody throng, haven't they got anywhere else to go for a connection?" She vented her anger on the growing heaving mass which seemed to be cramming every corner, but her annoyance also fuelled her presence there and Ariel decided to poke her fire a bit further.

"There is a young lady here." Milton's voice spread across every seat and all faces were upon him. This could be their moment. He scanned back and forth, their heads turning as if at a tennis match.

"Josephine. Come forward."

Everyone was looking around to see where he was indicating but his arms had dropped to his sides and he turned slowly and faced Jo. He raised his upstage hand and beckoned.

"What me?"

He nodded. "You. Come and pass your message."

"I haven't got a bloody message you idiot."

He smiled then turned to the audience "She's very shy, never done this before." A ripple of laughter was heard as this was a moment of relief during the intense moments the people had experienced. But all expected a young person in body to walk onto the stage.

"Perhaps I should explain." He gave one of his disarming smiles causing a few hearts to flutter. "She has passed over."

"I didn't pass over, I was bloody murdered. Tell them that."

"If you wish." His calmness was having an effect on her almost as if she was being hypnotised.

All eyes were on him now. This was something different, something they hadn't expected. Nobody had seen this on television before or even at one of his shows.

"This lady," his left arm went out again beckoning her to come onto the stage, "this young lady was taken tragically before her time. Not accidently, but by the hand of another."

The gasp shook the room and many put their hands to their mouths in horror, but all wanted to know more. Milton had them in the palm of his hand like never before.

"Come forward my dear. Don't be shy." he coaxed.

"I'm not shy and I'm not a showpiece," she was floating towards him as her anger rose.

Ignoring her outburst he said "Would you like to tell us your name?"

"You've told them. What are you getting at? You're not such a clever sod are you?"

He coughed. "I won't repeat that word for word. She is - um – shall we say a lively soul."

A few giggles were heard but most wanted to know more. He let the air settle again.

"The name by which you are known is Jo, you hate Josephine don't you? I was expecting you to correct me."

The air currents being stirred between this exchange were being felt quite strongly now and the true Milton was monitoring every attention it was attracting, sifting out the simply curious while concentrating on the evil he was enticing. For they would in turn be monitoring his activity and he knew he was going to be trailed until the final confrontation.

Ariel was satisfied that her efforts were bearing fruit but knew she had to keep the momentum going or the attention may drift.

"So Jo," Milton waved towards the audience, "what would you like to say."

A sudden inspiration wafted over her, not of her own doing but from Ariel although she prodded the girl into using her own expression.

"Well that woman shouldn't have nicked that teaspoon on the way in here. Got it in her bag she has."

"Um," Milton looked straight at the lady in question. "I'm not sure if I should divulge that."

"Oh please, "she called out "I'd love a message, is it from Bill?"

"Er, not exactly but Jo says she'll think of you next time you have a nice cup of tea."

"No I didn't, what a load of shit! Why don't you say it like it is?" Jo exploded and wished she could give out messages in her own way, not all this prim and proper false stuff he was spreading. Close up he didn't look so attractive now and she felt rather silly at her previous feelings.

The lady had gone quite red and was explaining to her companion that Bill always liked his tea, but knowing full well that wasn't what had been meant.

"And that old cow. She's fiddling that that chap's….."

"Yes all right Jo, maybe that's enough for now." Turning to the audience he said "She is such a lively soul but doesn't always express herself in the way we would appreciate."

"You mean she swears?" came from the back of the hall and everyone laughed.

"Well you could say that, very much so." Milton said.

"Then lets hear it how she says it." Again laughter but Milton held up his hand.

"Sir, there are limits as to how we portray messages and we don't want to give offence to those who wouldn't take it too kindly."

"One more and that's it then." Jo was pushing Milton.

"She says one more, what do you say? Do we let her have the final word?" The applause filled the room with cries of "Yes let her" and "swear words and all."

"Go on then my dear. Who to you want to address?"

"Eh? Oh who do I want to speak to? Well then…." Her thought trailed off as she pointed to the front row in the direction of the man and his dog. Milton followed her gaze then turned back to her for the seat was empty and both had gone.

Knowing he had to cover this, Milton said "I'm afraid the gentleman who was to receive the message has stepped out for a moment so we may have to come back to that." Then hastily he said "Well thank you for visiting us Jo, I hope to encounter you again."

As the clapping rose from the hall she hissed "Not if I have anything to do with it, you're nothing but a boring old fart."

Milton waved in her direction then took his position at the back of the stage and as the lights dimmed the first part of the show was finished.

Daryl's mobile had been vibrating in his pocket and as soon as he had escorted his boss back to the dressing room he whipped it out and looked at the messages. They were from his sister and the tone showed some concern so he excused himself from Milton and rang her. She answered as if she had been waiting for his call.

"Oh, I'm sorry to bother you, with you having a show and that, but something's not right and I felt I should tell you."

"Ok Sis, I'm listening, now say it slowly" then with some urgency "it's not junior is it?"

"No, No he's fine now ta. No it's Flop."

"Flop? What's the matter with him?"

"That's just it he's been acting sort of strange."

Daryl took a deep breath. "In what way strange?" He knew it must be weird enough to cause her to ring him on tour.

"Well it was about seven o'clock, he looked straight at the wall as if he was watching something, only there wasn't anything there, then he turned round slowly, but that's not all. He went to the little table and there was a flyer you'd left there. You know the one of the tour. You always bring one for junior."

"Yes, I know. What happened then?" Daryl wished she would get to the point as they hadn't a lot of time before the second part.

"Well, that's just it. He picked it up in his teeth and took it to where he'd been looking and sat down with it under his paws, Then he lay down with his head on his paws, still watching the wall. Now he's got up and gone and eaten his meal, been out and now is curled up on his bed as if nothing happened."

"But he's OK now?"

"Seems normal enough. He's asleep and looks contented, almost like a different dog. Don't know what came over him. He must have got into bad habits when you had him at your office."

"Oh that must be it." Daryl gave a small laugh to give the impression he wasn't worried and said "Look I'm glad you rang, but don't worry any more. Everything's fine here. He was probably just doing one of those unexplainable thing dogs do. He's clever you know."

"I guess you're right. I feel better now – talking to you – you know."

"I know, and sis you did the right thing. Got to go now. I'll call you tomorrow."

"Thanks Daryl, Night."

He may have fobbed off the dog's behaviour but this new Daryl was aware something was going on beyond his understanding. Something was niggling at the back of his mind that he would find out before long.

"Everything all right?" Milton was gazing at him enquiringly and he jumped.

"Oh sorry. Flop's doing strange things, nothing to worry about."

"Dog's rarely do strange things, they only seem strange because we don't understand. He will be fine." and he turned back to the mirror checking his hair was in place.

"I wish I did understand. You'd think working with you all these years would have rubbed off a bit more wouldn't you?"

"Who knows my friend?" Milton smiled stood up, put his jacket back on. "Let's see what the next session brings."

Although it had only been two days since Simon's trauma, the spiritual powers had done a magnificent job in restoring as much of the original character as possible. Physically he felt tired and his mind was settling for it had been virtually cleaned down to nothing and restored with only the necessary memories needed for his future task. He would not remember the horror of being trapped in the time lock unless it was deemed important at a later date, meaning that any knowledge would be fed to him like data into a computer. He would re-enter the world in his old format, not wasting words, always studying a monitor and treating most of those around him with utter disdain.

With a little intervention from the spiritual source, the doctors decided he was possibly suffering from overwork and eyestrain causing him to hallucinate at bit, but there was no sign of a stroke or anything serious, and as they studied his records they could find no reason to refer him to another unit or keep him, and with beds being needed urgently they said that if he was still the same the following morning he would, after being discharged by the duty doctor, be allowed to go home and he would be under the care of out patients. They would have liked him to have had somebody at home and were concerned about him living alone but he assured them that was how he liked it and he had a couple of friends who were only on the end of the phone if he needed help, or just someone to talk to. There was still a question mark over his lack of relatives, and the only contact number in his wallet seemed to be his solicitor who had been informed, but obviously it was the man's business and they were not going to find out anything further.

Milton was pleased with the way Simon had progressed and praised the work of the restoration group. It hadn't been by accident or chance that his two aides had come to work with him, as the whole circumstances had been planned many years before, even to the fact of both being made redundant at the same time. Now all the players were falling into place although they didn't realise the importance of their roll, past present or future.

It was often necessary for a highly intelligent spirit to take a form other than human, thus able to mingle at will and draw less attention to themselves than they would as a man or woman or even a child. Flop had also been part of the jigsaw and had been placed near enough for Milton to have him to hand at a moment's notice, not in the physical sense but Fluke, to give him his soul name was an expert at this kind of operation and had used many guises in the past, all with a very high success rate. Working in conjunction with Ariel they had given the illusion of a man and his dog at the performance whilst soaking up even the tiniest suggestion of being monitored or any attention coming from the evil source. Flop's behaviour was simply mirroring his movements and when Fluke returned to the body, the dog appeared at peace and happily asleep. That part of the job done, they let the visual images evaporate at a moment when Milton had the audience's concentration at its height. This pair had executed it so masterfully that even Jo had not seen through the façade, but she was of too low a level to be aware of such things.

Appearing as Min, Ariel joined Jo as she was floating near Milton's dressing room. The young spirit jumped as if she had be caught doing something she shouldn't. Up to this point she had almost forgotten her, so involved was she with what was going on in the stage area.

"Well? What have you observed?" The tone was like a teacher checking on the pupils.

"Eh? Oh yes, you wanted me to keep an eye out, so to speak didn't you." Jo realised she had noticed very little and felt as though she had slipped up.

"That was the general idea." The tone was cutting and Jo was beginning to dislike this one wishing the dishy young man had been allowed to stay with her. She felt her back come up and felt like telling Min that if she wanted to know anything, why didn't she do it herself. "Boring job anyway," she mused "thought it was going to be something important."

The next thing shook her back to attention,

"It may appear boring to you and not full of exciting action but you are here to do a job and you do not have to be informed of all the details."

"How..how…. did you know what I was thinking?" She would have gone bright red had she had the body to do it with.

Her question was ignored and Ariel knew she was churning up all sorts of emotions in this girl which would keep either her temper or her attraction to any tasty male just under the surface. Anything that would keep the enemy guessing would suffice, because she reckoned that they wouldn't dare disregard her just in case. By donning the mask of a disciplinarian she knew she could keep her on her toes for now until such time as she may have to fight for her very existence in whatever form. But she felt a warmth for this feisty young thing and would love to have praised her for her actions up to now but that may have left Jo complacent and she couldn't take the risk.

"Well, I have other jobs to do so I'll leave you for now, but please remember to stay alert, if you think that won't be beyond your capabilities." The image of Min disappeared.

"The old cowbag. Who the hell does she think she is" Jo ranted "if it's so important why doesn't she do it? She's like one of those frustrated old virgins that used to be in charge of the office and made the junior do all the shitty jobs while they sat on their perches pretending to work. I've seen them. Never had a man and jealous of those that do."

Ariel was amused as she watched. This was just what she wanted and now Jo would be belligerent and take risks just to get her own back on Min and with a little poke to help her on her way, the game could commence.

Nan was still feeling a little put out at not having been brought up to date about the evil mass which was becoming more threatening by the second. She had requested a conference with Za to voice her concerns about the concentration on the Peterborough venue and she felt they were letting Milton walk straight into the trap, although he must surely be aware of it. Also why had he been in hiding and now had suddenly appeared when he was in the firing line. It didn't make sense.

"And I would like to know why Jorg has been seconded to one person when we have numerous tasks for him."

"It is essential to the operation for many of us to remain uninformed." Za gave his usual non committal reply but she picked up that even he didn't know the answer. She felt brave enough to push it further.

"So the orders are coming from a much higher source." She was making a statement not expecting a reply.

"I imagine we will all know when the time is right." And with that he had gone.

She turned to Tabar who didn't share all of her curiosity and had guessed that secrecy was one of the main tools for she had encountered it before and knew it had to be that way regardless of individual feelings. For now she tried to coax Nan into carrying on in her own efficient way saying that they wouldn't want to jeopardize anything by interfering. Nan wasn't totally impressed as she had expected more support from her companion but knew she was right and she returned to her other pressing tasks.

It was time for the second half. Daryl escorted Milton to the stage and watched him take his place in the usual spot and as the lights came up the cheer from the house was deafening as everyone eagerly awaited more action. There was such a positive vibe in the place being fuelled by the spirits in attendance but the audience didn't realise it thinking it was just the talents of the man they were watching.

Jean Paul had been especially diligent and may not have appeared to have been playing much of a part, but he had been the main contact to the real Milton who still had to keep as far away for as long as he dare. Also it was Jean Paul's job to keep the persona believable and whilst Ariel was relaying the messages, he had been making sure Holland as Milton had reacted absolutely correctly in every detail. Jorg would not have been aware of this as the two were working on such a high level, not many would have been conscious of it.

But one thing had come to their notice which was now a major threat, something that none of the lower levels had the power to see. As with earthly devices, spirits for whatever reason can have a kind of antenna attached to them, either for tracking them to extract information or simply in cases of security to keep an eye on their movements if their actions are suspect. The ones used by the good powers are of a pale blue and less than a hair's width so go unnoticed to the untrained entities. But the ones attached by the evil are of a dark charcoal colour and it was one of this kind that Jo was connected to now and must have been put there during her recent experiences, so all her movements would have been monitored since then and up to this time, and no one had been aware of it.

Milton contacted one of his elite group who did an immediate check and confirmed the trailer was of the highest kind which was why it had not been detected even by them until now. Also it seemed to have been lying dormant which would also cloak it and if they now knew it was there it could only mean that it had been activated. If this was the case, it meant that Milton's plan was working and Jo was now being used as a mole right in the heart of the operation. In a way it was a major step forward in crushing the evil, but it also put the souls of those closest to it in danger of eternal extinction. Therefore the tactics now moved up a notch and everything to the smallest detail must be monitored and each move executed with maximum precision.

"Ladies and Gentlemen" the announcement floated across the hall, "will you please welcome again to the stage – Milton Warner."

The applause was tremendous for most of the audience were avid followers and the sceptics had mostly given up on him during previous shows, regardless of whether he was appearing live or on television. Any defamatory comments were now dismissed and only budding reporters would try their luck at exposing him but it was always to no avail so they turned their attention to more profitable pickings.

"Milton. Milton. Milton." The chant was so strong the floor was vibrating and continued until he raised his arms and everyone fell silent. The man and his dog had been forgotten and the seat in the front row was now occupied by a plain looking studious young man to whom nobody gave a second glance.

Holland was now so well groomed in his role it was becoming second nature to him and he didn't have to concentrate on every move, or how he spoke for he was a puppet and his strings were being pulled for him. It was almost as if his true self had been put to sleep for a while and he was simply in a dream. He addressed the audience giving out several messages to please as many receivers as possible before selecting one or two to specialise. Suddenly a voice came through with some urgency and Ariel picked up on it immediately.

"Tell Sadie, her friend is in danger."
Fortunately Milton was in the middle of the last message she had given him and her attention turned to this voice.

"Who are you?"
"Her Mum. Please tell her." And she had gone.

The applause followed the reading and Milton stood waiting. It was silent and he put his hand to his head and played for time.

"I do apologise my friends, there are so many and they are all trying to pass their messages but they are so eager they are all talking over one another."
This brought a little ripple of amusement and one gent called out "Bring that Jo back, and let her tell it how it is." This caused even more laughter and Milton was glad of the interlude giving time to receive his next message. Ariel sent him two in quick succession to keep him going then appeared as Min at Jo's side.

"Bloody hell…I mean you startled me. Good isn't he?"
Ariel was tempted to remind Jo that she thought he was a boring old fart, but kept to Min's manner as she replied "You shouldn't be startled if you have your wits about you. That is why you are here in case you had forgotten."
Jo felt her proverbial back rising. What was it about this creature that rubbed her up the wrong way?" Being Jo she could never keep the lid on her emotions

for long and as Ariel had hoped her temper flared strengthening her protective shield but attracting normally unwanted entities.

As this was being acted out the true Milton warned Jean Paul to guard Holland even closer while he could scan the surrounding area. There was no doubt now, Jo's antenna was growing in size and power and would soon be perceived by some of the higher levels although many would not know what it was, never having encountered one. He sent a message to Ariel to get away from her at present.

"Now where have you gone?" Jo turned a complete circle but there was no evidence of Min.

"Oh piss off then, frustrated old cow!"

Had the man in the audience heard that he would have been delighted but she only said it to herself, or so she thought for Ariel was glad she had shown this reaction. But on the darker side Milton realised that this was fuelling the evil and he now had the bait well oiled to attract it even more.

"Come on squire, get Jo, we liked her."

"We want Jo. We want Jo. We want Jo."

The crowd were in full swing some on their feet waving their arms. Milton slowly raised one arm and everyone sat down again and when silence resumed he turned almost on a pivot as though he had been put on a turntable and equally slowly brought his arm down until he was pointing directly at Jo and this time he could actually see her very clearly.

"Did you hear that?" he called "They want Jo."

Ariel gave her a slight push and as she was caught unexpectedly, she almost shot forward until she was almost pressed against him.

"Steady on my dear," he gave the impression of pushing her away "let's take it gently shall we?"

"I was shoved out here, you know that......"she stopped and turned her attention to the audience, mostly who had their mouths gaping open.

"She's looking at you now." Milton told them.

Jo's humour rose to the surface. "Tell that bloody lot they look like a load of fish with their gobs open."

"She says I have to tell you......." Holland trailed off as Jean Paul took over and put him in a trance. He stood now with his head down his arms hanging loosely at his sides. Ariel moved Jo to the side of him and let her inner voice come through him.

"Can't I speak for myself?" The shock of hearing her words coming out of a man's body made her stop, but if it shocked her it was nothing to what it did to the audience. This was another 'first', for Milton was not known as this kind of medium, he merely passed on the messages, he never had his body taken over with wandering spirits and this would have really given the disbelievers food for speculation. After a moment she felt a little more adventurous.

"Oh don't mind him. Bit straight laced for me don't you agree?"
Nobody moved.

"Christ Almighty, have you all been turned to stone?"
Again the whole audience was as if frozen to the spot.

"Well, this is a barrel of laughs I must say. I come here and you won't even talk to me."
There was a slight stir from the back as the man who had called out earlier rose to his feet.

"I'll talk to you Jo."

"Bloody Hell. A live one among the zombies!"

"Have you come here with a message Jo?" He didn't know what to say now she was here.

"Do I know you? No, I don't think I do, well then I haven't got so much as a flying fart for you so sit down and shut up."
This caused quite a stir in the room as it wasn't what anyone expected. Milton still stood motionless. The heckler wasn't going to be made a fool of by some playful spirit and called out "Then you'd best be going back to where you came from you common little bitch."
If he thought that would be the end of it he was mistaken. Jo didn't take that kind of crap from anyone and she certainly wasn't going to from a voice in the back row.

Extracting her self from Milton's body she flew to the man and hovered over him. Although he couldn't see her he could feel her presence as if she still had her own body, and as she struck him across the face he was knocked sideways and if the person next to him hadn't steadied him he would have gone to the floor.

"Why you nasty common little bastard." He shook his fist into the air.

"Bastard yourself, bastard, dirty bastard." He felt the words almost spitting in his face and he struck out blindly now trying to make contact.

"Jo. Return." The voice echoed across the seats and everyone gasped some almost sobbing in fear. The voice was deep and powerful and not familiar.

"Jo. You will return."
There was something very unreal about the whole proceedings and every person was transfixed wondering what would happen next.

Milton slowly stood bolt upright and his hands raised to chest level. He looked round the stage, then out to the audience, gave a slight shake of the head and said very quietly "I apologise, I don't know what happened then. Is everyone all right?"

Relief was spreading quickly through the room and there were nods and whispers of "Yes thank you," as they settled back.

"Good. Can you give me a moment please?"

Daryl was beckoning from the wings for Milton to leave the stage but all he got in return was a shake of the head and a hand gesture which showed Milton would carry on. He moved his chair nearer to the front of the stage and sat, taking a drink of water. As if on cue the whole audience burst into a round of applause.

Holland had no recognition of what had taken place and carried on in his Milton role.

"I will find out later, but I regret I have no knowledge of that episode and I thank you for your support." He cast his eye to the young man in the front row who gave the slightest nod in response.

The man at the back stood up. "May I say something squire?"

Milton stood. "Please do, but won't you come and join me here and he pointed to a sofa at the side of the stage."

"Oh well, I don't know about that. I just felt it was my fault you see"

Milton didn't reply but repeated his invitation by nodding to the sofa. Whoever was with the man must have nudged him into going and within seconds he had shaken Milton's hand and they were both sitting together.

After the usual introductory pleasantries Milton asked what the man had meant.

"Well, it was me what called her."

"That doesn't make it your fault. These spirits have a way of their own you know and some of them are very powerful, which is why "and he faced the audience as he said "you should never, never indulge in any sort of practice with which you are not familiar."

"Well I don't" the man said "only we like you, you see, you don't come over as a fake like some. You ask the missus." His tone lightened the atmosphere so Milton built on it.

"That's good to hear my friend. So you won't be wanting to meet Jo again."

The laughter rose higher now.

"Not likely. She's a bad 'un she is. Not what I expected."

"Which reiterates my previous statement. Some things are not to be meddled with."

"Well I shan't be meddling with her I can tell you."

Milton stood up and shook his hand "I'm sure your wife will be delighted to hear it."

The man left the stage to a standing ovation which he acknowledged thinking it was for him which caused more mirth in itself. As Milton closed the show with a very poignant message to a young couple who had been very close to tears most of the time, he left to an even more deafening appreciative crowd.

Although people may have left in a happy mood, the true Milton was anything but light hearted for he had just witnessed some of what the evil could do with one of their pawns. Although the act may have seemed innocuous enough, he was aware of the underlying power which was about to be unleashed.

Jo was not pleased at being controlled, she never had, and she would be rebellious in whatever situation she found herself. Just when she was having fun she was yanked away and held in the body of the young man, but it was his spiritual power that had pinned her down and had her in a tight grip. The more she fought, the stronger was his hold on her until she felt she was in the jaws of a ferocious animal, which wasn't all that far from the truth. She had no option but to settle down a little until the end of the show.

Ariel was pleased with Fluke's performance. Being on the same level, they both had extra skills to most and if he was told to arrest a being he did just that and nothing would have made him let Jo go until instructed from the right source. His basic animal side always came to the fore, and in every instance up to now had been supreme to any invader but Milton wasn't at all sure how much a match he was against this new evil. However this little test had either taken the enemy by surprise or they hopefully hadn't the power to confront him. Now that would have made a show to remember.

The levels around Nan, Tabar and Jorg would not be able to witness Fluke's role but they could see Jo and wondered why she had gone to a certain place at the front of the hall, but their experience told them there was more than they could see so had to accept it. Jorg was staying close to Daryl who also wondered what was going on at this show, but if the paying public liked it, why question it. Also they were both being fed instructions as to what to notice or be aware of and what to ignore.

The word was already getting around that Milton Warner had played the act of his career and disappointed people were trying to get seats for the next three shows without success.

Milton was satisfied with the part Holland was playing and was not homing in on every bit of trivia as he knew he could leave that to Jean Paul, but busied himself with putting all the players in place for the finale which may come sooner than he planned, so he had to move quickly now for it to succeed.

As no good power could safely infiltrate the evil mass or its tendrils, they could still only speculate as to its power and intentions and most felt they were no wiser now then when it was first noticed. A feeling of frustration was evident in the lower levels but those slightly higher had no option but to accept that actions were in place of which they had no knowledge, so curiosity was of little use and provided no answers.

To the trained high levels, the tendril attached to the De Lux Cinema complex in Peterborough had doubled in thickness proving it was getting ready for its attack. To Milton this showed it was preparing for the last show of this tour but looking at the overall picture, it was only the second of the six targets. His aim now was to stop it before it was able to have its effect on the other four, especially the climax of its programme. He had observed that you could work out the route by the colour of the arms. It was as though each one was programmed in order. As the one over Peterborough started to grow, the charity run one was following it and after that the theatre. The two television events seemed to be last and looked identical, but on one of his instantaneous inspections he saw there was a distinct difference when examined from a close range. So it figured that the international sports meeting was fifth and the 'Hymns from the Cathedral' followed it.

Judging by the slight similarities he estimated the theatre attack was almost immediately after the charity run, then a slight gap coinciding exactly with the sports meeting and cathedral the following week end. He could now form the pattern with the information he was piecing together. Knowing the dates of the two television venues, it meant the attacks on the charity run and the theatre were planned for the weekend following Peterborough, leaving only the Friday untouched. At first he wasn't sure if this was comforting or not but on the positive side it did give him an advantage as he could plot a mental chart as to the movements of the thing.

But time was also an enemy. He knew that to stop this evil now, he must overcome it at the Peterborough session. One question kept niggling at him. He knew he was the target for whatever reason, so why were there selected places under threat that weren't connected to him? It didn't take long for the answer come. The evil knew that wherever they were, he would go to them, so had he simply taken their bait and walked straight into the biggest and most lethal trap ever known?

CHAPTER 17

The media had jumped on the success of the Derby evening and headlines were already going to press."Medium Taken Over By Evil Spirit" and "The Devil In Disguise" were going to be on the front pages the next morning and one even sported "Who Is Jo?" But they were beaten by the breaking news on the television and phone alerts. The new look Milton Warner was news.

Simon sat watching the television assured he would be going home the next day but as the newsflash hit the screen he jumped up showing more life than he had since he arrived. A young nurse rushed into the TV lounge.

"What are you doing here? You're supposed to be in bed."

"That's my boss." He pointed at the screen.

She stopped for a minute then said "I'm sure it is, now then shall we go back to bed like a good boy?"

The look he gave her brought her to a halt, both verbally and physically.

"I am not a boy and if I go to bed it won't be with you." Then turning away he sat back down and watched the screen. Daryl would have been overjoyed at that interaction for he would have known the old Cyberfart was back, even if he had used more than his quota of words for the day. There would be no doubt about his going home, that had been taken care of already. One good thing was that, like many others, when infected by the virus and survived, people both in soul and body were then immune from any future invasion from the same source.

Fluke had an urgent message to impart and sent a certain code to Jean Paul who relayed it to Milton. With his special senses, Fluke had detected something but didn't know what it was for he couldn't see it but noticed the tiniest of a disturbance of the surrounding space when Holland was on stage in front of him, especially when he had turned and moved to the sofa. Jean Paul immediately confirmed acceptance by Milton.

Even the likes of the elite forces sometimes received information that made them apprehensive. Not exactly afraid but extremely cautious and it was this factor that had kept them in constant operation. Milton now pondered his message and praised Fluke for his diligence by only contacting him when Jo had been released back to Ariel in the form of Min. What he knew now told him the net was closing for what his ally had sensed was that Holland, with the appearance of Milton had now an evil antenna attached to him. In a split second he had visited the dressing room and assured himself that this was indeed the case and although still in its dormant state could not only relay anything back first hand, but be used to control Holland. So two of his work force were monitored and he knew it wouldn't be too long before others may be targeted.

He took stock of the general situation. Jo and Holland were tapped. Daryl and Simon should be immune, so the next level up would be Jorg and he was monitoring Daryl who was immune. His thoughts turned back to Jo, which meant Ariel although of a higher level, was in line and unprotected but with her talents they would have quite a task to pin her down. Alongside her was Fluke but they didn't know what they were taking on with him and the longer that remained the case, the better. Jean Paul although not anywhere near Milton's status, was pretty high up in the pecking order so hopefully he would escape for now by which time Milton would have destroyed the evil thing altogether.

Another factor was emerging. The rest of the planet seemed to have been switched off from any attention from the mass. The fantastic work of the elite teams around the globe had restored most things to normal and succeeded in wiping much of the knowledge from people's minds. It would only be when they were spiritually aware that they may have some recollection of the horror they had experienced. So the evil had homed in on its source, but would it be playing for time or did it know its exact movements? This was something even Milton couldn't fathom, and hoped the truth would soon emerge, but for now he must keep full control of his part of it.

As soon as Milton was in the dressing room Daryl took the opportunity to ring his sister. She answered almost straight away.
"Oh Daryl, thank you for ringing."
"Anything the matter?"
"Well no, that is I don't think so."

A feeling of dread came over him as he asked "Flop OK?"

"Well that's the funny thing, he seems happy enough but he keeps looking at that flyer. I was wondering whether to throw it away, but do you think that would bother him?"

Daryl thought for a moment before saying "No I'd leave it. He's a canny one you know and he does have an affinity with Milton so perhaps he feels close to him." The excuse came over rather lame he thought but it seemed to satisfy his sister.

"You're probably right. Oh, that reminds me, I must get some flea stuff for him tomorrow. Been scratching at his back something awful he has."

"Ok. Junior all right?"

"Oh he's fine now, playing with that new toy you brought him, even takes it to bed."

Daryl smiled to himself "That's good. Speak soon."

"Night bruv and thanks for ringing."

Jean Paul was hovering near Holland and picked up on the conversation. Although it was probably nothing, he knew that the slightest remark could always lead to a clue of some sort so he relayed the chat to Milton who didn't take it so lightly. If Flop was scratching his back, it could be fleas or ticks, or it could be an indication of something trying to get a hold on Fluke.

"Nice little job for Nan or Tabar" he thought "they feel left out so lets give them something to chew on."

The message was received and Nan paused in disbelief.

"What is it?" Tabar asked.

"Will we check to see if Daryl's sister's dog has got fleas!"

Although the situation was serious, Milton couldn't help being amused at the reaction and hoped they wouldn't make a meal of it but get it done as quickly as possible.

"Do you want to do it?" Nan asked.

"Why not send someone else?"

"Can't, it's us specifically."

"I don't mind, but seems a bit menial, although orders from above are generally not so." Her wisdom told her to execute the task with necessary attention so within a blink she was back.

"And?" Nan was still mystified.

Tabar gave the impression of scratching and with a humorous vibe said "Not much, he's crawling with the things."

"Right I'll send the message up. Really, as if we hadn't got better things to do." She gave a shrug of disgust and to her the subject was closed.

Although Milton received the news with some relief, he knew the guard must be kept up even more as this could have been a red herring thrown into the mix to distract him into thinking all was fine when in fact it wasn't.

Jo had been returned to her safe holding area and was venting her anger on Min.

"So where were you when I was being attacked? Fine teacher you are."

Ariel welcomed the anger and frustration being used at the right time but for now she needed the girl to attract as little attention as possible and when Jo paused for breath she appeared as herself.

"Where in hell did you come from, I wish you'd warn a person when you're going to swap like that. There's things I'd have said to her I wouldn't say to you."

"Not your favourite companion I gather?" Ariel's light hearted manner soon calmed Jo and she was glad Ariel was back, she liked her.

"Well, she's not like you. Bet she was a school ma'am on earth. Typical sort she is."

The whole air surrounding them had slowed to a murmur and Ariel said "Feel better?"

"Course I do. But don't bring her again she gets on my tits."

Ariel paused then said "You did well."

"Well? Well? I didn't do anything except get...."there was a pause "mauled, defiled."

"Brought it all back didn't it?"

"You know, so why did you allow that cow to let me get raped all over again, and by an animal. What do they think I am?" The young spirit would have sobbed in human form, but the pain was just as deep in her soul.

"I'm sorry. We didn't expect that."

There was a long pause now. "What did you expect, what had I been sent to do?"

"Would you believe it if I said you were just required to be there?"

Jo thought. "There's a lot I don't know. I mean you get asked to do things you don't understand but somebody knows why."

Ariel sent comforting vibes over her and assured her that she had been very valuable and was much appreciated by the higher powers which lifted Jo's spirits considerably.

"Now, you will rest. Stay here and remember there will always be somebody with you, whether you are aware of them or not." She saw Jo's face change and said quickly "All right, it won't be Min."

"Well thank God for that at least. Hey can you send that dishy young man again, now I could do things for him."

Ariel showed her amusement but knew that was the last thing that would happen, for the girl's attention would be on anything but the job in hand.

Milton was in shock. After all the careful planning the truth was beginning to dawn on him. The pattern of things seemed so clear now and he was angry he hadn't seen it before. He wasn't just a target to be destroyed; he was the almighty power the evil planned to use for their own ends. All the building up of planned attacks coincided with the tour. The devastation had been solely to show him that if he didn't comply with their orders the outcome on the world would be unbelievable. Added to which they would harness all his skills but use him to execute them for ultimate evil not good. It would be a spiritual blackmail.

He could see now that they would use the next two venues to plant their seeds and move in for the kill at Peterborough. The remaining four tendrils would not only be activated, but he would be the one controlling them, or else. It seemed that the future continuance of the whole spiritual and earthly life of this entire space area as they knew it, however large it may be, could be eliminated if he didn't comply.

So the sample acts they had dealt were warnings, and it probably didn't matter that the elite forces had undone most of the sadistic results because what they had done once, they could do again but probably to a greater extent. This may only be the very tip of what was in store. The thought of working under their control was unthinkable, but to resist would destroy everything and probably even him, although that didn't come into the equation. His own destiny was irrelevant but he knew there would be no way to refuse with the stakes so high, unless……

With a fresh thought in his mind he sent a request to Jean Paul for every detail regarding the Nottingham and Leicester shows. He would deal with those first, then concentrate on the Peterborough one as a separate issue.

The other important factor from now on concerned the players in this game. It may mean they would be in almost the same danger as he, but it had got to the point where that unfortunately could not be included in the strategy for he needed enough reliable diversion at all times. He would make full use of the antennas already planted and be on the alert for any more and if anyone could sniff them out it would be Fluke.

Again he was aware that the enemy would want to harness the animal super power for their use, so Milton would have to use him in a restricted way so that he couldn't be monitored more than was absolutely necessary.

While he was conjuring his thoughts another fact emerged. He knew that once someone had been infected with the virus and managed to survive, they would be immune so why had Jo and Holland have antennas attached to them. He could only think that, as the individuals couldn't be controlled, they must just be being used for relaying information but that couldn't be so or why did Jo react the way she did and have to be caught by Fluke. Also they might now be aware that it was Holland who had it when to all appearances it was supposed to be Milton himself who was in body.

That made him even more concerned. It could mean that they had seen through the deception, so he must now step up his plan to a higher degree. Just when he thought he had the answers, more questions seemed to appear.

The doctor had completed his Tuesday morning round and Simon sat dressed in the same clothes he had worn when brought to the hospital for there had been nobody he wanted to go to his home and rummage through his belongings.

"Well, you'll be going home soon then." The duty nurse came to give him his last dose of medication before he left.

"Correct." He was getting back to normal, wondering why she stated the obvious.

"I expect you're looking forward to it."

"Stupid woman" he though but simply repeated "Correct."

"Don't say much do you. Strange one, you are I must say."

"Must you?" He was looking straight ahead doing his best not to get into conversation as his mind was already thinking about his computer.

"Must I what?" She stopped, looking rather bewildered.

"Say."

She had absolutely no idea that he was twisting the simplest word without giving her the information she had probably been sent to extract. Now he turned his head in the opposite direction and ignored her completely. With a shrug she gathered up her tray and moved on to the next patient.

It wasn't deemed necessary to provide him with transport so he booked a taxi having checked he had money on him. The last days were such a mixed up blur he felt he   must double check every detail and looked in his wallet before giving the address. As soon as they pulled up outside his home he knew he would be on familiar territory and he could use his own skills to adjust.

He had never been one to welcome visitors. His home was private and any communication could be done elsewhere. This was his and it would stay that way. In fact everything about him was private. He never discussed any family or friends and wasn't the most sociable of people and when Milton offered him the job that had been preordained for him, he was glad it didn't involve many people. Daryl, he could cope with as long as he had little to do with him and Milton left him alone pretty much so he could escape into his cyber world and shut out anything that didn't relate to him personally. He lived in a small house on the outskirts of Mayfield and if you didn't know where it was you would drive or even walk past without finding it. The access was down a small lane between two large houses with just enough room for a medium sized van to pass, then the lane turned to the left and his property was situated behind one of the houses and was out of sight from the road. There was a small mail box just inside the lane so the postman never had to go further than that, and as no parcels were ever delivered and he didn't take newspapers, getting all he wanted from the computer, there was never any need for anyone to get even a close look at it. If one ventured to walk down out of curiosity, the house was hidden behind trees and a sturdy gate in the high fence kept out any nosey parkers.

The taxi dropped him at this gate and he fumbled for his key. The garden was quiet except for the odd little breeze that stirred the grass. Once in the house he let himself fall onto the sofa with weariness. He didn't realise how exhausted he was until he had tried to take those few steps outside. He pulled his legs up onto the cushions, rested his head and was soon floating in a place that was calm and relaxing.

It was time for Milton to select a bodyguard for him and for now he delegated Fluke as he wanted to know immediately if an antenna was placed. Also he put Jorg into Fluke's command so that they could monitor both Daryl and Simon together and Fluke could flit from one to another telling Jorg to swap at an instant. That covered everyone with the minimum of staff for if he drew in too many high powers it would send out a warning before it had even been put into place.

As Simon left his body and floated just above it he was aware of a protective force keeping him from straying too far and a sweet voice in his head was telling him that everything was going according to plan and he had played his part well. Now it was time for the next step. Information was gently fed into his system that Milton was in danger and they needed the help of those close to him to protect him. He was assured he would not be asked to do anything beyond his power, and if a task was too great, more power would be applied to him. Asked if he understood he gave a mental signal of acceptance and felt himself slowly lowered back to the sofa.

As his eyes opened, he was now fully aware of what had happened in the office and he knew this was all part of the same game. He wasn't afraid and something told him he had to follow orders however strange they may be for the plan to succeed and keep his boss safe. His mind turned to Daryl and before he could ask the question, the answer was put in his brain. At least he would be working with someone he knew and not a stranger.

"One thing you should know." Fluke put the thought there.

"Which is?"

"Don't expect the same man."

"You've swapped him?"

"Oh it's him, but a new assertive, less timid little soul."

"Interesting." But Simon was wondering if he would like him more or even less than before. But it sounded a challenge and his growing energy would accept it and see what happened. He got up slowly and moved to the kitchen to make a decent cup of tea which he would take to the room he called his office and boot up the computers as they must think they'd been deserted being off for so long.

No one would have recognised him as he opened the door and stepped in, tea in hand for the Simon the world saw bore no resemblance to the man now moving to sit in front of his array of monitors and keyboards. This was his true image and he had come back.

"Hello Son." The presence was behind him.

Without turning Simon answered with a question. "Been waiting here for me?"

"You are in my charge."

"Not from choice then?" The retort held bitterness.

There was a pause that made him feel uneasy and after a moment he said "You still here?"

"I'm here and you should know by now our work takes us where we are ordered, not just to follow our whims."

The computers were coming back to life and Simon became frustrated at his lack of ability to operate the keyboard.

"What the hell is going on?" he almost screamed.

"If you will calm down a little, I'll explain."

It was obvious he would learn nothing until he complied so he sat back in his chair and looked straight ahead. Fluke positioned himself so that Simon could just see his head above the main monitor.

"There is no time for pleasantries or proving one's feelings. There is something so important going on we have to be on our guard the whole time. We are sent to our tasks with the understanding we obey to the letter."

"That sounds familiar." Simon was calming with the tone of the message but something was distracting him.

"What's the matter? Looking for something that isn't there?" Fluke smiled. "Sorry son, you won't find it."

"What happened?" Simon felt as though part of him was missing but he appeared to be intact physically.

"Listen carefully. You were trapped in a time lock, and when they got you out, part of you had to stay there." He waited for the truth to sink in knowing this lad would soon piece it together.

"My tail. Part of my tail has gone."

"Your spiritual tail from your alter ego. Your body shows no signs of trauma but your canine soul has been – to put it mildly – docked."

"Oh Christ!"

"While we're on the subject you may as well know why you cannot work the keyboard properly. Your paws have not properly retreated from your hands, oh I know you can't see them but spiritually they are hampering you so why not try that new voice control gismo you were playing around with?"

"I'd forgotten that!" The realisation came like a breath of fresh air but Simon still had reservations.

"What about my voice?"

"What about it?"

"Will I bark or something?"

"Only one way to find out." Fluke's image disappeared as Simon tried a simple command and was amazed when it worked. He used more words in the next few minutes than he had done all the time he was in hospital.

Having let him settle into his familiar mode, Fluke explained that they were both needed to combat the evil that had attacked Simon and that those he knew best like Milton and Daryl along with spiritual ones unknown to him at present were about to execute the most daring scheme imaginable. He asked if the lad felt up to it in his present state and was assured there was nothing would do him more good. Simon asked who was at the helm but was told they didn't ask questions, just followed orders.

Fluke explained he had to go as he had more tasks and would leave him to acclimatise but assured him he would be back soon. He knew he couldn't hang around one area too long so did a quick switch with Jorg.

As he left he couldn't help be amused as he remembered Simon's first encounter with him in the office when he had entered as Flop.

"And no, I don't have fleas, any more than you young man." flitted across his thought as he joined Daryl.

When an event was being set up it rarely ran completely smoothly. The crew knew exactly what they were doing and their work ran like clockwork but at every venue there always seemed to be one member of staff who wanted everyone to know they were in charge, usually knowing less than they would admit.

"You can't run that bit of wire across there." The order was snapped out by a young lad with very little experience of dealing with such a large company. Cal appeared at the side of him and said in his very precise manner which was a sign he was not amused, "For your information sonny, that is not a piece of wire, it is an electric cable," he turned the lad round and pointed "which is then connected to another electric cable," then swung him back to his original position "which is then covered by a protective little bridge, so that people do not fall over it."

"Well....I....I'm sure you know what you're doing, but be careful" he added as though he was not going to be put down so easily.

Cal indicated to one of the larger members of the crew who put his arm around the lad's shoulders and whispered in his ear. What he said can only be imagined but there was no doubt as to the last word which was spat out "off!"

"Why is there always one?" The crew were used to it but had a way of carrying on as though the offender wasn't there, making them feel so in the way that they usually cleared off after a while.

"And one still in nappies!" They shared a laugh and concentrated on the stage.

The Victoria Theatre was quite old but beautiful in it's architecture and if there was a lack of wing space elsewhere, this made up for it. The ceiling was high and very ornate causing audiences waiting for a show to admire its beauty and wonder how it could be painted. There were boxes for special guests either side of the stage and the general seating was not cramped, a fact much appreciated by those with long legs.

Daryl was doing his usual checks in the dressing room in readiness for Milton's late morning visit and overseeing that the proper displays were being erected in the foyer. The young lad who had received his marching orders from the crew was trying to tell other members of staff how the job should be done. When he saw Daryl approaching the posters he blocked his way.

"I'm sorry sir, we have to get this complete before Mr Finn arrives and to put it bluntly, you are somewhat in the way, so if you would be so kind as to…."

The sentence was never finished for Daryl held up his hand, fixed his eyes on the lad and said very precisely "And I young man am Mr Finn."

There was a deathly hush as everyone in the foyer froze. How long they remained still was debateable for Daryl was like a tightly would spring which was slowly uncoiling.

"I don't know your name, and I have no wish to, but one thing I will say, take your puerile little clipboard, your self imposed attitude and get yourself as far away from this event as possible. I do not want to see you again for the duration."

As Daryl's arm raised and pointed to the entrance, the lad, bright red in the face scurried away almost in tears dropping his things as he went. Subdued whispers soon ran round the place and Daryl turned his attention to the promotion material whilst directing everyone else to carry on.

"Well done." Fluke was still with Daryl at this point and was impressed with the way he had followed his mental instructions without question. Daryl took the praise without flinching but acknowledged the message mentally.

This was one of the reasons Milton had put Fluke and Jorg on a switch routine, not only to protect and monitor Daryl and Simon but to use Fluke's nose at every opportunity for he was so adept at finding the slightest threat, and he now returned to Simon to change his location. The innocent nuisance of a young lad was in fact an evil scout placed at the theatre in readiness but was too inexperienced to pick up on the higher powers he was dealing with. He was supposed to have been on duty near the dressing rooms but had been foiled, partly due to his interfering approach.

Milton mused on this. Surely the evil power couldn't be slipping. If he had been organising this he wouldn't have used such an inexperienced creature if the ultimate goal was to get nearer to Milton. There could only be one explanation. This was a distraction and he sent Jorg a message to get Daryl back to the dressing room immediately. There, they could direct him to look at physical things whilst they took stock of anything spiritually evil. He chastised himself for not realising that the most innocuous players were often important in their role.

Holland was relaxing before going to the theatre, but there was now no sign of his former image and although he was still in presence, his mental state was completely that of Milton. There was no double identity, he now believed he was this person and although he was being manipulated from above, he believed that everything he did was of his own choice, even to the extent that he thought he was receiving messages from relatives, not ones that were fed via a third party, and he was the medium that was passing them on to the waiting relatives. But this was exactly how Milton was playing it for the mental image, properly used can be stronger than any physical one, and this had been so perfected that even if Holland had been using his own body, the mental image would have erased the truth from interlopers. However, as so much hung on this project, the fact that Milton's body was being used just supported the whole façade to an even stronger extent.

The elite forces viewed the evil mass as the tendril over Peterborough grew, pulsating with the most horrible force imaginable, but something was changing. So much evil had been brought to strengthen this arm that many of the cells arriving could not get a proper grip on the main structure with folds of it hanging down as though it was being overloaded and chunks were dropping to the ground then trying to get back to the main stem. The anger between the different entities was becoming almost destructive in itself and to those able to see it, it was the most horrendous form of everything disgusting and horrifying that could be imagined.

Other members of different elite forces were offering to try and destroy it as it may be at its weakest but Milton had to refuse as he knew that even if they were successful it wouldn't end there. With the evil having an objective, they wouldn't stop until they had succeeded, and with him being the prime target, they would get him, even if not this time, they would be back so it had to be now or never. He looked again at the terrible sight. It was so intensely dark that details were disappearing into the solid wall of one colour. It was nearly ready.

Daryl's mobile vibrated in his pocket. He looked at the screen and couldn't believe his eyes. Quickly entering his code he connected with the caller.

"Cyberfart! Is that really you man?"

"It is Simon."

"Oh you're OK. You are OK aren't you?"

"As well as can be expected, thank you."

"Where are you?"

"Home."

"When did you get out?"

"I wasn't locked up."

The thought crossed Daryl's mind, "Oh God it's him alright" but said "I know that, from hospital of course."

"Just."

"You're having a rest aren't you, before coming back to work I mean."

"Possibly."

The old Daryl would probably have entered into an argument by now but this man wasn't having any of it.

"Well you know best as usual. Have you spoken to Milton?"

"Not yet."

"When were you thinking of doing so?"

Simon sat back in his chair. "They were right, he has changed" he thought but answered

"Is he there?"

"Not yet. Still at the hotel. Expecting him in about an hour or so."

"OK."

The call ended and Daryl wasn't too pleased at being cut off without the usual farewell but he wasn't going to let that bother him and from now on Simon would learn that.

Holland answered the mobile and as Milton recognised the voice.

"Ah, good, I'm glad you're home. Did they find out what was wrong?"

"Only guesswork."

"Which was?"

"Eyestrain."

"Hmm. Can have funny effects that. You know, you spend far too much time with your eyes glued to a computer screen, then you are on your phone then I expect you watch TV at home, so your poor eyes don't get much of a chance do they?"

"Probably."

"Well, we're doing alright, Daryl has everything in hand as usual, and thanks to your preparation before the tour everything has slotted into place, so you just take it easy. No rush to get back before you are fit. I'll come and see you when we get home."

There was a hush. The last sentence hung in the air. Fluke hovering over Simon had picked up the hitch and he knew something wasn't right.

"Don't answer." He instructed and Simon obeyed.

"Hello, you still there?" Holland called.

"Ok" Fluke said "but don't give anything away."

Simon took a breath "We'll see." he said and ended the call.

There was a strange silence in the room.

"That was odd." Simon was the first to communicate.

"You noticed." Fluke told him to do nothing for a moment and he sent a message to the real Milton. Within seconds he had his reply that Milton had already picked up on the slip but he hoped that nobody else would have. The only person who knew Simon didn't have anyone to his house was Daryl and he hadn't been witness to it so Milton told them to clear their thoughts and told Jean Paul to keep Milton's communications with everyone else to the minimum for now.

Although Holland had assumed the role of Milton admirably, even the best laid plans can have the tiniest of flaws and it was hoped this would go unobserved or the whole programme would be in danger.

The day passed without any further incident and it was soon time for the audience at the theatre to take their seats. There was the usual hum of excitement as the house filled but backstage Milton seemed very composed as he dressed in his show clothes. Fluke and Jorg were exchanging places at irregular intervals so both were in constant touch with Daryl and Simon. On instruction Ariel had brought Jo again, anxious to see what effect her presence had this time. She told her she was leaving her with another guide, a young man although not too good looking as to distract her but at least an improvement on Min.

"Do I just hover around again?"

"Yes, just watch and tell your companion if there's something you aren't happy with and he'll call me."

"What's his name?" Jo felt she had to whisper.

"Cyril."

"What, how can I call him that?"

Ariel laughed "What's wrong with it?"

"What's right with it? It's bloody awful."

"Don't worry, call him what you like, he won't mind." and with that she went and returned as the unattractive young man.

"Hmm." Jo wasn't impressed. "You the best they could find, bloody hell fire!" Ariel was amused but glad that Jo was already firing up her emotions, and disappointment comes over quite strongly.

"I'm sorry."

"Oh I suppose I'll have to manage. Done this before?"

"Not much."

"Christ Almighty, I deserve better than this, and don't expect me to call 'Cyril' every time I need you. You can be Cy and like it." She shrilled the 'Cyril' which must have been picked up by anyone who needed to know her whereabouts and Ariel secretly praised her for doing a difficult job so well, yet without her knowledge.

"I like that. Thank you."

"Yes, well, keep on your toes, there's strange things go on at these dos." Jo had a vivid memory of last night's fiasco and wasn't about to let that happen again.

"I'll do my best."

"You'll have to do better than your best. Oh well, just stay alert. Watch everything. OK?"

Ariel thought what a good teacher this girl would make and knew she wanted to use her again in the future; that is if she had a future. Milton at this time was more concerned about the antenna fixed to her which seemed to be activating as he watched.

It was his intention to keep all concerned on as low a profile as possible during the next two shows to give the impression that not too much attention was being paid to any threat and to the average soul going about their business this may have been viable. But he knew he was fighting a much more intelligent force who would not be hoodwinked into such a cheap ruse. However, they seemed to be using less powerful pawns in some areas and that could be the crack in the armour needed to gain the information he must have before the final strike.

Jean Paul moved the Holland/Milton into position for the pre show inspection and when everything was agreed on stage he went to the dressing room to check his outfit for the evening. Daryl, who was still doing his usual flying around double checking everything, nearly collided with him.

"Oh sorry boss. Just got to see Cal. Be back in a tick."

Holland/Milton looked at his reflection and smiled thinking that age was being very kind to him, but noticed a few lines in his face that were creeping in.

"Don't be vain" Jean Paul whispered "It isn't you." The innocent phrase held more weight than it appeared and the guide had chosen his words carefully.

"I can admire what God gave me." was the reply.

"It's only on loan, as are all bodies for the time we use them." Again Jean Paul was covering any trace of suspicion. Thankfully Daryl came breezing back at that moment.

"Would you believe it?" He threw his papers on the side table.

"What now?"

"Another frigging mike has gone. Who takes these things?"

Holland/Milton turned. "Not one of my radio mikes?"

"No, no, the ones they put on the boom to pick up the audience."

"No problem then. They have spares of course."

Daryl was getting more exasperated with the man's calm attitude than with the loss of the equipment.

"Not the point. It costs money, your money."

Before Holland could give the kind of retort that Jean Paul felt was coming he took over and turned the reply to "Well, it is important of course but let's just concentrate on the show for now."

"Right boss, "Daryl was a bit relieved as this was more the kind of thing he expected and settled down to finalise his notes. "It's a sell out, but you know that."

Holland/Milton mused "I wonder what's in store tonight, we never know what to expect do we?"

"Just depends on how lively the 'other side' are."

"Oh there's always plenty of activity, it's just a case of sorting it out."

Daryl was only half listening and said "Good, good." before suggesting Holland/Milton went for his rest before coming back for the show but as they left the building the antenna attached to Holland started to activate unseen by his companion but noticed immediately by the real Milton. The game was on.

After a short weighing up of all the known facts, Milton had come to a conclusion. One of the main rules was always take notice of the minor things; don't overlook the obvious as not being important and that was what he now realised was the most important factor in this case.

He had been wondering why those immune to the virus had been able to have antenna attached, but why not? The two situations were not important to each other. It didn't matter whether any person, in body or spirit was immune. The antenna was a completely different tool so it could be placed exactly where the enemy required at any given time, and up to now they must have imagined they were invisible to all good levels. If or when they were not longer needed they could either be removed or just switched off and as they were not controlled by any physical means they simple operated by the will or command of those placing them.

So now the question was as to why certain ones were being chosen. Holland as Milton seemed fairly obvious, but Jo was a mystery, although having had her in their power she may have seemed to fit their plan in some way. Milton put himself in the opposite position. Who would he have wanted to track? The two lads? They didn't seem important enough although they were close to him, but again was it wise to dismiss them so quickly? As soon as his thoughts turned towards Ariel and Fluke he dismissed them from his reasoning in case by any chance the wave could reach out and hit the evil.

But now it was time for the performance and the air was electric, not only around the Victoria Theatre but stretching far out into the universe, for this was no small objective but would have repercussion beyond anything man had discovered.

CHAPTER 18

Jo was having a great time. Ariel had been clever in her image selection and Jo was bossing her young man around delightfully, attracting a larger audience than was now transfixed on the stage. Holland/Milton was really on form and this had the makings of one of the best venues yet. The audience was buzzing and after every message the whispers could be heard.

"He's so good. He couldn't have known that."

"Only I knew that, he's got to be the real thing."

"I know that was my Mother, only she called me by that name and she's been dead over thirty years."

The atmosphere in the room was building by the minute and Ariel began to wonder if all the good vibes were acting as a shield, for nothing untoward seemed to be affecting them at present.

"Keep up your guard."

She knew who was ordering her and immediately did a multi-person scan of the room leaving the image of Cy with Jo, but there was absolutely nothing.

"Stay in the auditorium." Again an order.

Fluke had been told to swap with Jorg and cover the stage and rear passages leading to the dressing rooms. He knew better than to question and immediately did an instant sweep. Nothing.

Everything was too quiet. It was approaching the interval and it seemed as if no evil presence was in the place anywhere. Milton did an instant check with Jean Paul who assured him Holland/Milton was fine and nothing to report but Milton knew his friend wouldn't see the antenna and so he had no option but to do a micro visit himself.

On his return he was concerned and did a spot check on Jo. Although no evil was actually there, their two antennas were extremely active, so they were being monitored. Milton ordered Fluke to move close to Holland and report, knowing he wouldn't actually see the attachment but he may pick up something different to what he had noticed before when he had been watching him on stage.

Within less than a second Fluke confirmed there was an air disturbance at the back of Milton, in the same place but stronger. Next he told him to do a quick check on Jo and the reaction was the same. Milton knew he had to check everyone himself to confirm the antenna but he would use Fluke as an initial source to sniff out the air movement as he now knew what to expect. The result was negative, nobody else had been fitted with anything.

The thunderous round of applause hailed the end of the first act and Holland/Milton returned to his dressing room, Daryl at his side. Jorg had returned for the interval leaving Fluke to monitor Simon.

Jo was floating around following her orders to just be around the place and thinking that perhaps this new life wasn't so bad after all. But the rebel in her was still part of her being and she decided to wander out of the auditorium and take in the rest of the theatre.

"Where are you going?" 'Cy' asked.

"Too bloody boring here, I'll come back for the next lot so you can stay here."

"I'm not allowed to leave you."

Ariel knew this would raise Jo's back and it was producing the required effect.

"And I suppose if I was in body you'd be following me to the shit house!"

Ariel wanted to show her amusement but feigned embarrassment with a quiet "Oh No, I don't do things like that."

"Well I should hope not. Don't like perverts."

Ariel pushed the chat on further. "But you don't have to go to the toilet."

"I know that. Now do me a big, big favour and push off. Leave – me – alone!" She tried to move away with a loud "Christ Almighty!" but Cy was right behind her.

Milton was watching the antenna, for as Jo's temper rose the antenna was going into overdrive as if it would take off. But why would such a simple exchange activate any interest. This needed watching and he instructed Ariel to keep up the pace while he checked on Holland.

The air in the dressing room was calm but Holland's antenna was reacting the same way as Jo's but a strange thing was happening. It was pointing in her direction whereas hers was completely upright as if sending a message.

There had to be more surely, how could the evil gain all its knowledge from two sources? But all that Milton could do at the moment was to monitor every minute movement of these two. But wait. What if that was exactly the plan and while his attention was onto these, he could be missing something much more important. Were these just decoys?

The evil would be playing with his intelligence, testing him to the limit, probably setting traps which had no bearing on anything other than to get a complete picture of his power. So this could be a double bluff. If they thought he had worked that out and would now ignore the antenna they could move in knowing they had a clear run for whatever action they had planned. But which way to turn? He favoured the idea of appearing to lose all interest but in this case that would not be the answer for they had the power to flush him out with the threat of total devastation if he didn't comply.

It was time for the second act and he placed all the players in their allotted positions. If the atmosphere in the hall was electric with enthusiasm, it was the opposite to the one surrounding Milton for it was like the calm before the storm and he was waiting for the first lightening strike.

Simon had rested and was back at his computer. Checking through his notes he reminded himself of the route of the tour and wondered how all was going. He didn't want to ring Daryl any more than was necessary, and as he had nothing to inform him about, felt there was no need for idle chat.

"So, get Nottingham out of the way and we are just left with Leicester and Peterborough. Then what happens?"

He had been aware of the exchange between Fluke and Jorg and when Fluke next appeared he said "Ok. What's going on?"

"Nothing much to report at present."

"Hmm" Simon's grunt was full of frustration and displeasure.

"You'll know, when you have to."

Simon tried to ignore him and carried on at the computer. Fluke gave him a moment then said ""Glad to see your hands are almost back to normal."

"Are you?"

"Do you know, you are the most insolent young pup I've ever known."

Without looking up Simon retorted "More like than you've ever spawned."

"You had better loose that attitude young man, you weren't brought back to be useless. People went to a lot of trouble to rescue you."

"For what purpose!" The reply was spat out with such a force Simon's teeth were bared in a vicious snarl. "To use me? Ha. So I have to be grateful."

Fluke eyed him suspiciously. "We have a job to do, whether you like it or not."

The sarcasm hit the room as he said "But you can't tell me what it is. Great"

Neither communicated for some time then Fluke said almost sadly "I've waited a long time to have you alongside me, but this isn't going to work.

I will say we are unfit to help Milton in this fight." As soon as the thought had left him, Fluke disappeared leaving Simon apparently alone. Jorg had been instructed to watch but not communicate in any way and he now hovered a safe distance away but still in the room. He couldn't understand what was happening to this man whom he thought would have jumped at the chance to help his boss, but he seemed to be changing by the minute. One moment the old Simon was there, and the next it was if he was having an inner fight with himself and everything around him. Perhaps it was merely a period of readjustment, after all he had been though hell and most souls wouldn't have had the nerve to even fight there way back from such a trauma.

"Are you there?" The question left Simon without vengeance, more like a cry for help. Jorg called Fluke who transferred immediately but did not reply.

"Dad. Dad, please help me." The cry went out like a howl in the night.

"I'm here son, I'm always near to you in some way."

For the next few moments they exchanged thoughts, fears and eventually the love that had been put on hold for so long and even in their spiritual state the emotions flowed like pent up tears between them. Fluke had known what he was doing when he left, hoping it would show the lad he was not only loved but needed so much.

It was if Simon had be cleansed from his torment and he was drawing on the strength of his powerful father to rejuvenate himself, and as the feeling washed over him he grew in stature and determination.

"I guess you were all I needed." His eyes were soft.

Fluke looked towards his back and said "And I need you, even if you have a little bit missing." That broke the tension and from then on they both knew they were working on the same team. Fluke explained that he was following instructions as they were fed to him so they had to be on their guard all the time.

"How will I work? In body or mind?" Simon was wondering what his job would be.

"Whatever lad, we don't know until we are asked, but whatever it is, we'll do it. Right?"

"Too right."

Tension was mounting as the evening drew to a close. Nothing seemed to be happening, and in the lower levels of the spirit realm there was almost an emptiness. On searching the higher levels there was no evidence of evil intrusion and some were wondering if all had been abandoned, but Milton knew better, and those on the high levels could see the evil mass pulsating until it seemed to be sucking in any weak soul who ventured too near.

The evening finished with the usual standing ovation for Milton and the theatre was humming with satisfied patrons. Slowly they reluctantly left as if they still wanted more, but eventually the place was clear and the crew started dismantling the set. Milton warned everyone to be especially vigilant as this could be part of the plan to promote a feeling of false security and just when they least expected it, an attack could be made.

Holland had been whisked away and was already on his way to Leicester for the next show. Daryl was driving but the car was fully occupied. Jean Paul and Jorg were in attendance along with Fluke and Simon in his spiritual form.

"Brought the dogs I see." Jorg joked but was soon warned by Jean Paul that flippancy was not welcome.

Daryl checked them both into the hotel and for a while the entourage stayed close.

Milton then instructed them to come and go in turn so as not to attract too much attention but Simon must be with Fluke or Jean Paul due to his inexperience.

Jo had been taken back by Ariel who again praised her for her actions, and promising her that she would be able to go to the next show at least.

"And what about the last one? I know there's two more." She almost demanded.

"We'll see."

"Oh I get it. Let her do the work and then ditch her when the going gets a bit rough eh?"

The last thing Ariel needed now was any attention to be drawn to the girl, it was fine while she was working but now she needed the calm to return. Using one of her many tricks she calmed her right down to a hibernation state and watched her drift into a spiritual sleep.

Other elite forces were flitting about during the night and informing Milton that nothing unusual was happening so he was assured that any action would be from the horrible mass awaiting him at Peterborough. The possibility occurred to him that maybe nothing would happen at Leicester, in other words it may be a repeat of the Nottingham show which was in one way a relief but didn't take away the fact that the attack would still be made unless.......

He was still worried at the thought that he would be made to make the choice between being used by the evil and thus save the planet and the surrounding spiritual area from utter demolition or stand his ground and fight this foe, but he knew that was impossible for even if he summoned up all the elite forces, it was unlikely they could rid the area of this fiendish power so the fight would go on. Also if the showdown was at Peterborough, he would have to take over his body again and release Holland to be properly adjusted before he could progress.

Even if the evil had worked out that Milton was using a plant, they would be sure he would be there to face them at the end, for what use was it to use a dummy for such a task. It seemed as though his fate was sealed.

There seemed to be a sigh of relief amongst the various levels as Wednesday dawned with no sign of any disturbance and whilst some were a glad, the higher ones in the game were more than apprehensive. Milton instructed Jean Paul to double check everything and pass the message down the ranks with the exception of Jo as she was only a puppet in the play and would soon be returned to her own area.

Holland fancied taking a walk. He hadn't seen anything of the places on this tour and he understood that Leicester had a lot of historical interest surrounding Richard the Third in particular. Daryl was immediately told to stop him doing any such thing but was worried in case he took matters into his own hands whilst he was checking everything at the Calgary Hall during the day.

Jean Paul took over and programmed Holland's mind into believing he was rather tired and needed as much rest as possible as he had two more exhausting nights to complete. This worked and Daryl breathed a sigh of relief and uttered a little "Thank You" to himself as he would have had no idea who to direct it to.

Everything was going along like clockwork as if nothing had ever threatened everyone's existence and Milton was afraid a little complacency may creep in but he was pleased to have a calm atmosphere around and only let Ariel stir up the vibes when necessary.

She was doing her multi tasking to perfection and although Jo may have felt she had left her many times, she was always at her side in some form or another.

Simon was still not strong enough physically to undertake any strenuous task but his spiritual side had been given a boost by Fluke who was injecting energy into him by the second so they would be used entirely in the supernatural sense in their own particular field. Daryl was now being pulled under Fluke's command and although he hadn't the animal instincts he had enough loyal energy towards Milton to fight to the bitter end. Jorg was also in this little group as he couldn't be allowed to return to Nan and Tabar's level at present where he would be bombarded with questions as to why he had been allowed to have special jobs and they didn't.

It would be Jean Paul's job to remove Holland from Milton's body at the precise moment Milton re-entered it. Any other arrangements Milton had made remained a secret from the group as any escaping thought could jeopardise the whole thing, so everyone knew they had to act as directed at that moment.

The usual checks had been made and Holland/Milton was already in the dressing room awaiting another great show. Jo had arrived with her usual gusto and the air was being nicely stirred up as she moved around.

"Thank God you didn't send that long streak of piss you sent last night." She exploded.

"Not your sort?" Ariel put it mildly.

"Let's put it this way." Jo drew her nearer as if she had a big secret to impart. "I'd rather shag a stuffed kangaroo."

Where this girl got her expressions from Ariel couldn't imagine but it was working for now so she fuelled the fire a bit more.

"You could have Min again."

"Come on now, you promised."

"Yes I did, now let me see, who's free."

Jo pulled close again. "Go on let me have that dishy one. Make my night that would."

"And just what would you do with him may I ask?"

"Whoa. What wouldn't I do with him?"

Ariel laughed. "You'd have a job."

"Go on."

"What if I said I would be here instead."

It was Jo's turn to be cheeky. "Oh well, I suppose I could just about cope with it."

This was such a lovely open hearted humorous girl who could bring a breath of fresh air to any situation and she feared for her safety. Although she was just there to cause a diversion, Ariel couldn't help but remember the night when Fluke had been forced to restrain her. So from now on she would have to watch, not just the girl but everything in the area around her so that she would be ready to ward off any future controlling entity before it had chance to get a hold of her.

It was now or never. Milton knew that this was his one chance to purge the earth area of this demon and he must not fail. If he didn't succeed tonight there was no way of stopping the programme of events the evil had lined up. He was aware he may have to be the sacrifice, but he would do everything in his power to destroy the evil from the inside should he be captured spiritually. His body was of no consequence for that was only on loan and could be discarded at any time. Now he waited.

The hall was filled to capacity and as the house lights dimmed a sudden hush filled the room.

"Ladies and Gentlemen, will you please welcome the one and only...... Milton Warner."

The silence turned to the usual applause and only settled when Holland/Milton raised his arm towards the audience. Immediately he homed in on a lady in the centre and brought gasps of amazement as he related details of her past before giving messages from her late husband and her mother. She stood where she was, tears streaming down her face and called out "God Bless you Milton. I've waited for twenty years to get a message. Only Fred and Mum would know those things. God Bless you." If her companion hadn't pulled her back to her seat, who knows how long she would have gone on. Someone whispered she was a 'plant' but was quickly told to shut up.

All those in Milton's group were getting a little edgy as it seemed nothing was going to happen, and they were in for a repeat of the Nottingham show but he calmed them and told them to be patient. When the first act finished they began to wonder just what he had planned and they began to feel rather small in comparison to the evil power lurking at Peterborough and beyond, but he reinforced his orders. Had it been anyone else in control, they may not have had the loyalty but they trusted him implicitly, still unaware of his true status. But he seemed to be hovering almost like an animal toying with its prey until it was ready to kill.

The second act was about half way through when suddenly all the electric power went off. Holland/Milton was standing at the front of the stage at this time and on a signal Jean Paul took Holland and passed him to Tabar who was waiting to receive him, whilst Milton himself re-entered his body. Fluke and Simon were either side of him and Ariel, or most of her was behind. She had left a small portion of herself with Jo although it didn't seem necessary but she was taking no chances. She would pass her to Nan at the first opportunity but for now she must concentrate on protecting Milton. Jorg had taken control of Daryl's spirit and they were hovering over him leaving the body of Daryl slumped in the wings. As the floor was protected by resident elementals, the only space between Milton and his foe was directly in front of him.

If any of the audience had been in a position to reach for a mobile phone or camera they would have found that they were all inoperable, but there was no chance of that for every person sat slumped in their seats, heads bowed and totally oblivious of what was going on around them which could only be classed as a blessing.

"MILTON WARNER" The wave vibrated throughout the entire building as a beam of light was directed on the target from the balcony area.
Milton had no need to speak to communicate and all his companions, being in their spiritual form, including Daryl and Simon were tuned in to the conversation.

"Thank you for accepting my invitation." His acknowledgement was curt but full or sarcasm.

"So you have seen reason at last."

"I know what you have come for."

"We warned you we would return, but you paid no heed. This time you will not escape."
Milton was trying to draw out the objective without confirming he knew.

"You will have to remind me, it has been a very long time."
The light changed to a misty grey colour and started to materialise as it moved towards the stage thickening as it went until the group were enclosed in a thick fog.

"Do not play games. You are well aware."
At this point Milton sent out a signal to members of his elite force who called in as many more forces as possible in the area. They were all used to working on a split second command and had not needed to be prepared previously. This was one weapon Milton had been relying on.

Few could have related what happened next as the group stood motionless on the stage. The entire elite focused on the main evil cell which was controlling the arms and attacked it with such force it was caught unawares and before it had time to fight back, the tendrils were dropping and disintegrating until there was no trace of them ever having been there. The area was then spiritually purged and cleansed. Those able to view the scene from the higher levels were stunned by the successful result in such a short time and many wondered why it hadn't been executed before. But Milton had known there was more to it than that.

"Very clever. And what do you think that has achieved?" The mockery in the evil power proved that the main reason for their presence had not been resolved.

"It's a start." Milton was equally snide.

"The games are over. It's time to deliver."

"And if I don't?"

The anger was rising in the mist and spirits felt a freezing chill run through them confirming the evil presence that was threatening them but they hung on to their objective which was to protect Milton whatever the cost.

"You are in no position to bargain. We will take what is ours."

"I'm not yours to take. You do not belong here, I do."

"Give them up."

"Them?"

"Oh we will take you and destroy you so you can no longer use your power against us, but we want those two. They are different and you know it. They are ours. They belong with us. We have come back for them."

Fluke and Simon had risen to twice their size, their backs raised and red eyes flashing through the mist. The sound of their howls echoed throughout the atmosphere and most would never see such a frightening sight again. Milton stretched out as a sign of protecting them.

"Never. They will never return to you."

The most horrible laughter echoed as the mist retreated and the light faded.

"Too late. They are ours." Again the peel of sadistic laughter was heard.

Most of the group were bewildered as Fluke and Simon were still there so what did the evil mean?

The audience was still in a hypnotic state but the lights were coming back on as the equipment slowly came back to life. Quickly Milton despatched his friends saying he must reassure the audience as they came round. Strangely although all the power had been off, the equipment clocks and all watches in the place were now showing a time near the end of the show so Milton took advantage of this and gave the people a quick explanation of how some of them may have experienced an unusual happening but not to be alarmed as it was quite common with those who were in touch with their 'other' side. Most left feeling they had always known they were gifted, while others just wondered what had happened but as the general mood was of awe and satisfaction they kept their thoughts to themselves.

Having made his exit from the stage he hurried to his dressing room to a very agitated group. Daryl was back in body but fully aware of what had gone on but Simon had been returned as he had been out of body for too long already. The most distraught was Ariel.

"She's gone."

"I know. I'm so sorry." Milton tried to comfort her but the fact that this had obviously been part of the plan was not pleasant.

"I felt her wrenched from my grasp. I should have passed her on before but we were trying to concentrate on you as a primary target and I'd only got a little of my strength holding her."

Milton paused before asking "And Tabar has asked where Holland is?"

Fluke answered, "She was concerned, thought she'd missed him somehow."

Daryl was trying to piece it all together in his mind. "So it was Jo and Holland they were after. But I don't understand. They are low down on the levels, the same as us really."

"In this realm yes, but in their own area they are probably as high as Jean Paul and I or even higher." He still had to maintain the secrecy of his status.

"Had they already tried to get Jo?" Ariel was still smarting at the loss of this lovely girl.

"Several times actually."

"And what about Holland?" Jean Paul enquired.

"Oh he'd been a plant for some time, that's how they got so much information about us."

"But wouldn't it have made sense to leave them here, to carry on relaying messages, whether they knew it or not?" Jorg was also trying to sum it up. "I would have."

Milton was silent before saying "They must have a good reason and that's what bothers me. Also I had been warned that my talents would be harnessed by them and I thought that was mainly what they were after."

"So they will be back." Daryl asked.

"Undoubtedly."

"One thing I'd like to know." Jorg was still pondering everything. "Did you plant Holland on purpose?"

"I'm afraid so."

"So you knew he was in danger, and you put him in the front line where they could pick him off?"

Milton could understand Jorg thinking this was callous and calmly replied. "One day you may unfortunately be put in that position. You may be the one having to make that kind of decision and it won't be easy."

"But he was a good man."

"Are you sure of that?"

The reply made them all stop. Fluke was first to ask the obvious.

"So you're saying there was more to him than we knew?"

Ariel cut in before he had chance to reply. "And what about Jo? You're not going to tell us she was bad. I won't believe it."

Milton silenced them with a gesture. "Nothing, and nobody is ever what they seem. Trust me, you are all safer with them gone."

The mood was somewhat sombre as they departed leaving Jean Paul and Daryl with Milton.

"What happens now boss?" Daryl spoke audibly now.

"I believe we have a show to do at Peterborough."

"So we carry on the same?"

"What else?" then with a smile said "Welcome to the world of spirit."

It took just over an hour for Milton and Daryl to arrive at Peterborough and both were ready for a good night's sleep. Having checked in, Milton locked the door to his room and sat in front of the dressing table admiring his reflection.

"Good to be back, I missed this body he mused." But to the spiritual world the face staring back at him was that of Holland. Another spiritual figure appeared over his shoulder gently caressing his hair.

"Good work, two birds with one stone." Jo whispered.

"Yes, they were coming for Milton and got Ariel as well, puts us in their good books."

"Can you handle her tricks?"

"Simple, I've been studying her while she's supposed to have been guarding me. I've mastered most of them already."

Holland frowned. "The dogs could be a problem."

"We'll have to be wary of them, they can sniff stuff out. One nearly got me you know. Thought the game was up."

"They'll be in limbo for a while."

"How long are you going to keep this body?" Jo was caressing him now. "Seems a pity to waste it."

If there was ever any doubt as to what spirits are capable of in their world, it would have been proved in the next moments in that room, but there was no one to witness it.

CHAPTER 19

"Well I didn't expect that!" Avril Harker closed the book and placed it on the table.

"What's that dear?" Bert looked up.

"Just when you think you know what's going to happen, it doesn't." She stood up. "Cup of tea?"

"Oh yes please dear."

Avril went out to put the kettle on then popped her head round the door.

"Oh I've been thinking Bert, I don't think I'll bother with going to that astral person I was telling you about. They're all fakes I expect. Just want your money."

Bert smiled "Probably for the best. Didn't you say they were starting a little club in town, crafts and the like?"

"Oh yes for ladies, we show each other what we can do and then we learn off others. I think I'd like that."

"Good idea," Bert said "best not meddle in what you don't understand. Never know where it could lead. Best left alone I say."

Avril looked at the book on the table. "No," she said "I think you're right."

- -

Whilst you have been reading this novel, the events therein could have been acted out around you, but you will never know - or will you?

The author does not have anything to do with the occult; she merely writes novels but suggests you take Bert's advice.

THE END

Are you an Author?

Do you want to see your book in print?

Please look at the UKUnpublished website:
www.ukunpublished.co.uk

Let the World Share Your Imagination

LE3 2FP.

66 Narbirtl Rd
         South.

fri 28th

     10.25.
come earlier

Lightning Source UK Ltd.
Milton Keynes UK
UKOW05f1911290414

230812UK00001B/5/P